"Vivid . . . convincing" *Guardian*

Warfare Accomplished is the third in a trilogy of novels about World War II, originally published in 1947 to remarkable critical acclaim.

Each title carries the distinction – rare in any novels of World War II or any other war – of being written almost contemporaneously with the action. All convey the immediacy of journalism as well as the more profound qualities the reviews proclaim.

"The author is a master of the English language. Really amazing . . . fully lives up to the high standards of the first two books" *The Times*

Warfare Accomplished

Edith Pargeter

HEADLINE

ISBN 0 7472 3399 3

Printed and bound in Great Britain by
Collins, Glasgow

HEADLINE BOOK PUBLISHING PLC
Headline House
79 Great Titchfield Street
London W1P 7FN

CONTENTS

PART ONE

ENGLAND, 1944

"This curly childhood of the year,
These days of dancing blood,
Is Spring the proper time for breath
To be resigned for good?"
W. H. DAVIES: *No Place or Time.*

I

SERGEANT BENISON crossed the third meadow and let himself out by the broken-backed gate, and hoisting it into place under his arm, turned to look back at the camp from which he had come. From this spot beneath the curve of the fields the array of huts showed only as so many brown hummocks sharp-spined in the smoothness of the turf, and the movement of men always busy between hut and hut was seen not at all; so soon could the activities of the Midshires be dwarfed into a bustling of ants, and put clear out of mind. There was only the gold light on the crests of the hills, and the shadows of the approaching evening drawn purple round their shoulders, as they sat there motionless and complete, like an assemblage of kings, watching the sun go down.

The battalion had been in Westmorland over a year, and he wasn't used to it even yet. None of them were. For some of them there would always be the same regrets for lost cinemas and dance-halls and shops and pubs and street-corners, the same frustrated restlessness for their towns; a lack for which the Saturday-night hops in the village hall and the lonely inns full of the country tongue did little to compensate. And for the others—and there were many of these—always this starting of the heart within the body at morning, and noonday, and twilight, whenever they could raise their eyes for a moment from the work in hand, to find the disputed earth so beautiful and so indifferent. And of this company there were perhaps a few who felt that witchcraft in a different way; those who had been exiles, who had known other spells than this; for them this dreaming quietness was not all indifferent, though the rich land drowsed unaware of its own, and made its immense and incalculable contribution by obscure ways. Jim Benison had felt its calm rise into him as the soil feeds the tree.

I

It dispensed virtue after the manner of the bones of the saints, touched into miraculous grace by the lips of a believer. The antique blessing came by faith only; he perceived it, and it was.

Walking down the meadows from the camp he had thought only of tomorrow's inspection, and the list of names for the next battle-course, and Peterson's probable introduction to the glass-house by way of that Saturday-night riot at the "Royal Oak"; serious, in a way, that outbreak, for their record in the village by the lake-head had been exemplary up to now, and only the hills, whose calm was impervious to shocks, had been witnesses of the regular week-end brushes with the R.A.F. from the camp in the next valley, those breathless, beautiful battles which it was expedient neither to see nor hear until they became too whole-hearted for safety. After all, a company of high-spirited youngsters, corn-fed and bursting with energy, and shut away into the back of beyond with sheep and larch-trees for company on the pretext of preparing for what must seem to them a wholly chimerical invasion, must be allowed to let off steam somehow. The amount of blood-letting they did on Saturday nights up on the moor hurt nobody, and sent them to bed blissfully happy; it was not even an unheard-of thing for the Company Sergeant-Major to compare notes afterwards with the Flight-Sergeant from the R.A.F. camp, balance the debits and credits of the slaughter, and advance the time of interference for the following week if the casualties seemed too high. So even the Redcaps were able to enjoy themselves, if they did it discreetly. And upon this ordered and satisfactory scheme of things Peterson, of all people, must burst with a roaring drunk and a tale of damages as long as his own gorilla arms, in the sober and respectable bar of the "Royal Oak", in the heart of the village. Not one of the raw kids, but the sedate and responsible Peterson, himself an ex-publican, and something of a mentor to the rank and file of the platoon.

"It would have to be one of mine," thought Jim amiably, "who cuts loose and spoils the record! Blast him! I hope he cops it hot." Though he had said very different things, not an hour earlier, to a harassed Platoon Commander who professedly was at a loss to account for the outbreak; being just twenty-one, and himself a relatively simple youth who lived by the book.

"Oh, I don't know, sir. They've done pretty well to hold in so long," he had said. "It isn't so easy to sit here quietly

2

month after month waiting for action they don't even believe in, without kicking over the traces now and again."

"But a sensible older man like Peterson," objected Second Lieutenant Baird, wrinkling his forehead into a bewildered frown for the follies of his elders. "You would have thought——"

"Yes," said Jim. "They get it worst of the lot. After all, the kids can afford to wait; but a man of forty, with a wife, and four kids growing up without so much as knowing him, begins to wonder if he'll have any time left."

Baird might or might not take note of that; you could say for him, at least, that he was a fair and reasonable creature, open to suggestion, and an apology for exasperated middle age might easily strike an unexpected chord in his young but just mind. He frowned over it, and said uneasily: "Still, it seems a great pity. He was well in the running for his stripe, you know."

"I hope he still is," said Jim. "He could be a very useful man." And with that he left his brew to simmer, not without confidence in the result. He had Baird more or less where he wanted him.

So he was thinking when he lifted the gate back into place, and raised his eyes to the hills; and the camp, and the war itself, or its lasting significance, dwindled into the background of his mind before the overwhelming assault of the world's beauty. He drew breath and stood still, watching the sky grow golden, and dissolve into immeasurable remoteness of air and light, where distance sang like a vibrating bow-string after the arrow's flight, and the circling of birds was idle and faint and far, spun out like threads of floating gossamer against the zenith. Low along the flanks of the hills the larch-trees and birches stood up slender and green; and along the valley the chuckling, gossiping music of Green Ghyll scuffling among its pebbles made a ribbon of silver sound round the sleeve of the evening quietness. Always there was that sound. By night, when the lorries had left the cindered camp road, and there were no 'planes up, he could hear the rushing waters of Green Ghyll Force, half a mile away, insistent and ecstatic as the singing of larks. If the wind was wrong, and he could not hear it, something was lost from his peace of mind; but while the soft, absorbed song came in upon the fringe of his consciousness his mind relaxed from the cares of the day, and he slept content. What alchemy there should be in running

3

water to charm him into quietness he never troubled to consider; it would have been like enquiring into the nature of rainbows, or the obscure workings of the human heart. He accepted it without question, and was grateful; that was enough.

He turned, and walked on down the lane, the village lying below him half bright in the slanting sun, half drowned in the flowing purple shade, a sprawl of creamy cottages among the trees, a tangle of leafy roads, and a stammering brook going down to join the Ghyll before they both lost themselves in the silver-smooth waters of the lake. Towards that burnished expanse of water he made his way, leaving the lane, just short of the village, by a green path which wound downhill between birch-trees. At the point where the ground broke away into a short, steep slide of sand and grass there was a stile, where a track from one of the farms came down to join the path. Imogen would be there by now, for he was late tonight; she would be sitting on the stile, watching for him between the trees, herself a flower bluer of eye than the gentians, redder of lip than the tasselled scarlet of the larch flowers that swung above his head.

At the thought of her he quickened his step, unwilling to waste a moment of the time they had together, for at best it was too brief. On Tuesday she would be back in London, and who knew when he would see her again? Or, indeed, if he would ever see her again? For the adventure on which the whole country waited, only half believing, was now so near that he felt the wind of its approach lifting his hair at times. Himself he had not more than half believed; but now the thing loomed large, and he knew that he was sure of a part in it. They had not drilled and toughened and sweated the new battalion for nothing, battle-course after battle-course, ordeal upon ordeal, until the young men were hard and lean and desperate with unused energy. Even before Major Harben had told him the facts of it, he had known in his own mind that the 7th were for it. Well, they were ready, as ready as men can be who go into untried fires; they had known the pretence, but there was still the reality to come. And as for him—even he, when it came to the point, might feel his bowels wrung in that cold fist of fear the grip of which he had never yet forgotten; but it would take more than that to cool the exultation of his heart. He had lived for two years upon the certain knowledge that he would some day go back; back to all the

4

places from which he had been ignominiously driven, to all the prisons of the living, to all the graves of the dead whom he had been forced to leave behind; back to Brian Ridley in some French war-cemetery, back to Charlie Smith in the mangrove-forests of the Johore border, back to Miriam Lozelle's secretly tended grave in Boissy-en-Fougères. There was no life for him in the end if he did not go back; and therefore even the solemnity, even the terror of this pause upon the threshold was for him a kind of bitter and profound joy, never to be spoken of because words could not encompass it, never to be shared because there was no one living who had any justifiable part in it: not even she—not even Imogen.

When he turned the bend of the path he saw that she was there, perched on the top bar of the stile with her knees drawn up, and her dark-brown hair lifting in tangled curls to the stirring of the breeze. She had a grass between her teeth, and a demure devil of amusement in her eyes; and at sight of him advancing upon her she smiled broadly, as well she might, for she was looking at him over the head of a private of his own platoon, who lounged at his ease against the stile, close beside her knee. One of the youngsters, a big, fair, husky kid by the name of Mason, well built, amost offensively clean and healthy looking, and serenely pleased with his own appearance; a good enough kid in his way, but cocky, especially where girls were concerned. Just the man to discover a strange nymph in the woods, and make the most ill-advised and untimely pass at her; and to get away with it, too, if the girl had been anyone but Imogen Threlfall. Jim could have told him he would get nowhere with this one. Probably she would have told him so herself at the outset, with that disconcertingly blunt honesty of hers, if he had not somehow put a foot very wrong with her; for though she was not angry, there was that in the deliberation of her smile which told Jim that Imogen was displeased. But Teddy Mason, damn his impudence, didn't know how to read the signs as Jim did; he was ploughing straight ahead, full of his own innocent cheek, while she made a fool of him. Do him good, too! Ninety-nine out of a hundred fell much too easily.

She did not move until Jim was a few paces only from the stile. Then she suddenly sat up straight, and shook herself, and spat out the blade of grass. "Here's Jim!" she said; cutting clean through Teddy Mason's latest line as if it did not exist; and she slid from the stile, brushing the boy aside in

5

passing, and linked her arm in Jim's, and went on down the path with him and on to the strand.

Jim got a brief glimpse of Mason's face as he turned on his elbow, open-mouthed, to watch them go. It was everything she could have wished, ludicrous in astonishment and offence, round-eyed, and growing suddenly scarlet with embarrassed indignation as he recognised her Jim, for whom she had pushed him aside in mid sentence without so much as an apology or a good-bye. It was everything she could have wished, but she did not look at it. Even the deliberate affront had turned into something fierce and single-hearted and instinctive, more perfect than her calculations could have made it. She was looking up into Jim's face, the restlessness of the water a reflected quivering of colour in her eyes; and her hands were firmly content upon his arm. He thought, not for the first time: "For God's sake, what does she see in me? What is it she's going to look for some day, and not find?" For he knew he was nothing much; and she was surely too sensible to go on seeing visions for ever, and asking for no proof. He had found most things bend under his weight; supposing, some day, she found him bend under hers?

"I thought you were never coming," she said, as the pebbles began to chatter under their feet, and on their right hand the lake-waters, burnished silver, soared away to the dark leeward of the hills opposite.

"Yes, I'm sorry I'm so late. I only got away at the last moment. But I see you managed to pass the time away all right." He jerked his head back towards the stile, and the misused youth who was even then plunging away to console his hurt vanity in the village. "That was a bit hard on young Romeo, wasn't it?"

"Serve him right!" said Imogen unfeelingly. "Don't worry about him. He's suffering from swelled head, that's his trouble. Do him good to find himself smaller beer than he thought."

"Do him no end of good," agreed Jim. "In fact, you seem to be doing my job for me. I have to go to quite a lot of trouble to deal him one in the wind like the one you just landed."

"I can see you'd have to," she admitted, "regularly." And a shade drily she added: "I gathered he was one of your lot."

"That wouldn't be hard. He hates my guts. With a sympathetic listener he wouldn't be able to keep off the subject."

"He hadn't got one," said Imogen, "but I suppose he

6

wouldn't realise that. Anyhow, I've learned a lot about you that I didn't suspect!"

"I daresay! Hope you didn't have long with him, at that rate, or my number's up!"

"Oh, I expect a lot of it was fiction, even to him. He didn't seem to me a bad-natured kid, if only he wasn't so bumptious. But why are we talking about him, anyway?"

"Oh, I don't know!" He looked down at her thin brown hand upon his arm, and it seemed to him that even the character of her hands had changed in the last two years, had grown mature, and responsible and acute, and with these things had gained a more than ordinary tranquillity. When he was with her it was as if something which normally endured in him as a single purpose of revenge gained for a time a significance which was of the future, as well as of the past, and fruitful, or at least potentially fruitful, where it had been merely sterile. She was all the future he had. When she was away from him his view of life ended with the end of the war—for someday it must end—in a blankness, in a cessation of purpose; but with Imogen near to him he was aware of the possibility of life beyond, obscure and disquieting, but not entirely without interest. He believed she understood this, being clairvoyant where he was concerned; which was an excellent reason why they could afford to spend their time together talking about people like Teddy Mason, instead of about themselves. "Oh, I don't know!" he said, smiling at her. "Might do me good to hear a few home truths, as well as him. Sauce for the goose——"

But she smiled, too, and did not speak. He had known she would never repeat what had passed by chance between the bumptious boy and herself, and that not out of any consideration for Jim Benison, either. She could rap the offender over the knuckles pretty smartly herself, but she would never pass on a word of what he had said to offend. Not that Jim couldn't have supplied the bulk of it for her. He knew very well how they thought of him; he was a hard-as-nails professional bedeviller, impossible to satisfy, unappreciative, demanding the last ounce from the men under him, and after that an ounce more; sour-tongued, impassive of face, too old at nearly thirty to make any allowances for, and have any sympathy with, the young. For certainly he looked a good deal more than thirty, with his lean, weathered face, and his scarred mouth, and the sprinkling of iron-grey in his hair. And to an ebullient youth

7

like Teddy, who considered that he knew everything, and could if required do all things well, the shadow of this ugly, silent and unimpressionable sergeant would seem peculiarly repressive. Well, that was only to be expected; they would both survive that.

"He didn't really bother you?" he asked. "He's all right, but he can be on the saucy side when he tries—without even knowing it. He's used to having 'em fall into his arms, you see."

"So I gathered," said Imogen, and she looked across the water, and smiled into the sunset. "No, he was all right. I can manage worse than him, don't you worry. And anyhow, he won't come near me again in a hurry."

"When he recovers," prophesied Jim, "and begins to see the affair through a couple of drinks and an hour or two of his own kind of fun, he'll go back to camp and tell everybody about being slapped down by the sergeant's girl. He'll make it a pretty detailed story; and especially he'll wonder what the hell a girl like that sees in me."

She raised her dark-blue eyes to his face, and was silent, though he felt her fingers close steadily upon his arm. They had reached their particular spot, an alcove of sandy beach where there lay a felled tree peeled clean of bark and polished to a shiny bronze-brown. Imogen sat down, and spread her green skirt neatly, and dug the toes of her shoes into the shingle, and looked at him still.

"When I have time," he said, "I wonder, too!"

"Don't!" said Imogen. "Leave it to him. It's waste of time for you, but there's always the chance he might find out, if he wonders hard enough."

"And I never should!" said Jim. "Is that it?"

"And you don't need to; that's it. But no, you never would, if it matters at all."

He supposed that to her it did not matter at all. She knew what she was about, and there was no help for it, and she wanted no help for it. No one had ever seemed to him so secure of herself and of what was hers. He supposed it was because she demanded nothing, being so greatly endowed within. She had never asked him for anything, not even to love her; and such gifts as he had been able to give her she had received always with a child's startled delight, as if they had gone beyond her expectation. No, Imogen would never repent. She would never fail him, even if unwillingly he should fail her.

8

No matter how far he fell short of his own standards, he would still be what she wanted. So to her it did not matter that he must let her love him beyond his deserts.

But to him it might, he thought, matter rather a lot. He could not lose her, but he might hurt her, he might humiliate her more than he cared to contemplate; and he would not even know, for she would still look at him this very way, with her level, night-blue look that pierced him like a lance, and the fierce simplicity of her mouth at once firm and soft like the bud of a flower, and her forehead under the shaken curls broad and rounded and tranquil, betraying nothing. Just as she was looking now.

He sat down beside her slowly, and together they looked across the lake to where the village in its bronze and purple shadows was falling asleep as gently as the closing of a flower. The hills grew taller, gathering majesty about them out of the air. Little tremors of silver passed over the nearer reaches of the lake, and died in broken whispers among the pebbles not a dozen yards from their feet. They could see among the green of trees, in the middle of the village, a flash of gold upon stone which was the tower of the church, square and old above the legion of its celebrated graves. Age was in itself an added goodness in this land where even death was only a closer union with the soil, and the soil was the fullness of life. The yeoman behind the plough and the yeoman whose dust was turned up in the rich loam under the share were separated by nothing more substantial than the illusion of time; and in neither of them was there any disquiet. How could there be, when they had this secret in their blood, and all the craftsmanship and wisdom and strength of the ages in their lineage?

And from this quietness a man must go back into exile to bring back the part of him which was lost there, or lose the rest after it; because life in this incomplete state was at best a maimed sort of life, not worth retaining. What it was that had been cut out of him he had never troubled to question; there was his pride in it, he knew, his pride of manhood and his pride of race, and the inmost peace of his mind; but what mattered was that it was essential, that have it he must, out of the bodies of his enemies, out of the joy of their prisoners as they came back into the light of day, out of the reclaimed soil of France and the captive soil of Germany he must have back what had been taken from him; and then he would be able, if he still lived, to come back to this holy, antique, kind

9

and good-humoured land in peace, and be urged away no longer; and if he was one of those who inevitably died, well, at least he would be whole again. But now, as he looked at the hills and the village, and the conviction of their permanence filled him with calm, still they urged him away, they compelled him back into exile.

So he thought, and the solemnity and horror of what was to come closed in perceptibly with the twilight over the fells. He was in no way startled when Imogen suddenly put out her hand and caught him by the wrist. Why should she not see what he saw, and no less clearly? The thing was there to be seen.

She asked abruptly, but in a low voice: "It is really coming this time—isn't it?"

Then he felt her gathering herself towards it even as he gathered his own mind, square against its appalling shadow; he felt that she desired it, welcomed it. It was not at all new for her thoughts to go step for step with his, and nothing said.

"Yes," he said, "it's coming all right."

"When will it begin?"

"I don't know—— Soon."

"How soon? I believe you know. I'm sure you know something about it."

"We're moving after Easter—somewhere south. It means the beginning of the muster, that's all. After that I don't know; nobody'll know until it happens."

"No," said Imogen, "I suppose not. And anyhow I could hardly ask you to tell me. It's only the waiting that's so bad; and even that's bearable when you know there really is an end to it. But I wish it would begin!" she said.

Jim was thinking of his first plunge, four years past now; of the attenuation of waiting then, and of a twilit kitchen in a French farmhouse, and a woman who adjured him sharply: "Don't wish for it!" Well, he had learned to wait since then. Two years he had waited, and worked, and toughened himself, and schooled others, and suffered the sickness of delay upon delay, and not complained. And he had got something out of it, too, besides a fit body; a little restored confidence in his kind, a belief at least in the intent to conquer, better realised in this curious monastic world than among the civilians who were aliens now to him. Yes, he had got something out of it, the steadiness within him, the calm without.

"It will begin soon enough," he said; and again he recognised the voice of Miriam Lozelle, warning her over-eager young men that the hour would neither hasten nor lag for them. He had thought then that she was merely saying what any other woman might have said, that late was soon enough to suffer; but he knew her better now, well enough to understand that she had told him, as clearly as one can tell the innocent and blind, to make use of the waiting-time before the storm fell on him and found him impotent and astonished.

"The thing is," said Imogen deliberately, "shall we make a good job of it this time. If it's half done it'll be worse hell than ever; and then, the waiting again, for more years than we've waited now——" She fell silent there, but she had said enough. They had both of them seen things half done.

For a moment he did not answer, for it was what had worried him more than a little during the first weary year of battle-courses and boredom. But suddenly, looking into the heart of peace, into a sky whose loftiness dwarfed wars and rumours of war, into the folded hills whose antiquity swallowed up this momentary turmoil as the night silence swallows the bleating of a solitary sheep, he saw that the question had answered itself within him without thought on his part. He did not have to take thought to discover if he stood on solid ground. Even this time he might die, but it would not be of shame or lameness for what had been left undone.

Well, she was justified. They had made a mess of a lot of things in their time, beginning everything reluctantly and half-heartedly, before they were well awake; but they were well awake now. They could almost feel the awareness of the wind upon their faces, of the earth under their feet. This time, whatever the outcome, the storm was theirs to loose or bind.

"Yes," he said. "Yes, this time we shall make a good job of it." But he did not say: "This time we shall win." At that moment victory, on which the whole course of the world depended, seemed to him a thing of secondary importance. A crazy sort of obliquity of vision possessed him for one dazzling moment, and then passed from him with the descent of the sun; but even the readjustment of his values to their normal practical scale left him strangely comforted. And why attempt to sort out impressions coloured by the sunset, and shadowed by the possibilities of death in innumerable and grotesque shapes, when the event could not be averted and was not of great moment? What mattered was that the terrible thing was in train with all their weight behind it. The rest could wait; he had long ago got over wanting to see the end from the beginning.

"Yes," he said again, "whatever happens—this time it won't be half done."

2

On Easter Day they went to evensong in the village church. That was her doing; he wanted her to have everything she wanted out of this last week-end, the third she had spent with him in Westmorland; and to go to church with her was a very little thing to do, though he himself would have liked to take her up to the highest stretch of moorland he could find, and have her to himself there close to the sky, and be quiet with her for a little while. What he found there, he supposed, she could find in church. As for him, he hadn't looked for it of late years, partly from excess of niggling little worldly cares, and partly from disinclination. He had been a regular churchgoer in his unthinking days, like a lot of the lads now, going there because it was an essential part of the social life of the village, and something to do on Sundays; but he was no longer a man who did things unthinkingly, or because he had been wont to do them.

Imogen knew that she was taking him out of his orbit. He saw that when he asked her, as they walked home from the dance in the parish hall on Saturday night: "What shall we do tomorrow?" He saw it by the dappled light under the hawthorn hedges of the lane, as she turned her face up and looked at him with that long, long, contemplative look, as if she would have the soul out of him. Being asked, she never went roundabout at an answer. "I should like to go to church," she said. And he said: "Right, then we will."

It was natural in her to have a feeling for it, for she'd been brought up, so to speak, in a churchyard. The turmoil and crying of the rookeries round the Norman tower of Morwen Hoe, in Midshire, must have been almost the first sound she remembered. She'd played in a stone porch set with queer grotesque roundels of Flemish glass, and polished memorial brasses grown razor-thin and faint with age. She'd cut her teeth on a door-handle the size of a horse-collar, and cherished a dead-and-gone Crusader's sandstone hound before she acquired a Sealyham of her own. What he could draw out of the hills of immortality and security she had taken by touch, and taste, and vision, and mere breath from the day she was born; and certainly she did well to turn back to what was for her the first fountain of it, whenever she needed refreshment. As who didn't need it now?

So he went with her. It was a friendly village and a friendly church, mellow and warm, lit with oil-lamps in the dark recesses, and covered all over with jonquils and narcissus for Easter. The stone font with its square-bodied primitive saints, and the carved bench-ends, and the lower panes of the incongruous Victorian windows were almost invisible under screens of hyacinth and daffodil. Several Midshire men were already there to see Jim follow Imogen down the aisle. They were properly interested in the spectacle. There was Corporal Sloan, who had a sentimental eye on one of the young ladies in the choir, and was mending his ways accordingly. There was the slim young scrimshanker of a clerk who did less work for better pay all day long in the adjutant's office, and had discovered another nice line in self-service at parish teas and vicarage At-Homes, at the very modest cost of these Sunday evening appearances. There were Corbett, and Pike, and Weldon, all together as usual, honest family men acting after their kind; and the well-brought-up infant, Dick Shelby, acting after his; and a couple of young devils from B Company, in unsuspected attendance on him. Mischief was what they lived for, and an offensively neat and quiet young soldier on his way to church, prayer-book in hand, might be regarded as fair game. They hadn't discovered yet what a mule's kick he packed, on occasion, into that innocent and long-suffering fist of his. Well, finding out would be a new and salutary experience for them, and Sergeant Leigh, whose hair was greying for their sakes, would be duly grateful. And lastly there was Micky Lynn, who was nursing what would one day be a fine tenor voice by practising with the choir, to their satisfaction and his own.

All these observed the entry of Sergeant Benison and his girl, and made due note of Imogen's unexpectedness, for word of her had already gone round. Teddy Mason hadn't wasted any time.

Well, she was, Jim admitted it, sufficiently surprising. There were times when she still looked eighteen, even though her first wild bloom had been rubbed off in the London blitz, and left her so quiet and self-contained. In her best frock, and a wide-brimmed straw hat, sitting there gravely with her prayer-book open in her lap, what had she to do with him, a man irretrievably scarred in body, and perhaps in mind, too? And why was this awe of her so new and strange in him, when she had been so all these long two years?

He didn't pay much attention to the service, because he was so intent upon her. There were two Franciscan brothers visiting the parish; they'd been there all through Lent, running a sort of revival, and this was their last Sunday, so they took the service between them. Pleasant people, he had found them in casual field acquaintance, Brother Philip and Brother Gabriel, happy, absorbed people, usually surrounded by children. He listened in a desultory fashion to Brother Philip's sermon, but when it ended it was gone from him. His mind was on something very different.

What was it that had set him to thinking of the possibility of a new loss now, at this late hour? Teddy Mason had admired Imogen; and he was gay and young himself, and good-looking, nearer kin to her. Was that what had made her possession seem suddenly as precarious as it was precious? Not because she would ever voluntarily withdraw herself, but because in the nature of things so perverse an attachment could not endure. It was the first time he had thought of it in that light, and the possibility stirred within him a fever of fear, so that he turned and fixed his eyes on the clear lines of her profile, so child-like in its candour, so severe in its stillness; and almost he could fancy that already she was receding from him. But that was impossible, for not only would she never go of her own will, but she would never suffer circumstances to force her hand, never without a fight, and he knew how Imogen could fight.

She felt his eyes on her. He saw her calm troubled from within, as a sleeper is sometimes aroused by the consciousness of a near presence; and then she turned her head, and looked at him full, and warmth and life came into her face, and she smiled. He had seen that smile before, whenever she had half hoped it might be in her to give back the lost part of him and make him complete. It was as if, having found what filled her own heart with hope, and confidence, and joy, she offered it always to him with that eager look, as if she said: "Is this it?" She had been bringing her best to him so for two years, with no reward, but now he put out his hand and closed it over hers where it lay in her lap, and felt the response of her thin fingers with a strange, humble and bitter delight.

When they left the church the vicar was at the door with the two Franciscans, scattering good-nights among the members of the congregation as they filed out into the pale and lofty blueness of the spring evening. He was a big, handsome, straightforward sort of man, a bachelor who farmed in a small way up the valley, and had been on excellent terms with the Sergeants' Mess of the 7th Midshires ever since they came to Westmorland. He looked faintly surprised at seeing Jim there, as well he might, for it had never happened before in a year of acquaintance.

"Hullo, Sergeant!" he said. "I'm happy to see you here." His eyes lit upon Imogen as she moved forward in Jim's arm, and he accepted her with the same serene smile. "What a pity you couldn't get home for Easter," he said. "These travelling restrictions hit you fellows unfairly hard. Luckily they don't apply to your——" He hesitated only for a moment; no one was quick enough to help him out, and Imogen's hands were gloved. "——your wife," he said.

It was a strange moment, enormous as a grain of dust is enormous when seen through the microscope, expanded monstrously into a significance it should never have possessed; for the silence, though breathless while it lasted, was beautifully brief, and Imogen's bright assenting smile and murmur were everything the situation required. It was only a matter of a few words in passing, and then they were out in the fragrant evening under the shade of the trees, walking together beside the bracken-brown reaches of the Ghyll as it threaded the village on its way down to the lake. The vicar never knew he had guessed wrong; never suspected it, for he had been quite sure of his perspicacity. No, it was only on them the shock of the moment had fallen, this constraint following on its heels, shackling hand and tongue so that they went silently, not touching nor looking at each other. Imogen was deeply shaken; he knew that by no visible sign, but by a responsive aching within himself. Her breath came evenly, her colour had not deepened nor the lines of her face tightened, but he knew. He wanted to speak to her, but for the moment the constraint was stronger than his resolution, and he could not bring himself to utter a word.

They reached the little wooden bridge which crossed the widening Ghyll as it left the village. Under the flimsy hand-rail the water shone and flashed from its pebbles, and its mutter became a song again as it hurried down to the lake. Here Imogen hesitated, her eyes caught by that rich glimmering flow over agate and onyx of pebbles, and gold-dust of gravel and sand, and the darkness of the loam-coloured holes under the banks, where motion died into stillness. She set her hands upon the rail, and leaned over to watch, and was quiet so for a long time. She could never pass this place without lingering.

Looking at her as she stood there, he thought: "There never has been anything we couldn't say. Why should things change now?" But within himself something was changed, was changing at this moment, an excitement coming to life from within the heart, where he had believed all schooled to rigidity that was not already spent; an upheaval like the subterranean quickening of spring in the tormented earth, possessing with passion every live part of him.

His tongue was loosed suddenly. He said: "Imogen!" and she turned her head obediently and looked at him; and it was all resolved.

"My God, what a fool I've been!" he said. He took her by the arms, and held her. He felt, even before he saw, her soft, wry smile shine out at him ruefully. "I've been the world's fool!" he said.

"Perhaps!" said Imogen. "Why now more than usual?"

"You know damn well why! What he said ought to have been true—would have been true if I'd had a grain of sense. Why didn't you tell me the one thing I thought I was doing for you was the wrong thing? Why didn't you tell me it wasn't what you wanted at all? Oh, hell!" he said helplessly. "Am I still putting the blame on you? I should have seen it without being told. And now it's too late to put it right, too!"

"Too late this time," she corrected quickly and fiercely, as if someone had freshly pointed out that there might be no next time.

"But you knew why it was—didn't you?"

"Yes," she admitted with the breathless ghost of a laugh, "I knew that all right! It was so exactly like you! You wanted me to go free, without any visible marks or scars or amputations, if anything happened to you. As if I could! But it was like you to try."

"I'm sorry, Imogen!" He took her hands to his heart, and held them there. "I'm sorry like hell now, but what's the good of that? I thought I was doing what was best for you.

It wouldn't have made any difference to what I could give you, except for the pension. I made a will, eighteen months ago. I never told you, but you might as well know now. There isn't much, but what there is, is for you.'' All this he said as if he spoke of two other people encountered in a dream, so easy it was to discuss their dependency and death and life, the duty they owed each other, the gifts they could give each other. She listened as simply, though her tranquillity was gravely shaken, and the hands he held were tightly clenched. There was something more he could give her, he saw that now; something she would not accept in silence to her own regret, and keep with gratitude while it fed upon her substance; something which would be the right thing at last.

"It wasn't the will that was lacking, my dear,'' he said in a low voice. "I couldn't love you more, girl, if I put a ring on every finger.''

He heard the breath start and flutter in her throat for a moment before she could reply. Then she asked almost inaudibly: "You mean that, Jim? The same way I mean it?''

"The very same way,'' he said, for there could be nothing more final, nothing more comprehensive than that; and it was true now as it had never occurred to him that it was true until the vicar made his slip. Always she had been dear to him, but this was a different thing.

Suddenly she was in tears. They sprang to her eyes as abruptly and spontaneously as the spring had gushed in his heart; and she put her arms about him and clung to him, with her face hidden in his shoulder. There was no one to see them, nor would he have cared if half the village had passed by. He lifted the big straw hat gently from her hair, and smoothed back the brown curls. She was motionless, her inexplicable weeping quite silent, and again the very touch of her asked, with passion: "Is this it?'' For she had given him her love for him long ago, and once for all; but his love for her, this launched torrent, was a new offering. It was not what he had lost; it was something he had never had until now, nor ever dreamed of possessing, because he had not known it existed. He knew now why the vicar had been so confident. No ceremony, no ring could make the link between them more secure. He must have seen by the very way they moved together, by the serenity of their companionship, by the repose of their love, that they were one and indivisible. How had it ever been possible to suppose that she could be free of him,

17

dead or alive, merely because they were not literally man and wife? He could never again be wounded but she would bleed, never be angry but she would burn. It took a stranger to see it and say it, but it was true, it had always been true. Yes, he had been the world's fool!

"Imogen!"

She raised her face, and looked at him with a clear, strange smile. "This is damned silly, I know. Don't take any notice, and I shall be able to stop."

"I've kept you waiting a long time," he said, "for something that's been yours all along. Oh, Imogen, when I think of the time I've wasted—your time, too!——"

He kissed her; this at least was wisdom. But in the very kiss it seemed to them both that time, which he had invoked, the lost time and the time still to come, rushed in upon them dizzily, and their remaining day was snatched away from them like a leaf in a high wind. The shadow of departure fell upon them. The ordeal by warfare stood between them, and embracing each other, they took this also into their arms.

3

On Tuesday morning he saw her into the early bus, and waved her away down the winding lake-side road towards Keswick until the flutter of her handkerchief at the window dwindled into distance. He could go no farther with her; even this last half-hour was enjoyed on stolen time, for he had much to do, and should have been getting on with it. Easter on the moor between the two camps had been something of a civil war, and there was any amount of malevolent energy still to be worked off somehow. Baird, exasperated beyond his normal elastic patience, had bidden his sergeant for God's sake to take the platoon out and lose it while he recovered his sanity; a request which Jim translated into a full day's sweat up Helvellyn, to general good effect. He had plenty of little things on his mind, too, but Baird had been a good lad throughout, and deserved a day of rest.

He set them a pace deceptively easy on the level, and held them to it on the climb. To exhaust himself physically, as well as them, he found to be an excellent idea. The mind had less time and energy to look for trouble of another kind than the trouble they were always hunting. Not that he wished to forget about Imogen, or that forgetfulness was possible if he had desired it; but at least in the comfortable, tired, relaxed pause with cigarettes, up there above the world, the extraordinary twisted worries which entangled Imogen in his mind smoothed themselves out, and there was no more carefulness in him for survival or possession. At least he had it, the thing lots of people went through the world without ever seeing; if he lived he would live having it, and if he died he would die still possessed of it. And in the meantime there were other things he could be thinking about, since this one was settled once for all, and so much to his comfort.

There was Clure, for instance, a good enough little man as completely out of his depth in this army of young huskies as a bank clerk among prize-fighters. Maybe he was a bank clerk, at that; Jim hadn't yet found out. A married man, at any rate, fresh from some white-collar job, with tender hands, and inadequate body, and over-anxious mind; willing to be the best and readiest soldier that ever footslogged it through Europe, willing to enter into the boisterous fun of brats like the Masons and the Meades and the Pritchards, to shoot like a veteran, to march like a champion, to earn the respect and affection of this strange alien species; pathetically willing, but hopelessly incapable. If only some humane doctor could have had the sense and decency to certify him unfit! But he was sound enough; and after all, the M.O.s aren't concerned with the spirit. Besides, he wanted to be in the Army; he'd wriggled out of a job that probably fitted him like a glove to drop his roundness into this uncompromisingly square hole; and even though it had never paid him back anything but disappointments and ridicule and humiliation, he hadn't given up yet, and very likely never would. He was still game, even if he was, as Jim suspected, becoming depressingly sure that he would never make a go of it.

It was Jim's concern to give him, every now and again, something to do that he could do well, and preferably in full view of as many of A Company as possible; but the snag was finding the jobs; the things he did really well were so few.

And there was Teddy Mason, at the opposite pole, unsquashable, competent, cocky, badly in need of a few failures to pull him up a bit, and unlikely to get them. There was a kid who was heading for one hell of a nasty fall when the real thing started. Jim remembered only too clearly what it is like to think you know everything, and wake up with a shock to find that you have everything to learn. He didn't want that to happen to this lot. He'd helped to make them; one way and another he'd tried to drum it into them pretty thoroughly what they were up against; but there are some people who can't be told. They have to learn by the only method they understand; and they don't all survive the lesson. Well, he wasn't going to lose any of his that way if he could help it.

And there was Peterson in jankers, and his stripe, if not washed up altogether, at least indefinitely postponed. And Drury, who was grown taciturn and misanthropic over something private, something which wasn't just girl-trouble this time, or not the ordinary kind. Maybe direct questioning might get out of him what an attempt at pumping would only drive farther in; for he was an honest soul, and would appreciate being honestly tackled, and if his only reaction was a request to get to hell—well, Sergeant Benison could get, and no harm done. He was long past the stage where he had to be subtle about everything.

And infinitely more difficult than these cases with some reason to them, there was Morgan, for whose state there was no reason, whose black depression, constant and incalculable, was a reflection, a haunting, from the darkness of the world. He had a pleasant family, but was independent of them; he had no wife or sweetheart to worry him, and the lack of either certainly gave him no pain. He had no money worries, being better off than most, and no business worries, having left a competent family firm carrying on at home with a friendly eye on his interests. A few material troubles of that kind might have distracted his attention from the real trouble which was corroding his mind and soul. He was obsessed, being a contemplative nature, with the singular horror of living in this world; he was like a man who stares into a dark pool until he topples forward and drowns himself. As perhaps he would have done in good earnest, that night last winter by the lake-shore, but for Jim Benison's advent. Jim had often wondered if Morgan, left to his own company, would ever have come back into camp that night, for there had been something in his eyes, across the glow of the cigarettes in the dark, which was disquieting to remember. But suicide is one act for which you need as much privacy, almost, as for murder; and an audience of one is every bit as bad as a stadium full of onlookers. That performance might yet have to be repeated; and the eruption of the self-same inconvenient sergeant would certainly be suspect this time. Well, leave that problem to be solved when it arose. In the meantime he could at least work the queer creature halfway to his death in order to distract him from finishing the job his own way. He couldn't do himself much harm lying on a hilltop under the lightly clouded sky, with a Woodbine in his mouth and his cap over his eyes. Forget him, while the forgetting was good.

Take them by and large, they were a good crowd; he couldn't wish for better. What he could do to make them invulnerable as a force he had done, and remembering, he hoped, that they were individuals first. They weren't the old crowd, of course; he missed the Ballantynes, and there would never be another Charlie Smith; but since he couldn't have the 4th, he would back the 7th against all comers. Yes, between them they had done a good job; and pretty soon some other people would know it, too.

He took them back to camp at ease early in the evening, in very good spirits, and pleasantly tired. It was peaceful enough to set the war a world away; and yet in that one day it had drawn perceptibly nearer. He felt it, if they did not, his senses sharpened by this clear, grateful fatigue. He slept well that night, being untroubled by thoughts of future or past.

He was out on the range with them all the next afternoon, in weather grown cold and wild, watching them perform demure wonders under the handicap of violently changing cross-winds and abrupt rain-squalls. He was pleased with them, and glad to see that Major Harben himself was not unimpressed, though he was a man given to pointing out the faults in no uncertain terms, and leaving the good points unpraised; which, within reason, was Jim's own way, but he thought Harben overdid it. They weren't all as self-sufficient as Mason; a little stress on the one thing Clure did right, for instance, could surprise even him into doing better, though in his eagerness he would never learn to squeeze a trigger instead of jerking it. And where Teddy pumped three out of five slugs casually into the bull and looked up confident of his unassailable rightness, it did him no harm to listen, instead of praise, to a few dry remarks about the erratic nature of his grouping, and a request to use his sights, and not rely on his memory. Not that every barb went home, by a long way, but they must score a hit now and again, for he took care that every criticism, however unexpected, was a just one. Teddy might rage about that sarcy devil of a sergeant for ever picking on him, but somebody was sure to come back thoughtfully with: "Still, it's no lie. You *do——*"

For to do them right, they too had, on the whole, just and accurate minds; he, who had insisted on the importance of details over and over, was perhaps partly responsible for that. Even a sergeant was sure of a fairish trial.

Jim was leaving the range when he saw one of the khaki-clad figures ahead walking with a curious broken gait, bent a little at the hips, as if trying to conceal a decided limp. He walked close behind him for a while, observing the phenomenon; and then he moved up and tapped him on the shoulder. The instant uneasy glance of young Harry Brecon's eyes said clearly: "Oh, hell, he's noticed!" The kid straightened up at once, determined to ward off the inevitable, though it was easy to see that the effort hurt him; he grinned, too, but it was a wary, speculative grin.

"All right, you can drop that," said Jim. "What's the matter with you?"

"Me, Sergeant? Nothing's the matter with me! I'm all right!"

"Sorry, kid," said Jim, "but I'm not that blind. No use trying to tell me that crab action comes natural to you. What happened to you?" And seeing the boy still hesitate, he went on equably: "Oh, all right, let me tell you. You pride your-self on being a handy lad at shifting weights, don't you? You lifted something single-handed instead of getting some of the chaps to lend you a hand. What was it? Machine-gun? I've seen you toss them around pretty freely. Did you try your jitterbug act with a heavy-weight by mistake on Monday night?"

A fleeting grin sidled over Harry's face and away again. He made the best of it. "Well—matter of fact—it was when Mike and me was out with the little van day before yesterday, Sarge. We had to change a back wheel, and it was quicker—well, we was in a hurry——" He swallowed and sighed; it was out, anyhow, and maybe it didn't sound so bad after all; but a covert glance at Jim's face was not reassuring. "It's only a strain," he said as brazenly as he could, "it'll be all right in a day or so."

"The M.O. can settle that," said Jim.

"Oh, now, look, honest, it ain't anything. It was only the *little* van, and——"

"What do you really want to jack up—a double-decker? No, my lad, its no use shying. You report sick in the morning, or I'll know the reason why. What have you got to show for it anyhow? Come on, let's have the truth!"

"Nothing, honestly! Well, only a little swelling in the groin here, it doesn't amount to anything. Look, Sergeant, I don't want to go sick just when we may be moving off. I've waited a hell of a time for some action; I can't afford to miss it now."

"Fool around with what you've got," said Jim, "and you'll make sure of missing it. Be a good lad, and give yourself a chance, and the odds are you'll be fit enough by the time we see any action." Harry didn't believe that, he could see; the sulky, reluctant lips hesitated upon another appeal. "Don't bother to think up anything else," said Jim flatly. "You're wasting your time. You'll walk to the M.O. or be marched; you can take your pick."

Harry said: "All right, I'll go!" all the time meaning: "Blast you, what did you have to interfere for?" And clearly, as he limped away, Jim could see him thinking vengefully: "It's all right for him to talk. He isn't human. He'd just as soon soldier here as anywhere else—maybe sooner. What's the good of trying to tell him how a bloke feels about it? He wouldn't know!"

Well, that was all right; what's a sergeant for if not to take the blame for every kick circumstances aim at his men? Do him good to hate somebody for it; give him an interest in life, while he fooled around in Sick Bay or on light duties. And supposing it wasn't serious, after all, he'd be back in time for the kick-off; and supposing it was—well, poor devil, but at any rate his mother would be grateful. She set great store by that bone-headed brawny brat of hers; he was the only one, too. Somebody always wins, for what the consolation's worth.

Jim turned to look back at the western sky, where the next storm was gathering in smoky whorls of black and purple cloud; and coming down the field, close on his heels, he saw Brother Gabriel, the taller of the two Franciscans, in his rough brown hooded gown and rope girdle. He drew back a little from the path, and waited for him; they were, after a taciturn fashion, good friends.

"Hullo!" said Jim. "I thought you'd left us. They told me in the village you were going back south this week."

"We go tomorrow," said Brother Gabriel, as they fell into step together. "I came up to see if any of my friends were about. I've been watching your rifle practice for some time, as a matter of fact, from the gate up there. You don't mind?"

"Good lord, no! But I can't imagine why you should want

to. It isn't very entertaining—or have I been missing something?''

"I should say you miss very little," said Brother Gabriel, and gave him a long, thoughtful glance of bright brown eyes, shrewder eyes than the layman expects, perhaps, in a Franciscan friar. Their heads were much on a level; they were both tall men. The sensation of encountering eye to eye this representative of an old monastic system aroused in Jim unaccustomed feelings of curiosity and surprise. It was always faintly wonderful to him that they should be able to think so nearly alike upon so many subjects, as if he had expected to have nothing in common with this man beyond the mere mechanism of flesh and blood. It was no less surprising that he should feel no obligation to edit his conversation; the friar had no taboos, and no apparent wish to see any man's world conform to his own. But above all it was a dizzy reflection to Jim that they had, after all, so much in common; for he, too, lived in a segregated and celibate community, obsessed beyond all other problems by the necessity for self-adjustment to an unnatural scheme of living, where there must be much giving and little getting, as much patience as possible with others, and the least possible concern with himself. The language was different—at least, he hoped it was!—but the fundamental problem was the same.

"You're thinking of him," he said, nodding after Harry Brecon. "I know his gait well enough by now to spot when there's something wrong, I should hope. He's away now to lay it off to his crowd. I'm used to that!"

"I was thinking of them all," said Brother Gabriel, "not simply of him. How long is it I've been watching you in action now? Six weeks, almost. It's been an interesting experience, Sergeant, very interesting."

"Why?" said Jim. "They're the same people they were in civvy life, and nobody took much notice of 'em then."

"Are they? Are you?"

Jim considered that with a wry smile. "Well, of course, if it's spiritual differences you're looking for, I suppose we've all of us developed a bit; but maybe not more than we should have done in the same time even without a war."

"How have you changed? Only in your habits? Only in your opinions?''

"Oh, I suppose we've learned a few new qualities, if only in self-defence; patience, maybe, and how to give and take—

24

you have to bend or burst in this life. But that's bound to happen."

"It gets surprising results sometimes, though, when a crisis like war forces the pace. Take yourself, for instance. Did you have men working under you before the war? Were you as good at it then as you are now?"

"Good at it!" he laughed. "I wish I thought so. No, I never had this bother, exactly, before the war, thank God! I was an under-foreman; that's as far as I got. Anyhow, it's different in a technical job, you only have to worry about their work and wages, not run their lives for 'em. But what in thunder makes you think I'm any good at it? They're the blokes who should know, and they hate my guts. I wouldn't call that being an unqualified success, even if it's usual enough."

"I think you overestimate their dislike," said Brother Gabriel with his knowing smile. "They could hardly profess any affection or admiration, could they? I may not be very well up in these things, but one soon picks up the general conventions, just from looking on. It is essential to detest sergeants, even if one likes them very much."

"You've been reading the wrong authors, or something," said Jim with a grin. "That's out of date. I could show you at least one bloke in our mess that gets everybody's good word."

"Sergeant Raikes?" said the surprising friar. "They like him because they can get what they like out of him, but for the same reason they despise him, too. But he's useful to them, so they don't admit it to one another. Every human being who likes his own way knows perfectly well there are times when he shouldn't get it. Like your young fellow there. If you'd turned a blind eye there he'd have been glad, but his opinion of you would have gone down with a bang. It's a matter of choice which type of regard you prefer, but I should think there can hardly be two opinions about which is of more value to the community."

Jim said, after a moment of astonished silence: "You don't miss much yourself, do you? I didn't realise you'd paid quite so much attention to us."

"I like to learn," said Brother Gabriel simply.

"Learn? From us?"

"Why not? Do you think one is too old at fifty-five to go on learning?"

25

"Not that, exactly; but I wish you'd share your conclusions, then. Might be useful to the rest of us."

"I'm not sure that they're all communicable, but we can try. I've learned, then, that you can more readily induce a number of men to obey you if you are prepared to do yourself every last, smallest thing you demand of them—even when you do it less well than they do, which is not quite so obvious. And again, that you must not ever make a man ridiculous— or, which is much more difficult, allow him to make himself ridiculous—among his fellows in a community. I mean, of course, in a serious degree. I have seen you cope with that very successfully, though you may have thought your strategy primitive enough. And that if you lose sight of them as individuals you have lost sight of them as a body—which is surprising, to me at least. And that everything you may do is useless unless you have a certain feeling for your men, from which everything else proceeds, every precarious subtlety, as well as every inspired simplicity. Unless, in fact, you love them."

Jim threw his head back and laughed aloud at that, into the teeth of the chill wind that scudded up the hill to meet them. "Oh, I'm sorry, but it *is* funny! When I think of the times I could cheerfully murder some of the bright specimens among my lot, it *must* be funny! I'll recommend the recipe to the mess; they'll thank you for it."

"I realise," said Brother Gabriel, thoughtfully rubbing his chin, "that the word may seem rather unexpected in this connection, but I don't feel inclined to withdraw it. Let it stand. You might use a very different expression, and mean the same. Ah, well, my view of things is hardly likely to trouble you, after tomorrow."

"I shall be doing my job as best I can, and so will you. But they don't touch very much, do they?" Jim proffered a packet of Players. "I can't remember if you do. No? Mind if I do?" He had to turn his back on the wind to light up; the trees on the hill-slopes were threshing in a sudden squall, and distance beyond had become only a haze of rain.

"They touch," said Brother Gabriel, "in good will, I hope. We are by no means separate, you know. I should like to feel that you *do* know that. Yes, I know I'm beginning to ride the sort of hobby-horse you expect from me, but you're not the man to hold that against me. One conscientious craftsman respects another, I've found."

26

"Every man to his trade," said Jim. "You keep praying, and I'll keep fighting. One trade's enough—for a conscientious craftsman." He drew on his cigarette, deeply, for it was the first since dinner, and dropped the match into the wet grass at the friar's feet. The intent eyes still held his in a bright and quizzical regard, as if they expected from him something he was deliberately withholding; so sure of him, so confident of his mind, that for a moment he was tempted to wonder if he knew himself quite so well as he had imagined. Then the tremor passed; he knew that he had not made any mistake. "It's no good," he said, "I'm no use to you. I know what you're looking for. You won't find it here."

The demanding glance did not waver nor change. "And yet you did come to church," he said.

"Once, under persuasion—I admit I did. Hang it, the devil himself might do that every now and again. Was that all?"

"Very far from it! But you did come!"

"I came because Imogen wanted to. That was all. I'm sorry, but there it is. Now, you could have talked to her and been satisfied enough. That was one thing you were right about; they *do* still exist."

"We have nothing at all, then," said Brother Gabriel gently, "to offer you?"

"Nothing."

"You are quite sure." It was not a question, but a regretful statement.

"Quite. Why not? I've had the faculty, you see; I wasn't born without it. Maybe I got it too easily to begin with. It just stopped functioning in a natural manner, when reality got too much for it."

"In Flanders, perhaps?" The friar took his arm as they turned to the path again and it struck Jim there was not so great a difference between the browns of the two rough sleeves. "We had better hurry," he said, "the rain is overtaking us."

"In Flanders? Not exactly. It doesn't happen like that, in one thunder-clap. It's cumulative. Maybe it began then; I don't know. It ended a great deal later—if it is ended. There may be farther to go still for all I know; I daresay there is. All I do know is, where faith's concerned I travel very light these days; not from choice, either."

"At least," said Brother Gabriel, "you will not close your mind against it—if it should come back?"

"If it should come back, I'll welcome it with open arms. I

27

know what I'm missing. But I don't expect it. I've got used to doing without, now, and I can go on doing without. I don't go looking for it—what's the good? But don't worry, if it ever does show up again I shall be only too glad to see it. I shan't turn it out!"

They had reached the corner of the camp, where the brown huts showed beyond the green of the unclipped hedge in an incongruous serrated edge like the bosses on the back of some antediluvian monster. Jim paused with his hand on the gate, and looked at his companion with a bitter smile.

"You see, in the matter of poverty I go one step further even than your favourite saint did!"

"You have, nevertheless," said Brother Gabriel, narrowing his eyes at him, "some hoard of your own whose source, if it is not the one I supposed, I frankly do not understand. For I have seen you spend from it, Sergeant Benison, both prodigally and often, and it seems to me it is by no means exhausted, or, if I tell the truth, exhaustible."

"Now you're talking in parables," said Jim, giving it up; "and incidentally, here comes the rain. Why not come in and shelter? It'll soon blow over; the wind's too high for it to last."

"Shelter from an old companion? Thank you, but no, that won't be necessary." He held out his hand. "Good-bye, Sergeant, and good luck—as you would, I think, prefer me to express it. I shall think of you all, continually. And in particular," he said deliberately, "of you. For you are—you will let me say so—a very good man."

"I'd like to believe that," said Jim, "well enough; who wouldn't? But I happen to have discovered that it takes me all my time to be an even moderately good sergeant." He grinned as they shook hands; Brother Gabriel had, at any rate, taken him away from that job of his for ten minutes, and he was duly grateful, but when they parted here nothing would remain of their meeting but a memory of companionship as casual as his contact with the landlord of the "Royal Oak", and no more significant. "Still, thanks for trying!" he said. "I haven't often been considered worth it. Good-bye. Take the short cut down the lorry track; it's quicker by eight or nine minutes. Good-bye!—and better luck!"

Brother Gabriel went down the field-path to the cinder-road as if blown before the squall of fine rain that came riding at speed across the wind. His wet gown flapped about his long legs as he lengthened his stride, and at every step the rope girdle swung out from his waist jauntily and lashed the air in a wide, white arc against the blurred green of the distant trees. The rain, a visible curtain of drifting, smoke-blue fringe, swung between them and dimmed the angular lines of his figure to the softness of a dream. Jim, looking after him, thought wryly: "Why, in the name of fortune did he have to pick on me?" And again: "I suppose being a man like that makes everything easy!" But he knew he was no such man. He did not greatly notice the rain, being preoccupied with the weather in his mind.

So Brother Gabriel had cast him for a sort of religious liaison officer, had he? On what misleading evidence he'd ever reached that conclusion Jim couldn't imagine, but reached it he had, and now he was a disappointed man. It seemed a pity, when he could just as easily have picked on young Dick Shelby, or the ex-local-preacher, Corporal Higginson, who would thoroughly have enjoyed being called to his face a very good man. Ah, well, what odds did it make now? Whether a man believed in all the articles of faith in all the prayer-books, or had ditched everything but what he carried in himself, he still had to get on with this job ahead, ready or unready, like it or lump it. He wasn't concerned so much with faith as with works. They would get the works, all right!

The squall of rain blew by as suddenly as it had come, in a great gust of wind that spattered him with heavy drops of moisture from the hedge. The grey veil parted from the distant hills, shining darkly blue as periwinkles beyond the green and silver of the valley, where all the colours now were dulled and angry, but beautiful still; and from the torn and swirling clouds overhead a sudden lance of sunlight launched itself, quivering, and transfixed the green slope beyond the lake with a dazzling wound. It was as if a sullen woman had turned from her tantrums and deliberately smiled at him, blinding him with unexpected beauty.

"All right," he said, goaded, "I know! There's always you —waiting to be explained—damn you!"

Yes, there was always something left to be explained, and no time or wit left to explain it. That was the untidy way things worked out.

He turned, and went in. There was a lot to be done, and here was he wasting time wondering how the world came to be so beautiful!

29

PART TWO

FRANCE: RETURNING

"Et du nord au midi, la trompette guerrière
A sonné l'heure des combats."
Le Chant du Départ.

I

THEY had been sitting there below deck in their kit, staring at one another in the dim cross-lights and smoking cigarette after cigarette, for a long time, nearly seven hours now. At first they had talked a lot, jauntily, with exaggerated carelessness, then in monosyllables, with increasing strain; now they were not talking at all, except when they really had something to say, which was not often. Their faces were strained and still, past impatience with the long waiting, hanging minute by minute upon the time in a tension increasing but controlled. The motion of the ship was not great, only sufficient to remind them constantly that they were under way. They were lucky to be crossing in a fourteen-thousand-tonner, for it was, as even the Navy admitted, roughish out for small craft. That disagreeable part of the business was to come, and soon now. This was nothing, this slight rolling lift with which they moved through the waters, and the incessant rhythmic creaking of timber which helped to keep the outer, awesome silence out of their ears; there was no inconvenience in this. But wait until the L.C.A.s were launched, and set off at lowish speed through that unpleasant restless sea on the three- or four-hour devious journey to the beaches: wait until that ordeal began, before you congratulated yourself on a good trip. Almost any time now. It was twenty minutes past midnight. Ten minutes to go if they were on time; and they would be on time. Everything was working dead to the dot.

Jim leaned back against the bulkhead, and looked round the silent assembly. None of them, he thought, would ever forget that creaking of timber again, that irritating, soothing, significant noise that went on and on constantly in the background of their minds; nor the half-lit faces intent and aware, with fixed eyes seeing nothing of the past now, nothing of the future, only this present moment as it passed, and the beginning of a new

30

moment on its heels, told out like a solitary's beads; nor the curious shock with which their glances encountered across the charged air, as if they had been for seven hours sitting among strangers. These things would revisit them while they lived, long after the bigger things were forgotten.

Half past twelve, and the motion almost unnoticeable now, stilled to an alert quivering like a good terrier over a rat-hole; and suddenly a rattling roar, not loud but unexpected, that made Corporal Sloan stiffen against Jim's shoulder, and ask: "What in thunder's that?"

"Anchor-chain paying out," said Jim; "we're here."

"Well, thank God for that!" said Teddy Mason. "How much longer do they keep us hanging about now, Sergeant?"

"Till they see fit to move us. I'm not in their confidence."

But it would only be half an hour or so now, he was reasonably sure of that. They would feel better once they could get on deck, and see how the whole sea was alive with British ships at the anchorage; and a damned sight worse, of course, a little later on, in those beastly little L.C.A.s, but they hadn't dared think of that yet. At least they'd be able to see something more than their own company; it gave them a slight feeling of facing the adventure alone to be shut down here below deck, though every conceivable craft from M.L.s to sixteen-thousand-ton carriers, and part of the battle-fleet into the bargain, thronged the teeming sea at no great distance from them.

They heard the brisk but unhurried passing of feet, a sweet, shrill whistle rendering a few bars of "Swanee", the hollow burr of the loudspeakers. Then Baird put his head in. At the very sight of him they hitched themselves forward, heaving the weight of their waterproofed equipment into the truest balance, ready to move off.

"Ten minutes more," he said. "All set, Sergeant?"

"All set, sir!"

"Last chance for a fag, if it's worth while wasting half. They'll probably get spoiled in the water anyhow, if you try and keep 'em. Better make sure!"

He was making sure himself, and he handed the rest of the half-empty packet of twenty to Sloan. "Here, get rid of 'em among you."

Jim gave him a light. After all this time it was something of a miracle that the little white metal lighter with the scratched engraving of the Eiffel Tower on one side still worked at a touch. Baird must have seen it before, but little things like that were registering now with a new clarity. He circled Jim's wrist with his fingers to have a longer look at the design, narrowing his eyes the while against the smoke of his cigarette.

"Hullo! French! Was that from—last time over?"

"That's right. Bought it at a little kiosk in Paris. I'm taking it home now."

The young fingers tightened on his wrist in a long, deliberate grip before they let him go. "I hope so!" said Baird. "I hope so!" And for a moment the words and the voice sounded brittle and nervous, but that was a false impression; he was strung up, all right, but there was something there in reserve, and the words were considered and meant. He was speculating on the chances, and accepting the open risk with a quiet mind.

"You speak French, don't you?" he said.

"I picked up a bit, last time. I've kept it up and enlarged on it as much as I could, these last two years."

"You went to classes, if I remember rightly?"

"Until we went north, yes, but the last bit had to be just books."

"It's going to be useful. I wish I'd done more about mine," he said regretfully.

"Yours was good to begin with, sir; mine wasn't."

"Hmm! That's as may be. But I did try to concentrate on German, of course." He laughed, a shade self-consciously, drawing deeply on the cigarette. "Nothing like being prepared for the best. I don't believe in missing any tricks."

Well, it was something to have a platoon commander who looked at the thing that way. Jim would have chosen him out of the lot of them. Yes, on reflection, A Company couldn't complain; from Major Harben down, they couldn't be bettered by much.

"I'm getting cramped," said Teddy Mason. "I'll be glad to move off. It'll be a treat to get some action, all right, after this sardine tin." His voice was gay and confident as ever, for his assurance was practically impenetrable. Clure might sit there beside him with hands gripped tightly together and a dew of sweat breaking on his forehead, steeling his senses against the impact of something bitterly imagined and justly feared; but Mason was still quite sure of his ability to do all things well. "I was reading what one of these military experts says about the sort of beach defences they're supposed to be using," he said cheerfully, "and according to him they've got a new sort of mine that——"

32

"Shut thi trap!" said Peterson firmly. "We're noan interested. Time's up for military experts."

Their own time was up, too. Baird looked at his watch, which was close upon the hour. "Right, here we go! Everybody up!"

Up they went, orderly and silently upon his heels, into the chill of the June night upon deck. The air struck unconscionably cold; or was that also partly a nervous effect? It was windy, too, so that the clouds were moving fast, and with luck they would at least be spared the last annoyance of rain. Darkness and quietness hung heavy upon them as they filed along the deck to their appointed L.C.A., and mutely filled it; but both the darkness and the quietness were populous with evanescent tremors of light and sound, and the sea was in turmoil with the movement of almost invisible ships. In a few minutes, when their eyes were more accustomed to the night, they could see the whole visible surface of the water dotted with craft, and pick out here and there the recognisable lines of Tank Landing Craft, of big ex-liners carrying troops, and of smaller fry whose precise species they, as mere landsmen, could not in every case identify.

Jim was well forward in the L.C.A., close to where the coxswain, a leading seaman, stood fingering his telegraphs and cocking an alert eye at his officer, who was perhaps half his own respectable age, and looked, in conversation with Harben, like a serious-minded prefect talking to his headmaster.

"Hope you're a good sailor, chum," said the coxswain, giving Jim a knowing grin from under his straw-coloured quiff. He was a fine, hefty figure of a man, built like a bruiser, with an immense chest which filled his jumper to bursting-point, and a pair of arms on him that strained at his sleeve-seams so that he appeared to be wearing a navy-blue skin.

"Why, would you reckon this pretty rough?"

"Lay a few of 'em low, this will, but it might be worse. Wait till we turn into the weather."

"Thanks, it looks grim enough for me this way round!"

The loudspeakers hummed and crackled. A staccato voice gave hollow instructions to lower away numbers one and two, and before the words were well out the thrumming of winches took the air. The loaded L.C.A. sank slowly, and a cross-wind caught and swung her sickeningly as she went, so that for a moment more than one of her complement wondered if she was about to smash like a trampled nut against the hull of the carrier. A wavering whistle from among the ranks saluted the dubious moment with a few breathless but recognisable bars of "Someone's rocking my dream-boat". Somebody said in a half-voice: "Thank God we've got a Navy!" and the coxswain, fending off like a Titan, grinned to himself in appreciation. Then the gust passed, and the L.C.A., shuddering, settled in a wallow of faintly phosphorescent water, shipped it perilously for a moment, and then rode easily, shaking off spray in a stinging cloud.

The sub-lieutenant heaved a sigh that was audible for yards.

"All right, let go aft!—Let go forward! O.K., she's yours, Coxswain; let's go!"

The L.C.A. slid forward through the dark, heavy swell, and the solid black wall which was the carrier fell away into the night astern. From the same ship, and from others more distant, the long, low sled-shapes of many assault craft like their own were converging silently, drawing into double line ahead, marking the dark tumult of the sea with two parallel perforated lines of phosphorescence. On their port bow a minute white light began to wink. The coxswain translated:

"Stand by for a turn to port, sir."

"Right! Hold it!"

"Is that the flotilla boss?" asked Jim, bracing himself as the craft rolled.

"That's right," said the coxswain.

"And the one ahead?" The sea was running so high that periodically he lost sight of this further light in the trough, but at every nauseating heave of the L.C.A. it was there ahead, flashing busily.

"That's the M/S trawler that's piloting us in. She knows what there is to know about the minefields around this coast—we hope! If she doesn't, we're wasting our time."

On the turn they shipped water, and the spray slashed over them salt and cold, chafing their eyelids and lips, and the rims round their wrists and necks, where collars and sleeves rubbed them raw. A few grumbling voices from among the ranks expressed their views on the sea in no uncertain terms; but up to now they were not doing so badly, for not a man was sick. That record wouldn't survive long, at least on this course; a cork on a hill-stream in spate would have been almost stable by comparison. Sloan was beginning to wear the familiar strained look, for one. Young Baird had a kid's shock-proof stomach, of course, and Harben was cast-iron without and within, but

34

by the look of him Lieutenant Grenfell wasn't feeling exactly on top of the world.

"How's it going?" asked the coxswain, not without sympathy.

"Like hell!" said Sloan simply. "My God, I wouldn't have your job!"

"I wouldn't swop you, mate. Every time I get chocka I'll think of you chaps getting out of this here floating shovel and going up that beach. Me, I'd have to be shoved from behind!"

"Beach!" said Sloan wistfully. "If it's solid I'll take it, Jerries and all."

"Cheer up! There's another two hours or so of this yet."

They found that there was. The teeming shipping of the rendez-vous was long since left behind, and for a while only their own flotilla of assault craft was left to trouble the silence, a twin thread of pallor drawn along the sea. Then 'planes began to pass over, flights of bombers heading out at speed for the coast of France. After the first squadron had passed there was hardly a pause, hardly a moment without that fierce, friendly sound crossing them in the cloudy sky.

"Welcome sight, that!" said the coxswain. "Hope they won't leave much for us to do."

"How many more trips will you have to make after this?"

"There's no limit. Four will get that lot off, unless we lose a lot of craft first go; but after that we go back for another lot, and start over again. You're the first of the many, mate— you and the bombers. Stand by for a hell of a splash. The F.O.'s bringing us up into the weather again."

It was a sickening lurch and shudder that took her this time on the turn, and a heavy sea came inboard and by sheer dead-ening weight brought her up wallowing, almost motionless in the trough.

"Heck!" said the sub-lieutenant, "we'll lose her yet! Hold her on it, Coxswain, we're skidding."

The L.C.A. recovered herself gradually, and nosed unsteadily ahead, regaining her station in the line. She had taken aboard too much water for their comfort this time; at every roll it washed round their ankles and over their boots with a sickly, monotonous noise. It was too much for Corporal Sloan; he doubled himself over the gunwale with a groan, and was deathly sick. He wasn't the first; several in the ranks had already given up the unequal struggle, and been sick where they stood, lack-ing room to move aside. Clure was green to the lips, but had survived so far. Young Teddy had turned out, certainly by no virtue of his own, to be immune, and was finding the misery of his companions rather funny than otherwise; natural enough, but why couldn't his luck let him down just once, and give the others the laugh for a change? Circumstances were building him up for the fall of a lifetime unless something pricked that arrogance of his and let him down gently, and a little thing like a bout of seasickness could at least have brought him to the common level of humanity. But no, his malicious luck still held.

"You're doing all right, Sergeant," remarked the coxswain. "Been rehearsing this?"

"We all have, but if it gets you it gets you, that's all there is to it. No, I've been picked out of boats twice before, once here in the Channel, and once in the South China Sea. I'm used to it. I quit feeling sick my first trip."

"You're lucky. I've known fellows who never got over it in years at sea. Yes, I'd say you're lucky."

"I have been—often—very lucky."

"You'll need to be again, in just about an hour."

Jim grinned. "I'm thinking so, too." He ducked his head into the spray of a heavy sea, and spat salt water, and swore. "Must be getting fairly near now."

"Fairish. You can see the edge of a minefield yonder—that blue light. Yes, getting fair to middling near now."

The 'planes continued to pass over, in greater numbers now, and distant reverberations from the still unseen coast began to be perceptible as quiverings along the air even before they were sounds. The bombers were doing their part. In half an hour more it would be the official dawn, the grimmest hour of the twenty-four. Already the darkness had changed in quality, and a visible shade separated the sea from the sky. Soon they might hope to distinguish the coast of Normandy whither they were bound. They strained their eyes after it through the dimness and the spray, across a heaving sea-line which cut off at every surge and fall even the light of their guiding trawler. Even Sloan dragged himself upright, brushing off salt water from his haggard face to stare ahead and strain after sight where all was shifting illusion.

The Flotilla Officer's light winked busily, and the coxswain interpreted: "Increase speed, sir!"

"Right! Give her another couple of revs.," said the sub-lieutenant.

"Ay, ay, sir!" And he relayed into the communication telephone at his elbow: "Shove her up a couple, Tom!"

"Oke!" said the telephone, distantly but distinctly. The L.C.A. slid forward with an increased impetus. They could see their companion craft now as more than shadows of darkness and wakes of dubious light, a line of flat grey excrescences slithering swiftly through the water, holding station as rigidly as if they had been the knobs upon the spine of a great serpent swimming headlong for France.

"Look!" said Sloan suddenly, peering ahead. "They've got a hit!"

Several others had seen it at the same moment, and exclaimed upon it with him; a scarlet flash upon the horizon, and after it a new, sullen red star left upon the fading night, a star that pulsed irregularly, and sent up a plume of smoke into the sky. The light was now so far advanced that behind that oily black smudge the sky itself looked pale. By keeping their eyes fixed upon that fire they were able to catch the flashes and puffs of other bombs exploding to left and right of it, and by these to fix in their own minds the line of the coast. It was not yet visible, though to stare long enough against the lurching gait of their craft was to imagine that they saw it. A scarcely perceptible line of slate-grey, lost and recovered, and lost again, recognised at every recovery by its stillness where nothing else was still, but so tenuous that a flicker of the lashes could blink it away. It might or might not be real; the dazzled eyes could never be sure of it.

Jim closed his eyes for a few minutes to rest them, the better to capture that elusive thread of land. With reality shut out, sudden memories came in upon him, and he knew himself near to the satisfaction of one hunger at least among the many which made up his famine of mind and soul. The last interval of waiting, shrinking now to a mere breathless moment, seemed to him yet too long. When he looked up again the slate-grey line was still there, was steady, was clearer, had more of depth. There was no more illusion; he was looking at France.

Another flash of fire spurted upward close beside the first, and shortly afterwards a new, pale flame, white and brief as magnesium, burst out farther to their right.

"Doing a nice job, those boys up top," said the sub-lieutenant thankfully. "Better be ready to duck, sir, from now on; we're going in pretty fast."

The wisp of coastline grew before their eyes, and put on

shape and substance, though all the colours were still flat and void in the chill half-light. They saw the lines of beach and cliff at last, the stretches of shingle and sand, and dunes behind, with here and there the curious dead texture of concrete which meant to them emplacements, strong-points, and forts. This was France; this was the world's-end they had come so far to seek. They could see, now, the eruptions of sand and debris from the successive bomb-bursts. The sky was palpitating with 'planes in combat. They alone were still ghosts, moving almost silently into the battle, unseen and unchallenged; yet on them all things depended.

"Ten minutes more puts us within range of their shore batteries," said Harben, staring ahead. "The heavies could reach us now. How long can we hope to go on unnoticed?"

"Can't be sure, sir. A 'plane could have reported us long ago, but they seem to have been pretty well held inshore. Failing that, I doubt if they can spot us until we deploy."

"Good! Then we'll grovel when we have to, and not before."

The quietness about them held as they went in, while the tumult ashore assembled itself before them detail by detail, from the shingle and the surf tattered with pronged steel obstacles to the sheer faces of concrete high among the dunes. The flat grey light picked out at last every angular shadow of that fantastic coast, and even a faint shade of green came into the thin dune grass, before the first battery gave tongue. The shell fell well short of them, and a sheet of water ripped upward and cut them off from the shore.

"This is it!" said Major Harben. "Tell the men to keep down low." Half of them, and the more experienced half, were down already, crouched in the wash of sea-water, braced ready for the lash of the descending spray, which hung upon the air in an opaque expanding tower, almost motionless. But many were slow in responding to something which had never yet been more than make-believe to them. Jim knew that feeling of unreality; it was soon shed. A word and a peremptory gesture fetched them down fast enough. Only Mason was deliberately slow in obeying, staying upright out of sheer bravado as the surge of spray spattered down, and rearing his head out of it, as it passed, with a gasp and a derisive crow of laughter. He had to be different, of course, the brazen little devil; he had to go one better. The sort of kid who feels bound to walk on all the walls the sensible kids reject as too risky, and never falls off in time to learn some sense without getting hurt in the process.

Jim swung on him with a ferocity they had never seen in him before. "You—get down and stay down!" he said bleakly. "We're not interested in your heroics—keep 'em for the enemy!"

Teddy dropped fast enough under that thin look. He laughed again, surreptitiously, as he sat back on his heels; that was due to himself, and Jim could afford not to notice it, though it was meant for him to hear. What mattered was that there would for ever be the same job to do again, every time a pointless risk offered for a fool to take in bravado. One of 'em throwing his life about just to cut a figure before the others, and another worrying and scarifying that wistful conscience of his because it wasn't in his nature to be the same sort of idiot! The trouble there was in men, and most of it needless!

"Here it comes!" said the sub-lieutenant, as the F.O.'s light began to flash again. "We're turning into line now, sir. This is the last dash, and I fancy they've got our number. Anything can happen now."

"Right!" said the major. "In case I forget later, or leave it too late—thanks for a pleasant trip!"

The L.C.A. slowed, and turned with deliberation this time, wheeling steadily inward to face the beach. On either side of her the craft behind nosed in, until the whole array hung for a moment still in one long, regularly spaced line. Short of them a second shell, and a third, sent up sheeting fountains of water. The assault craft wallowed under the surge from the nearer miss, but held their station, straining upon the Flotilla Officer's signal.

"Smoke-float ready?" asked the sub-lieutenant. His voice had risen a note or two from strain.

"All ready, sir."

"O.K., Coxswain, here we go! Full speed ahead!"

The line of assault craft moved inward in one converging leap, quivering and hissing through the water towards the pock-marked beach and the towering fires behind. They were seen now; they were marked. From all the length of the beach a staccato of fire broke out upon them so that they were stunned by the impact of it, and could not for a while distinguish instrument from instrument in that orchestra of fury. They slithered at speed through a sea boiling with fountains of spume, towards a foothold upon the shingle; and as they went the detail of the shore leaped towards them in a bleak, bewildering clarity under the dawnlight, pinpointed with explosions of fire.

Even small arms could reach them now. They heard and felt the shot like driven rain scudding by them and stinging the sea. They crouched and craned, fixing their eyes upon the strip of beach where they would first set foot, and gathering their weight forward towards the moment; and their minds were a single mind, braced and still, turning even fear into a weapon, and the knowledge of fear into a formidable armour. All the work and weariness and schooling of two years culminated in this one moment; the time had not been wasted, they were a unit in more than name.

A smoke-shell burst upon the beach to their left, and began to pour black and stinging smoke down-wind, leaving a mounting grey wall across their front, and on the near side of it their landing place clear. The smoke-floats in the windward craft of their own line had also been lit, and the thinning drift moved gradually across them until they travelled in a bitter, billowing grey cloud, cut off from the batteries in the dunes and the machine-gun fire from the beaches. Low along the water it was clear, and the first shaft of positive light, brightly coloured in amber and gold, glimmered across the waves and picked out the steel teeth of trestle obstacles ahead, and the black web of wire, and shone in green fire along the cleared passages between.

The craft slowed. Here and there she was touching, lightly and stealthily, the grinding of gravel along her bottom an ominous sound. She shivered and stopped.

"Terminus!" said the coxswain. "This is as far as we go, chum." He slanted a smile at Jim from under the tawny quiff. "Good luck! You'll need it!"

"Down doors!" yelled the sub-lieutenant, and down the landing-doors crashed in a torrent of foam that swirled back to meet A Company as they ran down the ramp and into the sea. Harben with his long legs and his light load met the weight of the water gaily, but the backwash almost took the ranks off their feet before they could adjust their balance to the thrust of it. Pity they couldn't have got in nearer! They were up to their armpits almost before they knew, and the fine, braced impetus they had stored for the assault was lost in a welter of water as they struggled in with the flowing tide. Time was desperately precious now. They had the job of making a beach-head for the next convoy, and a cover under which the sappers could work; and they were slowed up, and the screen set up by the smoke-bomb on the beach was filling the upper air, but thinning below. Just in time, there went a second one, from the

40

last boat to land its tally; well placed, too, fairly high up the beach to windward, so that the streaming cloud blew wavering across their front along the whole visible expanse of the shore.

Jim kept close by Baird's elbow, where he would be looked for in due time. His eyes never left the hollow path he had already chosen up the beach and into the shingle, yet he was aware of things which happened to left and right of him, and behind. He knew the curious sound, half grunt, half sigh, which Pike made as he took a rifle-bullet low in the chest, the platoon's first casualty. He knew the stunning explosion of the mine, away to their right in the smoke, too high to have got many of the lads, unless they had touched in earlier on that stretch; an officer in the lead, maybe, and the nearest of his men, touched that off and went up with it. He knew, too, the burst which got one of the L.C.A.s as they pulled up their doors and sped away upon their next errand. The flotilla would return less one, at least; maybe the very one with the straw-coloured quiff, that held the killick, who had wished them good luck. Somewhere just behind Jim and to his left, some unfortunate not built by nature for wallowing through unquiet seas went headlong into a deep pool, and was hauled out—the sharp exclamation was in Welsh—by Morgan; no longer pre-occupied by death, this Morgan, but infinitely alive to life. And the victim, who laboured ahead half drowned and wholly distressed, was Arthur Clure. But no more losses yet; only Pike. And here was the last shallow, and the rubbish of surf, and sand in which they could dig their heels and hold on.

As the drag of the water released them they picked up their feet and ran, well up the sand of the beach, selecting as they went. Baird had not missed that shallow gully; it was all sand within, hollowed by the thin trickle of a stream, and narrowing gradually as it climbed; cover of a sort, at any rate, and making due inland for the dunes and the concreted strong-points they must reach at all costs. Somewhere up there the Atlantic Wall began. The stream looked like sweet water; it smelled like sweet water. If it was mined it was mined, for that was an open risk almost anywhere. Baird ran crouching across the open, and flung himself flat in the hollow, and the platoon followed him at good speed. Jim looked back then for Pike, and saw him being half led, half carried forward at a jog-trot between Corbett and Teddy Mason. He wasn't out, then; he just had his ticket home. A short visit, that, but Pike wouldn't mind, nor Mrs. Pike either. And someone else got it just then, as he

41

watched; took it in the side as he ran through the shallows, and clapped his hand to it, and went down in a flurry of spray. Two others hesitated and half swerved out of their way towards him, but Jim shouted and waved them on after Baird, and himself went back at a crashing run to pick up the casualty.

It was one of Grenfell's kids, young Thompson, and he was half conscious and quietly drowning in eight inches or so of water. Jim heaved him up by the armpits and let the salt water run out of him, and after a moment the kid began to draw hard, greedy breaths for his life. Jim carried him up the sand-hollow over his shoulders, and laid him prone in the best cover he could find for him, clear of the last brash of the tides, with his head lower than his feet, and his face turned to one side to give him air. Baird, who was already manœuvring a mortar-team into position up the stream, turned back to view the damage.

"Is he all right, Sergeant?"

"I think so. The medical boys'll be here on the flow."

"Good! We've sprung a fairish spot. Come on!"

The fire was still hot, but it was not entirely one-sided now. The mortar had not yet gone into action, but rifles were crackling angrily all along the smoke-shrouded beach, and the stutter and cough of machine-guns perforated the din in dotted line of indignant exclamation. From the sea heavy guns began to sound, as the Navy went into action dead on time.

Baird went up to the head of the little water-course at a spasmodic run, dropping flat at intervals to hug the earth; and Jim followed, and the platoon, those who had not already gained on him, followed Jim as blithely as they had done on Westmorland fells two months ago, and on southern beaches last month. They knew their job, the 7th. The last stage of that advance was made flat on their bellies, for they had penetrated to the thin edge of the shroud of smoke, and by the ferocity of the fire that engaged them they were already observed. They had come, by virtue of that promising path, near to the lift of the dunes; the detail of their sector showed clear, a deep nest of concrete under the fall of the coarse grass, sunk in an elbow of the sandy hills, and what looked like another strong-point above, where solid ground began. The open stretch between them and the prize, swept with fire, made them flinch; but they coveted that corner.

"A couple of machine-guns up there," said Jim, "and we could enfilade half their other emplacements."

"That's what I was thinking. Save the rest of the company a bad crossing, too." They searched the field of fire together for the least ghost of cover, but there was scarcely even an undulation in the stretch of shingle, or a high patch of sand where they could dig in.

"It's a longish run," said Jim, "but give me some more smoke, and five minutes grace, and I can get there with grenades and give you an opening."

"Not much time! Yes, we'll have to try it. Take Sloan and a couple of men."

Not much time, or Major Harben and the rest, less happily placed, would waste themselves in a frontal rush, or lose men where they lay. They had drawn the aces this trip; it was their funeral. He took Sloan, Peterson and Bennett, sane men all, too sound to attempt the impossible where it could be avoided, or shrink from it where it could not.

"Got your direction clear? This'll be mainly from memory. Right, sir, let her go!"

The smoke-shell burst close to the smudge of concrete in the elbow of the dune. They waited a moment for the wind to spread the cloud and then picked themselves out of the sand and ran, half blind but holding their course by guess-work, towards the hills. Their eyes, already blackened and sore with smoke, ran channels of silted grime down their cheeks until the copious tears washed their courses white. They ran at a fast but cautious crouch, and dropped into the first soft undulations of sand, where the grey, thin grass helped to cover them. Five minutes they had asked for; prompt to the moment the mortar went into action, and the range was good, but the first shell drew the whole fire of the double strong-point upon the mortar's position. With the better will, remembering the platoon grovelling in their hollow, Jim and his three moved in upon their stomachs, and came near enough to see through the shifting smoke the faces of concrete casemate and steel shell-plating, and a haze of wire. Jim selected the easiest climb and at the most approachable point he lobbed in the first grenade, and saw it burst within the shell of the outer wall. Sloan moved in on his right and followed it up with a second, and the others scattered to the left and joined in quickly, before they could be located and picked off singly at leisure. The mortar was doing its part, too, and just beyond the line of the dunes a bomber was giving its attention to the inland batteries. They could feel, though there was too much din to

43

let them hear, the platoon moving in at their backs. The fire from the dunes was intense but broken; only the wire was a formidable obstacle, as far as Jim could see from where he lay, and even through that there was a way clear if they could so enlarge it that attack from that point did not mean being picked off man by man as they crashed through. He wormed his way closer, and sent in his third grenade with care, just under the terminal iron tripod that held the wire taut, and flung it some yards aside from its place. When the dust cleared he saw the whole four-foot-wide mesh of wire sagging into the sand, and the tripod overturned. Even a moderate hurdler could take that obstacle in his stride now. How great was the drop within the concrete wall he could not be sure, but less than a man's full height, he thought, and at worst not much more.

Here came the platoon, bursting out of the smoke like elementals embodied from nowhere, Baird in the lead. It was up and in like mad now, and the faster the better; and in he went with them, scrambling out of the sand and leading them in with a shout to where the wire was down, for they came out of an almost total blindness. They accepted his lead instantly, and not only Baird, but three others, took the obstacle neck for neck with him, and fell down headlong beyond the wire into a concrete pit of yelling men. It was deeper than he had thought, being stepped to a height of four feet from the base for riflemen, so that the drop seemed endless; but he fell upon flesh, and went down headlong with his enemy stunned under him. The narrow space seemed full of men, for the stairway to the upper terrace was too narrow to permit of a quick withdrawal, and Baird, who had dropped at its very foot, was halfway up it with a dozen wild youngsters at his heels before the Germans well knew he was among them. After that it was bayonet business, warm but brief, in the pill-box above, a confused, unclean business from which they emerged in a matter of minutes dazed with noise and shock, to find themselves in possession of the coveted point, a light mortar, two machine-guns, and seventeen prisoners, besides eleven dead.

They turned the machine-guns along the flanks of the dunes, searching out point after point; and only when Harben and the rest of the company were edging forward under cover of their fire did they find time to look round and count their own losses. Even then it could not be a pause, but only a glance before the next move, which was already forming in Baird's

44

mind. A step along the dunes to their right, and they could let
B Company in with hardly a blow struck; the temptation was
to spread themselves too far, though, for their foothold even
here was precarious until they were reinforced. In the meantime they had lost seven men killed, of whom three lay far
down the beach still; Bennett was laid out within the concrete
wall with his back propped and his knees drawn up to close
a transverse abdominal wound; Gratton was unconscious beside
him with a broken head, snorting like a horse at every heavy
breath; Bell had lost half his battledress blouse from one
shoulder and arm, and was streaked with his own blood from
neck to thigh; but these would live, given average luck, and the
rest were as nothing, mere scratches and furrows never noticed
until afterwards, like the ploughed line of a rifle-bullet spiralling
round the soft part of Jim's forearm. They had been perhaps
the luckiest company to land that day in Normandy; and luck
is a strange thing, not to be wooed by any means but the
prompt acceptance of good chances and bad alike. What they
had been spared they owed it to the balance of things to repay
to the others.

The sun was high now. Colour had come to the world,
though the shore was a reeking crater pitted with paler hollows
and furred with smoke. Moving out over the crest of the
parapet, where the grass was longest, Jim looked back over
the shingle to where the sea glittered in a shifting pathway of
gold, and the dispersing smoke made a blue ceiling, miles in
air, for the evolutions of 'planes. Another flotilla was coming
in, mere black dots as yet far out in that mutable world of
water; and the stabbing flashes of the Navy's big guns burned
along the horizon beyond them.

It was then that he saw, as he crawled forward, the smear
his right arm left along the stems of the grasses, and the red
drops that darkened the sand for a moment, and vanished in
dull brown stains. This manifestation seemed to him to come
from very far away and very long ago, and to have nothing
whatever to do with June 1944 or the coast of Normandy. For
a moment he was blind and deaf to the dazzling and resounding
day, all his senses turned inward upon the recollection of something which in fact he had never seen, of gunfire he had never
heard except in his darkened and single spirit, within the drawn
blinds of his loneliness. In this withdrawal he was aware, as he
had not been until that moment, of the reality and significance of
what he did now, as if the present was real only by virtue of

45

the touch of the past. He saw a quarry in Artois, gravel-red beneath just such harsh, thin grass; he saw blood dewing the stems and spattering the ground even as his did now; but this was not his own blood, except as the spirit has blood-ties. He saw a still face, pale as a lily upon a pool of black hair, and against the waxen cheeks roses lying, roses from long remembering almost as holy, almost as miraculous as St. Dorothy's flowers from Paradise. Miriam Lozelle had watered the soil of France with her life; how could it but flower? Even as the life she had given back to him was a new thing, or a changed, not the unthinking existence she had touched and transmuted. It was she who had made it necessary for him to come back, to gather up what had been shed, to mend, or attempt to mend, what had been broken. It was she who had lifted her hand out of the soil and drawn him down to her now, with the first drops of his blood drying upon the hem of her sleeve; she who by requiring nothing of him had caused him to desire to make to the world a gift exceeding all he had.

A moment of dizziness went over him, and he put his head down in his arms until it passed. The sand was already warm under him; he lay breast to breast with France again. When he raised his head he saw the assault craft turning into line in a feathery fan along the sea, and on the horizon other ships standing inward at speed for the beach-head, numberless ships, laden with tanks and guns and stores and medical supplies, towing sections of pier and dock and landing-stage, bringing the equipment and arms the men had lacked once, and the men without whom equipment and arms alike were useless; small as yet in the far distance, but advancing by hundreds, the ships came. He saw what he had been unable to see while he was a part of it, the invasion of France, the first wound of the atonement.

2

He saw the same beaches again, two days later about sunset, the tide low, and the sighing ebb far out beyond the hard. It was a thronging world then, but the greatness of sea and sky dwarfed it still and the activity upon the shore was like an ineffective challenge to the early stars, whose cold, pale, unmoved purity gazed upon the might of men and was not disquieted. So it was and so it should be, if they were to believe they did well; for the deed was great only if the impulse from which it sprang was greater, and something of what they desired for the world was there in the lofty evening above the Channel for all to sense and see, a heart of peace, profound and permanent and still, durable as a diamond and limpid as a thought.

He had come back from Bayeux that evening with half a dozen men and a column of German prisoners to be embarked for England; and he was waiting to hop a lorry back to his unit, who were lying just west of Bayeux, in fields north of the road to Balleroy and St. Lô. While there was time, and because it was the first real pause they had yet encountered, he took the opportunity of walking back, while the lorry was loaded, for another look at the beach-head. History was being made there; the thing which was an accomplished fact now had been a dream only a week ago. So he walked the length of the country lane that brought him by dwindling hedges and warped trees to the bare, high point of the dunes, and looked down with the populous coast and the immensity of evening before him, and at his back the gentle, rolling fields of Normandy, so like England that but for the wreckage of houses and litter of steel debris, the torn soil and the swollen corpses of cattle, he might have been standing in any of the mid-southern counties staring across at France.

The beach had changed a lot in two days. Now that the tide was well out he could clearly see the jagged black teeth of the tripod and grid-iron piles planted thickly all down the tidal mud to rip the bottoms out of the assault boats, and he marvelled how they had come through with so few losses. There were clear channels now, plain as on a map, where bulldozers had towed out the obstacles and sappers drawn the teeth of the mines, and small stuff could come in safely as on a high road. There were the beginnings of piers and stages, built far out from the hard into deep water, and already some craft were alongside at the seaward ends, and lorries plying with ladings of fuel and ammunition, stores, instruments, medical supplies for the advancing armies, everything a man needs to invade a continent. There were whole encampments under the dunes, hemmed with erections of oil drums, crates, ammunition boxes, kitchen effects, alive with men, humming with the movement of lorries going and coming by the inland roads. Along the hard, tanks and guns rolled ponderously, moving up towards Bayeux; other Tank Landing Craft lay off in deep water, waiting until the returning tide should bring them in to empty their freight and ship another, the tale of the wounded going home. Far along the sands from where he stood, bulldozers were butting at the remains of a section of the vaunted West Wall, coming back to the charge time and again like goats until the standing fragments of masonry and concrete crumbled in columns of dust. On the fringes of the hard, engineers were laying flexible mesh track over a bad patch of deep shingle. Everywhere there was the activity of a populous but strange city, a city of technicians and specialists. Even the Infantry, footslogging it towards Formigny in the lane below him, had earned that regard now; in their line they were experts, one and all.

Already, too, the pivot of the battle had shifted inland. He would have known it even if he had not seen with his own eyes the tricolour flash out from the broken-hinged shutters of Bayeux as the invaders entered the town, and the women surging up from their cellars with incredulous joy in their faces, and holding up their children to see the victors go by. He would have known it by the ease with which these landings and movements proceeded, and the comparative quiet of the evening sky. Scattered dog-fights went on constantly overhead, but the full fever of that battle had been driven inland. Not this time were the Infantry to stem with their bare hands the whole flood of the enemy armour on land and in the air. Things were changed since that 1940 campaign.

They had met, during those two days, all sorts and conditions of men. Canadians, Americans from their right flank, Frenchmen of the Maquis erupted out of the very soil, their own airborne and parachute troops who had held inland points for sixteen hours unsupported before they made contact, all these moved about their single and yet diverse business without confusion or fuss; the beaches swarmed with engineers; the high points of the dunes were alive still with the spotters who had ranged for the naval gunners, one-man units living in troglodyte fashion with their R/T and their solitary brew-ups, and collecting between actions all the gossip of the beach-head from doughboys and Canucks they had never met and probably never would meet. A highly organised society had worked itself into firm holding in this state within a state.

He heard Peterson hailing him from the lane, where the escort party were busy feeding three or four little boys in blue pinafores with their ration chocolate; that was where most of the chocolate went, but who could wonder, when the small, dark, chattering, bright-eyed people popped up irrepressibly in their path before the enemy were well out of sight at the other end of the village street? To a man like Peterson, who had left four kids of his own behind in England, it was honey to be wooed by these children of the captivity, to be able to bestow on them what would make the voluble lips grow round and still in wonder, and the wary eyes glisten. They had known, the youngest among them, only one kind of soldier; possibly even the Germans had held out sweets to them sometimes, but they had been taught how to deal with that very early in their short lives, retreating with blankly smiling faces and veiled eyes. The Midshires were a new kind of soldier, and had to be learned all over again, but it was well worth the effort.

"If only," thought Jim, watching them as he dropped down from the dunes into the lane, "if only we could be sure of our footing here!" For though it had gone well in those two days, they possessed as yet no more than a beach-head, and the enemy armour was massing beyond Caen. A lot to do, and a hell of a long way to go yet, before the Norman children could be sure of anything more than chocolate.

Peterson looked up from the smallest of the boys, and reported: "Lorry's coming up. He just gave us the clear."

The child, feeling himself neglected, pulled at the nearest khaki trouser leg, and remarked insinuatingly: *"Chocolat!"*

"You've had it, chum! *Il n'y a plus!* Savvy? Chocolate no got! That's the lot." He spread his large hands, displaying their emptiness regretfully. "See? All gone! And your Uncle Pete's got to be on his way, too, so how about you getting off home, eh? It's past your bed-time. Come on, now! *Allez chez vous!* Buzz off home!"

They smiled, and chattered, and did not move. He scuffled his feet at the youngest one with make-believe ferocity, and the youngest one retreated two short steps and laughed at him.

"Just like me own!" he said complacently. "One word from me, and they do as they like! Wouldn't think they'd ever gone in fear of owt, would tha?"

But to young animals and birds, and elemental beings such as these children, fear was at worst only a temporary thing, short-lived, very soon lost. The mothers and fathers it was who would carry the permanent scars; and perhaps, too, those unfortunate young who had been forced by circumstances into the cast of an older generation. There were children in France who had taken upon them the cares of men. The oldest of this little group, for instance, a boy of not more than ten, had eyes in his head that might have belonged to a grandfather. He was thin, and growing tall, shooting out of his ragged clothes here and there; and he did not smile nor chatter, but only fastened his eyes upon Jim, drinking in his ribbons and stripes and scars thirstily, and so stared, visibly satisfying himself.

"You live near here?" asked Jim in his prim French.

"Yes, Sergeant, in the village down there." He pointed inland, away from the road, where trees clustered about half-seen farm buildings.

"And these little ones?"

"Yes, Sergeant, they also."

"It's dangerous for them on the road here. You'll see them safely home, won't you?"

"Yes, Sergeant!" The too-experienced eyes never wavered, but he smiled a pale, pleased smile.

"Keep them in the fields; there'll always be heavy traffic on the road, all hours of the day and night, so you'll have to be a good general, and take care of your troops."

"I shall be very careful, Sergeant. We shall go home now." And he called his pinafored army to attention in excited French as the lorry came rolling up from the beach and slowed to pick up its passengers. Peterson abandoned his intelligent conversation with the smallest boy, hitched his belt, and hopped aboard with a smooth heave of his long arms. The driver leaned out, saluted the children breezily, and jerked his thumb back at the tailboard. "Step on it, lads, I daren't stop here." They heaved one another aboard and crawled in among bales of Sommerfeld track and cases of heavy tools, and the lorry shot away again at speed, all but spilling the last man as he clambered after his fellows. The children waved, and the oldest boy drew himself to his full fragile height and gave them the most desperately solemn salute Jim had ever seen.

"Let's hope," he said to Peterson as he returned it gravely, "he'll never have to do that in earnest."

"Nay, I hope none of 'em will. Twice is more than enough." He took the half of a cigarette from behind his ear, and lit it, and drew thoughtfully upon it, his half-closed eyes watching the road unfold behind them, endlessly prolonging itself in a flow of tanks, lorries, armoured halftracks and motor-cycles, all spaced along the dissolving ribbon of dust like the knots in a flagellant's scourge. "My big lad's about that age," he said. A lot of fellows must have been looking at these children of Normandy and seeing their own flesh and blood, thought Jim. The child's voice, saying dutifully over and over: "*Oui, mon Sergent!*" was in his ears yet. The fathers weren't the only ones who were feeling uneasy about being hailed as deliverers too soon, it seemed; single men, too, had the next generation on their consciences and Caen on their minds. For even this benefit, the gift of a land pitted with shell-craters, soiled, withered, smelling of sudden death, littered with scrap-iron, limping and bawling with maimed cattle, but free of Germans—even this might not last; and of the future there was no guarantee.

As they moved inland the devastation of their coming grew more and more apparent. This should have been lovely, kind country, pasture and grain and woodland rich upon the eye and fat in fertility, full of standing corn mellowing towards its ripening, and mown grass sweeter than meadow-sweet, and placid matronly dairy herds moving back and forth unalarmed between farmyard and field. The cornfields were pitted with shell-craters, and torn to pieces with the tracks of tank and gun; the corn, what was left of it, would rot upon the stem, for it was not worth harvesting. The pastures were raw with wounds and littered with the wreckage of 'planes and armour. Guns, abandoned in that first irresistible recoil, still pointed ineffectively at the onward rush of traffic from the sea. Their fate was clear even now; they would stand so while the armies passed, they would stand so after the armies were gone; they would rust there and rot there in the untended fields, and fall to pieces at last under the rain and the sun, and the coaxing of couch grass and convolvulus, settling into their weedy graves. The hay, such part of it as had not already been carried, lay blackening and steaming along the ground. As for the handsome Normandy cattle, some had survived, no doubt, but the bulk of them were swollen carcasses putrefying in the pastures and by the roadside, or distracted strays running wild with shock and pain among the tanks, their bellowing an offence in the ears, their distended udders bursting with milk. Such of the Midshire men as were handy at the work, and they were many, had filled in the odd quarter-hours by relieving the beasts of that intolerable burden of milk, and saved a great many head of cattle for the Normandy farmers, but what they could do, and all the other country-bred units with them,

51

was only a crumb against starvation. France was paying heavily for her freedom.

They passed through villages along the streets of which they had fought their way house by house and yard by yard on the previous morning. The house damage was not so bad, considering all things, for the struggle over these few miles had been quick and even clean compared with what would happen inland when the heavy armour began its work; but even so there were gaps enough to recall the realities to mind. The population had emerged from its cellars, and taken up, as far as was possible, the normality of life almost before the last German soldier had been rooted out of hiding. From behind the slatted shutters at night sleepless children looked out upon the streams of British and American traffic passing through, excitement and noise keeping them at the windows half the night, and turning them into hollow-eyed elf children out of a ghost story. And somewhere in every village, in the churchyard, under the cemetery wall, or by the hedges along the roadside, were laid out in rows the sheeted dead still awaiting burial; and somewhere in every village were new-turned graves, with rough crosses at their heads, and a few flowering spikes of clover and vetch to soften their raw newness. Would it occur to any man, thought Jim, that a necessary item of supply for an invasion would be shrouds by the thousand? And yet someone had remembered them, for there was no lack; the dead were all decently clad.

Half a mile or so out of Bayeux the lorry slowed and turned off to the right, waved aside imperiously by a young M.P., the least travel-stained Englishman they had yet seen in France outside of a Staff car. His trimness suggested comforts they had almost forgotten, baths and clean linen, and a shave in warm water. The boys in Bayeux were enjoying these things, very likely, for the cave-dwellers had not come out of their cellars empty-handed, and people who would open up their last hoarded bottles of wine in honour of the liberators would certainly not grudge a tub of hot water and a towel, or a piece of soap to go with them. As for the Midshires' present billet in the fields of a small farm, with forward posts spread ahead into a thin belt of woodland, well, it was not without its compensations. The bathing, a stream going down to join the Drôme, was not only cold, but risky by reason of a playful habit the Jerries had of flying up and down it machine-gunning whenever the skies were momentarily free of R.A.F. 'planes;

and for the rest they had to rely upon the mobile laundries which had not yet reached them. But there was a good deal of satisfaction to be got out of those lightning dips, and at one point, where a bend of the stream had hollowed out for itself a deep pool, it was even possible to swim in fair comfort. Yes, take it by and large, they were not doing so badly.

"Does he know where to drop us?" asked Jim.

"Oh, ay, he's got his orders all right. Don't lack for land-marks, do we? Turn right by the Panther in the ditch, and put us off just past the second dead horse on the left!" His voice was grim, for he liked horses; but indifferent, too, for what was the good of liking horses, here in Normandy? Or cattle, either? Or your fellow-men?

"Good enough! He can't miss that."

They were nearing their station. The lorry slowed and pulled in to the dusty grass verge, and they slithered down over the tailboard and lit out across the fields. There would be tea up any time now at the farmyard, and travelling in the dust of Churchills and Shermans and the acrid after-smoke of fires was thirsty work. They made for the shelter of the hedge, for it was a warm quarter here, no place to wander in the open. A few 'planes circled overhead, drawing languid patterns across the deepening blue. A British battery was in steady action from their left rear; yet the night was almost ominously peaceful after the din of the first night along the West Wall. There was quiet and leisure to notice the furtive movement of small hunting animals in the hedgerows among the brambles and coarse grass. A great deal of busy, shy life came out at night, when the worst of the battle noises were stilled; Jim had seen harvest-mice climbing the corn-stalks after sunset, and once in this walk he checked upon the quick rustle of small feet, and saw a stoat peering at him through the stems of the hedge with its glittering stony eyes, malignantly inquisitive. Not until they were in the fringe of the strip of woodland did they sight bigger game.

Jim, who was in the lead, heard the bushes spring and recoil upon the passage of one coming urgently, and with more of haste and purpose than of caution. He drew back into the shadows of the fringe of trees, and the backward gesture of his hand checked the others in a moment. They waited in silence, peering down through the bushes into the pebbly green gravels of the stream, which was shallow here and very easily forded; and in a few minutes they saw a man with a rifle come thrusting out of the twilight beyond, and drop down into the water, and wade carelessly across. A middle-aged man, broad-built and bull-necked, hairily dark of cheek and chin even in the dusk; a piece of good solid French earth like any other, but for the rifle on his arm, which he carried as to the manner born. They had drunk with the like of him in Bayeux, after the hurried half-ceremony which raised the Cross of Lorraine on the market-place, where the brassards flashed out of hiding, and the first free company of the F.F.I. paraded openly and proudly in the light of day. But this man came from over there among the enemy; which amply explained why he should be in some haste, and moving in the first shadows of the night.

Jim let him come halfway up the slope from the water, and then stood forward out of the trees to meet him. The movement was enough. The man dug his heels into the crumbling clay, and heaved up the rifle in a flash, before even he had a clear glimpse of the figure confronting him; but his nerves were excellent, and the trigger finger did not contract.

"English!" said Jim, showing his empty hands.

The gun was lowered slowly; an answering smile split the square dark countenance upon a set of teeth startlingly even and white. He came up the slope in a quick scramble, holding out his hand. Beyond question he was glad to see them, and for more and better reasons than made them welcome everywhere.

"Very well met, my sergeant! You speak French, no?"

"Yes, but not well. Speak slowly, and I shall understand you."

"*C'est bien!* My name is Jacques Côtin, builder, of the village of Montry-sur-Aure. I have no papers; you must take me on trust, or not at all. This I can show, but this could have been taken from a better man." He flicked the familiar brassard with the Lorraine Cross out of his pocket, and as casually thrust it back, shrugging his broad shoulders over his lack of credentials. "I came in haste; it was a matter of life and death, with no time for authority. Sergeant, tonight fifteen men are being taken from the prison camp at Montry into Caen by road, and from there by rail to Paris. So much we know. It is possible they would go on into Germany, for they are valuable, and can give much evidence against certain Germans. Sergeant, if they go into Germany they will not be seen again."

"What are they? Maquis men?"

54

"Not all—not actively. But all fighters after their fashion. We need them."

"Sounds as if they need us, too," said Jim. "How many roads are there from Montry-sur-Aure to Caen?"

The slow, dark smile came again. He said promptly: "One only, for a truck of that size. And why should there be anything wrong with that road?"

"Why indeed? Why should they even consider looking for another? Come on," said Jim, "we shall talk as we go. My company is not far away." He was pretty sure that Major Harben would listen, too. It wasn't big enough to be anything but true, and in itself it was credible, for that very thing would be happening wherever the line of the beach-head drew near to imprisoned men who had too much to tell. There was only one weak spot. He asked as he led the way through the cool aisles of the trees: "Why don't they murder them in Montry-sur-Aure and save the petrol?"

"First, because they still hope to get something out of them. Also because it takes time to dig graves, and time is what they have not—and these are bodies that should be buried deep. At Montry was not a killing place; it was for questioning—a place of getting information. The rest of the prisoners they will abandon; but these are the ones they dare not leave."

That was reasonable enough. They went softly as he considered the next question, the rest of the party all eyes and ears at their backs. It was now more than half dark, and the palpitating flashes of the batteries on both sides made the night uneasy.

"What are you asking us to do? Take it up our way—or yours?"

"I need only a small party—half a dozen men with arms. The rest I will do. But for the arms I could have done all," said Jacques Côtin.

Yes, Harben would listen. A man laying an ambush does not ask for a mere half-dozen to walk into it where he could as reasonably demand a platoon, or with a better story a company. He did not bother to ask who the fifteen were, for it would only be to evoke a string of names which would mean nothing to him. Instead, he asked directly:

"What's your plan? You know the ground, I don't."

"The road is a good road, but there are places in it where it is not so good. Not more than four miles from here is a stone quarry where the trucks have cut up the surface very badly.

There is a narrow bridge under the railway siding there; a three-ton lorry could block it, but most completely. I have friends at the quarry, *Monsieur le Sergent.*"

"You have useful friends." He rubbed his chin thoughtfully. "Four miles cross-country? What sort of going? How long, if we allow for interruptions?"

"By my way, it might be an hour and a half—less, if we have little trouble—much less, if we have none."

"And what information have you? It must have been good enough to make this trip seem worth your while."

"My information is exact. There is no time to go into details, but it is to be trusted. The truck leaves Montry at one o'clock. It will reach the railway bridge within the half-hour."

"How shall we recognise it? There'll be a lot of traffic on the roads, and one lorry is like another." He said "we" already; it was a matter of some urgency if they were to cover the distance in time.

"This is not like any other. It is an emergency ambulance truck belonging to the town. They have taken all our transport, this among the rest. A man of Montry would know it in the dark, and tonight at its deepest will not be fully dark."

"Good! But what escort will there be?"

"Ah, that is another matter. *Le bon Dieu*, He alone knows. It is the thing we must risk. But first stop them, and after that we can count," he said grimly.

They had reached the farmyard which was Company H.Q., and by this time were trudging through the dust of the rutted lane which led to the barn. The major had taken possession of a small room opening from the farm kitchen, and by this time of night would be invisible behind the screen of smoke he seemed in his leisure moments to prefer to air. Jim dismissed his party before he went in. He wanted none of them on this job, not even Peterson, who was the soul of reliability but had not been designed by nature for moving silently cross-country by night. Sloan, perhaps, and Westwick the ex-keeper, and Freeman who made a hobby of photographing wild birds—— He went on selecting in his own mind as he lifted his hand to the major's door.

"You'll tell him all you've told me. Make it short; if I know him, he won't make it long."

He tapped, and led the way in.

It was as he had wished it to be. He had the men he demanded, and was allowed to do the thing in his own way, which was Jacques Côtin's way. From indolence or conviction, it mattered not at all which, Harben put back the job into his hands as fast as it was given to him, suggesting only in passing that a greater force might make for added safety, and being as firmly assured by the builder that a greater force would make only for failure. Major Harben was a shrewd man, and knew a shrewd man when he saw him. He was being asked to co-operate, not to rescue. And six men were after all not so much to lose, if the end was loss; though the sergeant had his value, no negligible one. It was trust and go, or stay and abandon, for the time was not far from midnight. He let them go. He knew by Sergeant Benison's levelled and calculating eye that he meant to go, and the conviction passed between them that so firm a decision would not have been taken upon false premises, for they knew each other's mind well. Sometimes Harben felt that he had a special personal use for Jim Benison as a glass through which to see, silently and unemotionally, into the minds of people with whom his own contact was imperfect; and sometimes this vicarious perception had proved so deft and so successful that he could afford to entertain it and lean upon its judgments. It conveyed to him now that the builder was genuine, his story true, his assurance justified, and that Jim Benison could work with him.

"All right, Sergeant. Choose your men. I wish I could give you more cover, but get off at once, and I'll see your platoon commander. You'll report as soon as you get back." He did not say "if you get back" but the suggestion was there.

So they were here, six of them and the builder from Montry-sur-Aure, here in the wake and wary night, under the fitful light of moon and stars and flares and the flashes of guns, lying among screens of rosebay willowherb and wind-sown baby birches in the twenty yards of waste ground between the edge of the quarry and the road. The four miles had occupied them barely an hour, and with good reason, for the British and Canadian batteries in the beach-head were giving the enemy more things to think about than a small party of woodsmen filtering through the lines under the guidance of a native. Their own barrage had helped them through in good time to view the ground before they went into action; and Jim approved the choice.

It was a lonely place, with no community at hand to be penalised for whatever befell there, and consequently no garrison to upset the calculated balance. From the spot where they crouched they could see, as they parted the unkempt saplings, the whole field they had to use; the road crossing them closely, from the point four hundred yards or so away on their right where it swung into sight left-handed round the sharp bend of a knoll, to the point low upon their left where it dived downhill abruptly into the narrow space of the railway bridge, no more than a dark cavern. Beyond the road, more silvery neglected bushes, in need of trimming, and beyond them again rising mounds of clay left by long-abandoned coal-pits, where by God's grace no one would have need to be at this hour of night, in this disputed country. In their left rear the broad wagon-track swept in from the main road to where the gaunt iron shape of the crusher loomed against the sky, and sheds, and a litter of oil-drums and wooden piles, and the sharp angular moonlight on the upper surfaces of the rock-face. In their right rear, the nearest raw edges of its bouldery scree not ten yards back from the low hedge that fringed the road, the waste dump from the quarry soared into the moonlight, sand-coloured, as regular in its cone as Fujiyama but for the single short, beaded scar upon it at the crest, where the chain of tubs was moored. The narrow line up which they were towed by a steel cable showed clearly in the gun-flashes, a pencil-mark, its tail nearer the road than its head.

Between the passing of convoys on the road Jim pulled at Jacques's coat-sleeve, and said in his ear: "We can seal this strip of road up with the van in it. Will there be anyone at the quarry at this hour?"

"Only the night-watchman. I know him; he will help us."

"But can he come away with us afterwards?"

"No. He has dependents; he must be protected."

"I get it. He shall be protected. Take me to him." And to Sloan he said in English: "Keep 'em here till we come back. If Teddy starts knowing better than you, hit him."

"It'll be a pleasure," said Sloan, still watching the road. "I don't know why you brought him."

"Because he's a good kid when he forgets how good. He's going to be useful just now." For Teddy Mason had been a quarryman himself before he was called up, and knew more

58

about it than Jim did; and even what Jim knew might have been enough at a pinch.

"Come," said Jacques, "we lose time."

Well, they had little enough of that, at the most only an hour. First, there were things they needed; and after, to dispose their little force to the best advantage. He followed the Frenchman, slithering soundlessly between the young bushes and the tall, flowering willowherb, to the curve of the wagon-track and the sheds under the shadow of the crusher. There was one window with a corner of light showing, dull and sullen as a horn lantern, but perceptible against the depth of shadow there. Jacques flattened his ear against the door of the shed, and was satisfied with the stillness within. He lifted the latch silently, and opened the door a few inches.

An old man in a black beret was sitting over a small, smoky oil-stove, waiting for a can of water to boil. He was very old to be still working, maybe seventy-five, and he seemed to have outlived all capacity for excitement, for he showed no surprise at all when a proscribed Frenchman and a British sergeant invaded his solitude, closing the door after them upon the noise of a passing German convoy on the road below. He did not move from his seat upon a packing-case covered with old sacking; only his light eyes brightened, and somewhere behind the venerable whiskers stirred what must have been a pretty grim smile.

Jacques spoke to him in French too rapid and idiomatic for Jim to follow, and received a reply admirably prompt and brief, and jerked out of the old man's lips as if the words themselves knew how short time was.

"It goes!" said Jacques. "What is here is ours. Ask for what you want."

"You have blasting material?" asked Jim, steadily watching the old, alert eyes. "I need a charge, fuses, an exploder, all the stuff to lift the top off your little mountain out there. Polar blasting gelatine I have handled, if you've got that. And a spade. Well?"

"You'll find all you want in the shed at the back of this hut," said the old man. "But I am a truthful man. I will not give you anything. I must be able to say I gave you nothing, I know nothing, I could do nothing. You will understand."

"I understand. That's an ingenious conscience you've got," said Jim appreciatively. "The store is locked? No, don't give me the key. Put it back in your pocket. So! It was taken from you, was it not?" He drew it out, and held it in his hand. "Also you were shut in here—and the door locked upon you. There was nothing you could do."

"It was so," said the old man peacefully. "There was nothing I, old and feeble as I am, could do to prevent. They cannot blame me for it."

Jacques was already out of the shed, and flattening himself into the shadow along the wall as he slid round the corner. Jim followed him, drawing the door to gently upon the old man's subtle smile. He heard the last words that followed them to the adventure, a mere murmur because of the closing door, but clear and low in his ears: *"Soyez bénis, mes enfants! Dieu vous garde!"*

The night was becoming noisy now; only in a shaken pause did he realise that a train was passing on the line beyond the road. That was all the better; the more noise, the more cover. All the time that they were loading themselves with loot from the magazine his mind was resting upon the old man's benediction. "Be blessed, my children! God guard you!" He knew, none better, what was in the wind. He would be listening in his placid captivity, piecing together the sounds from without, smiling over his solitary brew. Well, if they were indeed blessed he would not long have to circumvent his Catholic conscience for the sake of a German threat. Two days—three—no more; surely he and his would be free of that shadow at last.

"You have all you need?" whispered Jacques.

"There is another torch. Bring it. Now!"

They went back, sliding from shadow to shadow, to where the others waited, and a long arm opened the silver sapling forest to let them in. Just then it was quiet on the road, but the British batteries five miles back were pounding away regularly, and the vague skyline ahead pulsed with shell-bursts, glowing and fading in a relentless rhythm against the dark. Through the tracery of leaves the flashes of light fell strangely on the young, strained faces, making them haggard as death's-heads, and scored with whips of darkness. It was then that Jim fel' for the first time the weight of them upon his back. He had expected it; it was not strange, but it was still terrible, the burden of their lives.

"Mason!" he said.

"Yes?" The kid was by his elbow in a moment, braced and confident and quivering with eagerness.

"You know about blasting. We're going to bring those tubs

up there down the slope and on to the road after the van has passed. Take this lot, and plant the charge under the right rail, about, and towards the top, to tip 'em over left-handed down the steep. You'll have to pack it down hard as iron, or——"

"Yes—yes, I know!" hissed Teddy, filling his arms.

"All right—you know! But watch yourself. The whole hill will start sliding—it's newish and loose. You'll have to get well clear. Get moving!"

The boy was gone, light as a hunting cat between the bushes, sliding towards the deepest shadows at the foot of the dump. Jim turned to Jacques Côtin.

"You're the only one who'll know the ambulance. Get into cover on top of that little hill at the bend of the road, and flash us when it passes. Before it passes, if you can. It'll have to be the torch; I'd rather not show a light, but we can't rely on sound. Flash alternate shorts and longs until I answer you with the same. Then get back here, top-speed, the best way you can without being seen from the road."

"I go!" said Jacques without argument, though the affair had been taken out of his hands with little ceremony, or so it might have seemed. Had not he made the journey alone to bring about this attempt upon the prison-van? But he smiled as he went, for he was not dissatisfied in his allies, however they trespassed. Sidelong the blanched leaves hissed over his passing, and came again to rest; they heard no more of his going.

"What now?" asked Westwick.

"You get back to the quarry there. There are lorries parked along the track by the sheds. Bring one of 'em—the heaviest you can get hold of—to the head of the slope where the track curves down into the road. When the time comes you're going to set her going down there and smash her under the bridge."

"I get it! But I shan't see his signal from there, it's tucked too far in from the road."

"I'll pass it on to vou from here as we receive it. You'll see me all right."

"And how if the curve's too great? There's a good slope all right, but if she misses the bridge——"

"She mustn't miss it! If there's any risk you've got to ride her down and get clear as best you can. Get on with it!" Westwick departed in his turn. The diminished army watched

61

its leader silently, and waited through a burst of noise in which he did not attempt to make himself heard; but when it passed his voice took up the tale again upon the same low note, as if there had been no interruption. "Sloan, get over the road into cover, close to the bridge, where you judge we're most likely to stop the truck with our block. If they leave the cab to see what's up—as I hope they will—get that truck off the road and up into the quarry. If somebody stays in the cab—well, get it just the same. We want no shooting round that load. Morgan and Freeman, you'll stay here. I'll be with you inside five minutes, but just now I want to see how Teddy's shaping."

Sliding down between the saplings towards the road, Sloan froze to the ground with his Tommy-gun cuddled closely under his arm as the first of a convoy of German guns and limbers crashed by. Jim took advantage of the noise to break into a tearing run as he cleared the bushes and made for the shadowy recesses of the quarry, there to climb the naked face of the dump upon its shadowed side. The luck had been all upon their side so far. Had there been no railway bridge, or no happy bend in the road at four hundred yards distance from it, or had the prison-van not been an impounded French ambulance of no official pattern, they would have been forced to make an open attack at great risk to themselves and greater still to the prisoners. As it was, the trap would not be set until the quarry was in sight, and if the luck held good the way would be sealed again behind its passage, with no more than an accidental companion or two shut inside it. Three submachine-guns working from cover over that steel ribbon of road should take care of the rest.

And how long would it take Jacques Côtin of Montry-sur-Aure to run back to his allies after the signal had passed? Four hundred yards or maybe a little over, down from the knoll, within the cover of the thick hedges, along the edge of the scree and back to earth in the wilderness of birch-saplings, clear of the explosion and the fall which was to seal off the trap. Five minutes?—not so long—three. If he could spot the van before it reached the bend he might almost arrive before it, but that was a lot to expect; and three minutes could easily let in a score more enemies upon them. No matter, that fall should not be loosed until the builder was safely back at the rendezvous, whatever companions he brought back with him. There should be no avoidable casualties; Jim was determined upon that. He knew what he wanted; he wanted every one of those lives

62

that hung so heavy upon him. What sort of a feeling was that? Merely a craftsman's jealousy of the quality of his work? Or what Brother Gabriel would have called love?

He climbed up by the shortest and steepest way to the foot of the ramp, slipping among the loose rubbish of crushed stone, and came to the narrow track. He was well clear of the dwarf trees here, and there was an uninterrupted view of the road, clean from Jacques Côtin's vantage point on the knoll to where the railway bridge swallowed it. Young Teddy would at least be able to see the whole encounter, even if he was to be prevented from taking any active part in it. And that had been a piece of deliberate planning, for he would be exceedingly useful where he was, and out of harm's way, too. None of the others was at all liable to go off at half cock.

Once on the ramp going was easier, for not only was the slope much less considerable, but also the weight of the tub-chain continually passing and repassing had packed the ground reasonably hard; and being free from the fresh daily deposits which left the rest of the hill incurably raw, the soil along the track had put forth a thin but persistent growth of coarse grass and poppies, which gave it at least a surface security. If the kid had any sense he would pay his wires down here, and stow himself and his exploder just within the line of the starveling trees. Thank God there was no question of having to hide his handiwork or bury his cables; as it was there would scarcely be time to do a decent job on the planting of the charge, but with any luck they would make it yet.

Halfway up the hill he met Teddy coming down at a crouching shuffle, paying out his double cable as he came. So he had, at any rate, sense enough for that.

"All set!" he reported breathlessly, recognising the dark outline of Jim.

"Quick work, that! You're satisfied the charge is all right? Well packed down? We can't afford to muck this up—it's a once-only show."

"Sure I'm satisfied!" His voice was quick to offence and dislike more palpable than when his expression could be seen. "You'd better look over the lay-out for yourself—Sergeant!" And the last word was an afterthought, and spiteful at that. His professional pride was hurt, as well as his conceit; Jim knew enough to keep the two clear in his mind.

"No need," he said equably. "You know your job. Come on, get yourself out of this moonlight. Where's the plunger?"

"Back there, by the trees." He slithered downhill, the cable snaking out from his palms and whipping the ground.

"Got enough wire?"

"I think so. Won't go more than a yard or two into the trees, but it'll do." He dropped into the harsh grass, both wires gathered into one palm, and groped back for the exploder with his free hand. Jim heaved it nearer, and they connected up in haste. That was that; just in cover, and only just, and a little extra distance between the kid and his dozen or so pounds of polar blasting gelatine wouldn't have done any harm, either, but unless something freakish happened with that charge he should be safe enough here.

"That's that!" said Teddy, forgetting to remain sulky. "Now what?"

"You know what we're trying to do—close the road fore and aft with that ambulance in it, and as few other things as possible. Your job's to shut the door behind the van. But you wont fire that charge until you get the flash from me. Understand?"

"Yes, I get it."

"You'll see me answer Côtin's signal first, so be careful not to act on that. By the time I'm ready for you it won't matter how much light we show. You've got the direction all right?"

Teddy pointed out the very spot in the wilderness where the remnant of the party lay waiting for action. There was nothing the matter with his sense of direction.

"It's a clear line, I can't miss you. What'll you be sending?"

"I'll flash you Ks, and the quicker you go ahead then the better. But I warn you, no beating the pistol."

"O.K.!" said Teddy, and lay down over his exploder, and settled down to watch the road and the hillock from which the first alarm would come.

"Right! Come down and join us after, but take your own time. And take care of yourself—you risk being a mark up here once things start."

Only a disinterested and faintly derisive grunt acknowledged that piece of advice. Jim left him to it; he knew what he was doing, or he should do by now. A hundred and one things could still go wrong with the set-up, but there was no time to try and work up an answer to any one of them. Already the enemy were late on the road. For all they knew, reflected Jim as he dropped back down the sheer slope, the van never would come.

Not much of a barrage tonight, nor so many bombers about, but who knew if the odd shell might not have blotted out the prison at Montry, or caught up with prisoners and escort and all on the road? Still, wait they must, and wait they would; and now at least they were ready.

He went to earth with Morgan and Freeman in the cover of the birches, and settled down to the waiting, his eyes fixed upon the dark hummock of the knoll against the shaking luminosity of the westward sky. Flashes of explosive reddish light fluttered through the pallor of the moon there, and stabs of fire passing upward and flares descending made a complicated and changing pattern upon this vivid ground, like a new aurora; but no sign came yet of the deliberate pinpoint of light for which he looked. Morgan had worked a clear passage through the clump of saplings parallel with the road, so that the signal could be returned readily, and as speedily relayed to Westwick in his lorry at the head of the quarry rise. Freeman was as near to the road as he dared approach, lying still over his gun that the bushes might not shake and betray him, and watching the passage of the slackening stream of traffic towards Caen. There remained nothing to be done but wait; which they did, for so long a time that they began to fear they had had their journey for nothing; but they were all wide awake when the signal came, for the same tension seemed to shiver through the three of them and draw them taut.

Jim caught the first flash, sudden and infinitesimally small in the one patch of complete darkness, and his hands upon the second torch began to return the limping rhythm on the instant, while his mind leaped away automatically to the sounds from the road. There were tanks passing; damnable luck if they had to take them into the odds, and yet suppose the ambulance was already past the curve? He saw Jacques Côtin's signal snap off short, satisfied. He swung round and crashed along his silvery tunnel to flash the alarm on to Westwick, but held his hand for dangerous slow seconds in the effort to calculate how long it would take that diminishing roar of the tanks to pass the railway bridge. Thank God it was diminishing! The last was passing. Five more seconds! He dared not leave it any longer. He flashed, and in the same moment the muffling influence of the narrow arch dropped over the thunderous noise like the felt cover over a bird-cage, and produced what seemed complete silence. So they were spared the tanks; once past that stone funnel, the crews would never hear the uproar of the lorry crashing behind them; their own accompanying din would see to that.

There was a pause, it seemed a long pause, while they hung upon that precarious quietness, waiting for the crash. Nothing passed upon the road, and for the duration of that moment the sky was empty of 'planes. It seemed an interminable age before the lorry, invisible to them beyond the screen of bushes, startled the night with the screaming impact of its four tons against the masonry of the arch. A pity, thought Jim, that there should be no other sound to cover it; and yet to following traffic upon the Caen road that crash could surely pass without comment as one more shell of a desultory barrage; provided, of course, that the ambulance came too late to see the hurtling descent, and as yet his straining ears caught no sound of its approach.

It was a question now of which should reach them first, the ambulance or Jacques Côtin, and the betting was heavily on the ambulance. Between the leaves they could see the railway arch as no more than a low blackness on the moon-blanched night. They could not guess at the degree of their success; only Westwick, gone to earth again in the bushes close by, could have any clear notion of whether the road was adequately blocked or no. All they could do for this brief and lame moment was stiffen to the note of their quarry's engine as it came into hearing, and fasten their intent eyes upon it as it drew level with them and passed at speed.

There were excellent reasons why a man of Montry should know it in the dark. It ran smoothly, but not with the smoothness of an ambulance, and its shape was top-heavy, for it had been in its origin an ordinary open lorry, and the upper part of its sides and its roof had been built on afterwards. The windows let in to give light were therefore necessarily high, and would give nothing more. If there were guards inside with the prisoners—and there would be—they would have no outlook upon what went on about them on the ground, and not by any feat of agility could they take part in the battle until they quitted the van. But there were two men in the cab besides the driver, for Jim saw the faces oddly silhouetted one upon another in deepening shades of grey as the ambulance passed. Another full second went by, and another, and the van was just abreast of the turn into the quarry before the expected scream of brakes came, and it pulled up sharply in a scurry of dust, close to where Sloan lay hidden among the bushes.

There was a silence so abrupt and brief that it seemed to open a cavern of doubt and anxiety in Jim's mind as pits open underfoot in nightmare, and as suddenly conceal it again behind the stony surface of the senses. He was listening at strain for the first sound or sight of Jacques Côtin returning, and flicking back glances at the road below to assure himself of what the enemy did. And the enemy did what was required of him. What else could he do, finding the road before him blocked, but go forward to examine the extent of the barrier, and assess the chances of shifting it? Motionless in his screen of leaves, Jim strained to see how many men descended from the cab, but could not be sure of the third. If he alighted, he struggled past the wheel to do it, instead of dropping easily out of the left-hand door. It meant he had the advantage of Sloan if he stayed, and he was out of range of Morgan and Freeman. Westwick might get him, supposing Westwick had recovered a decent position to the left of the bridge. If not, there might yet be trouble they had not bargained for. And in the meantime, as the seconds arranged themselves deliberately in patterns of plan and movement and stillness, the small army in ambush maintained its admirable silence, waiting for as many of the enemy as possible to detach themselves from the van. The two from the cab—or were they three?—had moved forward at a run into the cavern of the railway arch, and the darkness hid them. Two had emerged from the rear of the ambulance and shut the door again after them, and dropped down lightly into the road. They carried revolvers, but suspected as yet no occasion for using them. There was nothing but brisk curiosity in the way they turned to set off after their fellows. An accidental hold-up on the road, that was all they had upon their minds.

It was time for the next move; Jacques or no Jacques, the rest of the plan could not wait. Jim turned to peer back once more along the road, and the dappled moonlight on the scree. There was the sound of another car approaching, part of the escort, perhaps. Well, he could cope with one; Freeman would have a bead on the driver before he could even suspect there was anything amiss.

The car was just in sight when the thing happened. A succession of gun-flashes, distant and wan, agitated the pattern of moonlight among the stones. A strange quivering rumble ran through the ground underfoot, and the birch-saplings shook for the fraction of a second without perceptible reason; then with a dull detonation like distant but intense thunder the whole crest of the waste-dump lifted from its place, and dissolved in mid air into a storm of gravel and stone and dust. The clean, cold moonlight was utterly blotted out, and from out of the darkness two indescribable sounds began to beat insistently into their ears, a rolling, slithering, grinding descent of avalanches of stones pouring down over hedge, and road, and farther hedge, and a sibilance of grit raining into the trees and grass. Jim, dropped flat into the ground with his arms over his head and his eyes in cover from the dust, heard but never saw the fall of the iron tubs, a succession of clanging, leaping concussions from the shattered summit to the buried road, with a more clamorous rushing of earth about it, and a filtering and whispering of lesser falls, like echoes, dying away gradually over the last impact. And then there was nothing for it but to raise himself out of the grass, and throw his whole weight into the turmoil below. No need now to look back along the scree. Wherever Jacques was now, dead or alive, that prearranged signal would not be needed. Afterwards he might find out why the charge had been fired too soon; afterwards, he thought in a mind as cold as ice, he might require a reckoning from Teddy Mason; but now it remained only to do what the Frenchman had brought him there to do, at all costs, at any cost.

He was the first to fire a shot. The two guards from the van had crouched against the sheltered side of it as the impact came, and with the cessation of the fall they leaped back to the door, and one of them yelled forward towards the cab in German, probably urging the absent driver to take the van up into the quarry. Why allow the odds to be raised again by two? They never got back into cover. The first of them Jim dropped as he was mounting the steps, and he toppled backwards and bore his fellow down with him. Then gunfire broke out both before and behind the van. Someone well forward—it must be Westwick—smashed the windscreen with his first shot. Whether he got the man within no one but himself could see, but it was significant that he did not fire upon the ambulance again. His next target was the foremost of the German guards as they ran back into sight from within the railway arch. The man fell, and was dragged back into the darkness by his friend; and there began a duel in which the advantage was with the enemy as far as cover was concerned, but in which Westwick could certainly prevent them from recrossing the clear space of road to the remainder of their force.

Freeman had opened fire on the following car as it approached, a ghost leaping grey out of the haze of dust. If the fall had been designed to engulf these reinforcements it had failed of its object, though the near window was smashed in, for they saw tatters of glass fall from their place as the car drew close, and the roof was dinted and scarred with stones. The driver had accelerated instinctively to outpace disaster almost before the threat could be realised, so that the target was a difficult one; but Freeman's burst was directed low, at the tyres, and by luck as much as by judgment was effective. The near front tyre blew like a gunshot, and the car screamed across the road and broadsided with its bonnet in the ditch not many yards from where he lay.

Slithering down the slope to join in the nearer attack, Jim heard the van's engine roar into life again, and spared a hasty glance for Sloan's progress. He was quite sure that it was Sloan. The second of the two guards had clawed his way from under his companion's body, and was in the doorway as the van started up; the forward leap upset his balance and threw him back a second time under the wheels. It was unfortunate for him that the driver of the ambulance had taken it alongside the turning into the quarry before he saw the block ahead. Sloan had to back a few yards in order to drive in now; the fallen man scrambling for a quick foothold in the dust never had a chance to rise. The bump set the open door swinging; it was swinging still as the van tore left-handed up the incline into the quarry, and there was the glimpse of a light within, and a swaying entanglement of bodies. The prisoners had joined in the fight.

There remained the car, and the two men under the railway arch. Neither of them gave very much trouble. Jim and Freeman took care of the car between them; the shooting was fierce, but brief, and only one man at last stumbled out from the back seat, one arm raised and the other clamped to his side to keep in the blood he was losing copiously from a torn wound in his ribs. He was an officer, and he had some French, for it was in French he offered surrender, croaking like a frog from a throat lime-dry with dust and gravel. They broke cover and came down to him, for here the fighting was over. The two guards in the road were dead; so was the officer's driver, fallen over his wheel; so was the soldier who sat beside him. They took only one prisoner. By the time they had driven him in haste up into the quarry, intent to cross the railway siding and approach the arch from the rear, Morgan had forestalled them and the affair was over. The two guards surrendered themselves sullenly. Jim saw, as Morgan and Westwick brought them along, that the wounded one was beyond moving; he came leaning hard upon the other and leaving a trail of bloody footprints behind him. All they could do was patch him up and leave him in one of the sheds until his own people or the French should find him. The second one was whole, and very angry. They wasted no time upon him, but made haste to take possession of the ambulance and its cargo; and even this, they found, had been done for them.

Sloan, wishing to withdraw his charge from sight of the road, had driven right through into the shelter of the quarry face before he stopped to investigate the state of affairs inside the ambulance. By the time he reached the back the prisoners were already descending, bringing three mauled and disarmed guards with them. In this blacker pocket of the soiled and dusty night it was hard to distinguish friend from foe; they came thronging down from the doorway and crowding about him silently, for they were used to the necessity for silence. The foremost addressed him in French, but he made haste to disclaim any knowledge of the language, and looked round eagerly for a sign of Jim's approach.

"*N'importe!*" said the spokesman, in a voice rapid, cool and low. "Also I speak English. Not good, but I speak him. Is it that you know of us? Or are the British here already?

But Sloan was not listening. He had sprung away to meet the others as they came in with their limping prisoners. Jim, Morgan, Freeman, Westwick—the tale was complete but for Teddy Mason and the Frenchman. Thank God it was over so well! Five movable prisoners, the whole number of the rescued, and only a few grazes and a flesh wound or two to show for it. And now they could get moving, if only the last two would hurry up; before the traffic began to pile up outside the two barriers, and the curious enemy found means to come at the quarry from over the railway line, or clambered over the new talus on the road to discover what was going on in this sealed space within; as would most surely happen in no long time.

"Everything all right here?" asked Jim as they met.

"Yes, all O.K. Three more prisoners here. The French chaps settled that for themselves."

"Are they in good order?"

"They can march."

"And the others? Are they all fit to move?"

"Didn't get that far, but I think so. Better ask 'em."

Jim ran his eyes over the mass of men, and their eyes shone back upon him with instant, alert attention. It was very dark here, but they were still, and some clear idea of them he did get, even in that brief moment, though rather as a weight of experience than as individual men. His impression was that the oldest of them was barely middle-aged, but the youngest had ceased to be young. The volatile patriotism he had thought of as French had here become concentrated, secret and violent. He counted them as he talked. Fifteen! The information had indeed been reliable.

"Is anyone hurt?" he asked.

There was a silence.

"Speak now if you are. We're going back through the German lines, and we're moving fast. I don't want to be held up."

"We have scratches only," said an abrupt voice from among the fifteen. "We shall go."

"Good! Sloan, I want you to get them back. One of the Jerries you'll have to leave behind in the huts here. He won't get far enough under his own power to do us any harm. Morgan's patching him up. The others you'll take with you. Any of you men speak English?" Two or three voices assured him that they could make shift to do so. "Right! You'll stay by Corporal Sloan and take your orders from him."

"What about you?" asked Sloan blankly. There was surely no reason for staying. They were only one short now. He had seen Mason come slipping through the bushes bright-eyed and breathless, and add himself to the group. The other one surely couldn't be far.

"We have to find Jacques Côtin," said Jim. "I don't intend going back without him, but it would be crazy to hold up the whole party. He may be injured. I must keep enough people to find him and move him, in whatever state he is. Morgan is staying. Mason!"

"Yes?" said Teddy cheerfully, moving forward at once.

"I want you."

"I have the honour to know Monsieur Côtin," said the soft-voiced Frenchman. "I would wish to stay and assist you."

"I shall be glad. No need to hold back anyone else, then. Get moving as quick as you can, Sloan. Tell Harben we're following."

He turned abruptly, and led the way back to the road, Teddy loping at his heels and the Frenchman scurrying after. Morgan came from the huts and joined them as they passed. Of their own company they saw no more for some hours, and scarcely spared a thought to follow them along the anxious road home. They had enough on their minds here. Even Teddy's impervious spirits had been brought up hard against the tone in which Jim had summoned him, and he was almost visibly going over the affair now, over and over the unprofitable ground to discover what had gone wrong; and his silence made it plain that he was not easy upon the subject of his own responsibility, or more probably of Jim's views upon the subject. In silence they went down through the wilderness of wild grasses and willowherb, and in silence came to the beginning of the stony desolation they had created.

"You think he was caught in the fall?" asked Teddy then in a whisper.

"Yes."

The angry haze still hung upon the air, and would for some time yet, for in spite of all that had happened in the interval, the fall was barely a quarter of an hour old. But they could see, now, through the murk of fine dust they drew in with their breath, how the smooth shape of the artificial mountain had been smashed from the top, hurling down almost a third of its bulk on to the road. Before them was a great mound of rubble, still quivering here and there with minor avalanches as some motion of wind without or collapse within caused its stones to settle deeper. Above this mound what remained of the flank of the hill shone now with a paler, raw luminosity, and its top was a broken edge still silting downward little streams of dust. To search through that expanse for what remained of a man seemed a hopeless business. They would have to quit all cover, and expose themselves to the bare moonlight altogether recklessly; but there was no help for it. Jim thrust the second torch upon Morgan, and sent him with the Frenchman over into the field upon their left, to work along the extreme reaches of the talus in case Jacques had been swept before the fall. He himself set off upon the more exposed face of the mound itself, with Mason still at his heels.

He wondered, then, why he had kept him. Not for his usefulness, certainly. He could only suppose that he had intended to rub his nose in what he had done, as the unimaginative school pups. If so, the impulse was already by. He knew he could not and would not make any accusation now; he doubted if he ever would. For one thing, the risk had certainly existed aside from any misdeed of Teddy Mason's, had been perceived and accepted before ever the builder set out upon his evening journey. But more gravely, more finally, he himself was deep in the same fault. He knew it, if no one else ever would. He had lifted the affair, unbidden, out of Jacques Côtin's hands, much as Teddy had taken it upon himself to lift a part of it out of his, against his express orders. With the best intentions! But that was not likely to be of any consolation to Jacques Côtin.

He knew how it had been. No need ever to ask. He knew as well as if he had been there with Teddy upon his godlike height above the battle. His impatient fingers itching upon the exploder, and the whole scene spread before him in the moonlight, the stopped ambulance, the men running, the inexplicable quietness, the absence of the orders for which he looked. A piece of pedantry was all that signal would seem to him. He had not been told why it was urgent that he should wait for it; and he who trusted himself so completely had not room for the same respect towards Sergeant Benison. And then the following car in sight, and still no Ks; and thought chasing thought in his mind, helter-skelter before the flight of the seconds. I could get that car. If he knew he'd want me to get it; of course he would. It's obvious. He only plans everything down to the last thousandth of an inch, and keeps all the strings in his own hands, because he thinks we're all halfwits. He thinks we can't be trusted to act on our own initiative. But if he were here now he'd say yes to it. I'll do it! I'll show him we can be trusted. Maybe then he'll leave something to us another time. And he had fired the charge with absolute self-approval, sure of being commended. Oh, God, why should simple things grow so complicated upon a little thought?

He hunted at Jim's heels uneasily now, but no way disposed to blame himself for the loss of a man, rather in arms against the conviction that Jim blamed him. "I suppose," thought Jim in bitter disgust, "we shall end by rubbing each other's noses in it."

It took them twenty minutes to find him, though at some time during the search they must have been very near to him, and narrowly missed flashing the light full upon him. Another minute, and he would have been clear of the fall, for he lay at the nearer edge of it, on his face, the upper part of his body grey with dust but uncrushed. From the waist down he was buried under the stones. They plunged upon him as one man, and began to tear away the weight with their hands, kneeling one on either side of him. He did not move, nor make any sound. They thought that he was dead; but when at length they got him free and were able to lift him over in their arms, they found a feeble pulse and a thread of breath. It promised nothing; they both knew that well enough; but it was more than they had hoped for.

They had forgotten the other two for the moment, as they had forgotten the desultory reverberations of the barrage, and the thrum of the 'planes overhead. Nothing now existed but the unconscious man, and their two selves working desperately over him, and the encounters of their eyes across the body. The legs were both broken; Jim thought there was also some worse trouble from internal crushing. And yet they could not leave him; they must take him back with them, or his death was a certainty. The dark face was bloody and thick with dust, horrible to look at; Teddy averted his eyes from it with an effort, and suddenly looked up at Jim and burst out:

"How could I know he was going to be here?"

Jim unbuckled his belt, straightened the twisted legs with slow care, and made no answer.

"You think this is my fault, don't you?"

"Be quiet!" Astonishingly Teddy was quiet. "Get the others. Go back to the huts and get blankets and boards—if there are blankets—sacking, anything to wrap him up in. And rope. Plenty of padding. Use your loaf! We've got to carry him back in the best we can make of a stretcher. Go on, look sharp about it!"

Teddy went at a run, without another word or look. In a while they came all three with the loot of the quarry, and with the aid of cotton waste, cement sacks and a narrow door wrenched from its hinges they made for the injured man as easy a cocoon as they could. Mercifully he remained unconscious throughout; even when they lifted him by painful inches on to the door he did not stir into pain. Morgan and Mason, as being the best-matched of the four in height and pace, were told off to carry him. Jim straightened himself at last and looked at the Frenchman, seeing him now for the first time as a small, thin person of swift and yet deliberate movements, and possessed of a calm which amounted almost to coldness; the natural protective armour a man would have to develop, he supposed, to survive years of the German kind of captivity. He remembered, too, that he had claimed to know Jacques Côtin well; yet it was not he who shivered to look at him now, like Mason, or studied him darkly and fixedly, like Morgan. He must have seen a great many of his friends turned into pulp like this, and by no accident, either. What was a fall of stones to a man who had come straight from Montry-sur-Aure?—"not a killing place —a place of getting information"!

The man's eyes—they looked hollow and large with privation in the moonlight, but they gave Jim a queer feeling of a meticulous, incurious intelligence, too—flashed from the stretcher to Teddy Mason's face, and back again to Jim.

"You wish I should lead? I know the country, but not the dispositions."

"No, I can make shift. Bring up the rear, but stand by me if I need you. Take Morgan's gun."

"I have a German revolver." He showed it, and his hand was adroit upon the stock.

"You'll need something speedier if we run into trouble. Take it!"

He took it without more words; submachine-guns were not unfamiliar to him, either. He fell into their pace lightly as Jim led them away into cover between the quarry and the dump, crossing the ramp at the foot, where it was only a hummock; and this pace he held relentlessly, and without apparent effort, throughout the two hours and more it took them to come back to Company H.Q. Taking a stretcher through the German lines was no such simple matter as filtering through unencumbered had been, and Jim's memory of the way, though good, was less perfect than Jacques Côtin's knowledge had been. Their own party had long ago passed beyond their overtaking. The only men they encountered were two parties of German troops, the first of which they avoided by dropping into cover and lying still for twenty minutes or so, a delay they could scarcely afford. While it endured Jim felt at the injured man's heart again, but could not reach it for the thoroughness of their wrappings; and sight told him nothing, for they lay blind in a covert, with only threads of the waning moonlight upon them. He believed he could feel the slow, slight rise and fall of the chest, and almost hear a thin hissing of breath moving between the open lips. He was sure that at this time Jacques Côtin was still alive. The second patrol they met was sighted in time to allow of a detour, so that they were not compelled to lose time.

Nevertheless, when they stumbled into the lines at last, and moved through into the farmyard, the coldness of the dawn was already fading the white of the moon; and the curious dead hour which was neither night nor day, but only the halt between, came down upon the world in a dispiriting silence as they laid their improvised stretcher down in the barn, and unloosed the lashings with which they had held it together. The rest of the journey the wounded man could make in better comfort than this, at least.

Neither comfort nor pain, however, neither heat nor cold, could arouse Jacques Côtin from his impassive silence. He never accused or excused either of them of his destruction; they would never know whom he blamed, nor take from him any reassurance. He died under Jim's hands as the wrappings of sacking and cotton waste fell away. There was no sound nor sign from him, but they looked at each other across his body, and knew that he was dead.

4

It was not to be expected that the praise and blame could be buried with him. Harben might purr over the exploit like a contented cat, gloating upon his five well-informed prisoners and his fifteen influential guests from Montry, and marking the breaking of the instrument only with a regretful shrug of his shoulders; but for all that, others less wise would dig Jacques Côtin up again before the affair was over. Jim wanted nothing so much now as to let the dead rest; whatever scarifying of conscience was to be done in the matter he could well do for himself and them all, in private and with no multiplication and epidemic of blame such as there would be if it came to words. He had told his tale to Harben without mentioning how expressly he had forbidden Mason to fire his charge until the signal was given; and the guilt of mismanagement which had settled in consequence upon his own head had seemed to Harben, for whom he displayed it, as merely a fortune of war, not to be laid as blame at any man's door. But Jim knew better. Someone else, too, had found more in the narration than met the eye; the little Frenchman had sat through it almost unnoticed, his hollow eyes moving from face to face, and no word out of him, but towards the end Jim had become aware that there was in the room a questioning intelligence which was proceeding methodically upon a path widely divergent from the Major's. He had turned his head, then, and found those eyes probing

76

him, and had the momentary startling impression that he was glass to be looked through at will; but Harben's calm reassured him.

Officially, then, no crime had been committed. A man of the Maquis had come by a most honourable death in action, and regrets but not recriminations were due to his memory; that was the whole of it. And there Jim wished to God they might be willing to leave it, but he knew that Teddy Mason was too raw and full of his own importance not to want to justify himself. When Jim came out from Harben's office he was hanging about the farmyard, and instantly he came over to place himself in their way, treading out his cigarette hastily into the yard muck. There was no mistaking his intention; he went at it like a bull at a gate. If anybody was going to have to sling that particular weight round his neck it wasn't going to be Teddy Mason.

"Can I speak to you for a moment, Sergeant?" he asked. He hadn't got off scotfree, by the look of him; there was a pallid seriousness about him that was new, even if it consisted largely of outrage on his own account.

"Carry on!" said Jim, stopping in his tracks. As well here and now, after all, as at any other place or time; and the boy was too set on getting it done to care how he did it, or how many witnesses he had, for that matter.

"About this business," he said. "I know you blame me for it. I know I'm going to be in trouble. I'm not asking you to let up, or do anything to get me out of it, but I reckon it's damned unfair, and I want to know what I could have done that I didn't do. That's all! How can you make out it was my fault? How could I know he was going to be under the fall?"

"You couldn't. You weren't expected to know. You didn't have to know," replied Jim, ramming the repetitions one by one with calculating slowness into Teddy's ears, and adding nothing. Let him work it out for himself, if he could see anything but his own injury.

The Frenchman had moved aside sufficiently to avoid the appearance of listening, but not so far, Jim noticed, as to be out of earshot. He might, after all, be regarded as an interested party, the holder of a watching brief for France.

"Then what the hell am I supposed to have *done?*" demanded Teddy with passion.

"Do you really need to be told?"

"Oh, I suppose you've told your tale already! My error was not sticking to the letter of what you told me to do. But God damn it! what was I to do? You couldn't take *everything* into account. I could *see* what was happening, and you couldn't. I took it for granted there was *something* left to me. There was this car coming, and I reckoned I could stop it. *Anybody* would have done the same—anybody worth his salt. If you'd *told* me he'd be crossing there—but you never said—and there was this car——"

He could have gone on for a long time, but somehow his stock of indignant words seemed to have thinned and melted upon his tongue under the look that met him. Not until he was already silenced did Jim answer him, waiting even then to be sure that he had for the moment no more to say. It was important, since they had to get it off their chests, that the thing should be done clean; and for the sake of what might happen tomorrow, when they moved, or any other of the uncertain tomorrows, it was worth trying to make some impression on the rudimentary mind hidden somewhere behind an almost impermeable self-conceit.

Very quietly Jim said: "I told you exactly what to do. You couldn't misunderstand your orders, could you? Did I say you were to hold your hand until I signalled you, or didn't I? Well, answer me! There's nothing the matter with your memory, and as far as I know you are at least honest. *Did I?*"

"Yes," said Teddy, almost inarticulate with hate, "you did, but——"

"There's no but about it. And do you remember I took the trouble to repeat it when I left you?"

"Yes, you did. If you'd used the same breath to tell me *why*——"

"Your job was to do as you were told, not to find out the why and wherefore—as mine is, and Baird's—and Major Harben's for that matter. There was no time for drawing you sketch-maps. All right, it seems you knew what you had to do, all right. Will you also agree that you deliberately disobeyed orders?"

"No!"

"Did you, or didn't you, fire that charge without waiting for the signal?"

"Yes, but—it wasn't deliberate. I mean, I know I fired it, and I know you'd told me to wait; but it seemed to be an emergency, and surely *something* could have been left to me—to my discretion. I thought——"

"If you'd shown any sign of possessing any, more could have

78

been left to it next time; this time something was, a great deal was—but not that. A hundred and one things not provided for could have cropped up, and you could have dealt with them. This one thing was vital and obvious, and it was provided for."

The young, inimical eyes stared at him painfully for a moment in absolute silence. Then he said in a thin whisper: "I know what you're saying. You're saying I killed him."

"Didn't you?" said Jim.

It was impossible to be sure whether the boy's quivering nervous anger was still entirely due to a great sense of injustice, or whether a small doubt had begun to creep into it; at any rate, he was unwontedly quiet as he said at last: "All right, now I know where I stand. But I may as well tell you, I still think I was justified. In the same case, I'd do the very same again. I shall say so when the court comes off. You can probably carry the case, but I still think I was right."

But did he? If the infinitesimal anxiety had really taken root in that improbable soil he would put up a good fight against it, and for weeks, months maybe, the growth wouldn't show; but it might be there, for all that, and there could be no harm in watering the soil a little round the spot where it might already be germinating.

"You're still taking a lot for granted," said Jim.

The aggressive glance wavered a little. He asked, a shade uneasily: "What do you mean by that?"

"What I say. Are you under arrest? Has anybody said anything about putting you on a charge? Has anybody accused you of anything?" He saw Teddy's face whiten slowly from brow to chin with shock, and was suddenly a little sorry for him. A charge would at least have given him the satisfaction of telling everyone how right he was, and feeling himself a martyr; but to be spared the ordeal by the grace of Sergeant Benison was an indignity he could hardly bear; and again, to be unable to suppress the desperate flood of relief that welled through him at the reprieve, no matter how he hated the agent, was a redoubled agony. It was a favour for which there could never be any forgiveness. "Except yourself?" said Jim, hitting him again without mercy.

"Do you mean—you haven't told him? But you've been in with him for ages! I thought—you were——Then what did you tell him? I mean——"

"We could have something else to talk about besides you, you know. You didn't enter into it."

"But I can't understand! You blame me yourself—you know you do! Then *why*——?"

"Neither does that matter to you." Though the boy was looking for a two-edged reason, of course, the kind he was given to attributing to sergeants; either some sort of axe to be ground, or some sort of fear to be placated. Maybe that was the right of it this time! Maybe Sergeant Benison wasn't sure of himself; maybe he was uneasy at bottom about tackling Teddy Mason in the open. Jim saw the flickering of returning self-confidence in his eyes, the curve of his lips in the beginning of a significant smile; and it was time to put a foot on that spark quickly, before it grew. "No action's afoot against you," he said deliberately, "this time. Smashing you wouldn't bring back Jacques Côtin, or I'd clinch the bargain and think myself damned lucky. He's dead, no matter who suffers for it. But if you ever play God again, my lad, by any part of any plan within my knowledge, look out for yourself, for I'll go the absolute limit against you. I warn you! And you'd better make a note of it, for it's the last warning, as well as the first, you'll ever get from me. Next time I will put you on a charge, and I'll finish it as well as begin it. Do you hear me?"

He had not raised his voice, nor marked these sentences with half the emphasis Teddy had used in his own defence; nothing they had said to each other had been spoken as low as this; but it wiped that incipient smile from Teddy's lips as if he had been hit hard in the mouth, and left him staring whitely at his enemy, with no words to answer him. An answer, however was expected and patiently awaited, and when the silence began to hurt him more than speech could do, he managed through stiff lips:

"Yes, Sergeant!"

"All right! Remember it. Now get back to the platoon," he said quite gently, but it was rather as if he had said: "Get out of my sight!" Teddy went upon the word, with startling suddenness, not because of any anxiety for escape, but because the mère matter of uprooting himself from the spot required an effort which amounted to violence.

When he was gone Jim and the Frenchman looked at each other eye to eye, without any attempt at dissembling.

"Well?" said Jim drily.

"You forgive! I could not but overhear." But he was pleasantly brazen about it.

"You didn't try very hard," said Jim, but his voice was

indifferent. He was very tired now; reaction, probably, on account of both the night and the morning.

"And you, I think, do not much resent. But one wonders!" He stroked thoughtfully at a chin on which a brown stubble of beard showed, and his eyes followed Teddy's blind progress up the farmyard and out of sight. "That one, he will have our poor Côtin on his conscience."

"I hope so. But his conscience is resilient enough for two."

"And yours also?"

"Well, not resilient, perhaps. But durable!" He offered his cigarette case. "You're going after the others, to Bayeux? Oh, well, leave that to the Major. Why not come and see what we can scare up in the mess first? You must be hungry, and I know I am; and at this hour we ought to get the pick of the breakfast." They leaned together over the Parisian lighter. "You'll find the coffee hell, I expect, but the sausages are all right. And on a fine morning like this you won't mind the hole in the roof; we got a mortar shell two days ago, by mistake. They usually concentrate on the front line or Battalion H.Q."

"I shall like to come, yes. I forget you do not know me. My name is Amadis Cahusac. It will not be known to you; why should it? A second-rate poet and third-rate farmer from the Orléanais!"

"Which first?" asked Jim.

"Poet, alas! And Parisian by long necessity! I shall be truthful at all costs."

"And mine's Benison—Jim Benison."

They ate the prophesied sausages, and drank the coffee, over which Monsieur Cahusac made faces of appropriate horror, alone in the derelict shed which was the Sergeants' Mess by courtesy; and afterwards smoked another cigarette together comfortably in the lee of the hedge, and out of range of the smells and bustle of the farm. But they did not either of them for a moment forget the extraordinary conversation in the yard.

It was Amadis who harked back to it.

"You are, I think," said he with abrupt emphasis, "of sergeants the most peculiar."

"I hope to God you're right," said Jim bitterly, "for the sake of the others."

Amadis sat watching him for a while in silence, a strange little figure, of no identifiable age though possibly somewhere between thirty and forty-five, nondescript but for his eyes with their happy hunger and unvarying restlessness, and a certain quality he had of appearing debonair even in the old blue suit which now hung upon his emaciated body in folds.

"It was because I had seen the beginning," he said at last, "that I stayed to watch the end. I am of the curious. It is how I have lived. I ask the questions; I am incorrigible. Why did you not, as he said, tell all the story to your officer? You made him a case—though not great, for war is war—against yourself. I knew that was not so; I saw you both by Côtin's body, when you found him. It is that your baby firebrand, he would be so much crushed by one little rebuke that you must at all costs protect him? I think not!"

Jim smiled wearily. "I think not, either! You saw him!"

"Yes. However, he will have things to think out. It will perhaps last longer than the other would have done—and have more effect."

"I hope so," said Jim again.

"You agree too much with me, but you do not answer my questions. I think you play your own way with him, yes. Is that all? No, you invite blame because you feel him."

"Maybe."

"It is not maybe, it is yes. Come, we are together in this. It is too late to throw out Amadis Cahusac."

"All right, it is yes. The business belonged to Jacques. It was his idea, he made the journey to get hold of help, and all he was asking for was material. It was troops he wanted, not rescue. He never made me boss of the expedition; I took it from him. Oh, I never meant to. You know how it is. Suddenly we were there, and time was short, and I started laying out the field without thinking; and then it was my field. Well, that makes it my funeral, too."

"Also your success, I think," said Amadis.

"But there needn't have been any loss; there shouldn't have been any. Least of all, his."

"He protested, perhaps, when you took from him the leadership?" asked the soft, provocative voice.

"No. He didn't curse me afterwards, either, and for the same reason he never had a chance."

"That may have been an excellent reason—afterwards. It was not so while he was alive. I tell you, I know my Jacques."

"You may be right," said Jim. "That doesn't let me out."

"Ah, you mistake! I would not go so far. I am impertinent, but not presumptuous. You shall keep the millstone round your neck until it is to fall off of itself. No, I am concerned only

82

to understand. It has been my business. Also I was, you will remember, a part of the stake; it is natural I shall require how you played for me."

"I gather you were satisfied?"

"I am here. I am whole. And of fourteen others, all free and all whole. You are greedy, I think. You have not been in prison at Montry, or you also would be satisfied."

"But when you've said all that, still he shouldn't have died."

"Ah," said Amadis, "that is a mystery more profound than I can argue. We are not the first by many to say so. Millions have so complained for millions in this one century alone. It has been going on ever since Cain, I believe. But it may be that we lack proportion in evil. To die is not so grave a matter as many. In France it has been infinitely less comfortable to live."

"Yes—I do rather lose sight of that. What was it like—in Montry?"

A shrug of the slight shoulders answered him eloquently enough in spite of the few words. "As you would suppose. One did not die. One was lonely; when one was not lonely one was with *them*. And one heard things—you understand?"

"As well as anyone can who hasn't been through it."

"Fifteen of us, my friend, you have taken from this. Come, is that so small purchase for one life?—even the life you would not wish to spend?"

Jim asked only: "Who were they—your friends? I never shall know unless you tell me."

A cascade of French names answered him; then, seeing that they meant nothing, Amadis told them over again in another strain: "Six men of the Maquis, from here, from there—men with knowledge of what caused bridges to blow up and collaborators to vanish. Two ex-ministers of mild importance; a judge; two officials of provincial cities; a Socialist politician; a surgeon of reputation; a bishop; and myself."

"Hm! A mixed bag. What did they want with you?"

"They did not like me, they did not like my poetry; they did not like my farming methods. I was altogether undesirable."

Jim smiled, a shade grudgingly, at the potentialities of this formidable little figure. "To them, I can believe you could be. But I don't mind betting they never got any change out of you."

"Change? But yes! One is reluctant, of course; one waits for the moment when speech becomes expedient for one's comfort; but why wait longer? One talks, certainly one talks. I have given them—but under pressure, you understand—certain information at times. None of it was accurate; I doubt if it did them anything but harm."

"I see! But that could be a dangerous sort of game for other people, as well as yourself, couldn't it?"

"Not if one is a consummate liar. I do not wish to boast, but I should be so. It was an arduous apprenticeship." He looked into the smoke of distant fires dissolving against a pale dawn-sky, and the convolutions of feathery light clouds afloat upon its purity where the smoke had not climbed. His face was bland, contemplative and sweet, his eyes were bright and devilish. "I have not been without success," he said simply. "I made them shoot one of their best collaborators. Also they distrusted what information he left behind, which was well, for much of it was good. It was a *tour de force*. I did not try to repeat it; one should not pester fortune, it would be ungrateful."

"It would be damned risky, too."

"That also. And life is a heavy risk in any circumstances. Me, I deprecate too much daring. I am a very cautious man." He turned and met Jim's appreciative grin with the most wistful solemnity. "Not like you, my faith, no! You make for yourself the situation with this one, and with that one. And already you have a war on your hands! Oh, no, Sergeant, it is a life too dangerous for my tastes." He stubbed out his cigarette, and rose. The daylight was now clear and golden, not yet fouled. "I regret, but I must go."

Jim got up, stretching himself hugely. "So must I. See you some time, perhaps."

"Assuredly we meet again. But let me say now my thanks. I am alive; that is much. I am in a part of France which is free; that is more. This——" He struck his heel upon the rich crumbling edges of the nearest furrow under the flattened stems of wheat, where soft pink convolvulus, life too tender surely to endure a breath of cold, survived and wound its cobweb-delicate way to the light. "This is a miracle!"

"It's a pretty precarious one, then," said Jim. "All we've got yet is a beach-head; and personally I'm doing no betting."

The disconcerting eyes lingered upon him with speculative mischief in their look. "Ah, but you are you, and I am I. You will find I have reason. I say it is a miracle."

"And you call yourself a cautious man!" said Jim as they shook hands.

"It is true. *Au revoir, Monsieur le Sergent,* of all sergeants the most peculiar."

"So long! Watch out in Bayeux, it's pretty hot in the mornings."

The rear view of him, loping jauntily back towards the yard and the Major's office, was a thing not to be easily forgotten. The narrow lancet of sky soaring over him was clean and blue, but from either side toppling stone-work of smoke leaned upon it, threatening to fall inward upon his head. His gait, perhaps from undisplayed injuries, was broken into a droll, irregular half roll, half shuffle, and the too-baggy suit flapped around him like a sheep-dog's fleece as he went. From the back he looked a little like Charlie Chaplin setting off indomitably into one more sunrise at the end of another tragi-comedy. But though that in itself was enough for thought, Jim remembered the eyes.

In the days that followed he remembered them from time to time with supernatural clearness, perhaps by reason of the kind of mental weariness which brings back unsubstantial things to mind when the body has learned to move, and move to all appearances methodically, without the conscious co-operation of the brain. For from that day began the expected forward movement upon Caen.

The distance, according to maps, was roughly seventeen miles. It took them exactly one day short of a month to cover it. Half a mile a day was their average rate of advance, and even that they had to wrest away painfully with their hands inch by inch from the growing concentration of the enemy. What had been done upon the beaches and in the complicated warrens of the West Wall was not fighting at all by comparison with what followed at Caen. This was an advance upon the belly, hand over hand, hedge by hedge and bramble by bramble, a fight for every tuft of scarlet pimpernel among the stubble; and the night was as the day. Peterson, with his square face so often and so long pressed into the ground that he swore his beard began to strike roots, complained on behalf of them all that he'd never taken on to eat his way across France. Nevertheless, they moved, those infinite crawling tediums punctured by the passage of rivers, the Drôme, the Aure, the Seulles, where they splashed into the fords in a hail of mortar shells and scrambled ashore against flame-throwers and machine-guns; and having fought like devils to create a bridge-head, were compelled on to their faces again before they could go farther. By which means they found themselves in the outskirts of Tilly-sur-Seulles upon the 19th of June, the day before the Americans began their attack upon Cherbourg.

It was as if from all over France life-blood of armour and men drained along bursting veins of roadway towards this hinge of the attack. The pattern, so clear afterwards, was then by no means apparent to the Midshires and their fellows as they pushed forward in that almost motionless deadlock of sheer strength against the mounting mass. Nor would the taking of Caen in any way end or slacken the growing tension; so much was clear. But for the relays of bombers soaring south-eastward day and night to smash the congestions of inward-moving reinforcements, the flood might easily have swept the attackers away, as it was meant to do; but this time the air was the chief ally of the British, not of the Germans. Even so, they could feel the pressure of the defence rise steadily as the converging masses moved in against them. Everything was being forced in here, and if anything broke on their side they were in the sea again, and France was back in the dark, maybe for good. But nothing broke. They hung on grimly to their precious inches of soil, and lay patiently under their tattered and blackened hedges, mortaring and being mortared, moving on when they could and never moving back, while the guns steadily and methodically pounded Caen to pieces.

They knew there wouldn't be much of it left when they reached it. Even before they crossed the Odon on June 28th and began to creep round the western suburbs of the town, the smoke of its burning went up like a black tower and splayed its darkness along the sky. When they stumbled into the streets at last on the 9th of July they mustered only a few stunned prisoners from cellars and heaps of masonry, for almost all the surviving enemy forces had been withdrawn across the Orne into Vaucelles. Caen, for what it was worth, was theirs.

And what was it worth? They had seen destruction before, but this was beyond anything they had imagined so far. In parts of the town there was not left one storey standing upon another. Only fragments of lower rooms here and there remained, by courtesy, habitable; the rest was rubble, with cramped angular fingers of masonry standing up out of it in tortured gestures, and a pall of smoke hanging over all.

"I know now," said Dick Shelby, staring at it, "what it means in the Bible about a city becoming a ruinous heap."

So it was as they came into it, lifeless and awful in the dark-

ness which was noonday by the clock; but before they had
herded forty-odd wretched shell-shocked Germans into the first
open space they could clear, and seen the first of the Canadians
come clambering and cursing along the ruinous street, ghosts
had risen out of the earth and stood about watching them.
There were still, it seemed, some of the inhabitants of Caen left
to celebrate their terrible liberation. They came out of the
cellars, old men, women, children, silent at first, and stood in
strange little groups looking on, with motionless faces and
opaque, tranced eyes. But in a little while some degree of life
came back into them. They spoke, they moved, they looked at
one another. A woman leaned forward and spat at a German
prisoner as he was prodded along to join the line. A child crept
into the sagging ruin of a shop-front, and emerged with a dusty
two-day-old loaf, and sat gnawing it steadily under the lintel,
her great, hollow eyes fixed ravenously upon her enemies. A
middle-aged man marshalled half a dozen others, men and
women, about him, and they moved off purposefully along the
line of what had once been shop-fronts, and began to forage
there. Two young men in berets, with shot-guns on their arms,
appeared from nowhere with a German officer between them,
and with no words thrust him into the arms of Peterson, who
was nearest, and as silently disappeared again. The petrified
city was coming back to life.

Late in the evening, crossing the brick-dust wilderness from
Battalion H.Q. to the cleared street, Jim saw how already the
place had changed. A continuous stream of traffic was passing
into the town, gun and tank moving up slowly, lorry and limber
and motor-cycle and Staff car—yes, a veritable Staff car pulling
in beside what remained of a large house to drop some officer
or other. Half a dozen parties of soldiers were at work clearing
more road-space. As many groups of French civilians, men,
women and children, stolidly searched through the rubbish for
means to continue living. The smoke had thinned a little, but
the upper air was still dusty and dun.

He met the officer from the car, a dapper little Frenchman
in a uniform of bewildering neatness, almost face to face as
they clambered over the wreckage of beams; but what light
remained was behind him, and the silhouette was not immediately recognisable. Accordingly they would have passed with
merely a cursory salute had not the Frenchman greeted him by
name:

"Sergeant Benison!"

Then he knew him, uniform, medals and all. He bore no resemblance to Charlie Chaplin now. The droll gait had become a nimble, a soldierly limp, and ten years seemed to have slipped away from him and transformed his emaciation into a boy's wand-slimness in this dim dight. But the eyes, so incuriously observant, so receptive and so free of bitterness, were as Jim remembered them.

"You see? I tell you—you remember I tell you—yes, we meet?" He held out his hand. "You are well? I am glad."

"So am I! There were times when I wondered how much longer I was going to stay so well. You've changed a bit. It's Captain Cahusac now, is it?"

"As you see! I did not, I believe, tell you I had also been a soldier. Your general, he employs me for the time being. That is why I am here."

"Good! Then you're coming ahead with us?"

"As far as is permitted."

"Of course!" said Jim. "I forgot you must have pretty solid Maquis connections."

"We try to be useful. I am expected now, but—I shall look for you—here or at another place." His smile was brilliant in the dusk as he passed on. *"Au revoir!"*

"Good luck!" said Jim, and walked on refreshed. Even the desert of brick and ash and human misery seemed to be somehow transmuted by that touch of Amadis. It was possible, having seen him again, not only to believe but to rest assured that the spirit of man is indestructible; and in that light suddenly the dusk upon Caen had a grandeur of its own, almost a beauty. In the fading of a day which had never seemed less than half night the broken and contorted fingers of masonry reached up vengefully and knotted themselves in the smoke of the upper air. Every standing wall seemed to grow taller, terrible in a motionless dignity. In a cleared square two Canadians stood guard over a dozen prisoners waiting to be moved. The guards were still, gun on arm, bronze figures against the strengthless iris light. The prisoners were still, sitting on their haunches under the wall, with drooping shoulders and pallid masks of faces. There were stretchers ranged along a half-cleared by-street, and a walking case, a big Canadian private, sat upon a kitchen chair beside them with his hands laid patiently open upon his thighs, palms upward, and his face raised to the sky. A little girl in a torn pinafore, her face intent and immobile as a somnambulist's, her eyes fixed with shock, passed by him close, and without lowering his gaze he turned his head slowly after her going, listening after her with the hungry listening of the newly blind. And that was Caen.

Jim wondered what the tongues of men and of angels could do for that scene; he doubted if even Amadis Cahusac would venture to try and record a desolation such as this. Seen, it was absolute; it could not be forgotten. Reported it might be only a desolation, and that was not the whole of it by much. He walked slowly; it was the first time for a month that there had been no haste, or any possibility of hurrying; and Lieutenant Grenfell overtook him as he turned a corner and lost sight of the blind man.

"Hullo, Sergeant," he began blithely, "I see you're picking up celebrities!" And he nodded back to the spot where Amadis had disappeared.

"Who, Captain Cahusac? Well, I can hardly say. He was one of the prisoners from Montry-sur-Aure, that's all I know. Why, what about him?"

"You mean to say you don't know his reputation?"

"Well, he told me he was a second-rate poet, and came from the Orléanais, but I'm afraid it didn't mean much to me."

"Second-rate poet! He's nearly as famous as Lorca, and very nearly came to the same sticky end. I got it from one of the liaison chaps. Regular army, too. He was at Sedan in 1940. And covered with medals and decorations, from the Croix de Guerre to the Legion of Honour. I can tell you," said Grenfell cheerfully, "I'd feel a couple of inches taller if he stopped in the street to recognise *me!*"

"Good lord!" said Jim, and walked on in silence, wondering why he had. It hadn't been necessary; men meet and separate in war with no claims on one another, unless they choose to establish ties for their own comfort and pleasure. And this, it seemed, was no ordinary man, but one of the flaming spirits set apart from the rest. The more reason, of course, why he should light where he liked; but why, in the name of all that was crazy, should a man like that choose to set one crumb of his favour on a mere sergeant of Infantry—and of all sergeants the most peculiar?

5

After Caen continued the long, monotonous nightmare of slow tension, without pause to consider gain and loss. The advance they made was not a lance-thrust; it was the advance of a screw into iron-wood, ground out by infinitesimal degrees, its progress often almost imperceptible, but every effortful gain fixed and unreversible. South-eastward they drove through the ruined suburbs of Caen, British, Canadians, French, Poles all together, and out again into ravaged fields, forcing their corridor by sheer weight into the congestion of German armour massed to face them. For three weeks they made little headway, but they did not give back at all. The Orne they crossed in boats, and a small tributary of it by an easy ford, and there dug in firmly and would not be uprooted.

The Midshires had not, up to then, fared too badly in the way of casualties. Over all, they were three officers short, and twenty-odd men, including the lucky ones who had been wounded only, and were now on their way home. No one could think of a sound reason for this low figure; and after August 8th, when the real push for Falaise developed, the charm seemed to fail alarmingly. They would never forget the Caen-Falaise road, never as long as they lived; the long, flat, straight, hedgeless road with the long, flat, straight, hedgeless fields on either side, the barren ruled line of white through the dusty, smoky, oil-smeared green, the telegraph poles lopped here and there, and trailing their thrumming wires in the grass, the sultry burning of farms and villages away to left and right, the occasional spectral trees which loomed out of the smoke, maimed by shell-fire and withered by heat, leafless at midsummer; above all they would remember the ditches of that road, the shallow dry ditches under the trailing wire where they went to ground for hours at a time, swallowing the dust of their own armour and the blown charcoal of fires, and watching halftracks and tanks and guns ploughing the pasture into deep furrows as they moved in upon Falaise. In those ditches they left, during the second week of August, Drury and Mansel and Soames, Butcher and Freeman, Clegg and Jenkins, and thirty more Midshire men who would never see more of home again than one of those English shrouds they had brought over with them in such numbers.

At this time they were, considering the difficulties, remarkably well informed about the general position, instead of being shut into their own circumscribed field of action as in a box. News had had ample time to catch up with them, for they were the most fixed part of the front, the fulcrum upon which the whole plan turned. They were the handle of a great sickle which was curving now to reap the German 7th Army, Von

Klüge and all. The Americans, operating along the blade of it, had swung round full through Brittany and borne about in a wide sweep eastward, and were now creeping north towards Argentan as British and Canadians forced their way southward upon Falaise to meet them. Maybe Von Klüge could have got his army out of that closing circle in time, but it meant abandoning all the north-west of France, and either he didn't dare to do it, or he honestly believed he could break the attack without losing so much ground or so much face. At any rate, he had gone west instead of east, striking with everything he had for Avranches, trying probably, to cut a swathe clear through the American line and separate the troops in Brittany from their only source of supply and reinforcement, which was still Normandy. They hadn't a port to their name yet but half-repaired Cherbourg and the fantastic city at Arromanches, where no city had ever been before, the synthetic, prefabricated city of Mulberry, so susceptible to every storm. Once cut off from these, the troops along the blade of the sickle would have been in a dangerous position indeed; but the enemy never got through. They had underestimated both the hour and the men. They never got beyond Mortain, and even that they did not hold long. So now they would have to go east, and faster than ever an army had moved in its life, or they would be too late. If all went well their fastest would be too slow to save them.

The British entered Falaise on August 17th. It was like Caen, except that it was burning better when they forced their way in, and there were, perhaps, more standing walls and fewer people. The civilians had fled into the countryside, anywhere, eastward out of the mouth of the trap. The German troops, having set the town ablaze, had retreated in disorder towards Argentan, where the Americans were straining to reach them. By the light of the fires the British and Canadian Infantry rounded up what was left of a broken garrison, while armour poured through the streets all day in pursuit of the fugitives. They felt then that the tightly wound skein had slipped out of control, and was beginning to unwind itself at a dizzy speed. With Falaise gone, something had broken that held all taut; and nothing now could stop the whirlwind. Three days later British and Americans rushed together in Argentan, and the trap was sealed with Von Klüge in it.

What had seemed so slow and difficult in the doing, an infinite sweating labour more remorseless even than pain or danger, seemed now as a great wind which had swept men and events before it like spent leaves, hurling them into a spinning circle about their enemies, sweeping the German armour into a vortex from which there was no escape, casting Patton's Third Army hurtling towards the Seine to lick up even the survivors as they ran for their Fatherland, and with a flung whisper of its terrible breath raising the patriots of Paris again to the barricades. It had a place for armies and men; it was inevitable, and they felt its inevitability in the things they did, awful and appropriate, as if they had been predestined. This once, if never before and never again, they were marching with fate on equal terms, doing all things well because they were possessed with victory, and could do nothing wrong.

The position the 7th Midshires held on August 20th was almost midway between Falaise and Argentan, east of the railway line by the width of a few flat fields. They were strung along the crest of a ridge, partly orchard and partly pasture, with a village at their backs, though it had now not more than a dozen inhabitants, and they the stubbornest, who would not leave their homes until they were carried out feet foremost. Before the slit trenches the ground fell away gently to a narrow road, and beyond that a few scattered pollards here and there fringed the sharp, deep cutting where a river wound along to join the Dives, somewhere away on their right. Not much of a river, only a miserable trickle in the bottom of its channel, but the drop to it ensured that no traffic should pass it except by a bridge, ready-made or improvised; and a bridge there was, full in face of their position, where a by-road from the village ambled off to join the main road between Falaise and La Ferte Macé, crossing first the river and then, in the distance, the railway line. By that road, as far as the Midshires were concerned, the avalanche would come, and if the strain looked too much the bridge would have to be sacrificed, for they were determined nothing should pass it. By that road already had several wounded German soldiers limped in with lifted hands and stricken, grey faces to give themselves up. The whole field of fire was scarred and pitted with steel scrap and littered with abandoned transport and guns, and a pall of black smoke drifted and shifted about ceaselessly over it, cutting off their vision at less than half a mile even at best. For two days and nights that darkness had scarcely changed its quality. The sky westward had not once been free of R.A.F. bombers, and their fires smeared the skyline continually with red and black. Out of that obscurity only a few derelicts and much shell and mortar fire had yet come into their positions; but in the ominous morning of the 20th of August, the barrage mounted wildly, and they worked and watched and sweated the early hours out with the conviction in them that the climax was very near.

In their rear the artillery massed solidly, pouring shells in upon the distant, desperate, invisible congestion of the enemy, as the bombers poured in bombs, without pause or haste. There was no longer any haste. The 3rd Army might scald away the miles on their way to the Seine; there was still motion there. But here even fury had become motionless; the one thing imperative was that they should not move. Everything else might, the sky, and the earth, and the enemy; only they must not.

The Colonel came lumbering along the ridge about mid morning, ducking his head under the apple-boughs and whistling tunelessly round a cigarette. He looked happy, and interested, and alert, as he was wont to look in Calderhope woods at home when the beagles were out, and his unastonished tenants, who knew him normally as a large, indolent, deep-drinking and slow-moving autocrat, beheld him pass a whooping, charging, thundering tornado of a man who could go all day and never tire. His mode of life in the army had made as few concessions as possible from that golden ideal; for weeks at a time they scarcely saw him at all, for as men they bored him and baffled him too, and where the business of the square and the office was concerned he was a strong believer in delegated leadership; but he could jump to follow the pack as nimbly as ever when there was real hunting afoot. The whole of him, that lethargic mound of flesh of which Falstaff would not have been ashamed, came to surprising life in an emergency. The mountain walked fast enough then, had even been known to run, and always in the direction of the hottest mischief. He had virtues after his fashion; he stood up for his own against all outsiders even though he took no trouble even to know them by face or name; he was afraid of nothing that walked, swam or flew, not even of ridicule; and he was frank about everything, even the dangers he himself never took into account. No one could approve of him, but no one could dislike him. He was about two centuries out of date, but then so was the part of Midshire which had bred him, and so had a great many of his Midshire men been until army life jolted their education forward much as the devil went through Athlone, in standing leaps. He had been able to lie back and refuse to learn, but the other ranks had had no option; yet they understood him still, and even the reddest among them felt

93

a little sorry at having to reckon him among the worn-out ideas of which the world was busy ridding itself at last, and with so much pain.

But Colonel Sir Robert Friedland, who would not under any circumstances have lifted a finger to stop the revolution even had he perceived it coming, provided it permitted him to eat and drink as well as ever, to follow hounds, and be amused as much by the wisdom as by the follies of his fellow-men, was in no need of sympathy. He came rolling down the orchard with what was almost a dance-step, looked at young Baird emerging flushed and grubby from a slit trench, looked at the two anti-tank guns set to cover the bridge, looked at the sappers splashing about like otters under the arch with their cables and their gelignite, looked at the smoky backcloth tattered with gunfire, and was a happy man. Harben came climbing up from the road and found him sitting on a gun-mount talking to young Baird as if he had known him all his life, and calling him Grenfell. Baird, who had never seen him like this before, was too dazzled to notice. Oh, yes, the old man had some of Falstaff's graces, as well as his bulk, once he bestirred himself.

"Pretty near, now, sir," said Harben. "There's hell to pay farther up the Falaise road. They're trying to ditch a column that was shot up there an hour or so ago, but the road's still blocked."

"Good!" said the Colonel happily. "Then they'll make across country with all they can take that way, and we'll get the shock here inside an hour. Then we shall know what really happens when the irresistible force meets the immovable object."

"They both die of exhaustion," said Harben.

"Eh? Not these! Time's too short for that, they'll be dead of other things before it can take effect. D'you realise, Harben, that so far nothing ever has stood up to these panzers? Nothing! According to all the rules and most of the probabilities they should roll us out flat—like that!" he said with his charming smile, and smudged a greenfly into a small coloured smear on the back of his hand. "Roll us out like dough, and go straight ahead."

"But just now all the rules and most of the probabilities are going by the board." He looked along the road towards the bridge, where a single unkempt figure on a white farm-horse without harness was riding in towards the village, with a rifle across his thighs, and a German officer's greatcoat tied by the sleeves about his neck. His pace was only a brisk walk, yet it

94

was clear that he rode like a centaur, never troubling to use his hands. He saluted the sappers as he crossed the bridge, and in the momentary quietness between rounds of shell fire they heard him singing at the top of his voice "Dombrowski's March". " Somebody else thinks this is the time," said Major Harben.

The song floated up to the other ranks waiting with their chests braced against the new-cut parapet.

"Somebody's happy," said Dick Shelby, listening, "besides our old man. What is that chap?"

"Polish" said Jim, watching the centaur wheel right-handed out of sight.

"But he's coming from off among the Jerries, and he isn't wearing uniform."

"Yes, imported with a forced labour battalion, most likely. Wonder what he did with the owner of the coat?"

"What we shall be doing soon to the rest of 'em," said Teddy Mason.

He talked a lot still, but not when Jim Benison was around; only the stress of the moment could have made him forget himself so far. And yet when it came to giving and taking orders they could be natural enough together; no one seemed to have considered that there was anything out of the ordinary between them. That was necessary, but a pity in a way, for it meant that Jim had no involuntary allies with him, no one to frown thoughtfully over his diatribes and give judgment with "Still, when you come to think of it he's right, you *did*——" No, he'd have to come to that decision unassisted this time; and if he managed it, there was hope for him; and if he didn't all the rest of their efforts wouldn't help him.

"Oh, ay, tha'll do wonders," said Peterson tolerantly. "We know thee! Personally ah'll be glad when it's over."

"When I was a kid," said Morgan, "I used to have nightmares about falling down in front of a steamroller and not being able to get up again. I feel just the same now."

"But think of the nightmare the steamroller must be having this time," said Sloan.

It was worth thinking about, even in this thunderous pause before the impact. Von Klüge knew now, and all his men with him, what the British had been made to endure in 1940; but he had no friendly sustaining sea at his back now as they had had then, no miraculous fleet putting forth to his deliverance. He would have to come through if he could; at all costs he would have to attempt to come through. Not even the steam-roller was going to relish this nightmare.

It was about midday, and the sun was bright on the clean belt of land between the guns and their target, when they came. The sound of the columns began a long way off in the drifting smoke, hardly distinguishable from the continuous bass of the shell-bursts; but it had a quality different from anything else as it came nearer, insistent, fretful, ferocious, screaming through the subterranean repercussions of bombs and guns, and torment-ing the ear-drums with its metallic monotony.

"Here they come!" shouted Baird, and leaned forward out of the cover of the trees.

A serpent of dust writhed upward whitely against the black of the smoke lingering above, and out of the obscurity the first convoy burst at high speed along the road, with racing shadows along its flanks where tank and halftrack had relieved the con-gestion by taking to the fields. As far as they could see to left and right there surged out of the distance every conceivable vehicle for which an army can have use, lumbering dangerously up the long curve of the fields, flattening what was left stand-ing of the derelict corn, gouging out the flesh of the soft pasture. A world of iron leaped at them in whorls of smoke and clouds of dust, fretting the skyline with dark perforations that grew and expanded, putting on recognisable form as they raced at full speed for the river bank.

The Midshires waited and held their breath, watching the space between racing armour and sharp-edged cutting diminish rapidly. The pace did not slacken.

"They don't know of the river," shouted Baird in excitement.

"They do, they must, sir! Either they're just running amok, or they're going to bridge it the quick way."

"But, damn it, it's suicide!"

"Yes, for the first of 'em it is, but I saw it done once." It might not work so well this time, though, he thought in his heart; they were winning then, and they're a damned sight better at self-immolation when they're on the crest of things. Nevertheless, the possibility existed; he put it into Baird's mind to suggest that the second anti-tank gun be brought to bear upon the lowest point they could trace along the bank. They were surely not so crazy with fear that they couldn't spare a glance to select the least of risks. The order given, Baird went back to the staggering contemplation of the road beyond the bridge, where the thickest of the congestion was. Yes, they were mad, they must be mad, to mass a target like that. Nose to tail, two and more abreast, overturning in the ditches, mounting the hedge-banks, breaking into open country, the panzers came back from the west. Every vehicle of war was there, field kitchens, field ambulances, workshop lorries, transports, unarmoured cars, assault guns and Hornets on tank chassis, mobile anti-aircraft guns, mobile pill-boxes in tow of tractors, Tigers and Panthers, Elephant guns, Panzer-Nebelwerfer rocket-guns with their many barrels ridged in the sudden sun like corrugated steel, everything down to the helpless little *volkswagen* in danger of being squashed like beetles under the tracks. There was the material for three armies, and they were not even trying to make use of it; all they desired was to smash through the Allied ring and escape. Something was gone from that arrogant master-race; now that they no longer had the initiative they threw everything else after it, their power to command courage, their faith in their destiny, even their methodical coolness, and with lowered heads stampeded like sheep for the nearest exit. Half that weight of guns deployed into cover along this stretch of country could have put up the cost of victory to a terrible figure; but they did not deploy, they ran; it was all they had left in their minds. They ran, and the British and Canadian artillery, which had waited calmly for the range, opened upon them full and cut them to pieces.

It was like slamming a steel door in their faces. The hurtling impetus was smashed instantly, still at perhaps a quarter of a mile beyond the bridge, and a tangled mound of wreckage swept up into air like a wave, and remained fixed. Those behind could not or would not stop; those before could not disentangle themselves. A fuel lorry overturned ponderously into the ditch, and threshed like the death-throes of leviathan, and a comet's tail of fire licked out from its smashed engine and engulfed the mound. A few vehicles which had escaped from the belt of shell fire rushed onward to the bridge; and out of the blazing barrier behind some heavy tanks withdrew themselves, heaving their bulk laboriously up the hedge-bank into the fields, and so circumventing the fire, to come back to the road when it was passed. These also swept down upon the bridge.

The sappers held their hand until the first lumbering Mark VI was dipping to the decline and lifting its long nose again clumsily to the rise of the narrow arch. Then they fired their charge. Some smaller fry following close were lifted and flung yards aside into the cutting, turning in the air slowly like slivers of some weightless wood, but the Tiger only seemed to hang still for a moment while the stones of the bridge dissolved from under its tracks, and then as abruptly to fall like a heavier stone, flat into the fissure which could not fully contain it, so that the barrel of its 88-millimetre gun still protruded grotesquely from the cutting when it settled in flurries of soil and spray. Over it poured transport and tank, spilling bodies, and horse-drawn gun-carts plunged and wallowed and screamed, churning up the shaken banks and fouled channel with flailing hooves until fear, exhaustion and wounds killed, and fall upon fall behind buried the dead.

A few men, crazed creatures still just able to crawl, dragged themselves out of the hollow and staggered into the open, their hands spread, shrieking surrender. The Midshires held their fire and gathered these in, and they were passed through the lines into the village and abandoned, for no one had time to pay them any attention, and they were past doing any harm. No one could spare glance or thought from the fantastic horror spread out before them. They watched in stillness, and trembled. Morgan was saying something to himself over and over, deep in his throat.

"The horses!" he said. "Oh, Christ, the horses!"

There was nothing anyone could do for the horses except make an end of it quickly, and then go out and finish them on the spot; and there were so many of them, literally hundreds, wound inextricably into the traffic of the road and going mad with fear. They dragged their carts out of the press here and there by main force, and smashing hedges and fences before them rushed headlong out into the fields, colliding with tanks and tractors, tearing a diagonal of terror and pain across the van of the armour now nosing along the edge of the cutting. Most of them went over into the river, and strangled in their harness, or were crushed by their own carts, or held down in the pitiful trickle of water and miserably drowned. Two yoked together crashed into the pollards, and one fell from his broken harness, and one hung like Absalom from the tree, kicking and plunging against the sheer bank which gave his hooves no purchase. Jim took a careful sight, and shot him dead, and felt thankful even for so much good; but they could not do that for them all.

And the men were as the horses. They drove anywhere, in any direction, to escape that barrage; they overturned their lorries into the gully in two places along the Midshires' sector,

and tried to bring tanks to ground across the levelled piles
of wreckage and dead. Such as did heave themselves out of
the slaughter were met by the anti-tank guns, and knocked out
before they could bring any impetus to bear upon the positions.
Numbers of Infantry threw themselves under the near bank
to shelter from the shell fire, and were killed there by their own
following traffic; others scrambled across anyhow upon their
hands and knees, and ran in their hundreds to give themselves
up. Some who had gone beyond fear brought up machine-guns,
and found what cover they could, and fought; but these did
not live long. But it was mainly the artillery's battle; all the
Infantry had to do was glean where the gunners reaped, and
endure as they might.

There seemed no end to the inflowing columns. Traffic still
piled itself up in swathes along the smoking road, though there
was no possibility of clearing a passage there. Heavy armour
driving in from behind seemed not to see the struggling, burning
mass already penned between the shallow ditches; the drivers
were either blind or crazed, for they hurtled on until they
ground bodily into the heaving wreckage, telescoping smaller
cars before their weight, and adding another aspect to the
portrait of death. As far back as the eye could see for smoke
and dust, still the panzers came, by road and by field,
demoniacal, possessed, busy destroying one another in their
panic. R.A.F. 'planes flew up and down the columns
unhindered, gunning as they went; and within A Company's
sight alone at least a dozen petrol fires had sprung to life after
their passing, great, writhing, rose-coloured knots in the string
of traffic. How was anyone ever going to unravel that string
again?

And why did they not, in the last extremity, when they saw
they could not break through by force, deploy their guns into
cover, and man them, and at least fight it out? True, the case
was past reversal by that or any other effort, but how was it
bettered by going raving mad and wasting even what chance
they had? A few teams did get out into the farmyards and
clumps of trees, and go into action, and did some damage
before the 'planes turned aside to nose them out; but for every
one that was manned a score were abandoned, while their teams
threw away helmet and arms and all that weighed heavily in
their haste to reach the apple orchards and be taken prisoner.
Elephants and Hornets, Nebelwerfer and Wasp and mortar were
driven into the pasture and left there, until the whole country-

side was littered with undamaged armour as the Wrekin with paper bags after a peacetime Bank Holiday. And in the village in the rear every house was crammed with silent, nerveless, broken prisoners, some still uselessly nursing the arms no one had even troubled to take away from them. Occasionally some casual private put in a head to take stock of them, but for the length of the day that was all the guarding they had, and more than they needed.

The surrender which had begun by ones spread to dozens, to hundreds. What else was there for them to do but surrender? High-ranking officers began to come in with the rest, and in little better case than the rest, with stunned eyes incredulous of disaster, and jumping hands, and the rags of dignity shivering on them as they ran to order and stood still when they were told. And this was the incomparable Wehrmacht, this ruinous, quaking thing beaten almost into insensibility and whining for pity!

"My God!" said Baird, almost sobbing from sheer excitement as they dropped lower through the orchard trees in mid afternoon, "it's incredible! It makes you almost feel sorry for 'em, in spite of everything—doesn't it?" It had got him in the wind all right; every breath out of him since noon was a drowning man's gasp, and his eyes filled up half his face with awe and wonder.

"No," said Jim stolidly, "not me."

"Oh, I know all that! But to come to *this*——"

"They were always this. They were this at Munich, if we'd had the sense. They were this in 1940, if we'd had the means." So he thought but he said nothing, for it was waste of breath and time to hark back to what was gone; only suddenly he wondered if perhaps some of the dead of Sedan and Dunkirk saw this, and were satisfied, and how Miriam's face would look —did look, where she was—at this moment. Not glad, not vengeful, only quieted with the infinite, slow, inexorable rightness of justice, the pattern of the wheel's turning; not joyful, only confirmed, only reassured, because the overturned processes of time had righted themselves and justified her.

"To come to *this*——!" said young Baird to himself, slithering down the slope towards the road. Even he, perhaps, who had seen only this readjustment, felt it ache in his body like an invisible wound; but what did he know about this other ache within the first, where the sacred shut-up memories were, at which it had been forbidden to look until now? What did he know of the dead men stirring as if they were minded to come back? Or of the dead woman's dark, intent, assuaged face?

The barrage lifted and lengthened, leaving the shattered fields where it had quested for hours, to search out the distant congestions of untouched material still piling up in the rear. The 'planes moved inward upon the same errand. Before dusk it grew almost quiet on both banks of the murderous little river, tor though there was several days' work there within the pocket, worrying work still to be done, and some killing and some dying, yet the battle was over. The British were moved down steadily from their ridge, gleaning the stumbling prisoners as they went, and passing them back in their hundreds; and after them the ambulances and field hospitals came creeping along the narrow cross-lane and began to gather another harvest. The noise rolled past and away into distance as a thunderstorm withdraws with threatenings, and they were left with their victory.

But how to begin to see it fully? To describe it was out of the question. It could not be grasped; they spread their faculties to encompass it, and still it eluded them and they took hold upon air. All they could hold by was the individual bits of it that fell one by one into their vision, and one by one could be assimilated. So they saw by laborious degrees the fantastic debris of the field, mile upon mile littered with frozen transport and jettisoned equipment, steel helmets by the hundred, rifles and small arms by the ton; the river an unspeakable sewer of mud and oil and blood, with the dead swinging slowly in the iridescent wash, and the living heaving feebly under the wreckage; the two improvised bridges and the remains of the old one, three indistinguishable barricades of wreckage damming up the water into red pools; the broken cars lolling in the dust like burst oranges, spilling men and weapons and equipment and the loot of France; the mindless men sitting uninjured under the river bank, staring vacantly at their hideously dead companions; the burning, quivering, reeking heaps of flesh and steel that glowed along the road to Falaise as the dusk came down; and the blown ashes acrid in the mouth. They had had everything, Von Klüge's army, every refinement France could supply, beautiful clothes to take home for their women, beautiful perfumes, wines, food, jewellery, everything but the means to escape with their plunder. Now a man could step over their bodies and pick up here and there whatever he fancied of this ruin of riches, he could roll them aside out of his way and drive off in their undamaged cars; he could photograph the scene with their cameras, or use their binoculars to search out the unimaginable detail of their destruction; he could pick and choose between the treasures they had assembled so jealously, and leave all but the best lying, just as he weeded out the living and left the dead. But presently, in this ripeness and rottenness and requital, he would meet another of his kind wandering the field like himself, and see reflected the opaque incredulity of his own eyes turned inward from the stature of the thing they saw; and he would wonder, and be helpless to discover, if indeed he dreamed.

There had never been anything like this; it stunned the senses. Even the victors sickened and were afraid before it, as feeling themselves mad or bewitched. They went their single ways about the plain at dusk, while the sound withdrew from them, and the complaint of the batteries grew fretful and spasmodic; they did what they had to do, whether it was rounding up prisoners, salvaging wounded, nursing undamaged transport, piling small arms, all as men struggling through a hashish dream, their minds half absent with shock; but they did it well, for their hands were the hands of craftsmen. They went singly because they had each his own job in this extremity of an extremity, without need of orders or any word said. The great wind that had blown them hither was spent here at last in the Norman fields, its course completed, its terrible breath perfected and stilled upon perfection.

They saw one another, until the numbness passed, without any sign of recognition, almost as if they believed themselves unseen. No comment would ever be made upon what was seen that day. No one would ever look back and feel any surprise at the memory of Morgan stalking along the river bank with a Lüger in his hand, shooting the maimed horses that stood drooping and waiting to die, his face stony, and tears streaming down the dark mask unnoticed. No one would ever think it strange that Clure should hold a seventeen-year-old Bavarian boy in his arms as he died, or walk away from him after he was dead with blank, bewildered eyes and uneasy muttering mouth, straight across the darkling field between the flung helmets, upon some unformulated errand known only to himself. It was natural that some should serve and grieve and be haunted, and some should decorate themselves with cumbersome, useless souvenirs while they kicked aside treasures; that some should look unmoved upon the brash of human flesh and horse flesh and iron lying like the wash of a wave along this desolate shore, and some should be unable to keep their eyes or their hands from the wealth of mechanical equipment inviting the covetous attention of the expert. They acted after their kind; men who have seen what they had seen are past thinking or caring that they may be observed.

Nor did anyone, except perhaps Teddy Mason, wonder to see Sergeant Benison standing motionless upon the crest of a rolling meadow, staring westward across the darkening vista of pasture and grain, orchard and farm and woodland, with the smoke upon everything, and the smoulder of the burned-out fires growing braver in the twilight; with the bodies of dead men, and their belongings, unnoticed about his feet, and the stars showing here and there grudgingly through the murk over his head. Nobody considered that he looked any taller than usual, though he was stretching up to see across a world, and across time, too, if that were possible. Nobody thought it unusual that his hands should be empty just then of weapons and labour and loot alike, and his heavy brows drawn level and low over his eyes to see so far, and the eyes themselves fixed in that look they all had now, and yet with something in the fixity, a focus, an awareness, which not all of the rest had. He was looking at the only battle-field he would ever see that looked like the old paintings, littered with dead and untidy with spoils for miles upon every side of him, with the night shutting in upon it unmoved, and the silence silencing it; an awful solemnity of indifference glittering upon it from the clean sky as the smoke dissolved away, and clear in its silence and impotence the rounding and falling of a moment which could as well have contained Slaughter Bridge or Kulikovo as the Falaise road. Old tragedy or new, it was all one. Only there was more for him to see than an atavistic racial memory of wars and deaths and revenges; something as deep in his fabric, in the fibre and bone of him, as that memory was, and more insistent and possessive. He saw the rightness, the inevitability, the beauty of that day.

As he moved down at last from his island of contemplation, one or two who saw him did note that he went lamely, but that did not move them to wonder; they did not question, nor he explain, that he had just come by something he had lacked so long that the use of it came unhandily to him as yet. If you believe in something long enough in your own mind without justificaton or encouragement, and sudden lightnings strike for proof, you may well be the first to be blinded.

6

They were withdrawn next day, and sent headlong eastward after the pursuit, leaving other units less fortunate to clear up the unconscionable mess they left behind, the still unexplored complexities of the field, the uncounted riches of guns and armour and loot and prisoners, the conglomeration of death. They made for the Seine at Vernon, north-west of Paris, where the Americans were already winding an arm about the town, and the British Second Army were moving deliberately across their lines of communication to mass a force for the crossing of the river. Here the avalanche loosed by the breaking of the tension at Falaise did check for a few days, but with such method and purpose that it seemed no check at all, but a part of the very impetus that bore them. And on the evening of the 26th of August they crossed the Seine.

After four days of rushing through sunlight, under clear skies, this was a return to the obscurity they knew so much better, and in which they were at home. The smoke screen and the barrage, both launched upon the pure evening with no warning, covered their embarkation with a double blanket of darkness and pandemonium, and the ducks and assault boats in which they crossed were familiar friends whom they could trust, after so many trials of faithfulness, with their lives and their success. The only thing for which they had not bargained was the rise in the level of the river, covering shallowly what were usually islands. These submerged lands they did not know, and several of their craft grounded on them, and had to sit helpless in mid stream throughout the first attack because no one had leisure, until the bridgehead was firm, to turn back and tow them off. Worse, they could not even curse their ill luck above a whisper, even in such a barrage, for fear they should be located and draw a fire they could not return. There was something gratefully comic about the spectacle of Company Sergeant-Major Groome, marooned and impotent, sitting glowering through the battle in his boat with all the burning words penned up inside him, and loosing them at last like a jet of acid upon the grinning crew of the Duck that rescued him. And anything that made them laugh was sweet, after Caen and

Falaise where their laughter had been withered up by the stress of events, and their jokes for a little while dwarfed out of existence by a darkness beyond measure.

The bridgehead which had been pegged out that evening was consolidated next day, and the troops which had crossed expanded it by ten miles or more in every direction, to cover the crossing of the armour. It was perhaps a messy base from which to launch a major thrust, but there was no time to tidy it up; they had minds for only one thing, and that was to make sure and doubly sure that the Boche would not be able to dig in and pin them down to static warfare again. They had got to start him running. They tumbled their advance armour across the Seine, not waiting for the main body, and went for him enthusiastically head down; and the Boche ran. He was in no position to do anything else. He ran, and the Second Army, gathering their main armour after them in intoxicating haste, streamed after him in full cry, scattering fringe-guards of Infantry along both flanks of their advance as they tunnelled east and north-east into France, and cutting the enemy garrisons into two, half penned between the British and American corridors, and half between the British and the sea; shifting ground either side, and the retreating units, such as fell out by the way, could choose which danger they preferred and make the best of it, for once passed they were helpless, and could be cut up later at leisure.

On the 30th of August the Second Army entered Beauvais, and streamed on all night to reach Amiens by first light of the following day. This was a city whole and intact, even to the bridges over the Somme, for which the Maquis had fought the retreating Boche out of the town by twilight, and sat down upon their prizes stolidly until dawn, when the relief entered. Amiens was memorable even in what had been a triumphal progress most of the way, complicated here and there by knots of resistance, but everywhere radiant with the joy of the French people. Amiens was all flags and flowers and smiles, girls running alongside the lorries as they slowed through the streets, hard-bitten fighters of the Resistance beaming from guarded doors, children shrieking and waving along the pavements, shrill and excited and honest as puppies. It was hard to remember Caen in Amiens.

The crossing of the Somme occupied the whole of the day, and gave them an opportunity, while the armour was being shepherded through, to drop out of their lorries and stretch their legs before the next burst of speed swept them to the borders of Belgium. The Midshires, among others, climbed out and were at once mobbed by chattering children and excited women, who thrust upon them flowers, sweets, eatables, wine, anything they could dredge out of their depleted stores to lavish upon the deliverers. They let themselves be swept away in the flood of emotion without resistance. Why not? It might not be the whole reality, but it was authentic enough. It might not be what they had come for, but they would take it in passing, by way of experience with the rest, and be grateful. Once there had passed this way lads like themselves, who had met this triumph before their battle, and been lost in it. These were spared that; they took only what they had earned, and even that with a good-humoured smile, and their eyes ready at a word to look beyond it for the next danger.

Jim edged his way out of the press of people in the by-street, and went down to watch by the main bridge as the armour came through. Hands clutched at him as he passed, for every British uniform was a talisman of power that day; children ran alongside for a few paces, holding by his trouser legs and shrilling at him like jackdaws, shouting with delight and clapping their hands when he laughed back at them in their own tongue, and only abandoning him to rush away in the opposite direction with another of his kind; a hairy patriot of the Maquis, blue-jowled, with bare arms muscled like Hercules, embraced him in passing with the hug of an affectionate bear; a middle-aged woman, plainly and poorly dressed but with the eyes of Melpomene, caught his hand to her and fondled it, and he felt her tears upon his fingers like dew, effortless and sweet; a young girl, flung breast to breast with him unexpectedly, gasped and laughed into his face, and he kissed her lightly, partly because it was expected of him, and partly because he very much wanted to, and so passed on. But when he came to the head of the bridge he saw that this unanimity of joy was not so complete as it had seemed, that Amiens was not free from the old complexities, any more than any other city.

A posse of Maquis men had been rounding up prisoners in their own time and their own way, and happened to bring them past this point on their way to internment. There were two obvious Germans among the eight, not soldiers but civilians by their bearing as well as their dress; but the rest were French, and two of them were women, and all had been somewhat roughly handled. There was also another woman, not a prisoner, one who followed distressfully along the fringe of the procession, crying and cursing by turns, trying to reach the younger of the two German officials, and being shouldered off indifferently by the solid Amiens shop-keeper who guarded the column upon that side. She must have been a very pretty woman once, slender and chic and vivacious; she was still noticeably well dressed, with a delicate figure and elegantly cut clothes to show it off; but her hair and eyebrows had been shaven. Another, like her but older, walked along the street after the procession, with a child in her arms and a scarf wrapped round her head to attempt to hide what could not be hidden. It was by no means new; they had seen the same thing happen many times since they came to France.

The townspeople watched the prisoners pass and made no demonstration; only a shadow seemed to pass with them, and the watching eyes were like stones. But the younger woman's cries cut clean through the rumble of tank-tracks along the road, and reached the ears of a knot of British officers who stood by the head of the bridge; and they turned as one man to stare at the source of that lamentable noise. Jim, who was not half a dozen yards away, watched their expressions change to disgusted and embarrassed pity. Half of H.Q. was there, it seemed to him: a Lieutenant-General of whose name he was not sure, Colonel Friedland, a couple of Staff-captains, Major Grant, and a small, slim French officer of whom he caught as yet only a narrow glimpse between two large and indignant Englishmen.

One of the Staff-captains was heard to remark upon the spectacle as a distasteful exhibition. The other one said that it was an inhuman practice which ought to be stopped at once, and treated as a crime if it recurred. Major Grant was understood to remark that it was un-British; it was the worst censure to which he could lay his tongue without notice.

"But of course it is un-British," said the little Frenchman, amused. "You, my friends, are distressingly un-French. It is to be regretted, but what would you?"

The voice, Jim noted, was the voice of Amadis; he should have guessed as much.

"Good God, Cahusac!" protested Major Grant, "you surely don't defend it?"

"I do not defend or deprecate. For my part, I am not concerned in it at all. It is not important to me. I have seen too much blood shed, by too many strange ways, to expend any fury over a little hair.''

"But it serves no useful purpose. You people are supposed to be practical, aren't you? This is just damned degrading.''

"You are not logical,'' said Amadis mellifluously. "It is damned degrading, yes, and that is a purpose most useful. It is what you call a hall-mark for the species, that. In your country one must, I think, have one's poisons properly labelled and in certain bottles? That is a useful purpose, no? We also make our poisons recognisable—so! Oh, but yes, we are always practical.''

"My dear man,'' said the first Staff-captain, reverting from argument to instinctive revulsion, "you can't persuade me that that is anything but a commonplace instinct of revenge, and a cruel one, too. And probably unjust!''

"Ah, then you can no doubt account for the two who have not been cropped, but only arrested?''

"I don't have to account for them. No one expects logic from a mob gone mad with hate.''

"Logic? Ah, no, revenge is not logical. But wonderfully consistent. It generalises. It would have treated them all alike. And you see they have not been treated alike. Let us say—these are the poisons which may be handled freely, but must be marked; those are deadlier, and are kept—in well-regulated communities, my friend—locked up.''

Not much use any of them taking him up on that, thought Jim, as the dolorous procession wound away out of sight between the cold-eyed watchers; he could talk rings round any one of them, even if he hadn't been sincere about his arguments, and he was sincere. Now the Lieutenant-General was moving across nearer to the bridge, his retinue a comet's tail behind him. Amadis, last to turn and go, checked abruptly as his glance fell upon Jim, and instantly came back to him. He was smiling, the curious smile Jim remembered in him, at once rueful, and enjoying, and cold.

"Your countrymen do not approve of mine,'' he said. "I am desolate.''

"It's hardly new, is it?'' said Jim, smiling in his turn.

"You heard, then? Well, what do you think?''

"I think it says a lot that they stop at the hair. I wouldn't have been surprised if they took a few heads as well. But we haven't been occupied.''

"Oh, you underestimate your people. If they were the

injured I believe their attitude would be as it is now. For you are a wonderful nation, my Sergeant, so kind, so sentimental, so shortsighted, so exploitable——"

"Yes," said Jim, "that's what I'm afraid of."

"Afraid? But it is an excellent name I give you!"

"Is it? You know," he said, his eyes on the tanks and guns which ground steadily by and rumbled hollowly across the bridge, "I can't help wondering what's going to happen when we do get into Germany. Even now, even here in France, little influences emerge as soon as the gunfire stops, and get hold of little strings of sympathy, and pull like hell. You don't need to be told, I know, but how often do my people, as you call 'em, stop to look below the surface and find out the rights of it? Sympathy's all very well, but ours goes to the first one that asks for it, more often than not; and you know as well as I do, or better, that the first one is usually the bloke who wants protection from the real victims. After all, there's only so much kindness and help to be had out of any man—just so much as happens to be in him—and I'm damned if I can see why we should let the first comers take a bath in it, and leave none for the rest, when we ought to know by experience they're dead sure to be the ones who least need it and don't deserve or value it. But that's exactly what we go on doing. And you call that an excellent name!"

"You are always unexpected," said Amadis contentedly.

"What's so unexpected about that? It's just common sense."

"And have you not yet suspected that common sense is the least common thing in the world? But go on, I am interested."

"Oh, I've finished. Only as I see it, this undiscriminating charity of ours is going to be about the biggest danger we're up against unless we do something about it—dangerous to the world, too—and anyway, an offence against everything we're supposed to be interested in, especially justice."

"No compromise?" said Amadis. "No parley with the enemy?"

"No parley with the enemy, or the friends of the enemy, or the hangers-on of the enemy, or the traders with the enemy."

"And no revulsion from—a little clipped hair?"

"No feelings at all about anything so unimportant."

"Good! Now you will smoke a *caporal* with me, no? You do not dislike them?" And when they had lit up he added suddenly: "I noticed your Colonel, he had nothing to say."

"Oh, he's not so soft as he looks by a long way. He may be

the shape of a bladder of lard, but he can get his ear to the ground when he likes. No, if he rolls off after non-essentials it won't be because he can't see the essentials, it'll be because it suits him to pretend he can't. And anyhow, he's too old a kind to have any feeling for the people who think everything can be bought and sold and bargained over, even with cheap hard-luck stories."

"But—obsolete, perhaps?"

"Oh, I suppose he went out with the Feudal System, but nobody's told him, and he wouldn't believe it if they did. Now what happens to you? Do you have to follow the band?" He nodded after the little knot of officers gathered now at the head of the bridge.

"It does not matter. They will not go away yet."

"Walk back with me, then, a little way. I'd better not stay away too long, they may want to move us soon." And as they went he asked: "Are you still coming ahead with the Group? We shall be in Belgium before so long."

"No, I go back to Paris from here, probably in a few days."

"I did wonder. There'll be plenty for you to do down there yet. I suppose I shan't see you again, then."

"Not for a while, I regret. But perhaps when it is all over you and I——"

"Oh, don't make any plans about afterwards," said Jim hastily, "not to me. It's the only superstition I've got left."

"So?" Amadis looked at him along his shoulder with a wistful, oblique smile. "You hope very much, then, for an afterwards?"

"Yes," said Jim, and no more.

"And I also. Always, in Montry-sur-Aure and worse places, I was sure of that. It is an incentive to doing, to being, to believing, that desire. I am glad it did not desert me."

Jim said nothing to that, for it was new with him, and troublous. To be ready to endure the future is one thing, to desire it is another; he had not yet got used to the change.

"My afterwards," said Amadis, "is something I have had already, and perhaps never yet appreciated. It is my farm in the Orléanais, that is all. But if there were time, and I should show you my mind, it may be I should talk to you of my French soil as your priest would talk to you of God." A soft smile touched his lips a moment, and passed, leaving him grave. "France is for me not the turmoil of cities and tangle of interests which disquiets you. France is the soil. The soil is her own deliverance. In every need she will breed her own saviours. And destroy them, it may be, when they have served their turn, but will they complain against her for that? I think not. There!" he said quaintly. "I have told you. And yours?"

"It's just as simple. But not as settled as yours. Mine is a woman."

"Ah!" said Amadis. "You are fortunate."

"Yes, I think so."

"Your wife?"

"Not yet; but when I get back—if I get back—she will be."

They picked their way slowly through the happy crowd in the side street, where the lorries were drawn up along the kerb. The Midshires were enjoying their moment. Teddy had a girl in either arm, and two more fast by the hands. Peterson was sitting on his heels between the transports, in earnest conversation with half a dozen small children. Morgan had an old man beside him on the running-board, and a fine sturdy mastiff pup between his knees, and the two of them in dumb show, for they had not a word in common between them, were going over the points of dogs they had owned and known. Two unusuals had come naturally together. Nor had Morgan ever looked, thought Jim, so resolutely and consciously alive as now; he had seen the reality, there was nothing the imagination could do to him now.

"I shouldn't come any farther," said Jim. "Not that they'll salute you if you do, but they might feel they ought to, and it's a pity to disturb 'em. You'd find it would take some time to get out again, too."

"Also I must go back quickly now. It may be I am needed." He held out his hand. "Good-bye, my Sergeant. I trust it shall be all as you wish—your afterwards."

"And your farm—you'll get there all right. Good-bye, and good luck! And my regards to Paris!"

"And mine—to your wife!"

His smile flashed once as he turned to wave his hand, punctiliously as to a woman; then he walked jauntily away, with that gait of his at once halt and nimble, and was lost in the crowd in a moment. And that was the last Jim ever saw of the great Amadis Cahusac.

It was early evening when the column moved on, over the bridge and out of the city, following where the armour had gone before, along the road to Arras and Douai. They travelled all night without making more than occasional contacts, and when the day came they opened up to speed again, tearing forward along the right flank of the advance, where they were open to attack, though less liable to it than the units on the left. The hundred and fifty thousand German troops shut between the 2nd Army and the sea were fighting wildly to cut through the corridor and get out of the trap; and there were times during that advance when a single Infantry division along the flank was holding sixty miles of frontage and more; but with every hour their hold strengthened, as more troops pressed after them along the corridor, and the break-through never even looked like succeeding. On the right flank the pressure was not so intense, for the enemy had plenty of room to run here, and the instinct by now was become almost a habit; and the Midshires were the more disconcerted, therefore, when towards evening they ran into a bitter and stubborn resistance south of Douai, and were held up for a few hours before they could clear it.

This was the worst time they had had, when they came to reckon the cost, since leaving Falaise itself; and coming as it did at the end of almost a month of continuous strain, it left them as a battalion shaken and weakened, plainly in need of a rest. A great many of their transports, also, had suffered damage, and it was expedient to move them aside from the main roads into one of the newly cleared villages, and give them a few days for breathing-space. Which was done; and they settled gratefully into the comparative quiet of the Artois countryside, and watched the growing tide of armour and troops flow by them, and slept as they had not slept since leaving England, three months ago.

The companies were scattered through farmyards, factories and schools, over two or three square miles of country; and A Company found themselves living in the empty buildings of a water-mill, removed only by a narrow field from the foot of a winding village street. The mill was still working steadily, as if no war had passed by its wheel with the stream. The cool plashing of the slats was a continuous music in the first autumnal mellowing of the high summer; and above the dark sluices the pool was green and deep and very still, with speckled golden lights gleaming through it when the sun caught the pebbles below, and small feathery ferns starring even the stones that walled it in. It was an enchanted place, a rest even to the eyes and ears. They accepted the pause with gratitude, with delight. Even Sergeant Benison, at first sight of it when they marched in from the transport lines, was seen to rear his head like a starting horse, and draw a sharp breath as if it had caught him unawares.

Jim knew then where he was. He had known for some days, of course, that he could not be far away, but not until he reached the mill in its hollow of willows and water did he realise that by another route and from the opposite side he had come back at last to Boissy-en-Fougères.

As soon as he could get away—and half of the company were out before him—he went to look at it. Across the field to the end of the lane, and so up the easy, meandering rise of the village street, with his memories crowding about him and clustering like bees in swarm, he walked through Boissy from end to end; past the little houses, past the doctor's brass plate, past the market-garden, past the apothecary-cum-herbalist, and the café, and Mère Jeantot's bakery, and the little whitewashed church with its garish windows made beautiful by the resplendency of their blue; past Papa Brégis's *bistro*, check-curtained and noisy as of old, but vaguely more prosperous in its new blue paint and gilt-lettered sign; past the *mairie*, and the post office, and the little depleted *épicerie*, to the end of the street, to the end of the rise, where there was the glint of white masonry through trees, and a slope of apple orchards, and the compact richness of beechwoods behind.

There was no latch left upon the gate, which sagged from one hinge as he put his hand upon it. It moved aside with a groan at his touch, and fell drunkenly halfway to the dust, and he stepped through the interstice and went down the farmyard, slowly, like a man in a dream. Not since Westmorland had he known such a silence; here the bumble-hum of armour for ever passing on the main road north was already distant, and once within the crescent of the apple-trees it was cut off utterly from his ears. He went down between the stables and byres, past the kitchen-garden and the little enclosure of flowers, overgrown now with rank grass; and he stood before the shell of the house, silent in the silence, with the shadow of the standing walls over him, and high in air the marbled fireplace projecting into the sunlight like the portico of a strange aerial temple. It was all as he had left it, except that he had left it living, and now it was dead. The fallen stones had acquired, in five years, enough soil to support a few shoots of willowherb and stonecrop, and planes of emerald-smooth moss. The well in the garden, untended for so long, had grown licheny and silted with leaves, and long-legged water-spiders ran over the surface, dimpling it lightly under their darting feet. The windows of the house were all empty and dark, as if its eyes had been put out.

In the flower-garden the grass had killed all but the delphiniums, which were grown straggling and tired, and sparse of blossom; only two of Miriam's roses thrust upward through the brambles half strangled, but these two were beautiful, full-blown and dark as blood. They were all that recalled her now in this house or this garden, for she would come here no more either in flesh or spirit. Her eyes were onward-looking eyes. Once recollection had been too strong for her; but when that was past she had become too strong for recollection. It was for him to remember; nor did he need this spectre of a farm to help him to keep faith with Miriam.

He took the roses, and went down to the crowded little cemetery behind the church. There was no one there, but he did not need a guide, for when he came to the corner of ground which had been newly added when he was first in Boissy, his eyes fell at once upon Miriam's grave. He would have known it even without the rough wooden cross which stood at the head, barren as a soldier's memorial, bearing only her name, for by other signs it was set apart. Where all were well tended, the grass clipped and the edges tidily turfed, hers was smoother than a lawn, and the edges of its brilliant green marked out with brook pebbles; and all the upper surface of the mound was sown with short, harlequin flowers which he did not know, a tremor of colour and life over her sleep, as if someone had wished to make it plain, in the teeth of her murderers, that Miriam too was already risen, that no grave could hold her. As he in his turn bore witness now.

Well, he had come back. She had said no word, to him or of him, that time, fate, God, whatever you wanted him called, had not justified.

He stood at the foot of her grave for a long time, watching the wind pass and repass like ripples upon water over the bright petals which seemed to aspire to flight. He felt within himself no change, but he knew that change was busy with him. Why not? Even she had had her phases before she came to rest, walking over her white-hot ploughshares of experience into her heaven of completion. What she had put into him of herself took hold of him now by the bowels and tore him; and that was as it should be, as he had wanted it to be, for how was he to know certainly that he had any part of her unless the growth within reminded him in continual pain? And he needed to be sure of his possession, of that little morsel of her heart which was to heal him.

He put the two red roses upon her breast, where they glowed like arterial blood; and then, because the Abbé Bonnard came in by the Presbytery gate, he turned and went quickly away; for it was not yet time to speak of her.

7

They were sitting along the bank of the stream in the darkness that night, smoking a last cigarette and listening to the purposeful passage of 'planes overhead with no more respect than if they had been stag-beetles blundering and bumping about the woods, when Teddy Mason and Dick Shelby and a handful of the others came back from the village like kids from a fair. They flung themselves down and dabbled their fingers in the water, and talked themselves out upon the subject of Boissy-en-Fougères, its drinks, its girls, its fruit and its beauty. It was the first real relaxation they had had since D-Day, and they had made the most of it. There wasn't a drunk, or even a near-drunk, among them, but they were all a little high, and chattering nineteen to the dozen. Jim sat in the shadows, and listened much as he listened to the clacking music of the water under the wheel, for his mind's comfort, and not in search of a meaning; and it was some time before any significance obtruded itself upon the pleasant starling noise.

Teddy was saying: "She speaks quite a bit of English—not very much, but we managed, thanks." He would have managed without a word in common, provided the partner was a she. "But it's a lie that she knows any German. She told me herself."

"Well, that's what the cake-shop woman said," said Dick indifferently. "Pretty nasty about it, she was. Called her a—what is it?—horizontal collaborator. Your peach isn't what you'd call popular round the place, exactly. They say she hasn't shown her nose out of the house since the Germans went, because she's frightened the women'll kill her. Doesn't even come in the bar if there's anybody there, she's so scared." The bar, eh? Jim began to take notice then. Of course they would automatically find their way into the only *bistro* in the town; and the name over the door was still Brégis. "But *I* don't know," said Dick cheerfully. "It's nothing to do with me. She's a beauty all right, whatever else she may not be."

Yes, if she had not changed very terribly in five years she would certainly be that; and still only twenty-four. Older than these boys, but that would make her all the more perilous. He remembered her only too well, Eliane under the lilac hedge with her pale head upon Tommy Goolden's shoulder, and her long, fair arms about his neck, straining him to her heart. Poor Eliane! She had been capable of a genuine affection once, at any rate; perhaps it had been the last as well as the first.

"Ah!" said Teddy vehemently, "now you've said it! Now you've hit the nail bang on the head in one go. She's a beauty. That's why the other women are against her. Aren't they always?"

Dick seemed to be learning fast, or Papa's *pernod* had put him into an unusually cynical mood tonight. "Did she tell you that, as well?" he asked, making circlets on the water with his fingertip. "I noticed you were doing all right together; for once you didn't seem to be doing all the talking—nor making all the going, either."

"No, she didn't. She didn't have to. But you know what she did tell me? She said the Germans they had here were kind to her and her father, and she didn't think they were such a bad lot at all. She swore she'd never asked them for anything, or done anything she shouldn't to help 'em, nor her father, either. But people were against her simply because she couldn't bring herself to join in the things they were doing—you know, the sabotage, the killings, and all that. There was a lot of it here, they say. No, *she* never said anything about her looks having anything to do with it, but *I* do. I know women! And after all," he burst out, indignant because someone anonymous had certainly laughed, "why *should* she have to go about killing soldiers and blowing up factories to show she's no traitor? It isn't every woman's cup of tea. But she hasn't done anything for the other side; she told me so. She swore it on a crucifix she was wearing, the way they do. I never asked her to, but she did it. And what's more, I believe her, too!" He shut his lips firmly, triumphantly, as if that made it so.

"Oh, all right," said Dick peacefully, "you believe it then."

"And you'd better, too," stated the belligerent squire of beauty ominously.

Dick came to his knees, by no means reluctantly.

"Now, listen! I've said nothing one way or the other. She looks all right to me. But if you're going to start telling me what I've got to believe, you've got a hell of a job on, my lad, that's all."

"You said she spoke good German——"

"I said the cake-shop woman said so."

"You said she was afraid to show her face. And how d'you account for her being in the bar tonight, at that rate?"

"She wasn't, not until it was full up with us chaps. Can you think of a safer place?"

They were both in the act of scrambling to their feet when Sloan took Teddy by the collar and spilled him neatly backwards into the grass, and Dick, taking the hint, laughed and sat down again.

"One more cheep out of either of you," promised Sloan, "and in the brook you go." He was a man of his word; and since neither of them was drunk enough to court his attentions, they heard no more of Eliane that night.

Nevertheless she stuck in Jim's mind unpleasantly. She was the thin end of a wedge which could split minds; she was one more of the little hurrying influences running for sympathy and help ahead of those who had earned both. Everywhere it happened; why not in Boissy-en-Fougères? Already the Germans were a little more than kind, and the French a little less than kin; that was not bad going for one evening. Desperation would make her as deft as luck had made her lovely. And yet what had she wittingly wronged or betrayed, except herself? She had willed no harm to anyone, only every conceivable good to herself, who in the end had been the worst sufferer. He could not conceive of her ever giving damaging information against her countrymen; she would take care never to have any to give. All she wanted was to shut herself up from the sight or sound or knowledge of suffering in an island of comfort, and to be fed, and cherished, and protected from pain, and loved by anyone who could and would undertake the charge; by the Germans then, by the British now. But it wasn't going to be that way; they couldn't afford it. Only too soon the issues of justice could be clouded and obscured by a thousand and one secret interests, until honest men grew unsure of what had seemed to them as secure as the rock, until they began to talk speciously about everyone being equally guilty, until the enemy became the wronged.

He put her out of his mind at last, and slept without dreams; and the next day he had forgotten her. It was not because he proposed to do anything about her that he went up into the village that evening; it was rather to look up one or two people who might remember him, and would certainly be glad to hear news of Simone Lacasse in England. Doctor Vauban greeted him with delight, for in a way Jim was his own creation; how, without his help, could Miriam have arranged that escape in 1940? He looked upon him as an artist upon his masterpiece, and they reminisced together until the dusk began to fall. After that Jim sought out Mère Jeantot, who wept with joy to hear that her friend Simone was safe in London; and on his way through the twilit village again he met others who recognised him, and exclaimed over him with a fiery devotion which puzzled him not a little until he remembered that he was sacred, because Miriam had died on his account. It was as if he had been set apart by a vision of the local saint, and marked with her visible mark upon him to be henceforward miraculous and holy. It frightened him, it oppressed him, but it was inescapable; they only confirmed the responsibility he had already accepted.

He was passing by the *bistro* when he remembered Eliane. Several of the Midshires were within, to judge by the noise, and enjoying themseves. The check curtains bellied out softly from the open windows, leaning to a faint breeze; the new paint, where no other paint was new, shone brazenly in its gilt and blue. He wondered if French custom ever passed that threshold now; and suddenly he was most bitterly sorry for Papa Brégis.

He stood in the doorway for a moment, looking in. The old man was there behind the bar, his fat flesh quivering as he moved, his hands and shoulders voluble as ever. None the less, he had changed; his hair was streaked with grey, and the folds of his face sagged, in repose, into a mask of anxiety and furtive grief. Perhaps he was wondering what he would live on when the British, as well as the Germans, were gone from Boissy; for he himself was, at this moment, the only Frenchman in the bar. It had not occurred to the youngsters to notice that peculiarity.

Then he saw that she was there, with Teddy Mason and several more solicitous about her, talking to them dutifully in her halting English, dividing her glances scrupulously to keep them all happy. She looked as she had always looked, like a pale golden trumpet-lily, like Jeanne d'Arc; more virginal than Diana, if you did not know how to interpret the one thing she could never control, the tragic candour of her eyes. He did not see them full until she suddenly reared up her head in that startlingly graceful way she had, and saw him standing in the doorway.

The words she had been speaking died in her throat, leaving her lips moving for a second upon no sound. They stared at each other in silence, and her eyes flared wide and dark in the translucent pallor of her face. They held everything that had happened to her, and could not hide any of it; pathetic, appealing, impenitent, seeking eyes, weary but calculating, sick with experience. They stared at him without embarrassment or shame, rather with eagerness, as if she had still something better to hope from him than from any of these, and could hardly believe that her luck had really brought him here in the flesh. He remembered that she could not know how much he knew of her. He was to her only a man she had known, and who seemed to like her, heaven-sent now to use his influence for her in the village, to give her his protection, to set her up again in respectability by the mere virtue of not being aware she had ever been an outcast. More effective a thousand times for her purposes than the boys who surrounded her! He saw her thinking it; either he was very expert in her, or the rest were very blind, for every shade of argument that passed through her mind made for him changes of light and colour in those urgent eyes. He knew what she would do next, and he did not wait for it. The sight of her recalled too many things. He turned and went out abruptly, and began to walk on rapidly down the pavement. He didn't want her to think he was going to be any good to her. He didn't want to have to talk to her. Tommy Goolden had been dead five years; there was no sense in digging him up again now.

He had gone perhaps twenty yards when he realised that something was happening for which he had not bargained; she was following him. He had known by the look of her that if he stayed she would put the others aside, and come to him; but surely she had not overcome her fear of her own townspeople, or forgotten it, so far as to follow him out? Yet she had abandoned the *bistro*, and thrown her admirers to the winds with it, and was running after him along the street, lightly and quickly, her high heels tapping a sharp beat that brought out shadowy figures from the doors to see. He heard her call after him: "Please wait! Please wait!" confidently, almost indignantly, as perhaps she had not given orders to a man since the old days before the Germans came south; but that was not why, in the end, he waited. He had one thing to say to her, and only one.

"You had better go back home," he said, "quickly, before you are seen."

She pulled up a yard or two away from him, hovering uneasily as if he had thrust her off by physical means, but her opportunist eyes glowed upon him in the dusk, and her lily whiteness was wraithlike, luminous with hope. She was plainly dressed in black, which became her as the sheath the sword.

She said in French, because he had used it: "You do not remember me? Me, Eliane Brégis?"

"Yes," he said, "I remember you well."

She came a step nearer. "Then why do you go away from me without a sign? I thought you had forgotten me. You looked at me and went away. I did not know you were here. Why did you not come to see us? You knew we should be glad." And as he looked at her and was silent she asked, with a sharply rising fear in her voice: "What is it? What have I done?"

"That is for you to know. But you must go home now. This is not the place for you to consider it. Surely you know that."

"Someone has told you bad things of me," she said vehemently, suddenly breast to breast with him, stretching upward to bring her bitter eyes on a level with his as nearly as she could. "When first you came here it was not like this. You did not look at me so, then. You were my friend then. What have I done that you will not even greet me, and ask me how I am, after so long a time?"

"It will be better if you go," he said, quite gently and impersonally. "There is nothing to be gained here. What you have done you know best. As for me, I would be sorry for you if I could afford to; but I can't, and it no longer matters that I should."

Tears broke suddenly out of her like rain, gushing silently and heavily; she stood looking at him through them as through clear glass, and she said in a whisper: "Something has happened. When you went away from here something happened. What was it?"

"Tommy Goolden is dead," said Jim. There was no help for it now.

"Dead!" It was almost a shriek of regret, but the time was gone by when he had troubled her, and the regret was all for herself and not for him; because his very death bore witness against her, and he was not there to be beguiled anew and translate his evidence; because the dead cannot be cross-examined, cannot be swayed, are implacable. She put up her hands and clutched her head, and moaned: "No, no, no! It cannot be true!"

"It is true. He died in the boat that should have taken him home."

"He told you—about me!" she whispered.

"Yes, he told me."

The night closed in upon them gradually, her blondeness shining torchwise in the clear dark. Certain palpable shadows had begun to draw near to them from the doors of houses, from the café, from by-lanes, quietly, ominously, shadows of bereaved women coming unnoticed and watching unreproved. The tapping of her heels, that one cry of dismay in a voice they were not likely to mistake, the slim body and pale head like an oriflamme, had drawn them from their hearths. They stood inconspicuous in the dark places, aside from the scene upon the pavement, and waited; they had been waiting for this for three days.

"I did not think he would have told anyone," whispered Eliane through the fingers that drew her trembling mouth awry. "It was only that night—It was true, he saw us together. But I did not betray him. I did not, I did not! Did he say that I betrayed him?"

"No, he did not say so."

She protested desperately "You do not believe that of me?"

"I no longer believe or disbelieve by the book. Why should you not make good use of him? It was a chance you might never have again."

"I did not, I did not!" she panted. "I swear it! I watched him go, and I knew he would hate me, but I did not say one word to them. Oh, believe me, this once believe me! I could not bear you should think I killed him."

No, he thought, watching her, that was no part of her plan. Do her justice, she had hidden herself, panic-stricken, from the thought of harming a single man or woman among them; she had only comforted and flattered the murderers, not helped them to kill. No, it was not to ingratiate this poor creature with her masters that Miriam had died; at least he was spared that last and most horrible irony.

"I believe you," he said.

He saw her eyes light up again with a frantic hope. "Then you will help me? You will come back with me? I need a friend, you do not know how I need a friend. They hate me.

Jim, be kind to me!" She had remembered his name in her extremity. "I have not done anything except live peaceably with everyone. Is that wrong? Is it wicked to want not to die? I am young, Jim, I am not good at being very brave, but I have not done any harm. You will help me? Please, help me!"

"Why do you not ask us for help?" said a woman's voice, cold, deep and deliberate at her back. "We are ready. We are here."

Eliane started like a shot bird, and sprang at once round upon the voice and back from it, pressing herself against Jim's body, holding by his left arm, while she stared wildly round the closing circle for a way of escape, and found none. The women had moved without plan or consent, but as one woman, so quietly that they had not been noticed until now, and even now, though they stood only three or four yards away, could have been for their very stillness no more than deeper shadows in the night. They also wore black, but not for its elegance. They were not all even middle-aged; there were girls among them as young as she, perhaps younger. She looked all round the circle, her eyes flickering from face to face, looking for any softening, for any wavering, but they were grave, patient and ferocious.

"We will help you to know what you are. To know oneself, that is good for the soul, is it not?" A big woman she was who spoke for them, middle-aged, gaunt of face, a respectable shop-keeper, and one whom Jim remembered from the old days, though he had lost her name. She folded her hands in her sleeves, and stood waiting; she looked like Nemesis. He did not know how his own face looked, but it was to him Eliane was clinging, upon him she turned for protection; yet she could not, he thought, look at him and hope to find any comfort there.

"Jim, tell her I have done nothing! Say to her——"

"She speaks your own language," said Jim. "It is for you to answer her."

"I am afraid!" she moaned. "I am afraid!"

"You will be less afraid, afterwards," said the woman.

"No! No, Jim! Let us go home! Take me home!" She threaded her hands through his arm and pressed her body against him, and shuddered. "Please, take me home!"

"You came of your own free will. You came alone. You must go back alone." If she can do it, he thought, if she has the guts to try, I don't believe one of them will touch her; but he knew it was not in her even to try. She had not realised until then that he really meant to abandon her.

"But you can't leave me! You don't know them. They hate me. It was only because of you I came out. I was safe until I came out to speak to you. You can't desert me now!"

"Did I ask you to come?"

"You meant me to, you wanted me to. You trapped me into coming!"

He unbent her fingers gently from his arm for answer, and stepped back from her, but she followed in panic, and would not let go of him.

"No, no!" she cried, her voice running up into a windy shriek. "They will kill me!"

"You are mistaken," he said with the same passionless gentleness, "these are Frenchwomen, not Germans. They will not hurt you." And he looked over her head at the big woman, and met her eye to eye, and she smiled at him, the briefest contortion of her lips, before she lowered her eyes again to Eliane. The pale hair, disarranged now by the convulsive pressure of her head against his shoulder, slipped from its neat coil and covered her face and shoulders in a soft cloud; upon that ghostly beauty they fixed their eyes, and waited still.

"Your officer," said the big woman, "your man was in charge of the firing party that shot mine. It was he who gave the order. Did you find any change when you slept with him that night?"

Almost it seemed that Eliane felt him withdrawing from her before ever he made a move to extricate himself; for suddenly she slipped down against him, clinging and weeping, and wound her arms about his thighs, and crouched there in the cloudy shining of her hair. She did not again ask anything of him, not even that he should remain with her; she knew now that she had lost her throw, that there was nothing for her but the justice of the women, who had waited for this ever since the Germans abandoned the village. She only crouched and trembled, half dead with fear, she who could have so little to fear from them; for surely she must know in her heart that she was no fit meat for them to flesh their claws in. Their disproportionate injuries made it impossible for them to do more than mark her and let her go.

He looked down at her without emotion, though it would have been a luxury to him just then to feel pity. Then without another word, and with long, deliberate movements which had almost a suggestion about them of ritual, he took her by the wrists and unwound her arms from him. She was not strong

123

enough to resist, even had it been worth the effort. He put her from him to the full stretch of his arms, and took his hands away, and so left her, crouched upon the pavement under the drift of her light hair. He did not hurry, and he did not look back; and behind him as he went there was only a single sorrowful sound like a universal sigh.

8

It was, he supposed, the dirtiest thing he'd ever done, and he wasn't disposed to be proud of it; but neither was it the first time he had found himself constrained to do things of which his private instinct was to be ashamed. For a little time, while he was still shaky from the effort, he wondered if he had not given her a stronger weapon even than her beauty; but that soon passed. They would be bitterly indignant with him, and bitterly sorry for her, but they were young and human, and not even chivalry can stand up to a reflected humiliation such as her champions would suffer from Eliane. It is all very well to espouse the cause of a hairless woman from a safe distance, but it takes a hero to make his position clear at close range. And for the units who came after the problem would not arise, for the poison bottle was labelled now. In the meantime the kicks would all be aimed at one person, and he might just as well start the ball rolling tonight, and get the worst over; for, curiously enough, he found himself caring a great deal for this particular smart.

He sat on his blankets for half an hour, and smoked a couple of cigarettes to soothe the nerves he hadn't known he possessed; then, when he was sure they would all be home, he strolled out past the sluices to where the brook rolled away under nut-trees, chuckling in the dark. They would be there until lights-out, for it was a fine night, starry and clear and warm; and they were there indeed, and vociferous enough until he came by and stood leaning against a tree for a few minutes to give them an opportunity to attack if they wanted to. Then there was a silence, subdued and strange, while all their eyes battered him, but no one formulated what was in their minds. They were too baffled as yet to know how to come at it, but there was no doubt that they all knew the facts.

Only Sloan came crashing on his heels as he walked on downstream, and fell into step beside him; and being a straightforward soul, and perhaps privileged where Jim was concerned, went straight to the point.

"What the hell did you do it for?" he asked.

"Oh, so they all know it was my doing? Well, thank heaven for that, anyway! They don't blame the village, then?"

"Well—they've lost sight of the village, you might say. It's you they've got their teeth in."

"That's all right," said Jim, "I expected that. She wasn't—hurt? But she wouldn't be!"

"Well, no, I suppose she wasn't *hurt*." He sounded vaguely surprised at the consideration. "No, she—it wouldn't have stuck in their throats so much if they hadn't been in the bar when she came running in, you see. She gave 'em such a shock. Trying to hide her head with her arms, she was, and running blind. And they'd seen her go out after you not twenty minutes before. You can't blame 'em for——"

"I don't blame 'em. My God, no! One time, I'd have had the skin off any man for less—or tried, anyhow. But if you're thinking dark thoughts about what she may do to herself, you can take it easy. She'll survive. Suicide was never any part of Eliane's policy, and never will be."

"You seem to know her pretty well. That's getting in their necks, too."

"I can guess! I do know her, but they can make up the rest as they like. What happened then?"

"She went to earth so quick they never had a chance to do more than stare, but I must say it knocked the wind out of me. The old chap just looked at her and burst into tears. What the hell *did* you do it for?"

"As a matter of policy; and I'd do it again. But strictly between you and me," he said with a wry grin, "I'd rather have had a kick in the teeth, any day. I'd welcome a damn' good scrap to get the taste out of my mouth. Think Teddy'd oblige?"

Teddy did not oblige; indeed, Teddy was conspicuously missing until Jim had left Sloan behind, and walked on from the nut-coppice into the first of the long meadows, where he all but fell over him in the dark. The boy, who had been lying on his stomach and dabbling gloomily in the water, wriggled hurriedly to a sitting position as Jim checked, and recognised him with a flaring of angry and bewildered eyes; and the bewilderment was uppermost. He was in no mood to satisfy anyone who wanted a damn' good scrap. Was it possible that he was no longer absolutely sure of his judgment, even in an issue so clear? Had he begun to look below the surfaces of things already? He said nothing, only sat and glared, rubbing his wet hands in the turf, as Jim sat on his heels in a collier-crouch against the nearest pollard, and thoughtfully revolved a grass between his teeth.

"Now," said Jim reasonably, "you can say anything you like and no holds barred, and no witnesses. Carry on! I'm here to be shot at." It was not what he had intended at all, but events were running away with him now, and in his experience that usually meant that they had a sound idea of where they needed to run.

Teddy said, after a long moment of thought: "I don't know what you're after, I don't know what game you're playing; but I think that was the dirtiest thing I ever saw anyone do. I suppose *you're* proud of it."

"I'm sorry to disappoint you, but no, I never was further from being proud of anything in my life. But I'd do it again tomorrow, if I had to."

"Had to!" repeated Teddy, inarticulate with rage, but quiet still. "Had to! Why, for God's sake, should you think you had to—to do that beastly self-righteous thing to a girl who's no enemy of yours? What harm had she ever done to you?"

"Can you really think everything's as simple as that?" He couldn't, either; he had once been able to see things that way, and he would have liked to keep that vision, because it made everything beautifully easy, but he couldn't, and it was the first time it had ever happened to him. It made him very miserable. "Tell the truth, kid, if it kills you," said Jim, and smiled at him.

"You can talk," burst out Teddy, "as long as you like, but you can't change my mind. It was a filthy trick to go off and leave her to be manhandled like that, and you can't justify it, no matter what you say. Damn it, I've got more respect for the women who did the dirty work than I have for you. They did have the pluck to touch her, anyhow, and *they* had a grievance, or thought they had. But there's no excuse whatever for *you*. You were just scared to stand by her."

"Think so?" asked Jim, still smiling at him across the cigarette-smoke. "Good kid!" he said, and hardly realised until it was out that he had said it aloud. "So I was afraid of monkeying with it, was I? I thought I was being accused of monkeying with it a good deal too much. You can't have it both ways. I'm either frightened or vicious; which are you betting on?"

Teddy looked at him desperately, and protested in a lost voice quite unlike his own: "You've got me all confused. I don't know what to think. I just don't understand the first thing about it."

"The first sign of grace, I believe," said Jim. "The unregenerate understand everything perfectly." And he thought it high time to go away from him then, and leave him alone. He hadn't come to bait him, even thus gently. By the time they left Boissy-en-Fougères Teddy might have it all sorted out for himself, but at the moment meddling would only addle it all over again. Besides, who would have thought they could have progressed so far in the time? It was tempting providence to ask for any more.

Nothing, however, could cure him for the moment of an unexampled wretchedness which was entirely upon his own account. He found himself hoping that the unit might be moved on next day, but Baird shook his head over the possibility. Probably Baird would have liked to ask a few questions himself; he could hardly help having heard the queer story of the girl from the *bistro;* but he held his tongue with commendable self-restraint, and left it to the Sergeants' Mess to flay whatever susceptibilities Sergeant Benison had still functioning, which were generally believed to be few and atrophied. It was a peculiar situation, negativing in advance any action they might wish to take; for as the indifferent pointed out to the indignant, he had not actually *done* anything except walk away from the spot before the crime was even committed. Everybody knew he had understood very well what he was doing, but what everybody knew was not, in this case, evidence. In the meantime they none of them went near the *bistro* that day, because they were afraid of having to meet Eliane face to face; only one person from the mill was seen to enter under the blue and gilt sign during the early afternoon, and that was Sergeant Benison himself.

He went in the hope of seeing Papa Brégis alone, and he was not disappointed. The old man was sitting at one of the tiled tables, with his back to the door. He had a *pernod* in front of him, and was sitting over it hopelessly, his big shoulders sagging in mounds of fat, and his chins, which were many and broad, overflowing out of his cupped palms. His grey hair stood up in shaggy tufts, as if his hands had been constantly tearing at it. When the latch of the door clicked he looked round slowly without moving, and his eyes, once as bright as shoe-buttons, were seen to be red-rimmed and dull, sunken in folds of swollen flesh. He did not seem to resent his visitor, as probably the young of the Midshires would have considered he ought to do; on the contrary, his doleful face lightened a little at the prospect of company of any kind. He began to get up, which was somewhat of a labour for him at all times; but Jim put a hand on his shoulder and pressed him down again.

"You remember me, Monsieur Brégis? My company was at Boissy Farm, five years ago, when the invasion began."

The lustreless eyes stared at him without recognition, for he was very much changed since those days.

"I remember the time, but there were so many. I cannot recall faces."

"Well, never mind. But I suppose you know I'm to blame for what's happened to your daughter?"

"You?" said Papa Brégis, and leaned forward to peer at him more closely. "But it was the women. Certainly she has not accused you—no, nor anyone! How could she? She is not a fool, she knew it would have happened sooner or later. Again and again I say to her, you are making a mistake, you will pay for it in the end; but she thought the war was over, and they were the masters. It is bad business to be so expert. Now we have lost, and we pay. But I tell you, mister, it is not easy for an old man," he concluded tearfully, "to see his life ruined like this at my age."

"Very few things are easy any more," said Jim. "But listen to me! I do admit responsibility for what happened to Eliane. I could have prevented it, and I chose not to. Now if you want me to go away you've only to say so, and I'll go; but if you're willing I want to talk to you."

The drooping shoulders lifted indifferently. "What does it matter? If it had not been you it would have been another. Talk if you want to. Will you drink?"

"No, thanks! I'm not going back on anything, mind; let's have that clear to begin with; but neither do I want you or her to be prevented from starting fair again. You know there could never be much of a life for either of you here, after what's happened. Have you thought, yet, what you're going to do?"

Another shrug, even more despondent, gave him eloquent answer.

"Have you any relatives who would give you a home? If I were you I should get out of here."

"I have a sister in Arras, but she would not be glad to have us. She has lost sons in the Maquis, that one. But," he went on, brightening a little, "she is a very religious woman, she

128

would not turn us away because of being afraid of hell. She believes in a family duty. If she would take my poor Eliane—even for a time, until her hair grew——"

It sounded a bitter and salutary sort of lodging for his poor Eliane, but it was for the mother of dead sons Jim found himself feeling sorry. Still, he wished for the sake of everyone concerned to get the girl out of Boissy, for she was a core of hatred in what had otherwise remained even under occupation a singularly sweet and wholesome fruit. The faces of the women worried him; for his own purposes he had allowed them to satisfy their detestation upon Éliane's person, but now for theirs he wanted to rid them of her. And even for her he was concerned through his heart, if not through his conscience; it was right, or at any rate so expedient as to seem the least wrong thing, that she should be ruined as an apologist for traitors, but it would not be right that she should be prevented from ever becoming anything else. By all means let her hide her head for a few months in the bereaved household at Arras; if that didn't turn her eyes inward, nothing would.

"And you?" he asked. "There'll be no trade here for you, you know that. Better make up your mind to it."

"Mister," said Papa Brégis in a burst of tearful confidence, "I have not been a happy man for many years. I do not want this thing. My girl, she begins it, and I am just Papa who has no say. Now I cannot change that, it is too late, I am old. But I have enough money for a little place. Yes, I will go away from here as soon as things settle down, as soon as we are sure the Germans are gone. I will go away and get a little place, and sell this *bistro*. And because there will not be very much money, she will have to work, my Eliane."

"You are wise," said Jim, but he could not help wondering if she would not, as soon as her hair and brows had grown again, look round for another means of protecting herself—marriage, probably, to someone who didn't know her at all, and had money enough to make her content. But that was prejudging her, a vice he found himself very prone to. "If you should need help while we are here, ask at the mill for Sergeant Benison; but I hope you won't—I don't think you will. If you want Eliane to go to Arras before we leave, I might be able to send her. I can try to arrange it; she need not know I've had anything to do with it. At any rate, you know where to find me."

He saw by the bewilderment of the flabby old face, as he took his leave, that Papa Brégis was completely at a loss to account for this solicitude in him. And indeed, he thought ruefully, he was laying himself open to the charge of being the king of all prigs; the hell of it was that he couldn't even afford to take notice of that. Still, he went away from the *bistro* a little eased in his mind, and quite unaware that he was watched from an upper window as he went on up the village, watched by strange, browless eyes coloured like gillyflowers, and as blank and repellent now as bread without salt. Nor did it occur to him that a second time he would be followed away from that door.

She had not ventured even down the stairs since she rushed up to her room on the previous night. She had not slept, not even shut her expressionless eyes, nor ever sat or lain still for more than two minutes together. She felt no shame as humanity understands shame, only the insatiable pain of an outraged animal spitting at the world over her mutilations; she was ashamed only of being made ashamed. When she saw him from the window she forgot that also, and was given over to hate as only a second-rate nature can feel it for something which, rightly or wrongly, seems to its envious vision to be first-rate. All night she had writhed and plied uneasily about her room, swerving from the mirror, pushed by an unreasoning pain which would not let go of her; but now she felt whole, capable, reckless. Never in her life before had she omitted to count the cost of an action; but now a shining wall of hate, glorious to her sight, shut out all consequences. She tied a scarf over her head, and took her handbag from a drawer, and went out after him.

It was market-day, which meant that the tiny square by the *mairie* was full of people, for to the local population was now added a good number of off-duty men from the mill. Jim, picking his way leisurely through the chattering groups spread over the cobbles, drew to himself unwittingly all glances. At the moment he was not thinking of Eliane at all, but of Doctor Vauban, for whose house he was bound; and he answered the many greetings in French, and avoided the khaki groups, without paying much attention to either. The possessive devotion of the one lot and the indignant disgust of the other would work themselves out, all in good time, to a true level, somewhere in the region of mere toleration. Why try to adjust them now?

Several of the platoon were there, he noticed, Mason and Shelby and the rest, missing nothing, not even market-day. They had been talking about him again; their sudden silence announced it. Probably still arguing that he ought to be put on a charge, or shot at dawn, or something drastic; as probably he ought, for being such a fool as to try to shift circumstances instead of letting them go to hell their own way. He felt oddly relieved now, almost buoyant; he was getting over the incident, he supposed. He passed by the boys, watched as he went by their wary, inimical eyes, and was almost on the steps of the doctor's house when a sudden flutter and cry broke out behind them.

She had stolen through the press with her head bowed and her eyes lowered, only looking up to assure herself that she still had him in view. She felt eyes like swords in her, and saw the edges of skirts drawn aside from her touch, but these things no longer frightened or hurt her, for she was possessed. The only thing that at all alarmed her at this moment was the realisation that Jim had almost reached his destination, for he was in the act of turning aside to the doctor's door. She quickened her step, groping with one hand in her bag. Everyone drew back from her, and therefore there was no one within immediate reach when she pulled out a pistol, and fired at his head from a range of six or seven yards.

The bullet cut a shallow furrow along his left cheek, nicking the lobe of his ear, and buried itself in the doorpost. He sprang round upon a bedlam of shrieks and a flurry of running, and saw one of the young men struggling with her, saw him twist her arm behind her because she clung desperately to the gun, and with a wrench which brought a lamentable cry out of her throw her face downwards into the road. Women surged in upon her, shrieking invective; one of them kicked her in the side, another put a foot upon her wrist with some force, and stooped to wrench away the pistol which her fingers still obstinately clutched. "Murderess, murderess!" they cried, and in a moment more there would have been murder done in earnest. Jim came back at a striding run, thrusting a way to where she lay, and shouting peremptory orders to leave her alone.

"No! Stop! Don't touch her! Don't hurt her!"

For a few seconds he had to fight for it, plucking away men and women alike as they barred his way; then the panic which had made them cruel passed as suddenly as it had come, and they fell back and let him in to her, standing about the incredible scene at last silent and awed, even frightened by the thing which had been let loose among them. He saw that the soldier who had first taken hold of her, and dealt with her so roughly, was none other than Teddy Mason. He motioned him aside without word or look, not noticing as yet any complications; the immediate concern was the girl.

Eliane's burst of sustaining energy had spent itself, running out like life-blood in that first wail of pain. She lay where she had been thrown, her skirt spread across the cobbles and dusty with the marks of feet, her head in its bright silk handkerchief still protected by her left arm. She was sobbing softly, past effort or hope, her last courage broken; and for the first time he was really sorry for her, freely, without need to stanch the flow. He had a proprietary right to his luxury this time.

"Eliane!" he said.

She did not answer by word or movement, seemed not to hear.

"Eliane!" He stooped, and gently withdrew the pistol from her hand, which made no resistance now. It was a German gun, no doubt left behind by the Nazi officer who had walked in the woods with her, or perhaps by another of his line of succession. Jim unloaded it, and slipped it into his pocket. Still she did not move, but her sobbing was quieted strangely by the lightness of his touch as he felt along the bones of the bruised wrist, and found them, as far as he could judge, whole. "Come!" he said. "This isn't so bad. Look up, now, and tell me if you're hurt. No one will touch you." And as she still did not raise her head, he went on tranquilly: "You haven't done any harm. You see I'm alive all right."

Now why should he know that she needed that reassurance, when it was no more than two minutes since she had desired more than anything in the world to kill him? Perhaps he realised that she was not of the stuff that can kill without revulsion; it was certainly against her nature, and only extreme misery had roused her to the attempt. But it seemed that there was more in it than this, some unquestioned impulse which took charge of him now, speaking for him, acting through him, moving with assurance through all complexities. She heard him, and became still under his hands.

The townswomen murmured, not with pity, but wonder; they had not moved back very far, nor did they intend to leave the scene while it endured. He felt the same hysterical anger which had moved them once waiting to seize upon them again; he had to get her away now, before worse happened, for he was no longer sure that she would be safe with them. It was not that they loved him so much, but Eliane in her desperation had put her hand upon the miracle of Miriam Lozelle. A local saint had been profaned.

"Get up, Eliane," he said, and it was an order this time. She made the attempt obediently, his hands helping her. She stood trembling in reaction, her pale face streaked with dust and tears, only his arm sustaining her upright; and her amazing eyes, stunned out of all feeling, stared at the threads of blood congealing slowly down his neck and cheek.

"You are not hurt? Can you walk?"

She said "Yes," almost inaudibly.

He looked round for a helper, and was surprised for a moment by the looks that met him from his own men, their shaken silence, their confounded eyes; but he had no time to trouble about their reverses. They could work out their own salvation, and his, and hers if they liked; he didn't need to.

"Shelby, run ahead and tell Papa Brégis we're coming down with his daughter. Tell him she's all right, she's with me." Dick hesitated, about to plead lack of French, but thought better of it next moment, and ran like a hare. "Mason, help me down with her. Take her other arm."

Teddy did venture a frightened protest. His orderly mind was out of its depth here at last; he had lost touch, and must double back to the conventional reactions for refuge. "What are you going to do?" he asked. "She—she tried to kill you. They'll charge her. You can't just whisk her away now, like this."

"Take her arm!" said Jim.

She moved between them like an automaton, the tears drying on her face as the blood on his. The crowd parted before them without protest, though he wondered if they would reach the *bistro* without encountering some surviving gendarme or other, or zealot of the Maquis, who would think it his duty to represent the law; but no one attempted to stop them, and the authority remained with him.

"You can't do this," said Teddy feverishly as they went. He talked across her as if she had been a wooden doll, without nerves or feelings. "You won't get away with it. Why, she—she may try it again, or anything."

"I am doing it," said Jim.

"But you're crazy! Why, she——"

"Be quiet!" said Jim peremptorily. "This matter is between us two."

She lifted her disconcerting eyes and looked at him dully then, one long, bemused glance and away again, as if he had dragged out of her this single acknowledgment of his presence. At Teddy she did not look at all, and he found it expedient to subside without more words, for he was astray in this situation as he had never been in his life. The very consternation of his face was a question mark. How could and why should the sergeant go out of his way to protect her now? He hadn't lifted a finger for her last night. And what, in any case, could they do with her now? What was going on in their minds? Neither face told anything; the sergeant's ugly mug never gave him away, and without eyebrows the girl's look was just a shattering stare. What, for God's sake, was due to happen next?

They were not followed. The hush and whispering of the cobbled market-place fell behind them, only a straggle of children, shaken to silence by the recoil of their elders but inquisitive still, trailed behind until they neared the *bistro*, and there hung back from the doorway to watch them go in. Papa Brégis, glassy-eyed with fear, was shouting at Dick Shelby in violent French, and rocking his quivering bulk backward and forward distractedly on his heels, for he had not more than half understood what was reported to him, and his instant excitement had knocked out of Dick's head what little French he knew; but at sight of Jim entering with Eliane in his arm the old man diverted the stream of his lamentations, and suddenly lost his head and began to curse her, a thing it was clear he had never done before. She stared back at him with her shocked eyes as if he had had no real existence, and made no attempt to escape from her arch-enemy to her natural protector. Jim reached out one hand abstractedly to move him out of the way, and put Eliane into a chair.

"Get her a drink," he said over his shoulder.

The cursing faded into a weeping mutter as the old man scuttled away behind the bar. He brought brandy, the cheapest and rawest, for the family had always conserved their best, and he had not yet got it into his head that he no longer had a business to look after. She seemed not to see it until Jim gave it to her, and then she drank as if she had no separate will from his, and spots of colour burned abruptly in her cheeks. She gasped and shuddered.

"What have you done?" burst out her father. "Am I not ruined already? Am I not a by-word? You have disgraced me, now you want to kill me."

"Be quiet!" said Jim, much as he had said it to Teddy, and

with the same effect. "You are no worse off than before. Nobody's going to touch you." And to her he said, taking back the glass: "Are you all right?"

"Yes," she said as before, her lips hardly moving. And suddenly she put her head down in her hands, and tears began to stream between her fingers like rain. He made no attempt to quiet her, but let her cry unhindered, so that afterwards she might be calm and ready to listen; until this passed he would get nothing out of her, nor knock anything in. He lit a cigarette, and was grateful for the interval; someone might still take it into his head to interfere, but it was no longer probable, and ten minutes saved now might in any case mean half an hour lost later.

"Leave her alone," he said to the old man, who was rolling ponderously up and down the floor spilling curses and endearments equally in her direction, "and sit down. There's nothing to gain by making a fuss. It only means that she's got to leave here at once. There's no putting it off now."

"Yes, yes, of course she must go. This very day! She——" It dawned upon him slowly what he was saying. "Go? But—you will let her go? She has done this to you, and you only send her away?—help her? She tries to kill you, so you save her? Are you mad?" he asked with utter simplicity.

"I hope not, but who knows? In two or three years' time she shall answer that for you." He saw how the bewildered old eyes, sodden with grief, dwelt furtively upon his cheek, and clapped a hand to the place. "Hell, I'd forgotten I looked like a slaughter-house! Don't worry, there's only a scratch under all this. Is there somewhere I could wash off the mess?"

"But yes, of course! If you will come——"

Dick asked him as he passed: "Are you all right, Sergeant? Is there anything I can do?"

"Never better," he said cheerfully; "but yes, there is something. Cut down to the lines, and bring up a car. Don't argue, just pinch one. Say it's for Major Harben if anybody interferes."

"Very good, Sergeant!" said Dick, and went upon the word. Orders had never been obeyed with more alacrity, perhaps because none of them was understood at all. Out of their depth, they kept their eyes upon him, and jumped to meet even his suggestions halfway. Teddy, for instance, left alone now with the girl, would not take his eyes off her for a moment until Jim returned, conceiving her to be a perilous trust to him;

and he was very much afraid of her because he knew she was fragile and feminine, and had found that she was desperate. He remembered the cry she had given when he hurt her, and felt sick at the thought. He wished himself out of this with all his heart, but knew he was well in it, and felt in dismay that Jim would keep him in it, if only for spite. There'd been a good deal of spite about, one way and another, though, and he was no longer sure that most of it was Jim's. Things had worked out so queerly, he didn't know where he was. He wished the sergeant would hurry up and come back. She had stopped crying. She raised her head and looked at him, and through him. Her silk scarf had slipped far back, leaving what looked like an enormously high white forehead towering into air, and for the life of him he couldn't keep his eyes off it, though it made him feel sicker than ever. If only she would keep quiet, and turn away from him.

Suddenly she burst out in a hiss like a spitting cat: "You pity me! *You!* You dare!"

Confounded, he began to stammer what could only turn into phrases of pity, and horrified pity at that, no matter how he tried to frame them. She swept his incoherence aside with a gesture of her hand, and a glittering like broken ice came into her eyes; but just as he was beginning to sweat with dread Jim came back into the room, and her glance flew to him, and became again shadowy and still.

"Are you better, Eliane? Will you listen to me now?" He went close to her, but did not touch her, and Teddy noticed that her hands folded quietly in her lap now, as if she erected no barriers against this man of all men; perhaps it's easier to talk to a man whom you have just attempted to kill, and who understands your motives, than to one who just stands by and is embarrassed and sorry for you. "I've been talking to your father, but in the end it's up to you. I think you should go away from here at once, right away where you won't be known. There's your aunt in Arras—I'm told she might have you; but is there anyone else, if that fails? Have you any ideas? After today I don't believe you'd be safe here any longer, and I want to see you somewhere where you will be safe. What do you say?"

"I will go anywhere," she said dully. "There is no help for it. If I stay here I shall certainly die now."

He believed she might; and it was better that the possibility should never arise. "Listen to me, Eliane. I will send you to

Arras—today—now, as soon as I have persuaded the Major to back me up, and I shall do that without any trouble. There's no time to warn them. It means getting off at once, and walking in on your relations, but the case is desperate. Will you go?"

Unexpectedly she said: "There are factories in Arras. I have a friend there also. She would help me to find work. She does not know what I have been, but when she sees I do not think she will throw me out. If one will not have me, the other may."

"Your good aunt is devout," said Papa Brégis, who had recovered a little of his composure. "She will not refuse."

"If she does, I can work. Honest work," she said with a bitter contortion of her mouth; "I am of no use to the streets now."

Of this, though the old man burst into lamentations again, Jim took no notice. "You'll go, then?"

"There is no help for it," she said drearily.

"You are responsible for yourself. Answer me!"

"Yes, I will go."

"You have no gratitude," moaned her father, clutching his hair. "You are stone, stone! One could do miracles for you, and you sit there and make no thanks. It is your life our sergeant gives you! You should go on your knees!"

Jim's hand upon his arm silenced him. As for her, she had not moved a muscle, nor withdrawn her eyes for an instant from the only face which interested her here.

"It is not a matter of gratitude or ingratitude between us. There is no question of giving or taking; it's no part of my plans that there shall be murder done in Boissy-en-Fougères, or feuds, or taking of sides, or hate of any kind. I want you out of here for the sake of everybody concerned, and you owe me nothing. Now go and pack some clothes, and anything you want to take with you. The car will be here any minute, so hurry."

Rising, she said oddly, as if impelled by something within her: "I would certainly have killed you if I could have done it."

"I know. I haven't blamed you; I shall never blame you for that. Now make haste."

And she also obeyed him, with no more words. Never did she express surprise or thanks, never look liking or hate upon him. There were no questions and no answers. She did not express regret for the attempt, nor for the failure; she simply

137

accepted her life from him as if it had been a cigarette, and
he seemed perfectly satisfied with her response. And yet what
a mountain of feeling there ought to have been between them.
Teddy wanted fervently to get out of this. It wasn't simple;
no part of it was as it looked on the surface. They were neither
of them human; human beings didn't act like that. When he
was alone with Jim in the bar he kept looking at him secretly,
wondering if he might not discover a cloven hoof or two, or
nubbles of horns beginning, or some other evidence of nightmare. But the sergeant stood there to all appearance unmoved,
finishing his cigarette and waiting for his passenger.

"Are you really going to send her to Arras?" asked Teddy
at last, for him almost timidly.

"Why the devil should I tell her so if I wasn't? Of course
I am!"

What she had not investigated at all Teddy could not for
the life of him keep from probing. He had to get hold of things
again somehow, chaos like this frightened him too much.

"But why are you doing it?" he asked, jerking the words
out in fear and trembling, for some newly sensitive part of him
expected a ferocious snub; but Jim turned and looked at him
thoughtfully, seeming to weigh the answer before he made it,
and adding thereby one more confusion to the fog.

"Because I want to. I seem to have made this my business,
and I can hardly push into it one minute and then withdraw
the next because things turn awkward. It's too untidy. And
I don't want this village goaded into doing things it never meant
to do, and getting tangled up with rights and wrongs it doesn't
understand. So I'm removing the cause." He smiled. "I
shouldn't worry about the other part of it, if I were you. She
owed me this. I never thought she was so particular about
paying her debts, but I know better now."

"And her hair," said Teddy with a burst of rancour. "I
suppose that was a debt, too?"

"Yes," agreed Jim with the same respectful consideration,
"but not to me. You might say it was no business of mine.
That's why she had to pay me back. Only me, you notice;
she bore no grudge against any of the women, because they
were only taking what was theirs. *I* was the busybody. Well,
now we're quits. There's something terrifyingly honest there,
you know, kid," he said reflectively. "Why not ask Eliane for
her side of it? I can make guesses, like this, but only she can
tell you at first hand."

"I don't want to know," snapped Teddy, feeling suffocated every moment with the desire to understand.

"Of course you want to know. Why shouldn't you? No need to pretend about it."

"Well, what does it matter? Anyhow, I shall never have the chance to talk to her again." And mentally Jim could hear him add: "Thank God!"

"Oh, yes, you will," he said peacefully.

"What d'you mean by that?" cried Teddy, taking fright again.

"I should think you could guess. Somebody's got to drive her into Arras."

"But I thought you—I understood—— Oh, hell, you can't mean *I*'ve got to go? Oh, listen, it doesn't have to be me, does it?"

"Yes," said Jim.

"But I'd rather not, really."

"I daresay you would rather not, but still you're going. Better make up your mind to it."

He knew what was going on in the boy's mind, and he felt some compunction, but he knew what he himself was doing, too, and it was going to come out right if he pushed it home now. If he relented, and got Teddy out of it, he might never get so far again. He therefore turned a blind eye to the sudden stricken look which met him, and was glad his fiat was accepted as final. There was no argument; the boy shut his mouth with a snap upon whatever further pleas he had been about to advance; and before more could be said upon either part they heard the car draw up outside the street door.

9

What he said to Major Harben every soul at the mill surmised, but no one ever knew; yet he got his own way, as some said he always did. Very probably he told the truth, but certainly not the whole truth, and questionably nothing but the truth. Harben, however, had one very singular and valuable quality; satisfied of good faith, he did not demand details, for he had no personal inquisitiveness in his make-up. He had far too complete and impervious a confidence in himself to feel the need of overmuch knowledge of other men.

He listened to the story of Eliane Brégis with a grave face, and that appearance of indifference which his reliance upon

Jim gave him sometimes in their interviews. Then he said: "I'm not sure you're not playing with fire on your own account, Benison. How if they interpret your interference as indicating which side you're really on? We're not here to love, honour and look after their quislings, exactly."

"It doesn't arise, sir," said Jim. "She's merely been removed in custody. They can work it out according as their minds run. The bloodthirsty can imagine themselves satisfied, and the merciful can obtain mercy. In a few days they'll forget to bother. And we shall be gone. Human minds aren't so very retentive."

"Sometimes I wish they were," said Harben.

"So do I, till I begin to work out how damned awkward it could be."

"Well, anyhow it's the only thing we can do with her. But I'd rather you didn't leave camp yourself. We expect a move tomorrow, and Baird will want you if it's confirmed."

"That's all arranged, sir. With your permission I propose to send her with Mason."

The level eyebrows lifted, but he made no comment; and with Mason she went, Teddy raising no objection, for if he couldn't get out of it any other way he was damned if he was going to beg. A few days ago he would have sworn that was what Jim wanted from him, out of pure wanton spite; but he knew better than that now.

Jim put his head into the car as Teddy started the engine. Eliane was in the front seat, huddled low, with her face fixed and hard, and her eyes upon the road ahead; a sort of inertia which seemed sullen, but which he knew to be stoical, had settled upon her now. He said, with gentleness, but without emotion: "I shall not see you again, Eliane. Good-bye, and good luck!"

"Good-bye!" she said without a glance aside, and her voice a monotone.

He closed the door. The car drew away.

It was early evening, but the journey was not long, and Teddy had promised himself to make the miles fly. Anything to get rid of her now, anything, anything! The minute he was alone with her that craven dread of her came back, and he dared scarcely glance at her, and yet could not refrain. The first look was almost reassuring, so pure and cold was the line of her profile between the readjusted folds of the triangular scarf; but when he tried it again, and met instead the hot blaze of her eyes, he swung back to the wheel so hastily that she could not fail to discover something of his mind. He knew he had been clumsy; but in the end what difference would it make? The very air in the car, without a word said or a solitary mile passed, was already so charged with feeling that he might as well try to silence the engine itself as disguise the pressure from her, or clear it away. She felt it no less than he; maybe her reaction was different, but it was just as intense. In panic he focused his attention upon the road so rigidly that the over-concentration began to tire him very soon, physically and mentally, and he had to relax a little. Then, without even looking at her, he knew she was watching him and smiling, hatefully, vengefully, as if—good God, as if it was he who had injured her!

He knew then that he was in for it. Her very stare, unacknowledged though it was, was beginning to rattle him badly; a dark flush started at his collar and climbed his face, agonising, humiliating. Nor did it die away soon or easily. Oh, she meant to take him to pieces slowly, nerve by nerve, to make him pay for everything she had endured, and with interest, too. She meant him to sweat blood before he got to Arras and was rid of her. Already the atmosphere was almost unbreathable, as if her personal hell was amply big enough for two.

"You are not happy, I think," she said suddenly, not venomous yet, only feeling at him, probing for the proper place to plant her knife.

"I'm all right," he said, feeling a fool and worse, and yet afraid not to answer her at all.

"No. You are ashamed to be with me."

He tried to say he wasn't, and simply couldn't get the lie out.

"*He* was not ashamed," she said more sharply. He knew who "he" was, especially when invoked in that tone; and somehow the attack did not even surprise him, though he had hardly expected to be dragged back to Sergeant Benison, unless to curse him. But it was true, too; even she had had to admit it. How did he manage it? Whatever had moved him in that last encounter, it had certainly not been shame or discomfort for his own sake. Teddy knew what had gone on inside himself; and wasn't it he who'd stuck up for her two nights ago, throwing his weight about, sneering at the enmity of the townswomen as feminine jealousy? A shade drunk, perhaps, but not more; not enough to let him off now. But he said nothing; she'd left him nothing to say.

She went on in little vicious snatches of speech, like minute flames bursting irresistibly out of her invisible burning: "You do not pity me now, no. You are concerned for yourself. There is not enough for two." It went on and on, turning and twisting, pricking him here and there. "You are so gallant, eh? You tell me you believe me, you stand by me. You! You are a fool. You talk big, but you do nothing. He says nothing, only does everything. And you dare to tell him what he can do, what he cannot do!"

He was beginning to sweat in good earnest; and staring out of the window at the greying evening, still clear and soft before sunset, was no help any more, for he saw her wherever he looked, as she meant he should, and anyhow he couldn't get away from her voice. He took courage at last, and tried to defend himself.

"Look here, it's no good you going on at me. I don't even know anything about it. I haven't done anything to you, and I wish to God he'd let you alone, but I don't see why you should take it out of me for what he did."

"What he did! That is all you can think of. *You* did nothing. *You* must be justified. Oh, I hate him, be sure of that! But you—am I concerned with you? You are nothing. You do not matter. You are right, you are wrong, you are innocent, you are guilty—am I to care? You are young, foolish, very, very small—nothing more."

"All right," he said, goaded into shouting, "that's what I am. Now leave me alone."

"Leave you alone!" she said like an abrupt echo. "Why should I? Maybe I like to see you blow about when the wind breathes on you. You believe you know everything, but you are so light you lean at a touch. I tell you lies, you sway one way, you hear rumours, you sway another; you see me not pretty any more, you lean back quick; I try to avenge, you get frightened, hurt me; you say charge her, do not let her get away. I hate him, but at least he is not straw. He goes only one way, the way he set out to go. He is not blown along. So you sit and judge him—*you!*"

It was no use answering her; and besides, things were getting worse, for they were passing through villages, and here and there a child would pay them too much attention when they were held up at a crossing, and recognise what she was, and shout the news. So far he had managed to avoid long hold-ups, and had not been forced to ask his way, but he knew it would come. She knew all the turnings, he supposed, but in this mood she wouldn't help him, even to save her own face. She'd drag herself through the gutter to torment him; and the hell of it was, she was right, what he felt was all for his own sake; there wasn't enough for two.

He groped in his pocket for a crumpled paper packet of Players, and found there was only one left in it. Damn! He could do with one himself, too. But at any rate it might stop her mouth for a quarter of an hour, or at least distract her attention. He proffered it warily. The main road was ahead, and they'd be lucky if there were no convoys going through; if he could only get her looking more normal for that crossing it would help a little.

"No," said Eliane maliciously, "I will not smoke. Have it yourself, it will help your nerves." That made him want to put it up again, but it would have looked too obvious, and anyhow he longed for it so that he couldn't bear to defer it. As he lit it she pursued: "You want me to be silent. You would like me to cover myself with a rug, to lie down on the seat, better, to crouch upon the floor, where no one can see me. That would be kind to you. You would like that."

"I should think it would be kind to yourself not to be too conspicuous," he said, and regretted it the next moment, for it was fuel to her fire; he ought to have known that she would go to any lengths now to make him cringe, and this was handing her the whip. But every word he said achieved the same effect, for dimly he was beginning to realise that she would take, for her own part, a morbid, inverted delight in degrading herself still further, provided every agony recoiled upon him. Jim might have been capable of dealing with that, but he wasn't.

"Ah," she said, "you are not proud of your companion now. The little girl from the *bistro,* she is pretty, no? You make the good advances there. You make big fuss of her. Now she comes out with you, and you want to hide her. No, that is not kind. You should show her off. She has made the careful toilette for this occasion. You should say: Look, is not my *mie* beautiful? Admire then, the complexion, the eyes, the coiffure of *ma belle amie!"*

Here was the main road, and half a village in the street to see floods of armour go by, and she must lift her voice to a shriek just as he had to slow to a standstill among the populace. Faces turned upon them, idly at first, and then with sharpening interest. Men bent to peer in at the windows of the car; children, as soon as it was still, climbed on the running-board and flattened their noses against the glass. Across the side road from which they were emerging columns of tanks passed steadily, and after them lorries full of troops, who hung over the tailboards and waved and shouted to the village as they were whisked by. He could see no break in the sequence; they were there for some time. And she—what was she doing? Was she quite mad?

"I will be seen," she said viciously, "you shall be proud of me." The tied ends of silk under her chin flickered wildly as she tugged at the knot, and then the scarf was whipped off and crumpled in her lap, clenched tightly between her hands.

It was the most awful moment of his life. Nothing he had endured even in nightmares approached it, and battles were nothing to it. This, he supposed, was what she should have been suffering, and wasn't because she had transferred the ignominy to him. All the exclamations from without, the anger, the ridicule, the astonishment, the ghoulish curiosity, bit into his very flesh. They forgot the convoy and crowded upon the car, pushing and jostling one another to get near enough for a clear sight of her, lifting up the small children, pelting her with obscenities which missed her and stung him like wasps, even though his tingling ears could make sense of only a few of the mildest. Eliane had straightened herself in her seat, and was rigid from neck to hips, her face even to the lips alabaster-white with strain, and set as hard, her eyes dark red as always in stress. Her composure was a brittle shell over a white heat of grief and bitterness which shone through it clearly. She could ease herself only by torturing him, and in that cause there was nothing, nothing she could not willingly, gleefully endure. This, and worse if she could think of worse.

"For God's sake," he said, cringing, "put it on again! Do you want to be murdered?"

"Perhaps," she said through stiff lips. "Why should you care?" And what did she care, either, now? She had always been afraid, of so many things, of poverty, want, pain, ungentleness, cruelty. She was free now, this fire within had burned away whatever held her. She had known ungentleness, cruelty she was learning without resentment or appeal, physical pain she had found to be curiously easy, poverty and want she could face in the conviction that they would not, after all, prove more than she could bear. It was strange not to be afraid any more, strange and intoxicating, so that even now, while she paid, she did not in her heart find the price too high. As for him, he should help to pay it; it would not hurt him, and it assuaged her.

"You're mad! If they started anything now I couldn't save you."

"I have not asked you to save me."

"But I'm responsible," he protested, wishing the nightmare would end.

"You think so? He said to me: 'You are responsible for yourself,' and I am. He will not blame you for what I do."

"Please!—— Put it on!" His voice was getting out of control. If she could only get tears out of him she thought her heart would be soothed, she might even be able to feel sorry for him, to comfort him a little. It was all new, unexplored, unsuspected. Never had she desired to comfort or to hurt before, only to be shielded from hurt, only to be comforted. What was it coming to life in her? What tremendous birth was convulsing her small, adolescent heart?

"No," she said, "not yet!"

He was losing his head. "Oh, God!" he said abjectly, wishing he could be invisible, wishing he had never set eyes on her, wishing he was dead. His skin was crawling with nerves. He believed he was going to do something awful, go mad, or break down completely and beg her to consider him a little, or strangle her with his own hands. But suddenly she said something which pulled him up sharply, and did him good without even being intended for him to hear, for it was said very low, to her own mind only.

"Responsible!" she repeated thoughtfully. "Perhaps I am responsible for you, too!" And she turned and looked at him, forgetting for a brief second the world outside the window. She did not feel sorry yet; that was still to come, and possibly some way off even now; but she felt interested in an almost analytical sense, curious to take him to pieces and find the springs of him. At least he had relaxed that rigidity upon which her heart had stayed itself until now; she could move, and breathe, and feel, and still endure. It was not necessary any longer to make herself a stock in order to sustain the burden. Everything was strange, even the workings of her own mind.

"What do you mean by that?" he asked sharply, for an instant forgetting with her; and then the desired moment came suddenly, the roar of caterpillars subsided, and the road was clear. He seized his chance eagerly, and with a warning fanfare on the horn to cast the crowd from under the front wheels, sent the car forward, and turned into the main road. The villagers fell back and were left behind, all their wounding eyes and lacerating voices soon lost from the senses. It was over, that appalling interlude; anything, anything to be in motion again, even if they must follow close on the tail of a truckload of grinning sappers, who would give him another sort of hell. That didn't matter for the moment; nothing mattered except this exquisite sense of relief which flooded him, and in which his remembrance of her last remark was now utterly lost. His reason righted itself gradually; everything was under control again. Even the atmosphere had eased slightly, as if she had withdrawn her malignance from him in some degree. He didn't understand, but he was glad.

She covered her head again, knotting the handkerchief under her chin with hands which shook a little in reaction. She heard him draw a frantic breath of gratitude, and felt him brace himself to steal a look at her, as he had not dared to do while she exposed herself so defiantly. He was only an inexpert child, after all, unable to judge her attitude to him without the evidence of his eyes; but he would make nothing of what he saw, for she could make nothing even of her own mind. It was all a trembling, a turmoil. Poor boy! And yet she hated him, she had not done with him yet. She almost wanted to be decent to him, and then that first dubious, hurt glance inflamed her heart against him afresh. It wasn't enough, nothing was enough to satisfy her. They had been put together, she thought, to destroy each other, unless they proved to be indestructible. He should bleed; she would smash him if she could, she would make him ask for mercy; and then her perplexed heart could break over him, and it would not matter that he did not at all understand.

The devil possessing her, she fished out a small mirror from her bag, and with a soft brown pencil began to draw in arched eyebrows into the blankness of her face. Certainly there was virtue gone out of him, for she had had no heart even to do this simple thing until now; and it was wonderful how meaning and feeling leaped back into her eyes at once. The delicate work of art achieved, she put her weapons away and sat still, letting her gaze dwell steadily upon those grinning English faces in the lorry ahead. They were near enough now for her to be seen and noted; and there was no hope of passing yet, so the car had to draw in closely and follow. The sappers conferred over the apparition, and were encouraged by her fleeting demon-smiles to give tongue. Pleasantries, whistles, compliments began to bombard Teddy almost before he was aware.

"Where'd you find it, mate? Any more where that came from?"

"Want a passenger, kid?" And the youngest, sauciest and toughest had a leg over the tailboard in no time, and was waving precariously in mid-air. "Eh, tell Charlie to pull up, I want to get out!"

"Not in your class, my son; make way for your elders!" He was hauled back by the collar, and there was the burlesque sketch of a fight in the back of the lorry, a confusion of high spirits round which several other admiring faces wriggled into points of vantage and the game went on afresh.

It was getting worse again. They couldn't know what they were doing, of course, and she did look nice again, even his one furtive glance had shown him that; but she was doing it on purpose. Again he could feel that oblique delight emanating from her, that ecstasy of torture. He hated her for dragging them into it, decent chaps who'd have frozen up like mutes if they'd known the truth.

Past pretending indifference, he said: "I wish you wouldn't."

The newly pencilled brows went up. "I have done nothing," she said, smiling deliberately.

"You know what I mean. Stick to me, and leave them alone, for God's sake! They haven't done anything to you, anyhow."

"But I am doing what you wished. You do not like it when I am honest, and show what I am. Now I pretend for you, I put a good face on it, and still you are not satisfied. What is it you want of me?"

In the lorry these exchanges were observed with interest, she making them significant with a flicker of her lashes.

"Fancy cruising round France with a kit like that," sighed the youngest sapper. "Some chaps get all the luck!"

"Come out of it, you're causing trouble, my lad. Can't you see her boy-friend's getting mad? It's your fatal beauty."

"Can I help it if I have that effect on women?"

If Teddy could have brought himself to swop even an occasional grin with them they would have called off the attack contentedly enough, and let him alone; but he couldn't. There wasn't a grin in him that wouldn't have looked like a grimace of pain, and he had just sense enough not to try and force one.

What the lads in front thought of him he could not guess, but still he knew better than to try to put on an act, with his nerves in rags, and this demented woman waiting to stick a knife in any miserable little balloon he might attempt to fly. He was learning; he set his jaw, and fixed his eyes resolutely away from all distraction, and set himself to bear it out, not to see, not to hear, anything but what he must. And in a little while he turned from the main road, and was rid of them, and they of him.

Not that that was the end of it. There was the cross-roads where he was unsure of the turning, and had to stop and ask his way because she would not help him; and the stout middle-aged wife who directed him called Eliane by a crude-sounding name and laughed pityingly at him. Also there was the awful minute at a crossing outside Arras where a cyclist with a Maquis arm-band waited beside them for passage, and she lowered the window and entered into blazing conversation with him. What passed Teddy never knew, but it was filthy, and it was about him. Their French cadences curled round him like whips and left him raw; and the patriot stared at him, and spat, and threw at him casually and contemptuously the most horrifying expletive he had ever heard. Its precise meaning escaped him, but it didn't need translating in its larger sense. And she laughed, blast her soul! Driving on was no escape from that laugh; famished and hysterical, it went with him into the streets of the town, and afterwards, driving back, it was still in his smarting ears.

But it was almost over. He found her street, unmarked by damage, narrow, growing dark ahead of the dusk because of the height of the buildings on either side. His spirits should have begun to rise at the sight of it, and indeed he was desperately grateful, but too sore to be able to feel any joy. Now that he was going to get rid of her he became aware that that would not be the end of it; everything was vaguely soiled, every movement his mind made was stiff and painful from bruises; he wouldn't get rid of that so easily.

"Where shall I stop?" he asked.

"Stop here, where it is dark." It was the first time she had answered him without a stab since they set out from Boissy. He saw her hands clench and whiten upon her bag, and almost he was truly sorry for her.

"Is this the house?"

"No, it is there," nodding up the street. "I will go on alone. I do not want you with me."

148

"But the suitcase; it's too heavy for you."

"You are a fool," she said contemptuously. "It is late for chivalry."

"Well, all right. But suppose she——"

"I am here. You have done your part. I want no more of you. Will you not understand," she said, inarticulate with rage all in a moment, "that I hate you, hate you, hate you? To owe you even a journey to Arras, even a friendly word, is hateful to me. I cannot bear to be in debt to you. I cannot bear it!" And it was true, that was the miracle of it. She, who had never hated before, hated his decency now, his little-ness, his smooth, well-meaning, conceited baby face, his arrogance. She, who had never paid off a debt in her life until Jim Benison walked away and left her no alternative, she knew now what it was to be independent, and the intoxication of it raised her hot heart against any favour from this unprivileged young man who had no part nor lot of love or enmity in her. She rejected him. It was an insult that he, who shrank from her very presence in fastidious aversion, should offer her any consideration. Where did this fiery pride come from? Was it hers, was it really hers? It felt to her as if a woman could live upon that alone. "You despise me," she said, "you feel shame at being with me. Do not pretend. I have asked you for nothing. I want nothing from you. Your cigarette would have poisoned me."

He was getting angry, too, stung even out of his misery. "Look here, this is out of all reason. I didn't want to come, I'll admit that. Neither would you if it had been the opposite way round. But I don't see why we shouldn't have made the best of it, and at least been decent——"

"Decent!" she mocked. "Cover it all up! Pretend it never happened! Waste it! Then you would not have to know what a foolish small thing you are, and for me there would not be this—this——" She leaned forward fiercely, clutching her heart, where the processional pains of that strange birth convulsed her. "You fool, you fool, do you think that is what he sent us here for?"

"I know why he sent me all right, and so do you. He sent me because it looked like a damned uncomfortable job, and he shirked coming himself."

"You dare," she cried, "you dare to say so of him! A silly child like you to *dare!*"

"Yes, I dare. What's the matter with you? Is he a god, or

149

something? Or are you in love with him, now?"

Eliane gave a thin shriek of pain, hardly louder than a bat's cry. Love to her meant nothing more than that weary, expedient fondness she had forced herself to feel for a big young Prussian blond with hardly more sense than this boy; love she had paid for, love she was rid of, finished with, and this was bitter affront. Her control snapped. She swung her arm and hit him in the face, jerking his head back hard against the door, and drawing from him a queer little yelp of astonishment and protest, like a slapped puppy's cry. For a moment he struggled with childish reactions he had thought outgrown years ago, his eyes blinking at her, his hand nursing his cheek; then everything began to change, as if the shock had addled his brains and every impression stored there was sorting itself out afresh. He dropped his hand, and let the unconsidered ache pass of itself in his preoccupation with the jigsaw within; for beyond question this was important. For one thing, he stopped trying to understand; he was out of his depth, and he might as well own it; and this once acknowledged, there was no longer any need to try and maintain that rigid hold over himself which he had found both exhausting and ineffective. His instincts took over from there, and he let himself relax into them gratefully. Everything began to slip into place, as if he had stepped back to get the whole field in focus. He looked at Eliane, sunk back in her corner and weeping through her hands as if she would never stop; the sight no longer made him want to sneak out of the opposite door and slink away, or even more fatuously attempt comfort. Why shouldn't she cry? It was a legitimate reaction, and he could wait.

He waited, and the resentment faded out of him, and the negative pity, too. He felt a new interest in her, an interest which no longer walked stiff-legged round her with hackles up, like a village dog inspecting a stranger, but sat down and contemplated, waiting for revelation. When she had spent herself, and at last uncovered her face, she saw him looking at her thoughtfully, with eyes no longer wary; and his smile, as she dried her eyes, was altogether dazzled and diffident. They were silent for quite a long time, and then he said almost shyly:

"Well—it's all right now, isn't it? You paid me, too, so we're square. Now can I carry the suitcase?"

"Yes—I suppose so!" She sounded surprised herself, but there was no hesitation. "But, please, a moment!" She sat up and began to tidy herself, and the mirror came into play again.

"That's all right, take your time." She was a woman all right, he thought, her natural instincts were still functioning.

"I am ready." She closed her bag with a snap. There were no apologies, and no recriminations, all that had gone by them into triviality. It would not have mattered if there had not been another word exchanged between them, but she did say, as he helped her out of the car: "When you go back, will you say to him what I did not say—will you say thank you? Just a little, little thank you!" Her voice was unsteady, but she went on reassuringly: "No, I shall not cry again. That is over."

"I'll tell him," said Teddy.

"And now, please, do not come right to the door. It is not that, but—it will be easier for me."

"All right." He gave her the suitcase. "Good luck—good-bye!"

But he sat in the car and watched until the door was opened to her, just to make sure that she had a roof over her for the coming night. A narrow light blazed upon her ravaged face; he watched the progress of a brief conversation, seeing only her side of it, for whoever had opened to her stood well within, out of his field of vision. She looked more like Jeanne d'Arc than ever, but Jeanne at the stake.

Then the segment of light swung wide, and swallowed her, and the door was shut. He began the drive back alone, in the half-light after the sun's loss, before the true night fell.

10

It was dark when he reached the mill, but luminously dark as early September nights can be. At the transport lines a few drivers were working over engines still, which was unusual at that hour, and he stopped to borrow a cigarette and extract some information from an oily corporal who was purring over a three-ton lorry.

"What's the rush? Are we pushing on?"

"Mm, tomorrow!" He emerged a moment from inside the bonnet, started her up, and crooned over the sweet quality of her running, which was to him as the music of the spheres. "Smooth as cream! Listen to that, will you? She was knocking like a nut in a drum when we pulled in here. We've been waiting for that car, incidentally, I've got to look her over. Took you a hell of a time to get from here to Arras and back, didn't it?"

"Sorry, but the traffic was pretty hot. I missed a turn on the way back, too, and lost a lot of time. I'll do it, if you like. I don't mind." But he did, he was dog-tired, and still a little sick with indigestible experience.

"Get off with your bother! Go on to bed! How was she going, though?"

"Oh, all right, didn't notice anything."

"Then I'll let her sit on her perishing haunches till the morning, and just fill her up. The first hop's only a coach cruise, anyhow."

"Oh? Where're we going?"

"Brussels—non-stop."

"I always wanted to see Brussels. Where after that?"

"How the hell should I know? Antwerp, maybe. Don't ask me!"

"Well, what time do we kick off?"

"Ten ack emma. Now quit worrying me, and get to hell."

"O.K.!" said Teddy peaceably. "Thanks for the smoke!"

He went slowly on up the lane to the mill. A stag-beetle bumped into him under the nut-trees, mumbled a somnolent apology, and blundered unsteadily on like an ancient and respectable gentleman on his way home from a celebration. Teddy felt like apologising too, he was so pliant towards the world. No more struggling to work things out; it was all mad, but it made a lot more sense if you let it fall into place of itself, and quit nagging when it didn't. For instance, why expect any one human being to behave, in given circumstances, like any other human being? They were not one, but two, and it was no strain to let them continue incalculable.

Major Harben was taking a last stroll over the mill-dam from his quarters in the miller's house. He was standing so still that Teddy, taking a short cut across, almost pushed him in before he saw the dark bulk of him making a solid shadow among the shifting gleams of innate light along the water. He pulled up with a gasp.

"Oh, hullo, it's you, Mason. Just got back?"

"Yes, sir."

"Everything all right? You had no difficulty?"

"No, sir, everything was all right, no trouble."

"Thank God for that! Quite an economical arrangement, as it turned out. Especially as we're off tomorrow."

"Yes, sir. Corporal Haines told me, down at the lines."

"All right, better turn in now. Good night!"

"Good night, sir!"

He was getting quite a useful liar; experience again. He felt as if he had slipped an irksome mooring, and was running with a confident and kindly tide.

Sergeant Benison was still up, for he came sauntering along the edge of the pool in a sliver of light from the open door, and Teddy knew that he had been waiting for him, and felt, though how or why he could not have told you, that the waiting had been coloured with some impatience and more concern. Naturally, even if he detested the wretched girl—and was it by any means sure that he did?—he'd be anxious to have her safely settled.

"Hullo, is that you, Teddy?" In a moment the question answered itself satisfactorily.

They looked at each other in silence. Then Jim asked: "Well, did it go off all right?"

"Yes—I suppose so. They took her in, if that's what you mean. I'm not sure, though, that she isn't in for a pretty thin time," he added candidly.

"That's the least of her worries, I'm afraid. I rather think she gave you a pretty thin time yourself, as far as that goes."

"I'm all right." This was the routine answer, of course, for anything exceedingly glorious or excessively bloody, and impressed nobody. Jim was sure already that this had been bloody enough for all practical purposes.

"Have any difficulty finding it?"

"Well, not much. I took a wrong turn on the way back, though, and lost myself. That's why I'm so late."

"Ah! Not having a guide on the way back, of course."

It occurred to Teddy that he was being laughed at, very gently but very deliberately, being jostled delicately off his dignity; and it surprised him that his dignity did not object. But he was relieved to find it so; he was too tired to freeze up again, and anyhow it was more comfortable this way.

"Yes—no! She was queer," he admitted, and flashed a grin at the remembrance; wry, perhaps, but still an indubitable grin. The signs were encouraging. Whether it was the night, or the tiredness, or the relief of having the beastly job over, this was a singularly relaxed and reasonable Teddy Mason. The last colloquy in the brook meadows had been far different from this.

"Want to talk? Say no, if you mean no, and I'll shut up. But if you do want to, now's your time."

Teddy scrubbed at his tender cheek uneasily, and visibly shied for a moment like a half-broken colt, but he came back to earth with determination. "All right, I don't mind. What the hell!"

"Good lad! There's grub inside, and a wee small brew. Mind if I join you?"

Suddenly Teddy minded nothing; even the sickish feeling was swamped in the realisation of his extreme emptiness. They went in together and he ate and drank in a sort of sleepy gaiety, and the strong, stewed tea might almost have been whisky by the effect it had on him. He forgot that the man who sat opposite to him was an ancient enemy for whose blood he had thirsted not so long ago; he talked with a sort of subdued, half-rueful sparkle, making fun of himself in a wry way as to a man and a brother. And the sergeant smiled and let him talk.

"Feel better?" asked Jim, when he sat back at last with a sigh.

"Much, thanks! They never thought of this off their own bat?"

"Must have. Here it was!"

"You're as big a liar as I am," said Teddy, marvelling. He caught himself up there with a jolt, for he hadn't meant to do more than think it; but the smile only twitched a bit, and in the eyes became almost a laugh. Funny the queer beggar had never shown himself like this before. Pity about that scarred mouth of his, he could have been quite decent-looking but for that. Teddy had heard that the Japs did that for him.

"What was I telling you? Oh, about when we got there——"
He hesitated over that, but told it just the same, for it was a relief to get it off his chest. It was not in him to delve into her thoughts or his own, but he stuck to the facts. "And then I—well, I said something I take it she didn't like, and she let go and hit me. It wasn't that what I said was so bad, really, but—well, it must have touched the spot; and I was just getting blazing mad, too—my nerves were a bit shot—but it pulled me up. You know, sometimes there's nothing like a real slam in the face to make you think," he said with profound simplicity.

"Teach your grandmother!" said Jim. "I've had my slams in the face, too."

Teddy looked up quickly, and ominous chance turned his mind from the smile to the lips themselves, again that shattering scar down from nostril into chin.

154

"Now, then! Want another cigarette? Or just bed? You're three parts asleep as it is."

"Just bed, thanks. I am sleepy; it's coming in here out of the night air. I think that's about all, anyhow, if we've got everything straight now. And you know, she—she got so independent and you-be-damned, I believe she'll be all right." He did not make himself clear, for "all right" could have meant anything from the millennium to martyrdom, but Jim understood him very well. "I hope you're satisfied," he said, recoiling into impudence."

"Quite satisfied, thanks!" And the lingering smile broke surface at last in full brilliance, and Teddy was warmed and comforted. "You made a good job of it. Now come on, kid, we're on the move again in the morning."

As they moved towards the door he fell a little behind to give Teddy first passage, steadying him with an arm lightly about his shoulders, for he was nearly asleep on his feet. The touch was casual, and did not worry him with too great intimacy; and not until long afterwards did it occur to him how significant it was. He stumbled over the doorsill, and was held upright.

"Watch out for the worn bit of the floor. Can you see?" For it was very dark now that they had put out the lights in the room behind them, only a glimmer and gloss of moonlight from a dusty window remained to guide them to their blankets.

"Yes, I can manage. Good night, Sergeant!"

"Good night, Teddy!"

But before he was quite lost in the obscurity he checked again, and the subdued voice called back in a half-tone: "Sergeant!"

"Hullo?"

"That thing I said to her—it was about you."

"You're welcome!" said Jim, smothering a chuckle.

"Don't you want to know what it was?"

"No, I'm damned if I do! Get to bed!"

"Oh, all right! It was nothing, really."

"I don't care if it was criminal slander. Good night!"

"Good night, Sergeant! But it wasn't."

This time he really went, and Jim, after a last glance out at the dreaming night, found his way up to his own blankets, and lay awake for a time, or half awake, in a haze of happiness which coloured even his dreams at last. A strange result, that, to come out of the precarious fortunes of the Brégis family.

He wished there was time to go up in person to Papa, and tell him that she was provisionally settled; but he could send a note up in the morning by one of the village boys, to set the old man's mind at rest. So she was going to be all right, was she? Wonderful phrase, all the meaning in the world in it. And it went for some other people, besides Eliane Brégis; it was true of the people of Boissy-en-Fougères, and it was startlingly true of Teddy Mason. Eliane had said thank you in the end, for her life or for something else, what did it matter? Half asleep, he said thank you to her in return, for she had eased his mind of a long-standing load.

The next morning they left for Brussels, and reached it towards evening after an easy journey. France was left behind in this new intoxication, and Boissy-en-Fougères in particular was soon out of mind, slipping away peacefully enough into the panoramic background of their lives. That was one virtue of the advance, that all the bad patches were lost to sight so soon, and round every corner there was sure to exist something new which clamoured for their attention. No stagnation here, no sinking into the landscape. Nevertheless, Jim looked back at Boissy, as the convoy got under way, with a distinct pang of regret. It was a wrench to him to take his mind away from it; or was it by the heart it held him fast? It was, after all, his second birth-place, as well as Miriam's grave. He watched until the crests of the apple orchards sank like a recoiling wave beyond the beechwoods, and the gleam of the house was quenched like a dwindling star. Then he faced about with a sigh, and looked towards the Belgian frontier.

Brussels was Amiens all over again, but on a grander, wilder scale. From the Porte de Hal, where they entered, to the Porte de Louvain, where they left it next day, it was alive and thronged and shouting, drunk with delight, dizzy with joy. It was whole, but for slight property damage from air-raids, for the Germans had left it without a fight; to be sure, they had fired one wing of the great Palais de Justice, and destroyed the copper dome, in order to get rid of Gestapo records they had had no time to take away, but apart from that the city buildings were intact. It was whole and it was lovely, with tree-shaded boulevards, gay cafés, high-gabled houses, expensive hotels, a city made for luxury. The Midshires hailed it with unalloyed pleasure, for they did not even have to fight for it; it had been in the hands of the 2nd Army for two days now, and even the desultory fire of snipers which had made the Sunday celebrations hazardous was now almost silenced. The happy Bruxellois could and did surge through the streets singing and dancing, climbing aboard every Allied vehicle that stopped for an instant, wreathing tanks, guns and men with flowers, handing up wine, cigarettes, food and girls, until the Chaussée de Charleroi looked like a carnival, and behaved like one. The Belgian White Army, still hung with rifles, pistols and grenades, paraded the streets and were cheered and embraced on all sides. The pointed gables and gilded cornices of the old houses were lost in a flutter of Allied flags, and at night fireworks materialised from nowhere and shed a dazzle of colours over the triumphing capital. The celebrations had gone on already without a pause for two days, but joy demanded more satisfaction. It would go on for weeks, probably, while Rexist families were dragged out of hiding and executed after summary trial, and the last snipers were picked off one by one, and charming Bruxelloises waltzed with British Tommies in the Place de Brouckère, and bands played "La Brabançonne".

The Midshires were convoyed at last into a by-street near the Place de la Monnaie, and had expected to spend their night in the transports, but before they had finished drawing up their line they were almost swamped by a wave of hospitable people proffering half-understood invitations, beds, suppers, parties, sightseeing tours, the run of the city and the freedom of their own homes. An early start was not contemplated, and there seemed no reason why they should not make a night of it. The lucky were haled away, the unlucky swore philosophically, and got on with their jobs; and the M.P. manipulating traffic at the end of the street was almost submerged in the flood of girls and men making for the Place Ste. Croix.

Jim, in the hour and a half he managed to snatch out of the evening, got as far as the Grand' Place, which was already ablaze with lights, torches and fireworks though the daylight had not yet gone. He wanted nothing more. Just the turning of a corner, and there was the splendid beauty of the Hôtel de Ville, with its carved façade and its steep roof patterned with little gabled windows, and the delicate grace of its spire against the pearl-coloured sky. He looked at it to his heart's content from the Brodhuis corner opposite, and then he moved round the Place in the hope of finding a drink at the Maison des Brasseurs, but every table on the pavement was occupied. An old gentleman with a pointed beard, who was sitting alone, beckoned him to his table and insisted on buying him beer.

"This is a good time for you," suggested Jim over his glass.

"Ah, you should have been here on Saturday and Sunday. That was the time. All day Saturday I remained here at this table, and all Sunday too. I could not bear to go away, there was so much to see. Monsieur, history is recorded not by those who make it, but by those who sit and watch, and I am of them. But this I shall never write. It was too near to me; I am satisfied to have seen."

"You are an author, perhaps?" asked Jim. The old man could have been anything from a prince to a lawyer. He was expensively groomed, with excellent clothes, severely cut but for a certain cavalierly curl to the brim of his soft black hat; a pearl pin in his white silk cravat; gold-rimmed eyeglasses dangling; a silver torpedo beard trimmed to a grandee point; altogether a very imposing old gentleman indeed, with a live and lightning eye.

"An editor. I was a journalist. Once I would have made a great story of this deliverance; now I am content to live it."

"At least tell me the story," said Jim on impulse.

"Can it be told across a table, I wonder? You have not been in Brussels long, then? You saw none of it?"

"No, we came in only this evening."

"Ah, it really begins as far back as last Tuesday, when I received a letter from the Rexists warning me not to take any action against any of their number should opportunity arise. Then I knew that their natural protectors were leaving them behind. We were all threatened, all we who had not been of their number and would have, perhaps, some influence when the Germans were gone. The same day we heard that the Gestapo at the Palais de Justice were loading up lorries in great haste with papers, despatch boxes, furniture. Also the women, those grey mice who had offended our sight for so long, they were massed here and there in groups waiting for cars to take them to the Gare du Nord to entrain for Germany. Their faces had changed in a night, my friend; from long regarding only of victory they now regarded ruin. Everyone knew by then what was happening. I came down to the Gare du Nord on Thursday, and stood and watched for hours, and they had no time even to hustle me away. All the trains for Germany were loading up with German officers, officials, grey mice, but there was no room for our Rexists. Ah, you should have seen them! They sat there on their baggage day and night hoping and begging for a place in a train, and always they were pushed off. They had

158

expected equal treatment. 'No,' said the Germans, 'we have enough traitors at home, why should we import more?' Some gave up the attempt, and went away into hiding, some tried to find road transport, some bargained with the German drivers for places in lorries already overcrowded, some still hoped a little until they were taken by our people when the fighting began. On that day, too, all the people of Brussels began to put on their best clothes, and come and sit here in the cafés as if in the orchestra stalls at a play, to see the German army pass through from France. What you had left of it was not imposing. The dregs of Falaise and Normandy, half their armour abandoned, half of what remained battered, the men dusty, torn, abject. We sat and watched them, we smiled, we applauded. All they saw of Brussels was our smiling faces, and I do not think they will forget them soon. It began on Thursday, but on Friday and Saturday it was at its height. They came through in tanks, armoured cars, trucks, carts, on bicycles, afoot, with stolen French horses; half their possessions gone, and what was left they tried to sell here. I saw them offer rifles, rum, bicycles, spare tyres, watches, cameras, anything they had, for a suit of civilian clothes, but we sat and smiled, and there were no barterers. We had not come to buy or sell, only to enjoy. Sometimes there was bad congestion ahead, and they were held up here. Then they lay down in the gutters and went to sleep, and nothing could rouse them. When air-raids began they did not wake, and we did not move. From Saturday we could hear the guns in the distance, and there were more air-raids, but we remained here. No one offered them anything but a smile, not a cigarette, not a slice of bread. I saw a woman go out with a pail of water, and give to two thin horses pulling a cart; but when one of the Germans jumped out and approached her she poured out what was left upon the ground, and he only shrank away from her and climbed back into the cart. Not a forgiving spirit, ours, but what of that? I have not suffered as many have, only the injured should preach forgiveness. My part is to observe. I have observed."

Jim admitted: "I've noticed people are quite ready to forgive other people's injuries, as a rule."

"Ah, but you do not deprecate forgiveness of sins?"

"I'm all for it, but not by a third party."

"Good, you encourage me. I have a theory that within a year the Germans will be forgiven freely by all those who have not suffered from them, and we who are less ready shall become the villains in their place. Perhaps, after all, I am needlessly pessimistic.''

"I don't guarantee it, sir. Shall we have some more beer?''

But the old gentleman would not hear of anyone but himself paying for it.

"No, no, I insist. Today I have you here, tomorrow maybe you will be gone, in a month I may be unable to find a single British soldier to drink with me. Do not remind me of that. Now, where was I? Ah, on Saturday! Yes! Our last German newspapers appeared on Saturday. And on Sunday our White Brigade began to be very busy, and the gendarmes took over the establishment of Brussels Radio. It is in the Place Ste. Croix, you have perhaps seen it. Before the tail of the German army was out of the Place we began to hang out our bunting and get ready our fireworks. All day there were the guns, and in the evening the first armoured cars came in and forced a way up to the Porte de Namur. There was a great deal of sniping all that night, and some machine-gunning; our girls danced through it all. After that it was all as you see.''

He fixed his eyeglasses, and beamed benevolently across the Grand' Place to the Brodhuis, over the heads of girls and men dancing in long festoons along the roadway. A breeze shook the flags overhead, and along to their left, on the pavement in front of the Maison de L'Étoile, a small band played breathlessly at a march tune, and a shifting mass of people sang. The old gentleman beat time with his narrow fingertips upon the table, and hummed happily. He was sorry when Jim thanked him for the talk and the beer, and regretted he had to go back to his company.

"Forgive me, I am a little drunk, as drunk as I still have it in me to be, otherwise I would walk with you. But duty is duty. Would you be so kind as to take that American soldier by the arm, as you pass, and direct him to this table? He seems to be alone. Thank you! *Bon voyage!*''

The G.I., who was one of the crew of a totally unexpected American tank, appeared gratified at the proxy invitation, but objected shyly that he knew no French; it was not necessary to add that he knew no Flemish, either.

"I wouldn't worry," said Jim cheerfully, "he's probably multilingual. He's an editor. And the beer talks good English, anyhow. Besides, the old boy's worth a bit of trouble.''

"Oh, well, guess I'll try anything once!" He hitched his belt, and was off.

Jim looked back from the Brodhuis, and saw that they already had their heads together across the table. He went back to the Rue des Fripiers, and worked his way along to the closed by-street where the column was, drawn in neatly nose to tail. It was much to have seen Brussels in her transports of freedom, but at the moment he was seeing something else, something he had not been able to see in England, even, because of the mountain in between. They were well up the slope now, and had plenty of impetus left to carry them over, but there could be no anticipation. The summit was still ahead, and only when they were past that point dared he look forward and fix his eyes upon the desired distant places of peace. Only sometimes when a wave of feeling swept him high did he think to catch a brief, elusive glimpse of them before he was brought down to earth again; so in the Grand' Place, listening to "La Brabançonne", he had seen clearly for a moment of stolen time the beauty and quietness of home.

PART THREE

HOLLAND

"Je te salue, heureuse et profitable Mort,
Des extrêmes douleurs médecin et confort."
RONSARD: *Hymn to Death.*

I

THE airborne landings of late September, remembered afterwards, like so many tremendous ventures, chiefly for that
part of them which failed, seemed a total and spectacular success
to the ground troops as they burrowed north and east into
Holland. They knew, confusedly but thankfully, how much
they owed to these landings in life and movement, for the
impetus which had carried them clean through Belgium was
inevitably becoming attenuated, as the most strongly flung stone
must slacken and fall some time. Something superhuman was
needed to keep the fighting open for one more leap before the
winter froze them down to earth; and if luck helped instead of
hindering, who knew but the leap might carry them clean
through on to German soil, and prick the bubble once for all?
The gamble was for a whole season of effort and waste, and
though it did not fully succeed, the Midshires among others had
excellent reason to know that it did not wholly fail.

On the afternoon of September 17th, when the first flight of
transport 'planes and Stirlings sailed north-eastward like a
murmuration of starlings through the mild autumnal air, the
Midshires were in their first Dutch town, clattering over the
cobbles of Valkenswaard and gazing eagerly ahead into the sky
filmed with haze and reverberant with sound. They compared
notes about aircraft and gliders, swopping Hamilcar for Horsa
and Halifax for Stirling, and disclaiming fervently any inclina-
tion to change places with the passengers of any of these. Even
they saw, as distant pinpoints of light infinitesimally small
against the faded blue, the parachutes unfold by hundreds and
float earthward over Eindhoven; and the following day they
stumbled upon abandoned gliders lying in the flat pastures, each
at the end of its ploughed skid-track, and began to touch hands
with their passengers at vital points by the way. North-east-
wards into Holland ran the corridor of heroes, fastening upon

key positions from Eindhoven to Arnhem, and in particular upon the bridges, for to pass that whole maze of waterways, the Rhine delta, in one leap meant to bring to bear an army upon the German plains running eastward to Berlin. If the way was secured, the weight could follow, mass and co-ordinate at will, no longer dependent upon the last flagging breath of an impulse which had aready done miracles since the last pause at the Seine. So the ground advance became a series of standing jumps from bridge to bridge across Holland, everywhere reaching for the stretched-out hand of the Airborne Division, and grasping it, and hauling strongly ahead. St. Oedenrode, Veghel, Grave, they were told off one by one, undamaged, plain signs of what could never be even chiefly failure; and on the 21st they came to Nijmegen, and crossed the Waal there, and sped on. Armour from the southern approach and parachute troops from the north secured there the greatest prize of the advance. There remained only one more effort to be made: if they could reach the airborne lads who were hanging on by teeth and claws to the bridge over the Lek at Arnhem they had everything in their hands; they could turn the Siegfried Line, the Kriemhild Line, and any other line, push eastward to Berlin, south-eastward to the Ruhr; they could dismember Germany before the winter closed down, or at least go halfway in the job and use the winter to finish it.

From Nijmegen to Arnhem is roughly ten miles; but they had already covered more than had been believed possible for a modern mechanised army to achieve in one forward surge, without any interval for regrouping, without any backward, cautious eye upon the supply lines, the forward units elongating themselves like elastic and never looking behind. There is a limit to the stretching power of elastic; these ten miles, this little, little distance was the last demand which their exhausted powers could not meet. Between the Waal and the Lek their failing impetus blunted its nose against ferocious resistance, and lay down under them in the first mud of a long rain, and died.

It was the 22nd of September. Before this they had been expected in Arnhem, and here they were in the dreary rain still five miles away, footslogging it wearily in the lee of crawling tanks, along roads cleared of mines only to the verges, and peppered thickly along the grass and hedgerows with unpleasant little anti-personnel gadgets which didn't kill, but contented themselves with blowing your feet off. Here they were, shoving their heads against what seemed to be solid rock, and all the while the parachute boys in their foxholes across the Lek were looking for them, and wondering why they didn't come.

They tried; they tried heavens hard. But it was no longer possible to go tearing along the roads in lorries, or ride passenger upon buttoned-down tanks. The armour had shot its bolt, too, for there are things only the Infantry can do, and this endless laborious probing of every bush, every copse, every house, every decapitated windmill, was their job, and no one else's. Every knot of grass, practically, had to be taken apart. There was nothing for it but to dig in where they stood, snatch their rest as they could, and creep forward as often and as fast as the pressure ahead would let them. The pressure ahead was how they thought of it still, but it was on three sides of them now, and they were strung so thinly up the country that the enemy on their flanks could, but disappointingly did not, shoot right over them into his own ranks. They wallowed in the new mud of slit trenches, shot it out with the stubborn knots of the enemy at great loss, and harked back in vain for that forward wind of inspiration which would not be recovered. Every day they saw supply 'planes pass overhead, bound for Arnhem with munitions, food and reinforcements; but they knew for what the lads would be looking most anxiously, and it could reach them only afoot. Alleviation flew towards them; salvation crawled, with its nose in the Netherlands mud.

Even the weather was against them now. It rained and rained day and night, pausing only, as Peterson said, for what had fallen to flourish. But for that, ten times the amount of stuff could have been flown in, ten times the air cover given to the besieged and the relief alike. Just when they needed the last ounce of luck it slithered greasily out of their hands, and they were left labouring forward from house to house, from tree to tree, frantic with anxiety and sick with helplessness, while the furious thundering of Hun batteries across the river brought them only too frequent news of how things went with their friends.

On the 23rd they gained two miles more, at considerable peril to the units on the flanks. The Midshires were well out on the right, beginning to edge towards the river bank above the town; but they knew, none better, how precarious was their hold even on what they had. "Limited objectives" was beginning to be a catch-phrase. Never since Caen had they fought for a few square feet of ground, a clump of trees, a haystack, a wood-pile, as they fought now. At night they lay down where they were, and those who could slept, and those who must watched, but the Lek seemed still far away, and the rain still denied them air cover. Before dawn they would be massing again. Tanks, guns, trucks, cars moved up in the night by all the inadequate roads. Command Posts seethed with officers popping in and out of the ground like rabbits. The Infantry roused early, and brewed tea in odd hollows wherever they could find shelter from the drizzle. In the midst of so much ordered activity it was strange to listen to the silence which brooded over everything, receiving and absorbing all these diverse and devilish sounds; a pliant silence, from whose yielding surface even the clatter of tanks recoiled defeated, yet an early blackbird, tormented for the dawn, could break it with a note as soft and pure as spring water, and the sudden crowing of a bantam cock from the nearest farm shattered it as with trumpets of brass, and for ever seemed to one at least of the Midshires to have sounded the true onset of that day's battle.

Jim was with Baird when the cock crew. The briefing, what there was of it, was long over; they knew without being told what was expected of them, only the details of the ground needed pointing. They had reached the inevitable pause, when all has been said that can be said, and when what has not yet been done to ensure success cannot now be attempted without damage; so they were sitting under a hedge, quiet with two mugs of boiling, stewed tea, when the strident enthusiast gave tongue; and Baird jumped so violently that he spilled scalding liquid over his hand.

"Hell!" he said, recovering, "I must be in a bad way!"

He meant it only as a casual bit of self-censure, but the minute he had said it he knew it was true, and it worried him. His spirit was as good as ever, but he was so bemused with tiredness that he couldn't be entirely sure his spirit would retain command; it might easily be left bogged in some mucky shell-hole at the end of the day where his flesh had foundered. They were all in much the same case, swollen-eyed and heavy from lack of sleep, mud to the eyebrows—all but Dick Shelby, who was the type to whom no dirt adheres—and stiff with chills.

"Maybe find a drier bit of house-room tonight," said Jim hopefully.

"Maybe! This side the Lek or the other?"

They wished they knew the answer to that; or maybe, on

the other hand, it was better not to know. They would move,
upon the operative word, with more conviction if they could
still believe in their own effectiveness. There was nothing the
matter with their hearts, at any rate; they came to their feet
silently, alertly, as the first thunderous outburst of their own
barrage began, the creeping barrage that was to waft them into
the southern approaches of the bridge of Arnhem. It was as
if the breath of the guns blew them to their places; and indeed,
at this close range the impact of the noise seemed almost to lift
the skin from the body, and gave them, as they hitched themselves out of the ditch, a distinct and lusty shove in the direction
of the river. Everywhere men were creeping out of hollows
among trees, out of hedges and shell-holes and slit trenches,
and shaking together the weight they carried, and moving into
place. First the deep bass bellowing of the heavies, then the
mortars with their savage staccato, then the twenty-five-
pounders joining in, and the sudden unanimous clattering roar
of the tanks moving forward; and the attack had begun.

The first few hundred yards never seemed real; there was
plenty of enemy fire, but never any enemy, especially by this
dismal, vague half-light before dawn, while they trotted at the
heels of tanks, and pried cautiously along ditches, intruding
into a flat, depopulated world where even the trees seemed cut
out of grey paper and stuck untidily on to paper of a paler
grey. The drizzle, never hastening, never slackening,
emphasised by its negation of emphasis that all was illusion.
Only death and mutilation kept reality in mind. When
Granton stepped astray in the ditch, and detonated a small
mine, blowing his foot into rags and causing minor wounds to
two who were walking close behind him, that was real enough.
The stretcher-bearers who had him away inside five minutes
recognised reality there as well as the victim himself did; so did
the doctor who gave him a dressing and a shot, and the orderly
who stuck a cigarette in his face as a matter of course. When
a chance three-inch mortar flattened Dobbs and Craddock, that
was real, too. The chaplain at the R.A.P. would find it out very
soon, when what was left of them came back to him to be
labelled with two little crosses, being too late for any other
rites. But these things bore no relation to the soiled tissue-paper
sky and the cardboard haystacks gummed against it, and the
spectral trees.

A sudden sparkle of fire, the only bright thing in the whole
landscape, burned up on their right front; a house, but already

abandoned, even by the Germans. They were nearing the area where the first wave of their own creeping barrage had struck, and fires, shell-holes, great gouts torn out of the scenery marked the line of it. This was where it always warmed up. Mortar and small-arms fire began to strengthen. The tanks had almost finished their job; they could sit back and help to cover the end of the advance, the A.V.R.E.s could close up and lob their clumsy "Flying Dustbins" into the buildings ahead; but from now on they could not accompany the Infantry farther. It was out of the ditches now, and off across fields as flat as a doll's-house lawn, with shell-holes for the only cover, and a withering curtain of fire between the Infantry and their objectives. They took a last deliberate look over the field of action, by the grudging light of the rainy dawn, before they must swarm out of hiding and spread to open order.

Meadows, still grey and dun for green, still curtained with curious whitish drifts of rain, extended away into a half-seen solidity which Jim took to be the southern dyke of the Lek. Colourless and dreary, spattered with shell fire, the prospect mourned with diaphanous tears of rain no bigger than specks of sand, and here and there clumps of trees stood thin and dark in it like covens of witches, their heads together. On the immediate right front, not quite screening the fire, was a small, half-grown plantation, too orderly for their taste; dead centre, and the chief object of interest, stood a windmill, some three hundred yards or so distant, or maybe much more, since in this two-dimensional world all was illusion. A full-size windmill, an intact windmill, with skeleton sails still upon the motionless air; and the very fact that it was standing, in an area where lofty observation posts were so precious, proved one of two things. Either it had been abandoned in great haste, or it was strongly and confidently held, and meant to give a hell of a lot of trouble; and since nothing here was being abandoned without a fight, the first alternative was ruled out in this case. That meant they had to get that windmill the hard way, and until they had it nothing in this whole sector could be reckoned safely held. Beyond it was a farmstead, probably derelict, and beyond that again a village. These they could command once the mill was theirs, but the mill they must have. And these, the mill and the farm and the village, which was only a cluster of cottages, were A Company's pigeon. They spread themselves cautiously along their ditch, prolonging their line eastward behind a low hedge designed to give comfortable cover

167

only to dwarfs. This they felt to be a grievance, as if the Dutch should have anticipated their need. They wriggled their Bren and machine-gun teams into place, and fixed their eyes ahead, wating for the moment. Behind them, on the road, Churchills moved up a little nearer, grinding and slapping through the mud.

It was going to be bad business getting out of that ditch, even in open order; nobody was looking forward to it. Bad visibility would make little difference, for there was so much stuff flying about that even if the enemy had been firing blindfold they couldn't have missed with all of it. The barrage had knocked the village about a bit, fired the isolated house, and chipped pieces out of the plantation, and was now pounding steadily at the rear areas, but to judge by the fire-power that remained it had left plenty for the Infantry to do. The platoon found themselves on the extreme right of the advance, stumbling along bent double under that accursed hedge, listening to the dull, neat plunk-plunk of bullets into the damp ground around them, and feeling the short hairs in the backs of their necks erect themselves at every smothered impact. Three men dropped out while they deployed their party, Sloan and his section to the farthest point they could go unseen, and then on their bellies towards the plantation, Jim and his lot holding hands both ways in the centre, Sergeant Alcombe behind with his. The stretcher-bearers came hustling along and removed the casualties just as the platoon broke cover.

There were only shell holes between them and the enemy, and they felt, as they trotted towards the windmill with tracer from the Brens ripping past them in spurts of orange light, great need of something more than a shell-hole apiece in which to hide their nakedness. Coming over barren meadows from a low hedge, what a target they must make! They ran steadily, keeping level, trying not to listen to the withering passage of bullets that lifted their hair afresh every second. The air was alive with fire; men dropped grunting out of the line and rolled in the grass, and the rest spaced and ran on. But it was a costly business. Halfway they had to check, partly for breath, and partly to bring up their Brens and machine-guns again. Sloan and his lads had left the extreme point of the plantation now, and were heading out for the shell of the farmhouse, to find themselves cover, and come about the mill from another point. There was a long run between, and the flank fire here was intense. There was no guarantee that they'd ever reach the farm, and certainly none

168

that they would ever leave it again if they did reach it. But the whole situation was in the same key. All they could afford to see was the solid rise of the dyke in the distance, and away to their left, where the main thrust was, the faint luminous outlines of the southern suburbs of Arnhem. A little colour, a little disheartened light was creeping into the world, and there were perceptible depths of space now between windmill and farm, and village and blazing house; a third dimension existed, after all.

Baird sprang up out of the mud and waved them on again. It was all the way and under the wall this time, already feeling for grenades and circling for loopholes; a smashed window-frame dangling here, the flour-doors sagging on one hinge there, they selected as they ran. Some went to ground under the batter of the masonry, hugging it like a sweetheart, and some fell by the way; and of these last some crawled lamely after their friends, and some lay where they had fallen. Peterson pulled the pin of a grenade with his teeth, and snaked along the wall until he could lob it in through the vacant window, from which a machine-gun had operated upon them to grim effect. Baird made straight for the door, with half the survivors on his heels, and blew in the lock with a sweep of his gun, and they went in blind over the splintered wood, firing from the hip. Jim went up the shaky light steps to the upper door three at a time, with two others, one of them wounded, climbing after him. The sooner they were inside this improvised strong-point, the better pleased he would be, for from the village, and from every bush and hedge between, a renewed fire was shortening upon them; and it was now broad daylight, though still raining and full of a watery haze. The door here needed no blasting open, it swung and yawned upon one hinge. He leaped in without pause, for darkness could not blind a man who had come out of so subdued a light. There were four in this high, musty place, and more climbing up, to judge by the din from below; and these did not drop their arms and shout "Nix shoot", at him, but sprang about on the instant with revolver and gun spitting; but he had fired first, flattened against the wall within the swing of the door, where it was darkest. One of them went down and did not move; a second dropped his revolver with a clumsy clatter upon the floor, and dripped blood from a shattered wrist. The other two, too late to have any choice but surrender or suicide, responded to his rapped order obediently but with deliberate slowness, put down their weapons where they stood, and stepped back from them with raised hands. Morgan slid through the doorway like an eel, gathered these in passing, and was standing over the trap with his Sten gun at the ready when the first head erupted.

This one, suddenly confronted with a straddling enemy, fired in sheer panic, and angry with himself for the lapse, reached out his hands unexpectedly, flinging the revolver far, and tried to claw Morgan's feet from under him. The Welshman had not played Rugby for nothing. To evade the curious tackle was easy; to shove a toe under the stretched-out chin and jerk the man backwards off the ladder on top of his companions was not, perhaps, so obviously the result of training, but it came naturally enough, and was executed with the precision of a ballet step. The fight was not over yet, but they had no more trouble upon this floor. Morgan shot through the trap before the commotion of the German soldier's fall had subsided, and dropped into the fray bristling with armaments. Jim left Rednall, whose static usefulness was no way impeded by a flesh wound in the leg, to watch over the four disarmed prisoners, and himself went gingerly up the next flight of steps and listened at the closed trap above. Most of the mills they had seen had been in ruins; but he thought there must be windows enough in this place to accommodate five or six machine-guns if necessary, besides plenty of room aloft for snipers, and shot-windows enough in the ventilation grids up there to keep them happy and effective for weeks given sufficient ammunition. He looked quickly at his prisoners, but their faces betrayed nothing beyond a blank malignant interest, certainly no anticipation of rescue or revenge. If looks could have killed he would have been dead enough, but they showed no hope of getting rid of him by that way or any other. Yet he knew, he was sure, there were more men up there. And these were not the ageing conscripts they had met sometimes recently, but young, lusty Schultz-Staffeln, fit as buffaloes and arrogant as Lucifer; naturally they would give nothing away.

He took hold of the iron grip nearest the outside wall, for the trap had no hinges, only two handles by which it must be lifted bodily aside; and with slowly released pressure he essayed the weight of it, and the snugness with which it fitted into its socket. It gave with comparative ease, and he checked his hand at once, and waited a second or two. Since it was not bolted nor held above, he paid them the compliment of deciding that they were waiting for him; and since there was still no murmur out of them, nor movement, he did not think, though he could not be sure, that they had noticed the very slight motion of the trap. He raised it a shade more, just enough to glimpse the lie of the light in a thin, diminishing thread along the floor. Yes, the window was the copy of this window below, at least within a matter of inches; so they would be in the dark corners of the outside wall, waiting with all the advantage of the light, unless they were fools, which he did not believe.

There was no point in waiting; only one man could get through that trap at a time, if he had a hundred behind him; and on the whole, upon several counts, he would rather it be himself than another. He worked his arm through the two hand-grips as into a shield, and hitching his Sten gun into his side with lifted muzzle ready to spring into place under this primitive cover, suddenly heaved up the trap and erupted head and shoulders through it. The thing was a devil of a weight, but it covered him to the eyes, and it was thick. A gun stuttered, and the running blow of the bullets plugging home in the wood across his chest bruised his ribs and almost drove the breath out of him. Someone with a revolver fired at his head, but his helmet saved him, and all he lost from the attack, in the long run, was half the camouflage cover of his helmet and a sliver of flesh from his right arm, which was imperfectly covered. He swung body and shield and all round in an abrupt arc, pivoting the gun against his hip so that the two dotted lines of fire stuttered into each other indignantly, and the German gun fell silent. Next moment it clattered upon the floor, and the body of its owner slumped over it.

There were four of them up there, two living, two dead by the time he could take note of them. Baird, with the ground floor nicely cleared up after him, came up the ladder as Jim was jettisoning his clumsy armour and disarming his prisoners; and they undertook the scavenging of the top of the mill between them, and raked down no fewer than four snipers to join the captives; but these, knowing themselves already cut off from usefulness, did not fight.

They possessed, then, an undamaged and as far as they could discover unmined mill. A beginning had certainly been made upon the usual elaborate lay-out of booby traps, but the garrison had apparently meditated no sudden move, and the job was only half done. They left two machine-gun teams in the windows overlooking the village, to give them cover as they pressed on, and a couple of men to stand guard over the prisoners until the second line came in and they could be shoved to the rear; and the rest of the platoon set off again northward.

Far on the right Sloan must be in the farmhouse by now with his handful of men; but there was a hell of a lot of flank-fire pouring in upon that unhealthy spot. It was full daylight now, or as full as it would be this day. The morning was slipping away from under them, and maybe they were doing well, but not well enough. For this village which as yet they did not hold was only the beginning of what they wanted. They strained their eyes towards the dyke. There was no quick or easy way to it, it was through the village or nothing. On the right there was a thin belt of trees that ran outward towards it, but they doubted if they could get to it. Sloan could, though, from the farmhouse, if he hadn't lost too many to make the attempt feasible. It would take him perilously far aside from any help, but he could do it. He was doing it. Baird saw him break cover and streak head-down for the edge of the tree-belt, with Mason at his heels, close and keen as ever, and the rest following—Dick Shelby, Mathieson, Courthope, Lees, Clure— He handed the glasses to Jim as they lay under the wall of the mill, steaming in a faint burst of sun, and waiting for the tanks to finish with the village.

"Take a look! That's them all right!"

Jim was in time to see the leaders of the section dive out of sight in some hollow under the trees, ditch or water-course, probably the latter, especially after all this rain; but at any rate they couldn't get any wetter if they lay in it. In the foxholes of Arnhem men had been lying in watery mud for seven days now.

"It's crazy," said Baird, "but if they can hang on to it we've got a section of river."

"He's right to try it," said Jim, but expressed no opinion as to whether he could hope to succeed.

"My God, yes, try anything once! The tanks are letting up. Come on!"

They went on. Sometimes on their feet and sometimes on their faces, held up at every hedge and every ditch, they went on into the village. There was no walking out and leaving them to walk in here. They had to fight for every foot of the approach, in a tedious, exhausting, costly reduplication of wounds and deaths, losing men wholesale. Even when they reached the one ruled street, they had to batter their way from house to house, and room to room, and cellar to cellar, while the precious day oozed away in renewed rain out of their hands, and they were scarcely nearer Arnhem. By late afternoon they had the place

cleared completely, and had attempted to thrust on a little
farther by stepping-stones of haystack and house, when enemy
batteries from over the river opened up on them in a deafening,
stunning barrage which did not slacken again until after dark.
It was directed chiefly at the centre, where British troops and
Canadians were trying desperately against an impossible tide to
hang on to the skirts of the southern suburbs; but out on the
flanks they got their share of it, and the enfilading fire, too,
and more than their fill of three-inch mortar shelling, which they
particularly detested.

They were helpless, and they knew it. Flesh and blood, tired
flesh and depleted blood, could not endure any more. When
their own heavies in the rear took up the tale it was only an
increase of agony, for by then every access of noise merely shook
their overtaxed fibres a little nearer to disintegration. Their
little advance patrols could hang on no longer, indeed they were
being flattened one by one. There was nothing to be done but
withdraw them into the village, and at least settle down to
ensure that they should have to move back no more. Precariously but doggedly held, the village represented comparative
stability by then. The Colonel had just come up from the centre
in a jeep, the back seat of which he filled to overflowing. Harben
was there, as dapper as ever, and still only slightly smudged
with mud. One of the chaplains, looking more like the conventional idea of a soldier than either of these two, loped up the
single street and dived into a doorway casually in passing, to
avoid a shell-burst. This was almost homely; even the din,
which was what they all hated and feared most, had less effect
when they could hold together among their own people.

They looked for Sloan, but Sloan did not come in, nor any of
his men. Jim and Baird looked at each other at last, and by one
accord turned eastward to see how things went along that stretch
of dyke, and the fringe of pollards along the water-course. They
had to climb to get a view upon it, for it lay very low; but from
an upstairs window at that end of the village they saw that there
were gaps in the line of the trees, and even such as still stood
were tattered and thin of leaf. A rainy haze began to close in
again. Of humanity there was no sign, only the rubbish of shelling thick between, standing fountains of mud; and significant in
the background, those pitiful threadbare trees.

Baird licked his blackened lips, and remembered slight exchanges, intimate sometimes, impatient sometimes, friendly
always; boys his own age who were yet his own children. They

173

had done so well, so miraculusly well, up to now; he supposed it was their turn. His head ached with confusion and noise and strain, but what could he do?

"I ought to have kept in touch with 'em," he said. "What do we do now?"

"Nothing until dark. Whoever went out for them now would be in the same boat, and we can't afford any waste. If there's anybody left alive there, they'll do better lying doggo than trying to get back in this. I think they'll ease up a bit when it's dark, and we can go out after them then; it won't be so long."

But it seemed longer than an age before the barrage slackened and let them go. There was to be no help for them; after a filthy day it settled in to be a filthy night, so that the search party had to proceed by guess-work, in open country without small landmarks. They took stretcher-bearers with them, anticipating casualties. However, they had covered only the first few fields out of the village when they met what was left of the missing section retiring in tolerably good order, and carrying its wounded.

The first of it was movement in the shifting murk ahead, and a step astray, slithering in the mud. A faint exclamation reached them, in a voice they knew, and a hissed appeal for silence hard upon its heels. Baird stood forward and challenged softly: "Sloan, is that you?"

"Yes, sir!" said a voice which was not Sloan's, but appeared to have taken to itself authority to speak for him.

There stumbled out of the darkness five men, three of them carrying a sixth between them in an elaborate system of belt slings and rifles, the fourth leading the little procession, the fifth bringing up the rear; all that was left of the section which had moved up under Sloan that morning. As for Sloan himself, he was beyond answering to his name just now.

"This is all?" said Baird, looking round the standing shadows as the unconscious corporal was lifted on to a stretcher and taken up by fresh bearers.

"Yes, sir," said Teddy Mason, a hoarse whisper in the night.

"You're sure? No one back there still alive?"

"No, sir, no good going on."

So Dick Shelby was gone, and Lees, and Wainwright, and others of his contemporaries. In the obscurity, as they set out back to the village, it was just possible to put names to the survivors: Sloan—if he lived—Mason, Clure, Courthope,

174

Mathieson and Pryde. Some of them certainly wounded, though they hadn't yet had time to consider it; all of them, at a normal time, bound for the M.O., after an ordeal like that, but of course this was not a normal time. There was nothing said on either side until they got them safely into the village, settled down those who could smoke with cigarettes, and poured them full of strong, hot tea. They still looked like ghosts, fixed and shocked of eye and ashen-coloured, but at least some warmth began to come back into them, and they could tell what had happened to them. Baird wanted to send them all back to the R.A.P., but they insisted that they were all right, and he knew how valuable was every man just now.

"We couldn't get out," said Teddy Mason, "when the big stuff began to come over. We were almost on the dyke, too, but we had to drop back into the channel and lie there. We were getting it badly from mortars, and the din nearly took your hair off. Then our guns started up, too, and—well, it was pretty bad. Sloan got it, and most of the others, but we had to stay put, it was the only chance; and there wasn't another bit of cover between us and here, and they were all round the other side of us. So we decided to stick it out until night, and then make a break for it. And we did, but by then there was only the few of us."

"You did well to get out at all," said Jim, to whom this recital appeared to be chiefly directed.

"I suppose so," agreed the boy dubiously. "Do you think Sloan's got it bad?"

"Can't say, kid, wish I could. I'm going back to R.A.P. with 'em now. Want to come along?" Though Teddy had come through it in better case than the rest, partly from having more natural resilience of spirit, and partly from having taken Sloan's yoke upon him. To have a job to do is to have a reserve of composure to draw upon at need. He would never submit to being marked down as "battle exhaustion" and sent back to the Casualty Clearing Post at this of all moments. Nor would the others admit to more than scratches and the murderous headaches which were the inevitable result of being caught for so long in a double barrage of such intensity. Pryde had a shot-wound clean through his forearm, but no bones broken. Mathieson had a gash from a mortar-splinter in his shoulder, an ugly hole but it might have been a lot worse. The rest were blackened and dizzy, but would own to nothing more; and Teddy's quick rejection of help was largely to blame for that, thought Jim, for who was going to own himself outdone by young Mason?

"No, thanks, I'm all right!"

An ambulance took them out the short distance to R.A.P., which had moved up almost into the village itself. It was scarcely quicker, but much easier, for Sloan's hip was in a mess, though Jim thought the thigh was not broken, and hoped to God the pelvis wasn't, either. He climbed into the back with the three of them, and kept an eye on the corporal as the car drew out from between the houses; and as they crawled down the congested lanes, their subdued headlights picking up forms of man and machine for a second to lose them again instantly in the dark, Sloan suddenly opened his eyes vaguely, and blinked at the light over his stretcher, and asked for a cigarette.

2

The conversation between them occupied perhaps twenty minutes, from that first reviving glance to the moment when the hypodermic needle closed his eyes again upon drowsiness. He seemed to have less pain than would have been expected, but it was bad enough to watch the labour of his breathing between words, as he struggled with waves of nervous nausea. The cigarette wobbled so much that Jim was constrained to hold it for him, an attention for which he sighed his thanks just audibly; and after he had drawn upon it hungrily for a moment words and breath came more easily.

"So you got me out, after all," he said.

"Not us. Teddy beat us to it. We only met you coming back."

"Oh, he made it, did he?" His lips, muddy and dewed with sweat, managed a queer little smile. "Better keep an eye on that lad, he's sickening for something."

"Meaning what? That he did what he was told?" asked Jim, returning the smile.

"Without a murmur, as far as I remember. But he must have done all right on his own, too—after I stopped remembering."

"He did. Don't worry about him; he's all right."

"Who's worrying? But I wouldn't mind understanding. What's come to him? Do you know? He's quit thinking he knows it all."

"Just growing up," suggested Jim, grinning.

"Did it in jerks, then. Just like me to pack up when he stops making me spit blood." He asked next moment: "How many got back?"

Jim told him; it was not cheerful news, but certainly it was not unexpected. Sloan shut his eyes for a moment upon an onset of pain, clenching his teeth until it passed. Jim held the half-smoked cigarette and put it between the blanched lips again as soon as the blood came back to them.

"How is it? Very bad?"

"Not so dusty! Comes and goes!" He relaxed slowly, exhaling smoke. "How do you think it is? You've seen it, I can only feel it."

"Long and messy. But I think you'll be O.K."

"Mean that?"

"Yes."

"No bones gone, then? I shan't be crawling about on a cork leg, or anything?"

"Don't think so."

"Thank God!" said Sloan, and abruptly and briefly wept, but without sound. He was ready for speech again when the ambulance pulled up, and they began to lift his stretcher out.

"Stick around, Jim, will you? That's if you can?"

"All right, I can and will."

He walked beside the stretcher as it was carried into the Regimental Aid Post, from the darkness and the rain outside to the hard lights and queer shadows within, and a mute distressing movement of the last walking wounded of the day's advance. The whitewashed walls of what had once been a solid little cottage looked blue and supernatural in the artificial and inadequate light. The tiles of the floor, once glossy-clean in the Dutch fashion, would not bear looking at now, for the flow of casualties all day had left no one any time for cleaning up. The doctor, poor devil, was mud to the eyebrows like everybody else, and hard put to it to keep even his hands moderately clean. What a job, thought Jim, what a hell of a job! Yet somebody had to do it; and better that, on the whole, than the chaplain's. All day watching men die, trying to help them not to mind dying, when they were young and lusty and minded desperately, and the chaplain's consolations sounded to most of them just the usual flannel. Honest men, or they wouldn't be here; but even the honest can delude themselves as well as others. He wondered if this padre, sitting wearily on a bench by the wall just now, drinking cocoa, might not sometimes in the wakeful night see in imagination the rows and rows of little crosses he had written names and numbers on in his time, and suffer an appalling vision of his own responsibility if, after all, the dead do not rise.

"Gosh, I'm scared," said Sloan, from his stretcher.

"I wouldn't worry; no nurses here. Wait till the Base Hospital!"

"Bloody comforting, aren't you?" But he grinned.

"You're looking forward to it, really."

"Sure, I go for nurses! Hey, come here with that cigarette."

He finished it while the first free orderly, a middle-aged man with red hair, came over and began to cut away the clothes from the mangled hip and thigh. The area itself he did not touch, for cloth and flesh were so mashed together there that it was not for him to meddle. He was gentle with a large, airy gentleness and used his hands with the casual deftness of a craftsman, one in whom the hands had usurped a part of the function of the mind. Also he contrived to be cheerful, which in this place was much.

"Better do your bit of talking fast, mate," said he, "before his nibs gets to you."

"Why, will he sling Jim out?"

"Bless you, no, he's all right. But he'll want you safely blacked-out before he starts work on this mess."

"But I don't feel so much of it now," protested Sloan fretfully.

"No, but you would. You take it easy, and leave it to him. He knows what he's doing."

"O.K., but can I have one more fag, first?"

They gave him one. He could manage it himself this time, for now that he lay still, and only this confident handling disturbed his body, the pain had somewhat withdrawn from him. The doctor came and leaned over the orderly's shoulder as he worked, and looked at the dark swamp of flesh without a word, without the flicker of an eyelash. A lean bare arm was outstretched; long, thin, spatulate fingers felt round the borders of the wound, pressed along the line of the hip-bone at the crest, dimpled the white skin of the abdomen. Sloan's eyes dwelt upon the doctor's face all the time, questioning and frightened. His hand felt for something on which to clench itself, and fastened gratefully upon the fingers Jim slipped into it; the grip was convulsive with terror, not of death, but of

178

crippledom. The doctor saw that; even in the rainy, bloody horror of the day he would have seen it, for he noticed more than he was ever given credit for; but at another time there would not have been leisure to respond to it. Now things were easier with him; now he had time, not time to spare but time enough, to dispense just one more thing besides dressings and morphia. Frugally, for even in general practice he had been a sparing dispenser, but justly, too. A little encouragement, perhaps; a few minims of comfort. Even then he might not have bothered, for he was very tired and needed to sleep; but that small gesture of the sergeant's hand was a spark which started in him an answering fire.

He smiled reassuringly.

"It's all right, son; with any luck you're a straightforward case. No plaster and crutches for you."

"Are you sure, sir? You're not just being soothing?"

"Sure as we ever can be. I may be on a stretcher myself by tomorrow, you know. Don't worry, D.V. you'll do all right."

He went away then to fill a hypodermic, leaving Sloan limp with relief and reaction, still clinging to Jim's hand. After that he didn't really care; by contrast, everything else was easy.

"I know it's daft, but I can't help it. I've always had it. I couldn't bear to be crippled—and the hip's such a queer place——"

"I know. But I told you you were going to be all right. With any luck you'll be home for Christmas."

"Sure!" said Sloan with a wry smile. "I'm lucky! Jim— don't go for a minute, will you? He's going to put me out now. I've never been ill in my life, I don't like it. I never knew I was scared of so many things."

"Who isn't? I've had plenty of this, and I still hate it. But trust him—it's his job."

"I know, I'm just being a b.f. But hell, if I can't be one now, when can I?"

The doctor came back, taking it steadily, not rushing him.

"All right?"

"Yes, I'm ready. So long, Jim—thanks!"

The spatulate fingers gathered a fold of skin; the needle went in quickly and steadily, and in a minute his eyes closed, and he went off muttering a little, like a child falling asleep. Jim kept hold of him until the tight clutch of his hand relaxed, and then freed himself gently and stood up. The other two were being bandaged by the orderlies and packed off to the Casualty Collecting Post. They were all accounted for; he supposed he might as well get back to the village, though it wasn't worth trying to snatch any sleep, for they were bound to try another move before dawn. Stuff was still being massed, for he could hear it passing on the road; they might pull it off yet, if only the sky would clear and let the aircraft get off the ground in something like force.

He stood for a moment to watch the doctor cleaning up Sloan's thigh; and the doctor felt him there, and did not seem to mind. He'd reached the point where he didn't mind anything but the whole bloody, barren, nonsensical business.

"Bad day, Sergeant!" he said.

"Rotten day, sir."

"They won't be able to stick much more, if we don't get through. If only it would stop raining!"

But Jim felt as he walked back to the village that it would not stop raining. The sky was all dark, dropsical clouds swirling low, jostling one another, without any sign of a break from east to west. Some desultory firing was still going on forward; punctures of red upon the skyline alone relieved the darkness here, but away over the river there was the crackling of small-arms fire and pulsating glows of burning. Blast the Rhine, why did it have to multiply like rabbits here, after being so long content to be one river? Why couldn't Nijmegen be all? Hadn't it been enough of a miracle to win that, that more should be required of them?

He went back to the platoon, and having reported to Baird, found himself a sheltered corner of a half-ruined Dutch kitchen to watch out the rest of the night. Of the others, some were sleeping. Teddy Mason was well out, sharing a mattress with two others as young and exhausted as himself, topping and tailing it boots and all. Peterson was curled up on the kitchen table like an outsize cat, snoring mightily. Jim didn't want to sleep now, for if he did he would have to rise and go on in a few hours still half stupefied with want, whereas while he resisted the temptation he could go on almost indefinitely if need be, and keep his mind brilliantly clear, as if in some glittering rarefied mental atmosphere he could not normally breathe. So he sat down and tried for a while to relax, but it was harder work in the long run than he could bear. Long before dawn he was out again, prowling the street and watching the supports and ammunition trucks move in. He went forward through the gardens northward to get a clearer view of the stretch of land between village and dyke; and sitting apart from all the rest of the wakeful, on a back doorstep against a closed door, he found Arthur Clure.

The little man did not see or hear him at once, he was so deeply sunk into himself, with chin in his chest and hands holding on tightly to his head, as if he feared it might fly apart if he released it for a moment. It was difficult to be sure in the dark, but Jim thought that long, regular fits of shivering went over the slight body, particularly shaking the hands and head, for once at least he clearly heard the chattering of teeth. Why hadn't he looked more closely at Clure before? He might have a boy's build, but he hadn't a boy's elastic spirit; it wasn't to be expected that he could live through those hours of nervous torture in the water-course and bear no mark. It was no use, with this one of them all, going straight to the point and asking: "Do you feel all right?" for in Clure's theory of heroism it was a point of honour to dissemble pain, fear or illness, even if you were obviously designed by nature to be softer and more vulnerable than the common run of men. For him there could never be any such confession as Teddy's simple and truthful: "My God, I was scared stiff!" But he had been, for who wouldn't? Now he had to harry his strained senses to hide not only the fear but also the sense of grief and shame it aroused in him; and all with the appalling physical shock still repeating itself through him nerve by nerve, coursing round his body in a tightening coil of white-hot wire; with a breakdown in the distance for him, unless somebody began to work miracles. Damn Teddy! Why couldn't he have had a scratch that would need dressing? Then the rest might have been cajoled along to the M.O., and this poor little devil wouldn't have felt impelled to be "all right". Yet he was pleased with Teddy; he had done very well, and it was hardly to be expected that he should develop this special kind of gumption at the same time as the normal sort. It wasn't a boy's quality at best.

He moved forward a few paces, making his presence known. Clure looked up with a start, and even in the dark the effort his body made was clearly discernible, a sudden straightening and hardening of lines as he drew himself together.

"Hullo, Sergeant!" he said warily, on guard against the world.

"Hullo, Clure! Had any sleep?"

"No—I couldn't."

"Nor I." Jim sat down beside him, and folded his arms on his knees. "What it is to have an easy conscience! Peterson's snoring like a pig."

Silence for a moment, and then Clure asked: "Is there any news of Corporal Sloan?" He was always punctilious about ranks.

"Yes, he's not too bad. Nasty flesh wounds, take a long time; but the M.O. thinks his bones are all O.K."

A long sigh came out of Clure, and a shudder after it.

"I'm glad! But you—you'll miss him."

"Yes," said Jim, "more than I like to think about."

Silence again, though the arm against his arm shook. To anyone else he could have said reasonably: "Look here, you aren't fit to go on, and I know it, and so do you. What on earth is there wrong with admitting as much? It isn't your fault, and you're just as legitimate a casualty as Sloan. Now show a bit of sense, and come on and report sick." But he didn't want to do that to Clure. This impossible and pathetic knight-errantry had survived ridicule, even its friends', and discouragement, even its own; was it possible he could bring it to heel by merely inviting it to human weakness?

He tried another tack. If he couldn't knock anything in, maybe he could get something out. Like bleeding a patient. He would be a leech himself, too, until he did get some satisfaction.

"You're a married man, aren't you, Clure?"

"Yes," said Clure, rearing his head in surprise. "Why?"

"Oh, I don't know! Just thinking! I hope to be one myself when this business is over—and if I survive. It's a funny thing! For a long time I kept putting off getting engaged. Seemed to me it wasn't fair to tie her to me, when this was coming off. I didn't want her to be a widow, or even feel like a widow, if I didn't come back. But like a fool I never thought she might look at it quite differently. Don't mind me talking like this, do you?"

"Of course not!" said the little man, more warmly.

"I may not have another chance, who knows? And you're married yourself, you'll understand. Here, have a cigarette!"

Over the flame of the little lighter, which he had used so often in this stealthy service, he marked the hollows and starting bones of the narrow face, all gaunt soiled eyes and top-heavy forehead. He went on talking; he didn't think Imogen would mind.

"We're engaged now; I came to my senses just before we moved over here; I daresay it was what did it. But if I hadn't been such a fool we could have had two years to look back on—poor substitute for two of the years you must have had, no home, seeing each other week-ends and leaves, and all that, but still it would have been something to hang on to." He felt suddenly in his breast for the small wallet which held her photograph, and flashed the lighter upon it against his knee. "Look, this is Imogen!"

Clure leaned over her almost eagerly, startled and flattered at being made the recipient of such a confidence from such a person.

"Imogen! It's a lovely name."

"Imogen Threlfall. She's an ambulance attendant in London."

"She looks so young," said Clure in a low voice.

"The photograph's three years old; I've been plaguing her for a new one. But it's very like her."

"It's a pity she's in London. They—these flying bombs——"

"Yes, but she wouldn't be anywhere else. It's her job."

"Yes, I know, my wife's just the same. I've tried to get her to go away, but she won't. If she did go, I suppose she wouldn't be happy. But it worries me a lot. They're such devilish things—so inhuman—I do worry about her." Now that he was launched he could admit anxiety on her account candidly enough, but never on his own. "And then she—she's rather shy. I doubt if she sees very many people, now I'm away, or keeps as cheerful as I like to see her. Not that she isn't liked, you know, but she's so retiring, if she was ill she wouldn't ask for help. Yes, she does worry me a good deal. I think I've got her picture here somewhere." He fumbled in various pockets, and brought out a small card. "There she is—that's my wife!"

The flame of the lighter showed a face like a flower, small, pale, wistful, with a soft texture like the flesh of a rose, and large, trustful but bewildered eyes; not remarkable of brow or chin, with small thoughtfulness and smaller strength, and yet a face not altogether negligible. Capable within her limits she looked, the hub of a small, circumscribed and hitherto comfortable world, now out of her province in this broad and savage time; a little faded from her first bloom, but still a pretty woman. It was easy to see why, her husband being the man he was, and she the woman she seemed to be, he should feel impelled to go to war for her against his nature and hers, and certainly against both their interests.

"She's lovely," said Jim gently. "You're a lucky man."

"Yes, I do realise that. She is pretty, isn't she?" He looked at her fondly, and for a moment the strained lines of his face were softened. How foolishly and magnificently in love with her he was, and after—how long?—of married life! And how clear it was now that she alone, who least desired it, had sent him out to subdue the world for her, just by looking at him like that, just by being so sure he could do it; to her own grief and his humiliation, for of course he couldn't do it. If she had been a different woman she would have loved him in a different way by now, and he could have been safe at home where he belonged, and useful, instead of heroic and useless here.

Jim snapped out the lighter. Clure sighed, and shut the vision back into his pocket-book, and shuddered again.

"I wonder," said Jim, "if my Imogen and your wife couldn't get together? They won't either of them have a lot of time to play with, I know, but—I mean, if she's quite alone it would be nice if there was somebody to pop in and see her occasionally, wouldn't it? You haven't any children, I take it?"

"None surviving," said Clure, after a moment of silence.

"I see. I'm sorry!"

"No, it's all right. Quite a relief to talk about home again, really, only you see that's where we've been rather unfortunate. We had a little boy, just a year after we were married, and Helen was so knocked about she could never have any more. He lived to be three, but he never was strong, and we—we lost him. He would have been a big boy by now, nearly sixteen. It's strange to think of it, isn't it? You know, my wife never really got over it—I mean in her own mind. And even now I can never be with young boys, and not keep thinking which one of them he'd have been like. Seeing a walk that might be his, you know, or hair the colour his hair would have become. He was a very fair child. It's silly, but there it is. I try not to do it, I know it doesn't do any good."

"You never thought," suggested Jim diffidently, "of adopting one? I know it can't be quite the same, but sometimes people have found it helps."

"I did try to get Helen to do that, but she couldn't fancy it. And I couldn't press it, you see."

"No, of course not. I never realised. I'm sorry!"

"No, really, it's been a pleasure to talk about them both. It doesn't do to put things away in one's mind so much. You—you mentioned about your fiancée, Sergeant—— Do you think she would?"

"I'm quite sure she would. Imogen's very much alone herself. Let me ask her to go and see your wife, if you're sure she would like it, too. It would be a load off my mind, I can tell you."

"I'll write the address down, if you'll give me a light." And he did so, with a hand which shook no more than was reasonable. Talking had done him good, not a doubt of it. "I'm glad you thought of it, Sergeant," he said, handing over the folded scrap of paper, "very glad. Really, it will be a relief to know someone is keeping her company now and then."

"It beats me why we don't co-operate a bit more," said Jim, "but I suppose it's too simple to think about." He stretched his legs, and yawned. "I shall have to move or fall asleep. Anyhow, it's time I was stirring. Coming back to the bunch?"

They went back, talking now freely, but of nothing in particular, which in itself was an achievement. And after all, Jim reflected, as the first dim pre-dawn assembly began, and the fires came on, and the tea was brewed, he had got something for his trouble; the snag was that he didn't know quite what to do with it now he'd got it. Imogen would do her part, he knew, without question, though it was something of a fiction that Imogen suffered from loneliness; and that would, as Clure had said, ease his mind of one anxiety. But the situation would still be substantially the same.

He looked for Baird, while the detail was fresh in his mind, before the briefing began all over again, and urged him to see to it that Clure got some back-stage job as early as possible that day, pointing a gun at prisoners or something equally innocuous, anything to keep him out of the worst of it. Baird was more than willing, being exercised in his mind over last night's survivors. He himself had slept for a little while, and looked all the better for it, being still young enough, like Teddy and some of the others, to take his sleep in short snatches and yet benefit by it. Jim was past that.

It had stopped raining for the moment, but every field was a marsh, and the sagging clouds had not lifted at all. The day was much like the previous day. The same painful slow advance through the shadowy hours before dawn, the same intense resistance, the same spasmodic fires. By midday they had a thin hold on the dyke in this eastern sector, and were trying hard to extend it both ways, but especially west towards the approaches of the town and the bridge. By early afternoon they were sure in their hearts that they could not do it, but they went on trying. They extended eastward as far as the water-course and won back the bodies of their dead. They made their hold upon the village itself secure, and struggled to close in upon the town by a meagre mile, as others from the western face of the attack were labouring mightily against the odds to join them. But air cover was still non-effective, and still there was drizzle and low cloud. They could do no more. Towards evening the word went round that the attempt was to be abandoned, that the remnants of the 1st Airborne Division were to be evacuated from Arnhem that night.

This was that failure, then, which like Dunkirk refused to be deprecated or smoothed over or forgotten. This was the reverse which swallowed up, afterwards, for those who only read of it without much imagination, all the achievements of that Netherlands venture, and caused them to speak of it as a failure, even though they spoke the word as if they meant a triumph; forgetting, in the loss of Arnhem, the gain of Eindhoven, St. Oedenrode, Veghel, Grave and Nijmegen, which Arnhem made possible.

But to the ground forces, sweating and agonising on the other side of the Lek on this early-darkening evening of September the 25th, the word failure seemed to attach not at all to the parachute troops, but exclusively to themselves. They were the ones who had set out to reach Arnhem, and never got there. The airborne lads had dropped into the town expecting to hold it, or their positions in it, for three or four days at most. They had held them instead for nine days, perforce half supplied and half fed, with little air support, drinking rain-water after their supply was gone, and they were asking no favours now. Was that failure?

When Baird broke the news to his non-commissioned officers his face was hard set and brittle and white like half-translucent stone. They were in the tattered remains of a little wood, with a disconsolate dripping of rain all about them in the leaves, and behind them a lane along which traffic was oozing towards the dyke with a dolorous sound. Engineers were moving up any amount of stuff. They would want boats tonight on this stretch of the Lek as well as downstream, for though the bulk of the survivors were below the town a few isolated parties were here to the east, and must be taken off from here.

"There'll be no job for us?" asked Jim.

"Only to hold this corridor open from the dyke to the village, and pass 'em through as they come. We're going down on the dyke, if that's worth anything, and it'll be damned dangerous down there, so be ready for anything."

He had said not a word of his own feelings in the matter, but there was no need; his face spoke for him. But some of the others, when the word was passed on to them, looked and spoke their thoughts. They had not meant to; had they been over the river receiving their orders to get out there would have been no murmur; in Arnhem there was none, the case being beyond complaint. But these were the men who felt that through no fault of their own they had let their friends down, and they did complain, bitterly and wearily, wasting their breath upon what gave them no ease.

Howbeit, they did their part that night. They were down along the road to the dyke, and over it, crouched in the mud-flats where the boats would come to land, ready to pass the rescued men back to the village. There would not, they were told, be a great number here; and in the village there were trucks enough standing by to take them back the remaining seven miles or so to Nijmegen, where they could rest and sleep for the first time in nine days.

The evacuation was due to begin around ten o'clock. All that evening the bombardment had never slackened, but towards nine it became intensified, and the British heavies joined in thunderously from the rear; indeed, thought Jim, sitting in the mud on the river side of the dyke, most of the row going on was from Allied artillery. There was a great deal of machine-gun fire, too, spitting perforations of light along the black and oily-surfaced water, and a confusion of fires glowing and flickering round the town on the southern bank. There was altogether too much light flooding the operation, from one source and another, so that while they waited for the engineers and their assault craft it was expedient, in spite of the mud, to lie down flat under the slippery curve of the dyke and look as much as possible like mere undulations in the viscous slime of the flats; which, by now, was what they chiefly resembled, even to their faces.

They waited thus for the better part of an hour, with Very lights soaring over them, and their attention straining between the tape-marked pathway over the dyke behind them, and the tumult on the opposite side of the river. The water was high, black and swift, mottled sullenly with reflections of flare and fire; and beyond it they could see by uneasy glimpses the raised line of another dyke like their own, something atop that might be a hedge, a wet shimmer of trees. Appropriately it was still raining, and heavily now, a steady downpour that hissed and sputtered along the flats. Under trees the leafy rattle of such rain would cover up any other slight sounds, such as the shuffle and sucking of feet in the mud, or the rustling rasp of wet capes.

The launching of the boats, which had been rushed up at short notice by field engineers, was easy but hazardous, for such an activity under the dyke could not hope to pass unseen. They lost two men while they were manhandling them down the slope, and one of the boats was hit, and filled and sank, before ever they got them away; but once out in the fast current and the fitful mottle of dark and light in mid stream they had a better chance. They were small, light assault craft, with outboard motors, and swift and single in passage they afforded no target; but the Midshires, splashing back out of the Lek and into cover, didn't envy them their wait on the other side.

It was past midnight now, and the lads across the river were due to move off at ten, so even allowing a couple of hours or more for them to wind a way through the German line and across the dyke, there should not be a very long wait. Most of the Midshires, whose chief job had been to get the boats to the water, were moved back now into the village, where Harben had seen to it that all the survivors of Sloan's party of yesterday were pinned firmly down with the odd jobs, whether they liked it or not. That was Baird's doing, of course. The rest could the more readily settle down to wait for the return of the boats, a small party on the shore, and others stationed as guides along all the turns of the path. Baird himself came sliding down the dyke on his tail, and joined himself to the half-dozen effigies of mud lying by the river. They shut up their senses, as completely as they could, from the din of the bombardment, and fixed their eyes across the dazzle of true and reflected lights, and waited; and after a long while the first craft shot out of the obscurity and became unmistakably real, coming solidly to land.

They went hip-deep into the water to steady it in and speed the unloading, for some of the freight were wounded and needed help, and all were exhausted with effort and starvation. They climbed out, none the less, vigorously and silently, gaunt, soiled, blood-stained men, stripped of all their belongings but one haversack each, their boots wrapped in strips of blanket to muffle them, mud caked over them so evenly that they seemed more unfinished bronzes than men under the sultry crimson light of the fires. They did not speak, there was no time nor need for speech; their eyes were enough, enormous, sunken, burned into their heads with wakefulness, seeming after so long incapable of sleep, for the cavity could surely not be closed by a mere eyelid. They were steered quickly up the path over the dyke, and passed on from sentry to sentry into the village, where they were filled full of strong tea and fed, though hurriedly, before being taken on into Nijmegen. Before the assault craft which brought them was well round into the stream again, another was coming in.

It went on for just over an hour before the last load was in. How many came ashore there Jim had not counted, but he thought it must be between three and four hundred; and this was not the main landing point. He didn't know how many of them there had been in the first place, but he thought that if they got back much more than a quarter of the whole force they would have done well. In the meantime they had lost another boat, in passage but on the empty trip, thank God, and the engineers, all but one who had been wounded and foundered with her, had been picked out of the river by the following craft. The thing might have gone much worse. But it would not do to think of those left behind without hope of rescue, over there; the wounded, the doctors and medical orderlies who had volunteered to stay with the wounded; the lost, the captured, the very many dead. Nor to look too closely yet at those who had come back and were limping through the night beside him, nor to expect of them, until they were ready, speech or notice or any part of comradeship. The heart and mind consecrated for so long to one narrow, implacable purpose cannot, when drawn back from their cavern into ordinary air, at once expand to take in all that was put away from them with the world. When for three days or more you have been, to all intents and purposes, as dead as the dead, it is gradual work coming to life again, and takes a lot of getting used to that while you are reprieved the dead themselves are not.

Baird made that mistake. He walked behind Jim, on the

way back, shoulder to shoulder with a young lieutenant; at least, he must have been young when he dropped into Arnhem nine days ago. Baird had possessed himself of all that his companion had to carry, and from time to time would speak to him, which might have been well enough had he never required an answer. Monosyllables came out of the muddy lips in reply, almost creaking with effort, as if his vocal cords had not been used for a long time.

"It's best part of three miles yet. Can you make it?"

"Yes."

"Must be ghastly to have to pull out like this, isn't it?"

"Yes."

"Hate leaving a job unfinished myself. As we have, of course. You did yours. Did you—do too badly?"

"Others had worse," said the labouring voice.

"I suppose you were on the perimeter, being taken off here?"

"Yes."

Black dark here, rain, the sibilant dripping of a wood; still a long, muddy trek ahead, and everywhere, more perceptible almost than the din of the guns, these soft sounds of universal mourning.

"I wish to God we could have made it!" said Baird, in an undertone which was yet almost a howl. "This is hell, to have to creep away with our tails between our legs. And to leave so many behind!"

"My sergeant——" began the lieutenant harshly, and something happened to his voice, and he couldn't say any more.

Somebody else's sergeant, walking beside Jim, started upon that strangling sound, and drew breath like a gasp of pain; and Baird was quiet then, and only the rain complained, and the shivering leaves. From the dyke to the village Jim did not say a word, except to steer his companion round a bend in the path, and even that was done more by the hand at his elbow than the word in his ear. They got on well together in their silence. Their paces, which had begun in a broken rhythm, soon settled down together comfortably, and after every interruption and halt fell back readily into unison. That was all the contact they could stand yet, and it was enough. They didn't observe each other by deliberate ways; they only felt the slow thinning and fading of the invisible veil between them, which was the barrier between the quick and the marked for dead. They knew only, and this without recording that they

190

knew, that when they left the dyke they seemed to be together, but that when they reached the village they were together.

The bombardment was beginning to subside when their walk drew to its end. Looking back, they saw no more of dyke or fires, only a smoky smoulder still shot with sullen red below, and the watery darkness starred with Very lights above. The night was full of silent men marching out of nightmare into reality, suspended in the pause between being dead and being alive, between a grief of experience and a grief of recollection. The rumble of the guns rolled trembling along the flat world like the reverberations of lost anger, and again the tearful epitaph uttered by the rain which itself had destroyed them sounded back from the rescued to the dead.

It was half past three in the morning of September 26th. The Arnhem episode was over.

3

October and November, after that activity, seemed to them to pass in unfathomable boredom. It was no surprise that they found themselves suddenly static, yet it was almost physically shocking, as it must be to a spirited horse which after a brisk gallop is pulled up on his haunches. There they were in the tongue of land between the Waal and the Lek, and could get no farther in this immediate direction, and would not give back; therefore they stayed there, strengthening their positions as best they could, digging in along the higher ground, and making the best of a wet and miserable business. And soon this protruding horn of the Allied armies fell subject to a dull reputation of being always "all quiet", in spite of the fact that there were places in it where enemy shells came over at the rate of about one a second all day, and not so very much less at night. It was the quality of stillness rather than of quietness that gave them their name; and by late October they began to wonder if they were still capable of movement. They had settled in the abominable mud like an abandoned tank, like some of the smashed German armour bombed out of action on that first rush north; sometimes during those weeks of sitting still they expressed a bitter fear that they also would sink from sight at last in a series of greasy bubbles. There was, to be sure, a sniper loose about a certain corner of woodland, who for a time made the passage of the road there an exceedingly uncomfortable adventure; but after they had hunted him from cover and sent him down to the cage at Nijmegen even they, who suffered the shelling, began to believe at last in the dullness of their lives. The tragedy was that the great effort to defeat the winter by keeping the fighting open had failed; all tensions seemed to have snapped with it, and here were they, like a tug-o'-war team whose opponents have loosed the rope, sitting in the mud.

The Midshires had their ups and downs during these two months. Apart from a fortnight of rest in Nijmegen in October, and certain spasmodic actions undertaken to widen their holding north and east of the town, not war nor peace made up their immediate anxieties. Others might, and did, essay the effective clearing of the port of Antwerp, storming Beveland at the end of October and proceeding to the watery and perilous adventure of Walcheren in the first few days of November, thus triumphantly restoring its usefulness to what had hitherto been only a paralysed asset. Others might and did break into Overloon, Hertogenbosch, and other unpronounceable towns, and prod gently westward into all the crevices of the Maas. But for the Midshires hope was the move from one deliquescent hummock of mud to another, and usually vain; adventure was the daily passage of the hot spots on the road, and often fatal. The Canadians who were their neighbours on the left provided a breath of new companionship, not a little genuine rivalry, and a great deal more which was worked up as an outlet for animal spirits. But the most remarkable, pervasive and omnipresent feature of their lives was still the mud.

Midway through November they did have a stroke of luck. They were discouraged by then where the possibility of better quarters was concerned, and one more move was to them only the exchange of one hole in the slime for another, probably worse; so that they could hardly believe in their luck when they were marched into a neat little village, scarcely damaged, and divided up among the available accommodation there. B Company, always sticky-fingered, got the private billets, of which there were not enough to go round to a second company, for the place was small. C got an inadequate school and the remaining floors of a damaged windmill. D took over certain larger outlying houses which had been abandoned by their owners and not yet reclaimed. For a week or two, they were told, while the shelling here had been bad, almost all the population of the village had packed its portable property and run for safety, but they had not run far, and had come back again as soon as the pressure eased. Some had never budged at all. The Van Doncks, for instance, who had a large farm just out of the village, did not shift a foot, even when the Germans in retreat drove off all they could of a fine dairy herd, and slaughtered some of what they could not take, and no doubt would have finished the massacre and fired the barns had not the British come so quickly. For which the British in the persons of A Company got an extra welcome when they took over the barns and part of the house.

Very nice quarters, too, even if a little cramped for nearly two hundred men; they were used to worse camps, and in any case winter was settling in by then with the first half-hearted frosts, and close companionship meant warmth. They had their share of shelling at times, but not as they had been used to it for the past month, and the joy of sleeping under decent cover was enough in itself to make them content with their lot. It wouldn't last, of course; nothing lasted, even in this interlude in which nothing really changed; but while it endured they settled down to enjoy it. A rainproof roof, clean lying, really hot tea and eatable meals—except, of course, for those on tours of duty forward, who perforce received it by van, or if the mud was extreme by tank, as much as three hours after it was cooked—red tiles and a fire in the kitchen, leisure to write home, Christmas coming and kids in the house: what more could they expect? Farther south along the two hundred and fifty miles of front there was activity still, and at Aachen and Stolberg the line had actually entered German territory; but since there was no possibility here of moving more than a few sticky steps between a marsh and a quagmire, they were thankful for the minor mercies of comfort as they came, and the mud alone kept their minds from fretting upon anything loftier or more important.

The farm stood somewhat higher than the village, though the difference was negligible, and both were low enough to make their inhabitants cast anxious eyes at the weather and the winter dyke from October onwards. At this time the Lek and the Waal were running from ten to fifteen feet above the level of the surrounding land, but the dykes, in spite of inevitable neglect, were still sound. No one by any stretch of imagination could call the view from the house pretty; it was a blank expanse of grey-green polders, flat as a table but for a raised netting of smaller dykes which made clay-coloured lines about the scene, and kept the land passable, presumably, even under moderate flooding. A few trees here and there, tall, solitary and leafless, only served to emphasise the excess of horizontal lines against which their straight trunks contested in vain. Usually the sky was another matching monotone, grey-white for grey-green; and the air was mist and rain. But when the clouds broke and the sun came out upon the steamy polders the whole scene seemed to change, to put on a demure house-wifely charm, like a plain, wholesome face smiling upon a visitor. The depressing flatness could become a plane of light then, the sky a limpid shining poring upon its own reflection. And then the children came out and played in the stack-field in their enormous clogs, luring the Midshires from letters they could perfectly well write in the rainy days, and chores over which they knew they could take their time; and there was a shrill, innocent chattering around the house, and much shrieking and laughter and clattering of clogs up and down the cobbled yards.

There were three of the children, Baartjen, Claes, and Cornelia. Baartjen was eleven, and had outgrown the podgi-ness of the little ones, managing somehow to grow leggy without growing tall; indeed she looked no more than nine, being under-sized as they had found most of the Dutch children after four years of German misrule. She would be quite good-looking someday, for her features were good, and her skin, though now pathetically pale, was clear and smooth. At the moment she was quaint enough, solemn-eyed as a Van Donck heifer, with straight straw-coloured hair cut in a bob and decorated with an immense bow of pink ribbon on top of her head. Her frocks, which were old and could not be replaced, were grown exceedingly short and skimpy on her, so that she seemed to stick out of them alarmingly at wrist and knee, and to be about to burst them with her bony shoulders. She was a responsible little person, and took more care of the younger ones than they always relished. Jim had seen her, on occasions, place herself firmly between them and columns of stray German prisoners passing through, as though she could avert in her own inadequate person the malignance of which these might still be capable. She belonged, after the first day or two, to Jim Benison; no one disputed it, however willingly she played with others when he was not by. It happened on the first day, when he came round a corner upon a tussle between her and her little sister, who was struggling to reach the barn and the strangers, and exercise upon them her undeniable fascinations.

194

Baartjen, with a face of fierce determination, held her back from the enterprise, gave desperate unintelligible orders, and finally slapped her; and Jim came just in time for the resultant howl. Where he was different from the rest was that he looked at Baartjen, not at Cornelia, and smiled at her, and asked very gently what was the matter, knowing he would not understand a word of the reply when it came. But the reply was a white stare, a crumpling face and a flood of tears, and he understood it all perfectly. She had spent at least three years of her short life hedging the two little ones about from dalliance with the soldiers on their premises, at her mother's express orders and with all her single-hearted might; how could she be expected to lose the habit all in a moment now, and remember that these were not enemies but friends? She had been told, of course, but telling is not enough, and her instinct had betrayed her into a mistake of which she was bitterly ashamed. Jim told her, quite incomprehensibly but very effectively, that it didn't matter in the least, that her zeal did her credit, that the best of us are liable to momentary attacks of absent-mindedness; while she wept into his solar plexus, which was as high as she could reach, and absorbed the sense of it all through the sound, and was comforted. From then on they were confederates; she would walk away from any game when he appeared, or leave a conversation hanging in mid sentence if he called her. and it was no use any rival attempting to seduce her from him.

Claes was eight, and at the stage of losing his teeth. He was plump, with brown hair clipped brush-fashion, for fear of vermin, which were all too prevalent among the children of these half-nourished and overworked villages. His eyes also were brown; his smile was gap-toothed but engaging; and he was seldom confined within the narrow limits of being merely Claes Van Donck. Usually he was a soldier; you could tell that by the enamelled basin inverted upon his head, and the roughly shaped hunk of wood he pointed at you from round corners and behind logs in the yard; and the shouts of "bang-bang" or stutter of "tat-tat-tat" would tell you whether his weapon was rifle or machine-gun. Once, in a crash-helmet which made him sag at the knees, and borrowed driving-gloves which swallowed his arms to the elbow and had to be retained largely by will-power, he directed real and imaginary traffic in the lane for four hours without stopping, himself supplying the noises of car and tank until they feared his vocal cords would give out. When someone pointed out how like his enamelled basin was to the white helmet of an American M.P., and further explained under pressure what these worthies do, he became an American M.P. at once, and remained one for three days. Peterson, whose third child was at this age, became Claes's especial crony by simple right. Off-duty these days he was seldom on his feet, preferring always to get down eye-to-eye with his fellow-conspirator. And if he gave Claes a delirious amount of happiness, there was no doubt that Claes did him good in return.

But Cornelia was everyone's darling, and yet remained a free lance. She was just six, and bigger for her age than either of the other two, perhaps chiefly by virtue of being the youngest, and therefore petted and protected by the whole family. She was a rotund little person, with round cheeks and long lashes, and two short straw-coloured pigtails plaited so tightly that they stood out from her head like the horns on a mine. They terminated, invariably, in huge bows of plaid ribbon which fluttered after her when she ran and gave her an appearance of imminent flight; and at least six times every day, having wrestled and romped them loose, she would turn the back of her neat round neck imperiously upon one or another of A Company, and constrain him to attempt their restoration; which invariably he did with unexampled meekness, for Cornelia was a great tyrant as well as being a shocking flirt. She had blue eyes, round and bright as gentians, which she used upon the whole of her male acquaintance to devastating effect, and a mocking, dominating small mouth which laughed when you expected solemnity and was solemn when you expected laughter. She was altogether incalculable until they had grasped the all-important fact that the end and aim of her being was to subdue men to her will; and since she was ostentatiously frank about this they soon got the idea, and admired her the more for it. And yet a plainer little body never breathed, for all her fine eyes; her nose was engagingly snub, her head as round as a cannon-ball, and her frocks, which were relics of Baartjen's past, were quaintly long and large upon her. But Cornelia had a personal magnetism which made mere beauty unnecessary.

The Van Donck family tended to keep themselves severely apart at first within their own rooms, as they had done with the Germans, though for different reasons. They were determined not to hamper their allies in any way, and their business-like Dutch souls found it courteous to keep even the children from being constantly under the company's feet. But this did not last long. Claes first took Peterson into the bosom of the family, and the Yorkshireman made a great hit with the ancient grandmother, who issued her fiat at once that he must come again; and Mevrouw Coppenol was, as they soon found, as complete an autocrat as Cornelia, and as shameless a flirt. Jim, coaxed over the doorstep at length by Baartjen, saw the old lady, fair and speckless in smooth black of dress and smoother silver of hair, sitting in the chimney-corner with Peterson, the pair of them obviously as thick as thieves already; nudging each other and swopping sallies and smiles, chuckling at each other's jokes as if every word was perfectly understood, whereas the only common language they had was dumb show and a wink or two. After that the situation adjusted itself naturally, and more than half the company became occasional guests of the family. And in this happy state they remained until the beginning of December.

They said afterwards that they should have known it was too good to last. Planting a few snipers and making merry hell of a few cross-roads for eight hours a day had never in itself been enough to satisfy Jerry. He dared not come at them just now, and it was out of their power to go for him; but it would have been a miracle if they could sit quietly around this Netherland farm for more than a fortnight together and not be disturbed by some trick or other of his devising. Where he couldn't get at them one way they had usually found he would work round and get at them another. But he did it very quietly this time; there was no upheaval, nothing but a few dulled explosions during the night, all but lost among the persistent grumbling of gunfire. The night seemed no noisier, the noises no more significant, than at any other time. No one knew or suspected what was to follow until a Caldington lad named Tyndall, waking in the barn before dawn and hearing a soft, watery noise which he could not be sure was rain, opened the door sleepily and stepped over the coaming into the waters of the Lek.

He did not realise what had happened, for it was dark, and he was still bemused with sleep; but he knew it was water, and he knew it ought not to be there. He drew back with a yell which originated in surprise but sounded like terror; and the company rolled over in its blankets and reached for its rifles as one man. Of the three sergeants in the barn with them Jim was the senior, and the lightest sleeper, too, and he was on his feet in a moment, and stepping nimbly over bodies in the direction of the door.

"What's up? What's the trouble?".

"The yard's under water, Sergeant. Honest to God it is! Come and look."

They looked, and when their eyes grew accustomed to the curious innate light floating upon the earth, and the great darkness of the sky, perceived that this was an understatement. As far as anything could be discerned there was this amorphous gleam, and with it a slippery, seeping, sibilant noise of water creeping through hedges and bushes, lipping at tree-trunks and walls, slithering over stones.

"The dyke's broken," said Alcombe.

"They've blown the dyke," said Jim at the same instant.

He reckoned the lie of the farm; there was nowhere much rise or fall of the land here, and already they were higher than the village. No point in making for the dykes themselves, for the upper storeys of the house, the lofts of the barns, were higher, as well as sheltered, and they might as well be comfortable while they waited for rescue. The house, he calculated, was the first anxiety, the stock the second. There was an old stable, lower built than these two big barns, where a ramp might, with some trouble, be rigged to the loft doors, though getting the cattle up it would be quite another matter. But they shouldn't lose what was left, he was determined upon that; if they had to rig slings under the beasts and heave them up by pulley and ropes, the rest of the cattle should not be lost. The Germans had done enough to the Van Doncks.

"You get all our stuff up into the loft, quick," he said to Alcombe, "and rouse the others if they haven't already spotted it. It can't be over eight or nine inches anywhere yet."

"What about the beasts? We can't let 'em drown."

"The stable loft—if we could rig up a ramp they can climb. There's the sleeping benches, if they were roped together— and there are ladders in the other barn—— see what you can do. I'll go and raise the house."

Half a dozen of the platoon splashed out after him. Some-where on the way they lost Morgan, who was always a lone wolf. Jim knew better than to worry about him now; he would probably turn up again poling himself along on a barn door with a colony of hen-coops as passengers, or be discovered floating down the lanes picking up stray calves as he went. Whoever could not be relied upon to make good count of his life whenever it was threatened, and never spend it needlessly, Morgan most surely could. Jim waded on towards the house, with Clure and Peterson and Teddy Mason close at his heels. By the yard door they could always get in at any hour, directly into the room where C.S.M. Groome and two sergeants had made themselves comfortable; and by now, unless Jim had miscalculated, Groome would be either awake or afloat. He was a little disappointed to find that neither was true, though the water was well over the door-sill, and swept inward in a long wave which slapped at the far wall when they let themselves in. All three of the occupants had acquired camp-beds, nobody knew how; and all three of them were very much asleep still, and clear of the water by inches. Jim left Teddy to shake them awake, sent Peterson after the officers, and himself splashed through into the kitchen, whence he could reach the back stairs and the family. Baartjen's cat was in a basket in the kitchen, with three fortnight-old kittens; she would never forgive him if he forgot Geertje.

He was rather surprised to find Arthur Clure at his heels. Never until now had the little man been among the first to spring into action where there had been no time for specific orders; but he was glad to have him, for there was a lot to be done. The water was now rising rapidly, and had begun to lap along the brick walls of the passages with an unpleasant sound. In the kitchen the cat was afloat in her basket, and rearing uneasily with a kitten in her mouth, afraid to risk a jump with it. Her paws were wet, and she was very frightened. When Jim picked up the basket and carried it to the staircase she dropped the kitten, swore at him viciously, and took a piece out of his hand with a sweep of her claws. He swore back, but abstractedly, and set her down high and dry, turning back to try and assess priorities in a hurry. The family were all upstairs, and themselves safe; but without food they wouldn't enjoy their isolation, or without water, or the means of cooking. Clure had snatched up a paraffin stove, which was not a bad beginning, and was hefting it halfway up the stairs to join the cat. Jim added a large can of oil, and besought him to make sure of reaching the drinking-water tap now, for it was set low, and would disappear early. The food could wait five minutes, for the larder shelves would not go under yet. He took the cat upstairs with him, and went to wake Mynheer and Mevrouw Van Donck. It was not yet even beginning to lighten towards morning, and the silence was profound; no wonder they had slept through it. Only in the front rooms of the first storey was there the beginning of a confused activity now, where doubtless Harben and his flock were rolling out of bed and groping for their boots.

At the last moment Jim felt the need of a few words of Dutch, but even the translation for "water" or "flood" was a mystery to him. It was going to be poor business shaking a husband and wife out of bed without so much as a sentence of explanation that they could understand. But he had forgotten that to them the Rhine was a natural enemy, not this year only, but every year, that always at this season they kept their anxious eyes upon the winter dyke and the water level, and stood ready to go to war. It needed only a shake of the farmer's shoulder, and a gesture towards the window, and the man was out of bed, padding across to see the damage for himself, perfectly comprehending all but the details. The woman, too, sat up in bed, pushing back her two long plaits of greying hair, and holding the quilt up to the breast of her nightdress as if to stanch a new wound. Jim left them, and began to carry up to the landing all that might be most useful from below, even to rope, which he found in the scullery. Clure had already done well, and the mound on the landing was growing considerably; and presently Mevrouw Van Donck appeared in her dressing-gown and began to take much of it on into the bedroom. Cornelia's doll, which was old, featureless, hairless but beloved, sat on top of the pile like Dido upon her pyre, and looked upon the bustle with the calm of hopelessness.

Van Donck came down in oilskins and waders, and plunged away along the brick passage where the water came halfway up his thighs now, and was still rising. A faint, soiled light began to filter through the windows, and helped them to see their way about without torches, and they knew, even before Baird and Grenfell and Chatterton came wading along to help and incontinently said it for them, that it was high time to abandon the ground floor. It was precious little that was salvable there now. They had done all they could do. As for the stock, Alcombe would be doing what he could about that, and he was a knowledgeable man who had had dealings with cattle in his time; and certainly that was where Van Donck had gone, though whether afoot or floating they had not stopped to think. He knew what he was about; they had better draw breath and think of their own next move.

Harben came along the passage from the hall and the front

stairs with a distinct bow wave washing before him; and every one of them remarked inwardly how characteristic it was of the Major to sport, at this juncture, not only a paratrooper's camouflage smock, but a pair of thigh-boots into the bargain.

"The appropriate order, I suppose," he said drily, "would be abandon ship. I'm inclined to shorten it to scram. Sergeant, how do we get out of here? Or do we? You've navigated it once. Can we wade back?"

"I wouldn't risk it, sir. We can float the kitchen table; it's big and solid. But even then we couldn't risk taking more than four aboard."

"How are things down there? Everybody all right? All in cover?"

"Yes, sir, right as rain. No need to come down unless you want to. All the stuff's high and dry now, and the lofts are good."

"Which means you'd prefer I stayed out of it."

"Perhaps if I might go down——" suggested Baird eagerly.

"All right, carry on. Take the Sergeant here, and two of the others—take Peterson and Mason. The rest of you, beat it back up the stairs before you drown. We'll be taken off by amphibians before the day's out, I expect."

Baird, when they had the broad windows open upon the flood, and the inverted table halfway through, suffered some qualms about its seaworthiness. The waste of rising water under the cold grey dawnlight stretched now as far as they could see, a mud-coloured floor from which the trees and bushes rose bare and black.

"I won't pretend I like it, Sergeant, I've never done anything like this. Can we really use this thing as a raft?"

"Why not? I've crossed flood-water in worse boats than this in the Sheel valley, and this is as flat as a mill-pond."

"You probably know. My education was neglected. All right, let her go.

She went, dropping with a flat plash into the water, and wallowing gently as she lay. Armed with broomsticks, shovels, curtain-poles, anything that could be used to propel their craft, they climbed aboard and pushed off. As they poled away from the house they heard for the first time the shrill voices of the children chattering excitedly upstairs; and when they were about twenty yards away Jim heard his name called, and looked up to see Baartjen hanging out of the bedroom window in her nightdress, holding up one of the kittens in her palms in a way which must have caused as acute terror to Geertje as ever the flood water had done. She screamed thanks and anxiety together in a torrent of words, waving to him until her mother dragged her away. He waved back, and laughed, for she was a funny little figure; but in the same moment it came upon him that this was no laughing matter. It was easy enough for the Midshires, vagrants with nothing to lose, humping their kit from one hole in the ground to another, to see the novelty and the funny side of this; even when they were wet through and cold, bumping unevenly about the yard on an upturned table propelled with curtain-poles could seem funny to them. They had been more often wet than dry during the past month, so that was nothing new; and they had no stock to worry about, no men out, only a lot of surplus energy glad to find a new outlet. But to the farmer this was much more than the possible loss of all his remaining stock, the certain loss of some, the spoiling of his premises; for this was tidal water, whose salt caress would leave the soil soured even after it subsided, and make future harvests meagre even with unsparing labour. It would undo all the toil that had been put into the land in past years, and make the future unprofitable for at least an equal term. The children would find that out, because of their parents' faces when they sat waiting after what could be done was done. Baartjen, he thought, knew it now in her heart, for she was already half a woman. He was all the more glad that the child in her need not, at least, be bereaved of three kittens and a cat.

They rode strangely down the yard towards the barns, heaving gently upon a surface in which no current, no impulse of any kind, seemed to exist. The by-waters of the Sheel in flood had been, as he remembered them, less quiescent than this, for broken as they were, the Lek dykes withheld a great part of the ruinous force within. He had seen pack-ice from the Welsh mountains come clanging down the Sheel in the first thaws of February, and swing outward over the football field, jostling in corners until fresh miniature floes swirled after and butted them back into the stream; all the new shallows, like the river itself, alive with malevolent energy. But here the flood water, like the land it covered, was flat, uniform and quiet, a dull plain of grey, its only voice that whispering among bushes and mild slapping against walls which they had noticed in the dark. Grudging daylight made visible the desolation which had come upon the world. All the colours were monotones, the clouded sky a void of dirty white, the watery earth a darker, muddier reflection of it, the trees rigid black skeletons casting no mirror image in that opaque surface. They could not see the roofs of the village from here, but they knew it must be deeper under water than the farmhouse; yet from the passing traffic it should have received earlier warning of the disaster, and made its dispositions accordingly. How far, then, did the flood already extend? They could not begin to guess, though it covered the earth as far as they could see; doubtless a good many unlucky lone wolves, Don Rs and such, were marooned about this stretch of country in trees or minute high points, waiting for rescue. Doubtless, too, there were not wanting drowned bodies, British, Canadian, Dutch together, floating among the brash of boughs and driftwood and poultry and cattle, patiently awaiting burial.

But they had not yet thought of all that. To young Teddy the whole thing was a joke of the elaborate kind his soul loved, and he poled gaily, with more vigour than science, wedging the raft into hedge and outhouse all along the yard, and as cavalierly bullying it out again, until Peterson took the curtain-pole from him and bade him for God's sake sit down and be quiet before he had them over. He sat down, but was not quiet. He treated them to all manner of nautical nonsense which would have driven Claes crazy with joy, and ended with "A Life on the Ocean Wave", with verbal variations attributed to the Royal Marines themselves, as they drew in close to the old stable. From the lofts of the two barns men of the company looked out and hailed them. A few had taken to the water, and in queerer craft than their table, too, stable doors taken off their hinges, planks, benches, anything that came to hand and would float. Van Donck had obviously risked the journey afoot, and was now wading steadily out from the cow-house leading a milch cow by the horn, with the water up to his waist, and his oilskin coat spread out blackly behind. She went where he led her docilely enough, though the ramp Alcombe had rigged to the loft-door of the stable was steep and difficult, and wobbled under her weight. Some rapid work had been done there to get it rigged at all, but the very long trestle tables which had been installed as sleeping-benches had come in useful, and there was no lack of rope. Van Donck pulling and an assistant pushing could get most cows up that slope. Yes, they'd done well; as well as they could do, there would still be more loss than enough.

Those who were established in the lofts had spent their time stowing the kit, making tea, and rigging knotted ropes by which the mariners could pass in and out. Baird went up as nimbly as a monkey, and was helped in at the door by a dozen willing hands.

"Now what?" asked Teddy, seeing that Jim made no effort to follow.

"Fancy a bit of cow-punching? We can't get much wetter."

"Don't mind if I do. But I don't know much about it." That was a thing he would never have said a few months ago, and Jim could not forbear smiling at it.

"That's all right. Neither do I. You take it steady, and they'll do the same."

They eased themselves down gingerly into the cold water, shivering at the touch of it in their loins, and went to help Van Donck and Alcombe. The cow-houses were half empty by now, for the calves had been carried away first, and the nursing cows had followed their offspring, bawling. Peterson was good at this; his big, easy touch roused no alarm in the mild brown bosoms, and his deep voice elicited soft complaints from them, as if they confided in him as they waded forth. Between them they helped to empty the remainder of the stalls, and coax the anxious cattle up the waving ramp, where two more of A Company received them into a pungent, steaming dimness fragrant with hay and hides and breath. All the Midshire farmers had reverted to type overnight. Courthope had been head cowman on a big dairy farm once; Pritchard had had a small-holding of his own. These two were milking again, as if they had never left the land for the Army. Yes, Van Donck had good reason to be satisfied with his lodgers. He might easily have had a unit of colliers or engineers, instead of a fragment of a battalion of an agricultural county regiment called up almost exclusively from the barn and the byre.

But his anxieties did not end with the cows. Morgan had come in astride a hen-house door, with a draggled sheep-dog between his knees and three coops balanced behind, and was understood to have gone back in search of more strays, but it was doubtful if any more of the poultry remained alive. As for the stock which had been out in the fields, it was dead loss; why hope for anything else? All they brought back from their voyages by the end of the day was one philosophical despatch rider who had been sitting in a tree for nearly five hours; all they had seen and could not bring back were two dead bodies of men and one horse which had been hobbled at a low level, and drowned early. The comedy was becoming less apparent, the tragedy clearer, with every moment that passed.

Early in the evening the kitchen table, which had proved easily the most navigable of their various craft, made its last trip back to the house with Mynheer Van Donck and Second-Lieutenant Baird. They had done all it was possible to do; they proposed now to bed down for the night. Jim and Tyndall poled them over, in order to take back the raft, which they would certainly need again in the early morning, having made themselves responsible for the cattle. Also Jim wanted to be sure that the children were all right; he expressed it so to himself, and indeed he was concerned for them all, but it was of Baartjen he was thinking. And it was of him she had been thinking all day, for as soon as he climbed up after the others and set foot in the bedroom she flew at him with her arms outspread, and hugged him, and would not let go. Geertje was sitting up superbly in her dried and re-lined basket, placidly licking her kittens asleep as if nothing in the world had happened. Baartjen confronted her severely with Jim's scratched knuckles, and she blinked, yawned, and looked coldly through them, denying all knowledge of the crime. Cornelia was discovering and exploiting the malleable nature of Major Harben; in a day or so he would be doing her will as meekly as any of the other ranks. Claes had been a shipwrecked sailor all day, and all that spoiled the occasion for him was that his mother would not let him emulate the Midshires, and embark upon the waters. All was very well with these two. Only the woman, having done all she could think of to do, sat now with her hands idle in her lap, and her eyes fixed upon the grey waste dimpling and rising languidly outside the window; and her face was drained and still, tired almost beyond sadness, for what she saw was the ancestral enemy in triumph, and all her own work undone.

When Jim left, Baartjen came to the window with him; and looking down at her as he sat astride the sill, he saw something of this same look in her face. She leaned her cheek against his arm, and stared at the water. She talked to him freely in Dutch, as she always did, not forgetful of his shortcomings in the matter of languages, but as a child will talk unintelligibly to a grown-up it can trust, satisfied with the response of touch and sympathy and affection, where literal understanding has become unimportant. But in the middle of this she suddenly turned to him fully, and began to try to express something to him, something for which only precise and vehement words were adequate. It was then that he fell short. He knew she was trying to tell him what the flood meant to them, but it was no longer enough that he should see that. She shook her head and lowered her eyes, and hugged him again more fiercely, because there was a lack between them; but he could not make up to her for the separation, nor she to him. There was no help for it. The child was his, but not the woman; with her he would have to make laborious logical contacts, like ordinary people, instead of taking her into his heart and walking into hers. Poor little Baartjen! Hers was the common disease of the eldest daughter and the eldest son in this new European civilisation, where they must become men and women at ten years old, and soldiers, perhaps, at thirteen or fourteen. Nothing he could do would ever be able to arrest that sadness in her eyes which was the mirror of her mother's sorrow. Not all the Allied armies between them could do it. They might set Europe free at last, but they could not give back to Baartjen and her kind their fleeting, ravished childhood.

He kissed her on the forehead; it was the first time he had ever done so, and she was smooth and cold to his lips, and held to him, trembling as if for her own loss. Then he slid down the rope, and poled himself back to the warmth and congestion of the barn, there at last to strip off his clothes and dry them at the stove. Rolled in a blanket among the clean straw, he lay listening to the buzz of voices round him, and fell asleep at last with Baartjen's gentle alien chatter in his ears and her wan face before his eyes.

4

They were taken off next day. Jim awoke early, the chill air disturbing him, and put on his clothes, and looked out over the floods. The night was frosty, and there was a moon, fantastically sharp and clear above the level water, transmuting to silver what by day was muddy grey. Given frost enough, every shallow would be passable afoot, but as yet there were only frilled edgings of ice along the margins of the land. He was sure they would not be left here, not because the actual conditions were much better elsewhere, but because it was uneconomical to have to supply a village so remote by water transport. They would be taken off and dumped somewhere else, maybe back eastward into the line at some spot where they could be more easily reached even if boats were still necessary, or maybe into Nijmegen for a spell before they were thrown back into the mud. Just as surely he felt that the Van Doncks, if they were given any choice, would elect to stay where they were; but it was by no means certain that they would be given any choice. They would be an embarrassment to the British if they stayed, for no one could any longer be responsible to himself alone even for his own misfortunes. They would be in the way, and they would be shipped out of it, back to the rear where they would be safe. But they would be resigned, not grateful.

In mid morning the expected happened, and the queer flotilla of amphibians, sighted first as dark sled-shapes slithering through the water some distance away, came nosing with difficulty along lanes only distinguishable by the trees that bordered them at regular intervals. Buffaloes, Ducks, Weasels, half of Noah's ark lumbered and swam into the farmyard, and assault boats with them. The men in the lofts cheered, for though the affair was still novel they were already growing sick of their close quarters, and another aspect of the comedy would be more than welcome. Moreover, their positions had grown more precarious during the night, for the water was only three feet below the loft level at dawn, though it had not seemed to gain any height since, and was possibly now at its worst. Their spirits, which had been high throughout, became uproarious at this happy outcome, and the nautical joke, which had been worked hard for a whole day but was to last them for many weeks before they were rid of it, blazed up again with renewed zest. Shouts of: "Ship ahoy!" and: "Sail on the starboard bow!" began to issue like missiles from the lofts, over the heads of the grinning crews. An officer in the foremost Duck looked up along the row of faces, and selecting Jim as the first sergeant he saw, called out: "Where's your C.O.?"

"At the house, sir. Take the left side of the building, or you may get stuck. There's a good window that side."

"O.K. if you know your way round, drop aboard and take us straight to it."

Jim swung out by the rope, and stepped aboard as they came alongside. There was a civilian there besides the two officers, a middle-aged man, probably brought along from the village to translate to the Van Doncks. He seemed to be a man of some authority, which was why he was being used to sanction military orders.

"How'd you get on here?" asked the officer. "Lose anybody?"

"No, sir. Acquired one. A Don R who got cut off between dykes. We found him up a tree.

"Hm! Did better than most of us then. This'll happen again

and again now, of course. Won't stop us, though, and will stop them coming back, but they haven't realised that yet. What's the family like here?"

"Sizeable, sir. Farmer and his wife, three kids and an old lady—the wife's mother. They didn't move for the Germans; they won't want to go now."

"Not much choice, poor devils. Now, where's your window?"

"Bear left! There! It's about the only clean turn, clear of the trees. There's the C.O. now, sir, at the window."

Major Harben was sitting on the sill. The lower windows of the house had disappeared altogether, and the level of the water must, Jim calculated, be about eighteen inches short of the floor of the bedroom; but the Major was reading a very ancient magazine with all the singleness of purpose which was his natural gift. As the noise of their engine came round the corner he looked up, and remarked calmly: "Ah, I thought you'd soon be here."

"We'd have made it yesterday, sir," said the engineer officer, "but for the cuffuffle in the village. We were rushed, somewhat. I hope you haven't been inconvenienced?"

"Very comfortable, on the whole, thanks. Coming in?"

The Duck drew in alongside, and was steadied by the sill while the Major gave his visitor a hand in at the window. Jim saw no reason why he should not follow; he wanted to see Baartjen again, and this was the last opportunity he would have. Accordingly he took it upon himself to climb in unobtrusively after the others, since no one seemed to notice or care, and left them to talk business in the Major's room while he slid softly out on to the landing, and called his friend's name. She came instantly, scurrying along the passage from her mother's room with the following light from the end window caught in her bow of pink ribbon. Mevrouw Van Donck came out into the passage and stood to peer at him shortsightedly, and recognise him at last with a smile and a sigh. She was about to go in again when the elderly Dutchman came out from Harben's room and addressed her in a quiet voice. Jim put his arm round Baartjen's shoulders and drew her aside from them; she would know all about it soon enough.

The conversation was brief, and pitched very low, and without understanding it was yet easy to guess what passed. He asked her to bring her husband and come into the Major's room; and in a few moments she did so, and the door closed upon them. Baartjen turned her face up to Jim, and he saw that she knew already. Her eyes were soft and wild with hurt, but she did not say a word nor shed a tear; he had never seen her cry but the once, and never expected to. She let him lead her back to the room where the younger children were, and sat down pliantly in the hollow of his arm there; and her gaze dwelt thoughtfully upon their untroubled greeting of an old friend, but of what was in herself she said no word and made no sign. Even when the father and mother came back and began in silence to hunt out the thickest clothes they could find, she did not complain.

It was the mother who broke the news to them, after a moment of steadying her mind upon the methodical movements of her thin hands among the children's clothes. She looked at her husband, and then began to speak in a measured, sensible voice, making no fuss, commanding them to make none; and Jim knew by their solemn, disturbed little faces the moment when she reached the point.

This was home, they had never been away from it before; it was like suggesting that they should set sail for America. Cornelia began to cry; Claes hesitated whether to follow her example, which was contemptible, being feminine, but contagious none the less. Mevrouw Van Donck shut her eyes for a moment, as if she had reached a precipice over which she was strongly tempted to throw herself. It was then that Baartjen went into action. Her small, cold hand relinquished its hold upon Jim's arm; she crossed the room, picked up Cornelia's doll, and planked it forcefully into her lap. She turned upon Claes with her customary brisk, authoritative tone, demanding some instant errand; and he was surprised into obedience, trotting away with his mouth still open for the first yell of crying which never came. Then she began to fold the clothes her mother had turned out, and put them ready to her hand for packing. Her father, who was rolling up blankets and strapping them together, smiled at her, but she did not smile in return. There was no mourning from her; nevertheless, there had been a death. Practical she knew how to be, but to be more was beyond her. Not once did she seem to make any reference to herself or to anything that was hers, any request or complaint, until Jim had withdrawn unnoticed and was going back softly along the corridor from them; and then he heard her voice, steady and quiet as ever, and Geertje's name passed, and he knew that she was asking if she could take the cat with her into exile.

All but the family were assembled in Harben's room when he re-entered; Harben, Baird, Chatterton, Grenfell, Siward, C.S.M. Groome and his two satellite sergeants, they were all there, and their kit was being hoisted out of the window into the Duck. Clure was there, too, doing more than his share of the heaving. Jim lent him a willing hand, for if there was one thing he wanted more than another just then it was to get the officers off the premises, and have the embarking of the family left to their countryman. It looked as if it was going to work out all right. The officer of Engineers appeared to be in a devil of a hurry, and they must have given the Van Doncks at least half an hour to get their belongings together. The junior officers were sliding over the sill and hopping aboard. Harben turned from conversation with the Dutchman, and prepared to follow them.

"Groome, we're sending back transport for the people here inside half an hour. Will you wait with the interpreter, and see them embarked safely? There's the old woman to look after, of course. Better keep Benison and Clure with you. You other two can come ahead with us."

"Very good, sir."

"Oh, and tell them we're shipping the cattle; they'll be glad of that, at any rate. Probably be beef before long if things get difficult, but at least they'll be paid for."

"Yes, sir. Where are we bound?"

"Oh, back to Nijmegen for the moment. More or less what we expected."

Well, that was true of the whole rotten show, except that they had waited so long for this typical Jerry trick that when it came it had almost grown to be the unexpected. Groome watched the Duck turn heavily and nose its way out and along the farmyard. He blew through his bravo moustaches, and said grimly: "It's a hell of a war!" It was a summing-up with which they could all agree. "Just to give these bastards a few months more for mischief!" said Groome with bitterness, looking at the grey barrens of water. "So help me! They ought to pay cash back on every acre when the settling-up comes, and make good the produce loss for ten years ahead. It'll take all that to put this in condition again."

They sat and waited, and smoked moodily, until the half-hour should pass and the time of departure come. The high spirits which prevailed in the lofts could get no purchase here. The company had the comedy, while these few were shut up with the tragedy.

"What will happen to these people?" asked Jim, turning to the elderly civilian who sat beside him on Harben's bed. "Where will they go? What will be done for them until the flood drops?"

"They will go with the rest of the village, to Nijmegen. After that, maybe stay there, maybe move farther south, I don't know. We shall live——" His shoulders lifted heavily. "—as refugees live. You must have seen for yourself."

"Too damned often! But when the water falls, you'll come back?"

"Yes, we shall come back. It may be a long time."

"And nothing can be done about repairing the dyke, of course, until the flood water has drained off after the fall?"

"Nothing can be done."

"So you just have to sit and wait! That's worse than all the fighting."

"There is this, Sergeant: that if we have not possession of our homes, neither have they. And we shall regain them in time; but *they* never will."

"I hope you're right there. I think you are. But I wish I wasn't so sure," he said bitterly, "that the Germans will do a lot more of this before we're through."

"They will," said Groome flatly, "as long as there's a dyke left they can get at. To slow us up, while it still looks possible; and for spite after they realise it's useless. What they can spoil for the rest of the world they'll spoil, and sleep a bit more content for every extra acre. It's the way they're made."

Clure, looking out from the window, reported: "There's another Duck coming round."

"That's ours, then," He looked at Jim. "You know them best."

"All right, I'll go."

But the Van Donck family also had been listening for that sound. Opening the door, he met them in the corridor, in solemn and pathetic procession, and stood back to let them enter. Mevrouw Coppenol came first, in her customary black, but with a thick coat over her gown, and a cape thrown round her shoulders. Her silver-white hair was smooth as ribbon under a high black bonnet, and she clutched an umbrella firmly under her arm. A lifetime of natural mischief had left her some sparks even at this crisis. She walked like Hecuba from the walls of Troy, heavily, perplexedly, a matriarch torn from her sovereign state without warning; but her old bright eyes roved over the three British soldiers, the Duck, and the two sturdy Canadians who looked in at her smilingly from its well, and something of curiosity and interest, almost of enjoyment, kindled in the faded blue irises. Divorced from responsibility and past much discomfiture with the new and strange, she could afford to enjoy her late adventures. Her daughter, who walked close behind her with a hand at her elbow, had no such comfort. She was quiet, grave and impenetrably unhappy. No one could do anything effective about it, and it would be better not to try. She would give no trouble; she knew what she had to do, and she would do it; but it was hardly fair to ask her to accept any second-rate comfort in the matter. She had the roll of blankets under her arm, and Cornelia's hand in hers. The small girl was still crying in a desultory fashion, having all but cried herself out in the interval; but she kept fast hold of her battered doll, and out of one pocket of the enormous checked woollen coat which almost swallowed her there peeped a rolled-up picture book from which Jim had seen her on occasion reading fairy stories to the doll. Claes had brought his wooden gun along, and clutched it tightly in both mittened hands, but his funny little face was still crumpled and uncertain with the desire to cry; it was doubtful whether even a Duck and a couple of Canadians could give him any happiness today. Mynheer Van Donck carried two large suit-cases with rugs strapped to them, and wore his oilskins over a greatcoat of thick wool. He had always been a very silent man, immersed in doing rather than feeling or thinking, but every action had been bound to this farmstead, and with that balance not even the passage of the Germans had interfered as did the floods now. He was still intent upon actions, the mere mechanical motions of hand and body involved in the carrying of cases, the lifting of children, the marshalling of his family; for by these means, at a pinch, men can live. His life, until he came here again, would be counted out from minute to minute without look-ing ahead; but the small severed roots would be ready to strike again as soon as this soil could receive them. His smooth-shaven face was resigned, not despairing, patient, not wretched; it was a little reassuring to look at him after his wife's motionless pain. But there was a small person bringing up the end of the proces-sion who undid all the good effect, and made them feel like murderers again.

Baartjen had Geertje's basket on one hip, clutched rigidly against her at the full spread of her short arm, for it was gener-ously wide. In her other hand she carried a small attaché case of brown fibre tied up with string, for its catch was broken. She was wrapped up in a very large scarf, and had her woollen cap pulled down low over her forehead and ears, as if to show as little of her face as possible; but the look was her mother's look over again, only sharpened and made more poignant by the young softness of her eyes and the immature lines of her bones, which had never been meant to settle into such an immobility of suffering for many years yet, even if they must come to it at last. She was like a dull glass window, half opaque, with a frantic child pressing her face against the panes from within and trying to see daylight where only twilight could come. No one could get in to her. No one could get her out.

The interpreter told them what he had been instructed to tell them, and reported that they were quite ready. Jim and Groome between them lifted the old lady over the sill, and the heftier of the two Canadians jumped her down as lightly as if she had been one of the children; she was, indeed, so unexpectedly light that the greater part of her bulk must have been clothes.

"There y'are, ma," said her porter, settling her as comfortably as possible. "First-class berth, and no extra charge. Now how about you and me eloping before the rest come aboard?"

He was a personable chap, big, vigorous and full of the devil; she had only to look at him to see as much, and she never missed an opportunity of taking stock of fine young men. The incorrigible light burned up in her old eyes. They were on her favourite tack in a moment, and kept it up until they parted in Nijmegen over an hour later.

"There's life in the old girl yet!" he remarked approvingly as he lifted down the suitcases and stowed them. "Who's next? Come on, young Piet, give us a hold of you!"

"Nicolaes!" said the owner of the name meticulously.

"Nicolaes, then. What about this young lady? Wilhelmina, is it?"

"Cornelia," explained her elder brother, the tension of his face relaxing a little.

"That's a big name for a little person. Here, what's this? Crying? You don't need to cry, honey, we'll take good care of you." Her wet cheek had rested for a second against his grimy one. She scrubbed at the prickle of his stubble of beard, but instantly put her cheek back again, settled her arm round his neck, and was in no hurry to be put down. "You know, you're an outrageous female, that's what you are. You're as bad as your granny. Between the two of you I can see I shall get into trouble."

He had these two smiling in no time, a trifle wanly, but still smiling. But Baartjen's face did not change; her calm and her desperation remained steadfast, and when he offered to take

Geertje from her she held on tightly, and turned her hunted eyes upon Jim. He put his arm round her, and smiled significantly at the Canadian.

"Leave her to me. It's all right, only this one's best left alone just now."

"O.K., you know 'em. How about mother coming first? That might make her feel safer."

Mevrouw Van Donck was lowered to their arms, and her husband followed. To them Baartjen consented to surrender the cat, and then stood shrunk into Jim's arm for a moment in such an agony of reluctance that he thought she was going to break. He was afraid to press her in case he pushed her over the edge of composure, and precipitated what he was trying to avoid. He turned her to him, and nodded to Clure and Groome to embark first.

"Please! She'll be all right in a minute."

They went, leisurely, filling up the struggling pause in a way he appreciated from his heart. The parents, who knew their child better than he did, attempted no comfort, did not call attention to her even by watching her too closely; therefore he followed their lead, only turning her to the window again as soon as it was clear, and making to lift her in his arms, but without forcing her will.

"Ready, Baartjen?"

She answered the tone, nodding dumbly, since there was clearly no help for it. The moment of panic was past; he had felt it recede, leaving her limp and acquiescent. He lifted her down to her father, and lowered himself from the sill after her; and one of the Canadians gave him a hand aboard.

The Duck turned, slewing a long, diagonal, corrugated ripple from its stern. They slid away from the wall of the house with a salutary suddenness, taking no farewell, only hurrying away. It was dangerous, perhaps, but it came out all right. Cornelia had meant to burst into tears again, but had no time for more than a gasp before the big Canadian drew her attention to the way the water ran backwards under their wheels, and the hilarious activities of the Midshires piling kit and men hand over fist into their unaccustomed transport, after the fashion of a middle-school club embarking upon a steamboat trip. Clearly they heard Teddy Mason's voice yelling: "Any more for the *Skylark?* Rahnd the lighthouse, back in time for tea!" Cornelia watched pallidly for a few minutes, but she forgot to cry. Claes, who had stood with his chin on his shoulder, staring back at his abandoned home, could not keep his attention fixed there for long when there was so much going on ahead; and as they slowed among the congestion of traffic and rode waiting for the column to form he folded his arms along the forward edge of the well, and began to watch; and a few of his old friends, notably Peterson, soon spotted him, and began for his edification to act the goat to a dazzling extent, skipping about perilously from fender to fender, pretending to push one another in or to fall in themselves, tripping over things, pantomiming sailors, pirates, fishermen, anything that went with water. They did things Jim couldn't have done without looking a fool, and got away with them triumphantly, which was a gift he envied them. He believed Peterson would have gone the length of falling in in good earnest to get a laugh out of Claes, had not one of Chatterton's youngsters saved him the trouble by going head-over-heels off the fender of a Buffalo by sheer accident.

It was beautifully timed, and the process of fishing him out was almost funnier than his flashing descent. Claes was not proof against it. He gave a thin little shriek of laughter, which fixed Cornelia's attention just in time for the hilarious rescue. She began to laugh in her turn, and for them the worst was already over. A return to grief is never quite the same thing as the first lost frenzy. Even the old grandmother, encouraged by the Canadian, was taking a lively interest in the scene; if there was one thing she enjoyed better than the company of one high-spirited young man, it was the contemplation of a lot of them together.

Everyone left Baartjen alone. Her parents knew better than to do anything else, and the rest were taking their cue from them. Groome, through the interpreter, was trying to get the parents to talk, but with no more success than elicited answers to questions and yet gave no lead for further conversation. However, he persisted, bothersome as it might be to them, rightly supposing that a minor counter-irritant might have its uses. Clure sat rather sadly watching them, but said nothing. That one night in their grievous company had done him no good; struggling with concrete troubles might stimulate Morgan into forgetting abstract ones, but it only overwhelmed Clure, enmeshing his diffident good will in strangling threads of inarticulacy and helplessness. Reality was too much for him, always had been, always would be. Jim, catching sight of the dispirited droop of his face, felt again that uneasiness over him which had bothered him ever since Arnhem in an aggravated degree,

215

and had been at the back of his mind ever since he had known him. But he dared not entertain it now. Clure was a long-term responsibility. With Baartjen it was now or never.

He could hardly complain that he didn't know what to do about her; the thing to do was clearly nothing, but the difficulty was to do it. There can be nothing much harder than to see someone of whom you have grown fond struggling with a trouble you perfectly understand, and yet to stand by without interfering; especially when you will certainly be separated from your friend within a day, and in all probability never see her again. It's hard to get over the idea that you have to do something yourself about every such trouble, in a world which is full of them, and few of them with anything to gain from you. But he was past that, too. He stood near to her, looking back with her at the house; and though he did not touch her, nor watch her too closely, his vision was infected to some degree by her reflected passion. How long before she saw it again? Six months? It sounds little enough, but it is a lifetime to a child, and within this stony miniature woman there was a child. She was cursed every way, not old enough to be philosophical about it, not young enough to forget; of strong, sensitive, immoderate affection, but compressed within rigid walls of duty. "Baartjen, look after the little ones. Don't let them out of your sight." "Baartjen, keep Cornelia away from the soldiers." "Baartjen, help your mother." "Baartjen, do this for me." "Baartjen, keep your eye on that for me." At eight years old she had known danger, and labour, and oppression, all the things she should not have known, and it was too late to go back on any of them.

She did not look round when the uproar of Robens' rescue broke out, not even Cornelia's shrill laughter brought her attention away from her lost home. The column formed and moved off, and all the effect it had upon her was to make her lean out and raise herself forward upon her hands, straining after the red roof as long as she could see it; and when it was lost to sight, and her eyes could find in that retrospect only the long column of amphibians making arrowhead patterns upon the water, she turned away and stood staring sidelong across the grey, cold floods, no longer noticing anything at all. After a while she seemed to become aware of Jim, and showed it by a slight movement of her head towards him. He remained still; and presently she moved closer, and settled her thin shoulder into the hollow of his arm and side. He was encouraged, and let his arm go round her shoulders as it had always done quite naturally when she made this gesture. She, upon whom events had leaned so early and so heavily, had a way of leaning hard into his side sometimes, that sharp little bone snugly pressed home, half of her slight weight hanging upon him confidently. She did so now, and he was glad; but she did not talk Dutch to him any more. To the person she was now it was a matter of importance that he would not understand.

It took them just over an hour to get back to Nijmegen. Part of the journey they covered upon higher ground, part by narrow roads along the crests of the dykes, several stretches afloat upon brown lagoons; but as they drew nearer to the town the level of the land rose clear, and the floods were left behind. The ghostly trees, lean and leafless as they were, looked instantly more substantial; the flat uplands with their ruled plantations were almost beautiful. The younger children, who had made this journey only once or twice in their short lives, and never by so exciting a method, were chattering together shrilly in front, and had almost forgotten that this was anything but a holiday. The Canadian was calling Mevrouw Coppenol "sweetheart" and getting away with it. He was also understood to say to anyone who cared to listen that she was a game old girl, and he hoped he'd have as much devilment left in him when he was going on for eighty. A curious patchwork happiness, not enduring but warm while it lasted, possessed half of the family; the other half were still in the position of having to get along without it, and would continue so.

Baartjen came out of her trance for the old inescapable reason, because she had to, and the time was now. She looked round her slowly, and sighed; her eyes met his at length, and he saw the child looking out at him from her prison. He thought she would not live long; he was certain she would never get out again.

They passed by a railway bridge, along the wall of which on one side had been splashed in white paint in letters a foot high: *"Wir kommen wieder!"* He pointed it out to her, though she could hardly have missed it. "We shall come back!" The Germans had left that message behind, but it should have something else to say to her just now. She said it over to herself soundlessly, and then aloud, and looked almost startled at the sound.

"Wir kommen wieder! Wir kommen wieder!"

"You will come back, Baartjen. You know that, don't you?"

"Ja! Wir kommen wieder!" she said again, suddenly, passion-

ately, a flame out of her lips; and she sighed, and drew breath, and stretched herself up to be taller against him. That was all there was, and it was so inadequate that he could not bear to look at it, and add nothing, but there was no gain in longing to deliver her, when she could not be delivered. When he parted from her at last, at the door of a house in the old part of the town, requisitioned now for relief work, nothing more had passed between them. It was just: "Good-bye, Baartjen!" and again her smooth, cold forehead under his lips, and a murmur of farewell in return; but at the last moment she put her arms round him with a sudden gasp, and for an instant he had the child upon his heart again. Then she was gone, hurrying after her parents into the doorway, the ends of her scarf whisking out of sight.

So that was over. If she stayed there long he might see her again, but there was no relying upon it. He might as well accept it now, and be satisfied, that she was merely one more echo in his mind, sounding on and on like all the rest, diminuendo along his memory long after she had passed out of his life. There were so many echoes, they set one another off in a ceaseless chain, as men touch and deflect one another in the business of living, sending a succession of consequences eddying through time, to end no one knows where. "We shall come back!" It was not new. He had said it himself more than two years ago, making the promise to Miriam who had herself been two years dead; and he had borrowed it then from her lips, repeating the promise she had made to the Germans on his behalf. He had made good her word, but that was not an ending. What her hands had set in motion could not be arrested. It has passed through him and into Baartjen, by a strange contagion, by a human laying-on of hands; and it would go on as all inspired things go on, flashing from heart to heart and impulse to impulse, the influence of one mind upon another, the impact of man upon man, world without end for all he could see. It might weaken in time, as spread ripples slacken and become feeble when the outer impetus flags; but he felt that it would yet outlast him, and everything he knew.

He went back to his platoon very soberly, surprised to find how weary he was.

"Well, seen your sweetheart off?" asked Groome, meeting him in the jostling congestion of a narrow cobbled street already half blocked with German scrap.

"Yes. Anyhow, they're on dry ground and under cover."

"Yes." But it seemed to occur him that there was more to it

than that. "Poor little devil!" he said, and pulled himself up as if he had been guilty of eloquence.

Jim let it go at that. It was just as legitimate a way of looking at it, and maybe no worse expressed in the long run; and it was infinitely simpler.

5

Three days later the Midshires were put back into the same old mud from which they had been taken and wiped clean; and the watery round began again. They were not actually in the water this time, but holding a position on a slightly raised plateau of immature pine plantation in the unpopular swamp between the rivers, which was already becoming notorious as "the island". They could be supplied only by water, they could be moved only by water; their patrols were affairs of assault craft, and certain individualists among them took to the sniper's life wherever there were evergreens to afford them cover, sitting up trees like stylites for a day at a time. It was not, at best, an active life. There were occasional adventurous voyages towards the junction of the rivers, from which they did not always emerge scatheless; there were minor brushes at long distance, where the rifle came into its own; but by and large it was a sedentary way of fighting wars. The joke, worn out in a week, was soon being used as a counter-irritant with no less vigour; they had to let off steam somehow. It reached the point where Colonel Friedland himself, sloshing along ankle-deep in water and slime, got: "Ay, ay, sir!" by mistake as often as: "Very good, sir!" and seemed to like it every bit as well. He even appeared to do what he could to contribute to it, with his waders and his fisherman's jersey, and that incredible padded leather coat he wore, the whole get-up making him more like Falstaff than ever, but Falstaff with a salt flavour. The watchword these days was: "Look out, here comes the Rear-Admiral!" and the old man knew it as well as anyone, and they suspected he liked it.

Theirs had become by mid December the dead-end front, compounded of mud and missiles, where they sat on their hinder ends in mucky slit trenches, and made themselves dug-outs among the half-grown pines. They heard of action, but they themselves were fixed as with glue by this all-pervading slime, the colour of brownish clay and the consistency of dirty lubricating oil. They were sitting in it drinking tea when the first news reached them of Rundstedt's counter-attack in the Ardennes, the push that was to sweep through Houffalize, Laroche, St. Hubert, Ciney and Celles before Christmas Day, bringing the German armour within four miles of Dinant on the Meuse, and only thirty from the ill-omened town of Sedan. There was an echo nobody wanted to hear, and they dwelt anxiously upon the news day by day, names of places they had never seen passing between them familiarly as the worn-out year declined. They noted the abandonment of St. Vith, the recapture of Echternach, the relief of Bastogne, all the fluctuations of the forty-mile salient. But what they felt was never more than anxiety. If anything, they had expected the counter-attack earlier, and had reasoned that somewhere behind the lines reserves must have been massing for some time, and a considerable armoured component among them. It wasn't to be expected, it never had been expected, that they would walk up to the Siegfried Line and into Germany without a determined resistance being flung in their path. It just happened to be the Yanks who were getting the hammering; it could as easily have been themselves. It might be bad while it lasted, but it would be accounted for. Still, they watched progress, and made no short-term calculations and no forecasts.

The trouble the U.S. 1st Army was having with Rundstedt was not the Midshires' main trouble. There were others too near and nagging to be lost; discomfort and inaction and mud between them made ready the ground by fraying their nerves and shortening their tempers. Christmas, though the separation had not been long, brought in too constant thoughts of their families and homes; for the flying bomb, the ugly traces of which they had seen for themselves near Amiens, had given place to a new and aggravated horror, the V.2 rocket projectile. Jim had never heard one word of it from Imogen; a newspaper posted on to him by his mother in Caldington gave him the first information of what had been going on in London, and the jolt it delivered made him feel physically sick. Just as they were getting V.1 out of commission and raking out the last bases from which it could be launched, here came this new and worse thing, from a greater distance, giving no warning at all, simply the impact, and good-night. And Imogen, who would be busy again in the thick of it, had never said a word. That troubled him with a hurt he did not recognise as jealousy. Why should she keep back any part of her own danger or anxiety from him? She had not always done so. True, she had never dwelt upon it, for that was not her way, but there had been no such deliberate silence as this. He reflected honestly that his letters to her had never been communicative, and the only stresses he had ever recounted to her were those which were well past; but that was because she loved him. Knowing that, how could he tamper with her peace of mind? And yet—was this her reply, now that she knew beyond question he loved her in return? And was this frustrated hurt what she had been feeling for his reticence all this time? Precious little good he had done for her if it was!

He wrote and taxed her with it. Her reply came just in time for Christmas, together with a supply of cigarettes and a khaki sweater hand-knitted in an elaborate cable-pattern; and characteristically most of her letter was concerned with the sweater rather than the rockets, or any complaint of his.

"There are at least four places at the back and two at the front where the pattern's gone wrong, but if I'd bothered to unpick it and try to put it right you wouldn't have got it for some time, and I gather it's cold round your part of the world. Besides, you'd expect at least five mistakes in any sweater I knitted. I hope to goodness it fits. It ought to, after all the trouble I took getting your measurements from your old working one, and adding on inches for width across the shoulders. Because in spite of not having an ounce of flesh on you, you're just about double the breadth you used to be.

"I saw Mrs. Clure again this week, she came along to the flat with me. She is pretty, just as pretty as you said she was. I like her, but I don't honestly think I could live with her, it would be too wearing. I think she must have been raised to a sort of domesticated uselessness. You know, she can cook, and sew, and look after a house all right—which is more than I can, at that!—but she hasn't an idea beside. All she reads is the more refined love stuff from the libraries, and she seems to me to have rolled all the heroes out of 'em together to make up her husband. She adores him, and honestly thinks him wonderful; I swear she tells him so, too, in every letter, and unloads all her troubles on him. Not that she's a bit selfish, and she's very loyal; but she just thinks he's the infallible cure for everything. But this is no use to you, I know. If he needs news, you can safely tell him she's very well, and all that, and I'm seeing her pretty regularly. It wouldn't be any good telling him she's brave and cheerful, because it's certain she'll have told him the opposite. But anyhow she's alive and well, and that's something these days.

"And now what's your worry? I thought you knew about the beastly rockets, and anyhow, what's the good of writing to say I'm worried? Who isn't? The whole thing's so definite, you see. Either you're alive at the end of the day, or you're not, and either way there's nothing you can do about it. I didn't set out to protect you at all, or not consciously, at any rate. I just don't think of them myself, except when I'm on duty, or when I hear one hit and go off somewhere around the town; and that isn't half so often as shells go off around you, and I don't hear much about those. I suppose you take them for granted; well, I'm getting almost that way about rockets.

"We have been pretty busy. They do an awful amount of damage, and the casualties are bad, but the heavy rescue men get the worst of it. It isn't in the least like the blitz, when we went crashing about through all the stuff that was falling. This is just an explosion without warning. We're no more in it than the public are. Shelters don't count. Every next one may be miles away; so you see there's no point in the world in worrying over risks that can't even be calculated.

"I'm glad leave starts in the New Year. I hope you and Mr. Clure will both strike oil. I suppose it's no use asking you to rig the ballot?"

So wrote Imogen, with a directness which he was bound to accept, but without comfort for him. How could she expect him to take it as benefit that her chance of death should be ever present and incontestable, not an adversary you could forecast and cheat, and breathe again, but always there, equally divided over the whole of the twenty-four hours, and at no time to be assessed by any feat of intellect? But the thing was there, and from her point of view she was right to try and turn it into something which had to be taken for granted. It was her job; had it been his instead he could have borne it.

Preoccupied with his own troubles, he almost lost sight of Clure for a couple of days; but on Christmas Day he was shaken sharply out of his personal depression and back to his responsibilities. They had made a sticky little advance eastward that day, to straighten out a dent from their line; a purely local affair which involved no barrage, and lasted them the better half of the day in cold and muddy discomfort after thin, fast-melting snow. They operated in small groups, and there were a number of prisoners, including the crews of two machine-guns which had caused them trouble for several days. Coming back through the battered plantation in early dusk, Jim saw them waiting in a hollow, disarmed and huddled upon the ground, with a solitary private standing over them; and the solitary private was Arthur Clure.

It was a good three hours since he had last seen him, and then he had been moving ahead with Baird; and how and when he had come back there was no guessing. But there he was, and pale as a ghost, his skin stretched over the bones like parchment over a drum, every line standing out like a glistening edge of ivory. It struck Jim forcibly that this was no illusion of the light; not only was Clure suffering under some immediate strain which exaggerated the sharp cut of his face, but also he had certainly lost flesh, must have been losing it gradually for some time. He ought to have noticed it before. Why hadn't he? He'd been too engrossed in his own affairs, stuck in the inescapable mud like all the rest, fretting about Imogen in London instead of about his responsibilities here.

But when had this physical change begun, this increasing frailty and translucence? Along that water-course in the polders by the Lek, most probably, for shock has strange effects. What a fool he'd been not to insist on sending him back to the M.O. then, even if nothing came of it. It would all be evidence, if——
He pulled himself up before the thought went farther, for its logical end was something he preferred not to contemplate, at any rate unless he had to. He sloshed through the slippery tree-lanes, down into the hollow, and Clure heard his steps deviate from the rearward track, and turned to have a quick glance at him; which, seeing he had no fellow, was itself an indiscretion, for they had found themselves up against young but sturdy and fanatical troops here, who would make trouble whenever they could. Some of these prisoners over whom he stood guard were S.S. youths, bitter boys of eighteen or nineteen. Some might have been younger still. One looked no more than fifteen, was almost certainly not above sixteen, for he had not acquired as yet the assurance of his fellows in captivity, and had nothing of their arrogant bearing or defiant confidence. He was slim and undersized, with straight fair hair which hung over his forehead in thin, divided locks, making streaks of unexpectedly clean gold over the mud-stains on his temples. He was ragged, dirty and utterly wretched; also he was hurt, for he nursed his right forearm in a bloody bandage. He was sitting in the mud, crying quietly and continuously, with his eyes closed, and tears oozing from under the lids and making pale furrows down the grime of his cheeks. And somebody, well meaning but ill

informed, had thought it better for Clure to stand and watch this boy by the hour than to take his chance forward among the bullets.

Jim's conscience reminded him of things he should have foreseen and made disposition for. The twilight was full of echoes, all too clear and close for a man to have much chance against them. "He would have been a big boy by now, nearly sixteen. I can never be with young boys, and not keep thinking which one he'd have been like. He was a very fair child."

"I thought you were up with Baird," said Jim. "Who put you on here?"

"He did—Second-Lieutenant Baird. He sent me back with a bunch of prisoners. There are more coming along."

Well, no one could blame Baird; he'd never been told but half a tale. Moreover, he was a reasonable soul who would stand by his sergeant even when his own orders were countermanded, provided the thing was explained to him in a sensible fashion.

"How long have you been here, then?"

"Nearly two hours, Sergeant." He licked his lips, and Jim saw the faint glimmer of drops of sweat upon the upper one.

"Well, I want you below there. Hang on a moment, and I'll get Courthorpe to relieve you here."

It was shutting the door a bit late, of course, but the analogy was not complete; for though the mental effect had been achieved and could not be undone, the physical strain was cumulative, and could at least be cut off here. They left Courthorpe, who hadn't a nerve in him, to contemplate the sorrows of the prisoners, and Jim sent Clure back upon a blameless errand which was almost but not quite fictional, and went to make his own peace with Baird, who was tramping back from the new terrace of foxholes, a large part of the clay excavated from which he carried on his boots. He was content with the outcome of the day's work, and accordingly as approachable as ever; but he was young himself, not complex, and after making repeated concessions against his nature on his sergeant's recommendation, he was liable to suffer a revulsion from so much painstaking subtlety at the wrong moment. In such outbreaks of human impatience he was apt to set out to have things out with people; and to start having this out with Clure would be to drive Clure into agonies of self-questioning and reproachful

224

introspection, to which he was prone enough without being prodded. So Jim was careful.

"Oh, by the way, sir, I borrowed Clure a while back. Courthope relieved him. I hope that's all right."

"The hell you did! After I'd gone to all the trouble to move him back there!"

"Yes, sir, but I wanted him for a nice innocuous jaunt, and I was pretty sure you'd approve."

"Well, I damn well don't! I don't trust all this individual finesse. You just can't treat 'em singly, Benison; it's asking for trouble to try. You only get yourself wound into awful complications of wangling and don't do them any good. It just can't be done."

Jim had been doing it, he sometimes suspected very badly, for over two years, but he didn't argue. In his experience it was impossible to get anywhere with a bunch of men if you did not treat 'em singly, but he admitted to himself that you were lucky if you didn't turn yourself grey in the process.

"No, sir, I know it's a bit precarious, but having started——"

"Come off it!" said Baird, more patiently than the words suggested. "I always know when you're up to something. Oh, it's all right, I know you've usually shown results, and you're welcome to Clure if you want him. But just as a matter of curiosity, what did I do wrong?"

"It's these kids we're finding among the prisoners. When they get down to fifteen- and sixteen-year-olds even the sound ones feel bad about it, but Clure lost a boy who'd have been just going on sixteen now if he'd lived; and in his present state he's liable to brood a bit even without any encouragement. So I took him off the guard."

"Oh! I see!" There was a dubious silence, and then he remarked: "You do get to know things, don't you? But surely it's a bit far-fetched, isn't it? Life's going to be too involved by half if we've got to work out everybody's past history, and arrange for 'em to avoid all unpleasant reminders. It isn't that I object to the principle in the least, but it simply isn't possible in practice."

"No, sir, I know I'm getting off my beat, and it worries me, too. But just give me a blank cheque on this one case, and I'll go gently. Seriously, I think it's well worth trying."

"Oh, all right!" sighed Baird. "I won't interfere. Do it your own way. But I'm no magician; if you want any help from me you'll have to put the request in nice short words I can understand. I'm not very gleg in the uptak', and I haven't time to be."

It was like him, however, that his nice mind did not follow the book of the words to the logical conclusion, and refuse help even if it was asked. He was uneasy about these methods, but he was loyal, and would stand by to the last ditch once he had given his backing. Jim felt the burden lie upon him all the more heavily for this talk, which was not the effect it should have had; for he now had Baird on his back as well as Clure. Suppose he made a mess of it, and dropped them both? It was not a merry Christmas that he spent, in spite of Imogen's pull-over.

Clure would talk sometimes, when there was no one else by. He talked a little that night, but not about the blond German boy who had been marched away with the others to Nijmegen. His main preoccupation was now, as always, his wife, and about her he could speak freely now, for Sergeant Benison's girl was becoming a friend of hers, and the roundabout link thus established held firm between the four of them. They sat beside a small, resinous fire in a fold of the plantation, with a lean-to of fir-branches sheltering them, and fine, drifting snow floating ominously past them upon the wind, hardly visible yet, but soon to cover the mud from sight. They compared notes about the situation at home, and Jim found himself offering for inspection the very intimate fears he suffered on Imogen's account. He had not meant to do it; it had not been in his mind to surrender any precious part of the feeling he had for her; yet he had done it, and the wrench of the resultant pain in him was the first he knew of it. What possessed him? Even to catch the rare fish he was after, did he have to use so extreme a bait? Or was it a gesture rather of repayment than incite-ment? For doubtless what he got out of Clure was just as sacred to him, and honesty demanded that it should be requited. When he talked of Helen you could almost smell the smoke of altar-fires. To admit anxiety for her was only the rim of his trouble, a desperate understatement of something graver by far.

"If I could be there with her," he said over and over. "I wouldn't mind so much. It's just not being there that does me."

"But there's nothing we could do even if we were there. That's the hell of it!"

"I forget sometimes," said the little man grievously, "that it's just as bad for you. I don't mean to, but everything goes

226

out of my head except my own worries. I can't help it. I do try, but I can't. Sergeant—I've been wanting to talk to you about this for a long time, but it's so difficult——"

Jim waited, saying nothing. The pinched face was sharper than ever with the cold, for it had turned frosty; the lagoons would soon be passable afoot if this went on.

"Sergeant, sometimes I don't seem able to keep my mind on what I'm doing at all; it seems to go right away from me. I know that sounds like an excuse, but it's true. I even forget what I am supposed to be doing. It frightens me. I've tried to fix my thoughts on the job, but I don't get on very well. I don't know what to do."

What made him think Sergeant Benison would know what to do, Jim wondered? If that could be answered, he wouldn't be just a sergeant, he'd be a superman. But he did attempt to answer by posing other questions.

"Well, I can't help thinking it's more a physical problem than it seems. I've been worried ever since you were caught up in that terrific barrage with Sloan, that day. I think you should have gone to the M.O. then, and I still think you should go now. If you will, I'll back you with Baird; you'll have no trouble there. Nobody can do his job properly when his balance is upset by the effects of shock. Honestly, are you really well?"

"Yes, I am, really I am! Oh, it isn't that! I'd like to get out of it that way, but I can't. My head was noisy for a few days, but I'm quite fit now."

No, he wouldn't leave himself any loophole there. He wouldn't go to the doctor unless he was sent, and if he was sent he wouldn't admit more than he was admitting now to the sergeant. The strong and confident can afford to ascribe weakness to sickness, but the weak may not; there is always a lingering fear that it may not be true.

"It isn't put off as easily as that. And on top of shock, worry can do all sorts of damage. I think a good many of us are a bit off-balance through sitting here rotting in the mud while this damned V.2 business goes on at home."

"Yes, it makes everything so much worse. But it isn't only that, even. I don't know what it is. Sergeant—I hope it isn't true, but I can't help it coming into my mind sometimes—it's as if my brain was going——"

"It isn't," said Jim almost too quickly, "or you wouldn't be talking about it."

"I don't mean exactly going mad—just losing control of my

227

mind, slackening up on everything. And I'm afraid someday it may really let go, you see." His hands, suddenly knotted together, plied their thin, grimed fingers agonisedly; his eyes, after a spell of wandering, came back to Jim's face and held on there. The truth came out in short sentences like puffs of frosty breath. "It might be in action. Suppose it did happen? It might be almost any day. It might be tomorrow. Suppose I lost touch under fire? It would be desertion—— I should be a deserter! I couldn't bear that. But it might happen. I can't be sure of my mind. And she—Helen——" He stopped upon her name, for it was enough, it was all.

"I know you're not mad," said Jim very slowly, for indeed he hardly knew what he was going to say, what he could say in this extremity, "but I'm just as certain you're not well. And I blame myself for not forcing the issue before. Will you, to satisfy me, go back to the M.O.? It would be a load off my mind if you would."

"I'd like to please you," said Clure, clutching his head, "but I swear that wouldn't help. It's too easy. I might be held back for a long time, and safe, but when I came back it would still be there. It might still happen. No, I daren't do that. It would be hanging over me worse than ever. No, I've got to go on. If I go right ahead it may go away. It's the only way I shall ever get rid of it."

That was as sane a thing as any man ever said. He was right, of course, it was the only way; but the risk was worse now than it would ever be again. Still, to yield to it would be, for him, as bad as the breakage he dreaded.

"Don't, for God's sake," said Jim, "imagine that this has anything to do with courage, or anything like that; it's just a matter of mechanics, the way minds are constructed, and the strains they have to stand. So whatever you do, don't imagine you ought to keep it to yourself. I can't do much about it, but at least I shall be around when you want me. Tell me how it goes on, tell me if it gets worse; and between us we might get it straightened out all right. I know it's your worry, and you shall treat it your way; I won't pull any fast ones on you. But for what it's worth, I'm here. Seems to me we can only go ahead from minute to minute, and do the best we can. And that goes for your wife and Imogen in London, as well as us here."

"It's a great help to me," said Clure, from between his rigid hands, "that Helen has Miss Threlfall to be a companion to her. I want to thank you, Sergeant, and the young lady, too, for being so kind."

"Good lord, do you think it doesn't help me just as much? We can't do much about them ourselves, but at least there are two of 'em. And we ought to be able to weather this between the two of us."

What more could he have said? He wasn't satisfied, but what could he have said? Doing was less important than saying at the moment, but listening was most important of all; and he thought that merely getting the fear itself off his chest had done Clure good. There are terrors, as there are joys, that will not stand inspection. And he thought that before they went to their blankets there was a shade more colour in the wan face, a little less of strain in the eyes, and the voice was less brittle than it had been. Not that he supposed the thing could be finished with by sharing it; he knew it was not so simple as that.

Before he slept the frost had set in in good earnest. There was scarcely any wind, and yet the boughs of the half-grown trees swayed together restlessly with a metallic clangour, and the needles tinkled like the glasses of chandeliers. In a few days the shallower lagoons were solid ice, and the deeper ones covered over sufficiently to bear. Fine hard snow came down grudgingly out of an iron sky, and turned the whole forbidding landscape into a Brueghel winter-piece, leaden-distanced, motionless, wonderful. Then a wind sprang up which cut like a knife, and searched out every corner they hollowed for themselves out of the ground, and every crevice of their clothing. They went into white camouflage overalls, and their new invisibility seemed to emphasise that they were an army of ghosts, put by in this desolate place and there forgotten, never to move again, never to get home again. Only letters joined them to the living.

In this bitter weather the armies on their southern flank fought out to a standstill their battle of the Ardennes bulge. The impetus which had dented their line wore itself out in January, until Laroche and St. Hubert, Houffalize and St. Vith, fell back one by one into the hands of the Allies, and the hollow was ironed out straight. It had not been an enviable job. Theirs was cruel upland country to fight in, enemy weather, and intense pressure of fire against them before they repassed their wintry forests, and left Rundstedt's guns standing frosted behind them like marble monuments under the tinsel trees. But at least they, neighbouring so closely with death, knew and could be glad that they were alive.

Late in January they were moved down, first south, and then south-east of Nijmegen. Though the weather was little improved, and they operated in alternate ice and mud, yet there was a breath of new interest going round which prophesied action. Some said that only the counter-attack in the Ardennes had held up the next move until now, and that further delay was impossible, however reluctant the generals might be to go forward in such filthy conditions. The Midshires as a whole professed no knowledge of what went on behind the scenes, but they caught the strong forward wind which came fresh upon them after four months of stagnation, and the awareness which had faded to a small spark in them was blown back into steady flame. By early February they were sure that the move was imminent. There were infallible signs, regrouping of units, massing of artillery and armour, especially great numbers of Buffaloes, renewed air activity, and a plethora of generals who invariably turned up in time to embarrass struggling columns upon half-submerged roads, more particularly where shell damage had involved copious repair labour and one-way traffic. What might easily be the last push of all was due to start any day; they had expected to find themselves wholly glad at the prospect, but there was a certain reluctance, too, now that it came to the point. They were human, weren't they? Still, it had to be done, and with all their hearts they wanted it by. The sooner begun, the sooner ended.

The battalion was holding positions on a long, wooded eminence overlooking the wide depression of the Rhine valley. There was a road running along below them, a raised road flanked on the far side by sheets of new flood water, for more dykes had been pierced somewhere forward. The river proper was visible only in gleams of continuous silver beyond fields, villages and woods away to their right front, probably as much as ten miles distant; and immediately before them, beyond two or three miles of low-lying fields starred with water, and a few villages, began the dark ridges of the Reichswald, a German state forest of which they knew nothing that was not evil. Air-crews could have told them much more, for its concentration of flak was murderous, and bombers returning from missions over the Ruhr gave it as wide a berth as possible; but for their own part they knew it as a nest of artillery and a warren of strong-points. They considered, justly, that it would be their responsibility to assist in the clearance of these southern reaches of its unpleasant shade; a prospect they did not at all relish. As for the German frontier, it was somewhere down there in the watery lowlands, along the line of villages, and they would need Buffaloes to get to it. It was, in their experience, as good a way of going to war as any.

They considered the lie of the land very seriously, now that it was business again; even the youngsters who would once have taken everything for granted were heard comparing notes about the direction in which the German cities lay, and the nature of the country in between. Jim was walking along the crest of the slope one day with Second-Lieutenant Baird when they saw Teddy Mason, and Pritchard, and Jackman down below them in the garden of a deserted villa, arguing where exactly the Ruhr lay, and swopping the names of Essen, and Mulheim, and Dortmund like a conference of generals. Their conclusions were very largely accurate, and their opinions not unsound.

"The Army's changed," said Baird, as solemnly as if he'd been in it fifty years.

"Yes, sir, so they say!"

"Young Mason's improving a lot. I don't know if you've noticed it, but he's getting over that cocksureness you used to object to. *I* never thought it was much damage myself."

"Yes, he has come on," admitted Jim austerely. It wouldn't do to be too enthusiastic if Baird thought he was making discoveries; it was his lead.

"I suppose you'd create, as Peterson would say, if I suggested he might be nearly ready for a stripe?"

"It's your responsibility, sir. I wouldn't offer an opinion either way without being asked for it."

"I am asking for it," insisted Baird. "Come on, Sergeant, be big about it! Admit you were wrong about our Teddy!"

"Well, sir, I suppose we might do worse. I have noticed he's been much steadier lately; and he did do very well with Sloan's section that time, I've got to allow him that. Yes, I daresay you're right."

"You know darned well I'm right, you old humbug! He was always O.K.; all he needed was a bit of practical experience."

Jim made no defence; it was just as he would have it. There wasn't a man in the platoon could be more valuable to him, properly used, than Teddy Mason; and if Baird liked to cling to the fallacy that Sergeant Benison disliked the kid and had a down on him, well, the result was the same, and no bones broken. Besides, it made Baird feel good to assert the superiority of his judgment now and then, and he deserved his crow.

On the 8th of February the expected offensive began before dawn, with a terrific barrage following on a night-long pasting of the forward areas by successive flights of bombers. The Midshires massed and moved while it was still dark, and were almost blown bodily down the slope by the blast of their own artillery. From the road they were taken aboard Buffaloes, and ferried across the lagoons behind a moving curtain of brown mud and water which waved twenty feet high and more, continually falling and continually renewed with a noise like the tearing of rhinoceros-hide. When they lumbered up out of the shallows on to dry land, or what passed for dry land by their present standards, the wave continued before them in a dull brown heaving of mud, as if the crater of a new volcano seethed and bubbled under their tracks. The din was like a steel curtain that shut every man into a separate, dangerous and chaotic world, for only by bellowing in one another's ears could they have any communication one with another; but it was their own din, and the worlds they inhabited, however forlorn and frightening, were worlds of which they were masters. They sat in their Buffaloes, wallowing along behind the heaving wave of the barrage, counting the minutes as they slid away behind in water and foam, and straining to see their first objective. Smoke generators massed up-wind dispersed a stinging cloud over the landscape ahead. Skeleton trees loomed at them out of the fog and rushed away again behind. The ground rose slightly, so that only here and there in hollow places lurked a few miserable shrunken inches of water in a basin of smooth alluvial slime. Germany was a dark smoke ahead, raddled here and there with the fires the bombers had started. In that invisible frontier village towards which they crept now at diminishing speed half of the dwelling-houses must be flat to the ground after such a pounding. The civilian population would most probably have been evacuated from this zone in haste, maybe as late as the previous day, just as the Dutch had been moved back from the Allied base area. This no-man's-land of smoke and shell-craters was populated only by the men of the opposing armies, and here came the first real clash between them upon German soil.

The frontier village—its name, though it meant nothing to

them then or later, was Erdenlich—had open polders on its Dutch side. The road which ran through the barrier and by the Customs Post could bring in the tanks to advantage, and get a company or two well up in that particular spot, but for the rest it was the usual open order advance for the last half-mile or more. Yet walking across fields as cruelly vulnerable as lidless eyes had never before been quite like this; the smoke covered them, the heaving wave of the barrage proceeded before them. Major Harben held them to a steady, even a slow, walk through this artificial night, and they felt almost safe, as if they had been protected by cloaks of invisibility and garments of immortality. Jim could not remember that they had ever walked into less enemy shell fire than this. Later, when the small arms came into action, it was not so uneven; but the balance was still upon their side.

Nevertheless, it took them three hours to enter Erdenlich, and the rest of the day to clean it up. For one thing they were concerned with effectiveness more than haste just now; but the chief cause of the delay was the quality of the resistance they encountered. The village was strongly held; artillery support might have thinned a little, but the men were there all right, fresh young S.S. troops among them, as vicious as Tasmanian devils and as artful as a wagonload of monkeys. Even as they withdrew house by house they missed not one trick that could harass the advancing enemy. Everything was mined, everything was booby-trapped; even the bodies of the German dead, two days old and still unburied, were made instruments with which to kill the invader. The Midshires lost several men that way, and left behind them, when they passed, warning notices for those who came after: "Lousy with Mines", "Don't Touch the Dead!" It was a habit they had met before, but never so lavishly used as here. The place swarmed with trip wires, tethered decoy animals, small, shallow, mutilating mines; and the men were equally ingenious and equally venomous. They were also very brave, whether from the fanatic devotion they felt to a creed, or mere desperate attachment to a country like other men, no one could be quite sure. They did not all withdraw when their positions became untenable; some barricaded themselves into houses and sniped from windows and roofs until they were winkled out one by one at the point of the bayonet; and they cost the Midshires several valuable lives before it was done, Lieutenant Grenfell's among them.

This was a bad loss, and should not have happened. A section

233

of Grenfell's platoon had been having trouble with a house full of Schultz-Staffeln in a strong position at the end of the village. They had a mortar in the yard, well covered by riflemen, and a machine-gun operating from behind ramparts of rubble in the smashed front room on the first floor, besides several snipers firing from the windows at the sides and rear of the house. Grenfell came trotting along as soon as the hold-up became apparent, and sent up a Piat mortar which effectively silenced the fire from the yard. The machine-gun continued to give trouble for some time, while they picked off with infinite patience every enemy who ventured to show his face; then Baird came along with a handful of his own men, and worked from the windows of the house diagonally opposite until the odds were so reduced that they could come in closer and lob a grenade among the bricks and rafters which held the gun. Down came a shower of masonry and dust, a solitary body and a snow of plaster; and the machine-gun sagged slowly into view, hung balanced for a moment and crashed in the yard below. A few very young German soldiers came out sullenly from the dark oblong of the doorway, raised their hands rigidly to shoulder-level, and gave themselves up. They were by no means broken men. Instructed to run, they condescended to break into a casual double, like athletes saving their strength. Nor were they the last. Adamson was shot dead from a loophole somewhere in the perforated roof as he stood to run his hands over one of the prisoners. The attackers slid into cover again, taking their dead man with them. A fellow who could shoot like that, singling out one of two figures which from his viewpoint must have overlapped, and leaving the other one untouched, was not to be sneezed at. Grenfell tried his German upon the invisible enemy, shouting that to persist was suicide, and for nothing, since the issue was already settled. After a long pause a voice, young and clear, but wavering, answered: "I am hurt. I cannot walk out."

"Crawl, then," said Grenfell, who had dealt with Germans too long to fall so easily.

"I cannot move. I surrender! Only help me!"

"You can show yourself. We will not shoot."

Through one of the gaping holes in the roof an arm and a head slowly come into sight, the hand clawing the dragged weight of the unseen body along behind it. They saw the gleam of his rifle-barrel take the light for a moment.

"Throw down your rifle," said Grenfell, and was instantly

obeyed. "Now stay where you are. We're coming in for you."

Those of Baird's platoon who had good positions on a parallel with the roof of the house held them, and kept the survivor covered while Grenfell and his men went in. Clure, who had the nearest station and very good eyes, could see that the man was in S.S. uniform, and that he was undoubtedly wounded, but whether as gravely as he alleged it was impossible to say. The roof was liable to collapse any moment, to judge by the sway-backed line its red crest made against the smoky sky, and either he was lying among rafters, or in an attic under the roof. Tiles slithered down in a shower as they watched, making the hole bigger, so that Clure was able to identify the moment when another figure, which must be Grenfell, loomed shadowy across the prisoner's body. He saw, too, the movement of the exposed arm, apparently the only remaining sound one, as the German youth pulled out a pistol from under his side, and fired pointblank at the newcomer.

Two of them fired upon him in return, Sergeant Brady from inside the house, Clure from outside; but it was Clure who got him. He gave a convulsive leap that dragged him halfway from his hole, and then fell slack; and the weight of his head and shoulders drew him slowly out until he fell over into the yard below, and crashed there with a sickening sound. But when they got down to him he was not quite dead, though both his legs were broken, and he had two bullets through him and a mortar-splinter embedded in his arm. Grenfell, brought out in his sergeant's arms, was seen to be dead already, shot through the heart. The German boy had made the better job of it.

He was unhappily a mere child, seventeen or so, well grown, and of a temper which marked him as a fanatic, but none the less pitiable now. It took him only ten minutes to die, but it seemed to Clure a long-drawn-out lifetime, for during no one of those minutes did nature see fit to soften the process by taking away his consciousness. His very vitality was enemy to him. He had abominable pain, and did not cease for an instant to throw himself about in torments as much of the mind as the body, threatening, cursing and crying through leaden, twisted lips, in words all the more monstrous because unknown. Clure stood watching him in a fearful fascination, unable to tear himself away; he even drew nearer to the boy he had so horribly destroyed, and the frenzied blue eyes lit upon him, and all the cursing and crying came beating about his head like eagles. He stooped to try and wipe away the sweat that rolled down into the boy's eyes, and with the effort of a dying animal the head was dragged aside out of his reach, and a long, indignant scream came out of the grimacing mouth and transfixed him where he stood. He felt something broken in him, or spilt, as if a vessel full of hot liquid had been shattered, and scalding heat had run down through his body. From that moment he bled his sanity away inwardly, knowing it passed from him, unable to arrest the draining loss, unable to confine it, unable to share any part of the horror which filled him.

Nevertheless, this had been only an incident like any other. They could not afford to dwell upon it. Grenfell's virtues, his cheerfulness, his personal kindness, his common sense, were hustled away into the background, as were the enemy's determination, and cunning, and courage, and treachery; and in due course they were both buried, together with the grim but brief memory of Erdenlich. Not much of a village; not much of a battle compared with some they had known; big losses for the gain of so short a distance, but small for the leap from Holland into Germany. In another day they were through it, and penetrating cautiously into the nearer reaches of the forest; and no man could expect just then to give his mind to anything but the Reichswald and continue to live.

The state forest lay over a range of low, rolling hills which at least lifted them out of the waters of the Rhine, though they found that it had a species of greasy, glutinous black mud all its own. Its roads, and there were plenty of them, had once been readily passable, but were now torn to pieces by bombing and shell fire, so that only tracked vehicles could possibly negotiate them. Its trees had once been handsome and closeset, but were now tattered and chipped, great gaps blown out of their ranks, and the standing trunks stripped of leaf and bough. It had had an evil reputation from the first they had heard of it, and it proved, by the end of the first day, to be worse than they had supposed; but they continued to shove their way through it doggedly, and at night dug in and hung on through crazy medieval counter-attacks which were unlike anything they had known; and in time the frayed aisles and cratered clearings wore away behind them.

The passage of this concentration of discomfort was made largely afoot, because there was no other way. Later, even a day or two later, it would be easy for supporting Infantry to ride in high and dry upon tanks and self-propelled guns, but all the units which forced the first entry had to footslog it gingerly along in the lee of their covering tanks until opposition showed itself, and then go to work on their own with everything they had but their teeth. The Reichswald was already full to bursting with every sort of gun, rocket projector and emplacement, the British and Canadians were pouring in as much again upon their own part, and yet here was a perverse battleground where head and hands and bayonets in the end decided the issue. The undulating uplands with their lavish cover of pines and conifers had been still further complicated by the Allied bombing and shelling; and every crater of the forest seemed to be inhabited by determined and well-armed troops intent on giving the best possible account of themselves even though the whole set of the tide was now against them. Opinion was unanimous that the enemy here fought well, "almost as well as we did". They fell in upon him unawares into shell-holes and dug-outs hidden under pine-branches and the trunks of blasted trees, and in narrow spaces of half-darkness fought him to exhaustion before he would surrender. They shot it out with him through the less damaged thickets from tree to tree, all day and half the night. They emerged suddenly into clearings, and saw him peering at them from the shadows on the other side, and charged at him madly with levelled bayonets; and as often as not he accepted the challenge, and rushed into the open to meet them, and they crashed together with a shattering shock that belonged by rights to the fourteenth century rather than the twentieth. Sometimes they missed his hiding-places and passed him by, and he emerged behind their backs to slash and kill without warning, by which means they lost many good men, and were much delayed in their passage through this horrible place. More and more armour lumbered up to their support, but it was still upon them that the responsibility lay. More and more rocket projectors played their thirty-two-barrelled withering barrage forward among splintered trees and raw black earth reminiscent of the nightmare landscapes of last-war artists. More and more heavies pounded the forward areas to an indiscriminate paste like the primeval slime before creation. But it was still the Infantry who had to go in with their hands at the end of it all, like dogs put to ground after badger, and finish the work in the honeycombed galleries below. And they admitted fervently as they lay round pine-fires in the hollows at night, brewing up the tea, that they did not like the Reichswald, and would be unconscionably glad when they were out of its shadow.

By the 14th they were pausing for breath on its farther edges, looking south-east across gently rolling country towards the Rhine, which seemed now more accessible. Only a few villages and a town or two stood between them and the symbolic frontier. At Erdenlich they had hardly sensed that they had entered Germany; but once on the far side of that swollen expanse of flood water they would know in their bones that the last campaign had begun. However, there was no future in haste, and they could wait. The last few German snipers were being winkled out of the forest; the first ditches and forts and systems of the Siegfried Line had been passed almost without a glance, forming in the end only a part of the multiple tribulation of their lot; and only this belt of land and water which was the Rhine valley lay between them and the softer plains of Münster, a clear path to the enemy's heart. On the eastern front the Russians had crossed the Oder and lay only fifty miles or so from Berlin. It was a race now; the western armies were in the picture after all, and with a firm thrust now would be in at the death. All this the young men had by heart, and to be held almost stationary by repeated counter-attacks, with all the interior trammels of the Siegfried defences still before them, and still this one more symbolic river to cross, was a fretful agony. They fought them off impetuously, creeping forward against the pressure mile by mile; and in a few days the counter-attacks lapsed, and they were able to go ahead steadily.

They passed through an eerie village on the 17th of February, under a damp drapery of white flags hung out from upstairs windows. The decision to display tokens of surrender and await the issue seemed to have been overthrown at the last moment by an instinct of panic, as if the inhabitants had secretly feared that the fate of the villagers of Oradour-sur-Glane awaited them with the entry of the victors. The Midshires had seen the effects of enforced evacuation at Erdenlich, but never before had they come into such a depopulated place as this. There was absolutely no damage; not one window had even been broken by blast. There had been no military installation here, for it could never have been tenable. The people had simply taken fright, snatched up their most prized belongings, and run for their lives, leaving gas-rings still burning under boiling saucepans, letters half written on their open bureaux, beds half made, washing on the line. The white flags must have been prepared in good order the previous evening, for they were heavy with rain, and dripped dispirited tears over the muddy heads of the conquerors as they tramped in; whereas this was a fine drying day, and the shirts on the lines were blowing merrily in a light breeze. The panic had manifested itself in mid morning, and abruptly; and the population could not have gone far, and would doubtless easily be overhauled and sent back home. In the meantime, there was only one person left in the village, and that was a tall, raw-boned woman of middle age, who stood at the gate of a prosperous-looking house at the end of the short street. She wore a bright-patterned handkerchief tied over her head, and high leather boots that came up under her skirt; and she stood there inside the gate, waving her hands as they passed through, and beaming on them as she called out incomprehensible things in a strange language. At first they thought that she was German, and either genuinely anti-Nazi or quite mad; but then they realised that she was Russian, and exceedingly sane. Within that house she had been a slave; now, perhaps for only a short while, she was mistress here. What would become of her if the villagers came back to their homes it was difficult to guess, for Military Government could only protect, not avenge her, and she would find herself still the alien, probably still the servant. Jim had no faith, now that he came to consider it afresh in her case, in the comprehensive nature of Allied Military Government. It existed to maintain order, not to create it, which meant making more use of existing systems than he cared to remember, confirming in office even questionable authority, rather than being left with none. In such a lame reorganisation would this woman and her kind be much better off? She would have a certain amount of protection, but how observant and how effective would it be? She would be able to look forward to ultimate repatriation, but after how long and weary a delay? No one wanted her to run amok among this hated community with a machine-gun; least of all did she want that herself; but a little demonstrative consideration offered to her, a little authority invested in her over a loathed enemy, was no more than her due, and might do a bit of good. He was pretty sure that she would not get it. It occurred to him to be very glad that he wasn't in Military Government himself; a difficult, thankless, unsatisfactory job it must be, full of abuses there was no time to set right, and offering scope for a vision and imagination far beyond human, with only human beings, and overworked and heavily handicapped human beings at that, to be its instruments.

So he thought, and was sorry for it, as they passed by and left her there; and all they could do for her between them was salute her in passing with any and every phrase of English, French or supposed Russian she might understand, and grin, and wave until they were out of sight. Which might help her now, but would do her precious little good hereafter, any more than her good will could help them to an easy passage into Goch, which was their next target.

This bastion town of the Siegfried Line, flanked by strong-points and infested with snipers, proved as tough a nut as they needed at this stage, even after it had received the attention of bombers and artillery for the greater part of one night. It suffered a great deal of damage, but it was not flattened like Erdenlich, for there were concrete emplacements deeply embedded there, and the barrage was perhaps more dispersed. While Scottish troops were attempting the entry of the town itself, the Midshires were deeply involved on the southern out-skirts with a group of heavily manned and armed forts, covered and complicated by snipers' fire from the outlying houses. All they could see of the town was a drift of oily black smoke from the generators which had hidden their advance, and a few tattered limes on their left front, which marked the beginning of the avenue leading into town. The forts were grouped in a triangle, greyish cylindrical hummocks lying squat to the ground, with a fuzz of leafless bushes about them, and their edges fading indefinitely into the smoke. The approach to them was across fields pitted with shell fire, and a slightly higher out-crop of broken ground, stone and clay and furze, behind which they withdrew themselves coyly like hermit crabs into their borrowed refuges. Over this negligible ridge looked slateless roofs and windowless upper storeys of houses, and a garage-roof, from the main road. The central and nearest of the three points, the apex of the triangle, lay lower than the others, a mere mound in the fields; the two more retiring were bigger, and carried almost all the fire-power between them. Neverthe-less, the smallest gave quite enough trouble before B Company broke into it at last; and they had still the main pair to attempt, if possible, before night shut down on them.

A Company had worked round to attack the right-hand fort, and were finding themselves heavily handicapped by machine-gun fire and sniping from the upper storey of the garage, which was of brick and concrete slabs, and had suffered little from the bombing but the loss of its windows and a spattering of splinters.

like flakes of lather, denting its near face. Possessed with urgency, for the dusk was already failing, they scattered singly along the meagre cover they could find, and moved inward to attempt attack simultaneously upon the fort and the garage; but at the last three hundred and fifty yards there was neither hedge nor ditch, tree nor bush, only a flat field and a sagging wire, and then the two surfaces rising obscurely out of a furry dark of bushes, the concrete and steel of the fort on the left, the concrete and brick of the garage on the right, with great black doors, and blank windows above; and beyond, the beginning of another lime avenue, and mountainous rubble, and the first houses of the town.

Within the sunken outer frame of the fort there was at least one mortar, more probably two, doing deadly work. They stood to suffer that all night if they had to dig in there, and yet it seemed impossible to go on in this failing light. They were reluctant to move back, but if wait they must, the waiting would be better done up among the scrub of the ridge. Harben hesitated, looked at the descending light, looked at the subdued, flat light of the concrete wall fading into it, looked at the only hint of cover across the open, a new hedge fifty yards to the right, not above eighteen inches high in shadowy saplings, a mere veil of leafless twigs, but leading straight towards the fence of the garage and the open-ended drive in from the road. He hesitated. The light was still good enough for one gambling throw, but it was good enough for sniping, too, and whoever crawled up that hedgeside might as well cover himself with butter muslin and believe himself invisible. Still, it was all they would get, even by daylight.

"Try it!" said Baird, following his glance.

"All right! But if it fails we'll have to throw our hand in for tonight, and shift back until dawn. Send up a corporal and half a dozen men with a Piat and some grenades. Who knows? Two or three may get there."

Baird sent the first he fell over at that end of the flung line, wishing to God he could go himself; but they'd lost Grenfell, and Chatterton was on his way back to the Casualty Clearing Station on a stretcher at this moment, and Harben was playing safe on platoon commanders as well as sergeants. It was a fair indication of the chances here that he had not left it to Baird's discretion, knowing that when it came to sending his men forward and holding back himself he had none. He sent Corporal Deveril, who was Midland Irish and possessed, usually, of the devil's own luck, and the six men nearest, without reference to who they were, or how suitable, for the case was urgent; and it is doubtful if he even realised until later that Arthur Clure was among them. Jim, for his part, knew nothing of the move until he saw the party slithering away towards the hedge, butting through it, which was as easy as tearing through tulle, and flattening themselves in single file up the lee side. At fifty yards and from the ground they could still be seen as moving lengths of darker shadow behind the tracery of young growth; from the upper storey of the garage and the loopholed roof of the fort they would be even more clearly visible. Perversely the smoke-clouds also drifted away in a changing wind, and left the sky clean in the twilight, eerie with a lambent yellow light for a brief while before all became dark.

Baird saw him rearing his head to follow their anxious progress.

"I know! But there it is! We could give 'em better covering fire if we took a machine-gun up right, but that's all I can see for it."

"Shall I?" asked Jim. "They'll welcome all the help they can get."

"All right! I wish we had another Piat to spare."

But the mortars were fully occupied replying to the shelling from the fort, and a machine-gun firing tracer was more than welcome. Jim took it as far to the right as he could, and the team entered into a duel with their opposite numbers in the garage. The party under the hedge crawled on, all but one who lay still perhaps a hundred yards away from the machine-gun team. One of the snipers—and there must be several, for their shot came thick as bees—had accounted for him. The light was burning up to a malevolent glow, and would fade as abruptly in a few minutes more. Jim left his team still industriously pumping tracer into the garage, and crawled along the ground to the prone man. The fire was uncomfortably heavy, and as he reached the spot where the private lay a mortar shell exploded forward, between him and the rest of the party. He dropped low into the grass, and the blast tugged at him with a violent shock; he heard fragments plunking into the ground around him, and the dull, precise impact they made was a thing that could still erect his hair. As soon as it was past he turned to the casualty; Price, of Sheel Magna, shot in the chest, unconscious but alive. Not much blood; maybe the bullet had struck a bone and been stopped short. He raised him gently by the armpits to get a purchase under his body, and the next moment had to drop flat over him again as another mortar shell went off, much nearer to the hedge. They had the range from the fort only too well this time; when Jim raised his head and looked forward again through the gathering dusk he saw the drifting smoke of the burst spreading slowly over a stillness which was a litter of bodies, and one man, only one, springing up and forward towards the lee of the garage fence. A small man, running like a hare, head down for shelter out of the smoking remnants of Corporal Deveril's party. That was all he saw, and even that was straining after shadows, for clouds had driven in and extinguished the lurid afterglow, and darkness had fallen over obscurity, making sudden night of evening. If the one whole man could let them in at once they might at least clear these buildings and have a taut circle drawn round the fort ready for dawn. A couple of well-directed grenades from close under that fence might do the job very nicely. He waited for a sign, but there was none, and to trace movement was not possible any longer. Maybe the survivor was manœuvring for place before he revealed himself, since he had the whole company, as it were, in his hand, and everything depended on his first move; for Harben would throw no more men in upon the off chance of success in these conditions.

Jim lifted Price back to the gun-team, and went to find Baird, who was sitting under a broom-bush with his eyes straining uselessly towards the garage. He blinked and shook his head.

"No damn' use! Did you see anything? You had a better line on it than I've got."

"Sniper got Price. He's alive, though. The rest ran into a mortar shell."

"I know, I saw it go up. Did any of 'em get through?"

"Can't be sure. I thought one did, but can't be sure even of that. Certainly no more than one."

"If anyone did," said Baird, "he'll have to go into action, poor devil. His life isn't worth much purchase, anyhow, he may as well sell out on a good price. But I've got orders not to shift until he opens the ball."

That was not surprising, for all the odds were on the defenders at the moment, and the chance of carrying the forts themselves before morning was already past. They waited, ready to attempt the garage at least if their man gave them the signal; but there was no sign. The machine-gun fire on both sides slackened, and what was almost silence came down over the approaches of Goch.

A quarter of an hour passed, and still nothing happened; nothing except that the fleeting rear view of a diminutive man running for his life became a more precise memory in Jim's mind. Without reason, without warning, he knew that the survivor was Arthur Clure, and that there had been no other.

"Looks as if we've had it!" said Baird. "Are you sure one of 'em got through? What the hell's he playing at if he did?"

"No," said Jim steadily, "I said I couldn't be sure."

"Well, that's that, then! We'd have heard from him by now if he was still alive."

Nevertheless, they waited for the Major's order before moving back to the ridge. Baird would have liked to move up and see for himself what had happened to Deveril's men, but it would have been only to throw good lives away after what was already lost. He did not notice the defection of Sergeant Benison, which was accomplished unobtrusively and in silence, until it was too late to question; and even then he supposed dispiritedly that he had merely gone back to the machine-gun, which was true as far as it went, considerably truer than Jim's answer to his last question.

Pictures are often clearer in retrospect; this glimpse of Clure diving under the fence stood out now with frantic clarity in Jim's mind. He had declined to be sure of anything, but there was no doubt left in him that Clure had reached the target alive and unhurt still, though there had been no sign from him, and no attempt to carry out his orders. What had happened to him? What was happening to him now? With anyone else you could at any rate make a guess, but Clure in this condition was incalculable; and if he turned up alive and whole in the morning, having lain hidden all night, what was to become of him then? It might not be actual desertion; there might be medical evidence enough to get him out of the worst of it, after that shell-burst which had killed the others; but for all that, and putting it at its best, it would be the end of him.

Something old, and feverish, and indignant, came to life suddenly in Jim's mind, something coming from far back, from Miriam, perhaps, in her great day, when she contested against the whole world for an unexpressed idea of the sacredness of man. No one, if he could help it, should strip Clure naked of his pathetic, dreamed dignity. It wasn't his fault he had been born and raised chronically unfit for this confusing world and this bitter way of living. In his incompetence, in his dread, he had already done things more heroic than had been acclaimed

in heroes, and Jim was damned if all this should pass unseen
and the one moment of failure be spotlighted for the world to
gape at and criticise. If he wasn't responsible, yet someone had
to be. Nothing, in Jim's belief, was ever so rigid a shape that
it could not be altered, if the attempt was made in time and with
all your might; and the time was now, and there was only one
person to provide the might.

He waited for another half-hour, and then he withdrew himself inch by inch, and slipped back through the darkness to the
thread-fine line of the new hedge.

7

Clure lay under the fence with his face pressed down among
the mortar dust of spilt masonry, and hung on with fingers and
knees and body until the reverberations of the explosion began
to fade from his mind. He wondered dully why he was still
alive. It was as certain as nightfall that the others, with as good
right to life as he, were all quite firmly and finally dead; yet
here he lay with his heart pounding thunderously against the
ground, and his head buried in his arms, and never a scratch
upon him. He was here under the very doors of the enemy,
but the enemy did not know he existed. The world lay upon
him; he had to lift the weight of it, and rouse himself from this
dazed lethargy, so that something could go on happening. What
was it? Something bloody and nonsensical and obscure, something as confused and helpless as himself. It had to do with
deserted villages, scattered letters in an abandoned house, dead
cattle putrefying in the fields, blown bodies of poultry mashed
into the ground by the barrage, children creeping out of cellars,
young men dying on stretchers, skeletons of towns, petrefactions
of forests. It was the murder of a continent, the invasion of
Europe. He was involved in it, in some way which he could
not immediately remember, but which hung threateningly over
his burdened mind; he had something to do, something immediate and definite, so that this crime, this horrible necessity, could
go on. He had it to do because he was the only one left, when
all he wanted was to lie down and sleep. And he didn't know
what it was!

He moved his hand along the ground, and the grains of dust
felt like mountains, and his hand itself like the earth in motion.
He took hold of a broken slat of the fence, splintered by
machine-gun fire, and his fingers, cumbrous as bolsters, found

it solid and ponderable, and held by it jealously. It came back to him slowly that there was some business about a gun, and some snipers; and in another moment he was helped to remember by a spitting arc of fire fanning out across the fields from above his head. The span of his thoughts, which had seemed wide as the poles, contracted to a glittering pinpoint of purpose. He knew what he had to do.

The fence was too high to let him see the upper windows of the garage from this angle, just as it kept him unseen; but by dragging himself round a few yards to the right he came to a place where the woodwork was broken away into splinters, and the remaining part of the planking stood only just over a foot high. There were a few scattered willow-shoots rooting close enough to confuse the dusk with a multiplication of shadows over him; and from there he could look in, and see the end wall of the garage just eight or nine yards away, dark maroon in the dusk, with its broad black doors tight shut, and gashed pallidly here and there by splinters. The top floor was a face of grey concrete, and had probably once been living quarters for the proprietor, but its near window, as broad as the doors, had been blown out frame and all, and it was there that the men with the machine-gun had ensconced themselves, probably behind barriers of sandbags, certainly in a strong and commanding position. What presented itself, therefore, as the enemy was a large oblong of complete darkness in a light wall in a world just past twilight; an excellent target, one not even he could miss, unless his hand shook too much to command his throw.

He lay still for a few minutes, to regain as great a measure of physical control as he could, breathing long and deeply to offset the noisy haste of his heart-beats, which shook him from head to foot. The night gathered over the outskirts of Goch in circling plunges, as a bird of prey falls, hiding the broken, lolling petrol pumps away towards the main road, and the skeleton roofs and scattered masonry of the houses beyond the garage, and the tattered trees. He lay with his head in his left arm, flexing the fingers of his right hand gently, and trying to keep his mind fixed on what he had to do, but it was an effort which took up all his energy, and from which his sick senses continually tried to turn back. He made within his shut eyes a picture of his wife's face, to keep his attention constant at least on that; but even these beloved lineaments seemed to shake and dissolve as does a reflection in still water when it is fingered. He could not focus properly, some vital part was gone out of his mind; and always, when he seemed about to get the better of his senses, the splintering crash of the gun broke out above him, and shook the atoms of his vision away again, disintegrating into the dark. Yet his hand seemed steady enough, and time was precious, and would not wait. He raised himself and lay close against the gap in the fence, leaving free play for his arm. The black oblong of the window spat fire again, fixing his aim vividly; then there was a moment of quietness in which he heard voices, low-pitched but curiously fresh and sudden, exchanging staccato remarks within the room.

He had a grenade in his hand, and the pin between his teeth, when the terrible thing happened, and it fell upon him as fiercely and with as little warning as the light that blinded Saul on the Damascus road. A head and shoulders came clear into the black framework of the window, leaning out recklessly, so that his eyes, accustomed by now to the dimness and always better than most men's, could discern, if not the features, at least the general outline and the dress. This was not a man, but a boy—no, a child, even younger than the sniper of Erdenlich whose death was still green and sore in his memory. About fourteen, by the half-developed lines of him, with thin arms like a girl, and attired in a lightish coat which was certainly not uniform. And in a moment a second figure came to his shoulder and peered out with him; someone with longish blond hair that seemed to shine by its own innate light as a pallor against the dark, someone even smaller than the first apparition, someone with a rifle in his hands, for a gleam of flare-light caught the barrel. He held it competently; it was clear that he had fired it often. He might have been ten years old; almost certainly he was no more. They held their places only for a minute, and then slid back into the dark, and he heard a word or two pass in a middle voice, deepening a little but not yet broken, and a man's fuller tones replying, and a secret, odious laughter, as if they mocked him.

He crouched there with the pin still gripped between his teeth, and everything against which he had tried to measure himself came clattering vengefully about his ears in ruin. What was he doing? What were they all doing? What sort of duty was this which called him to shoot down endless agonising simulacra of his son, and watch them die in agony? What was it that demanded he should throw this grenade in amongst children, mere children not even in uniform? Or were they terrible imaginings out of his own diseased mind? Had he so feared them that they had power at last to put on flesh for him? He closed his eyes

and was shut into a blind, maimed darkness; and then there was
no more perception of the eyes or the mind, only a shuddering
numbness that possessed him utterly, shutting him from the
world as if a steel curtain had fallen between. He lost at a blow
all that had been his world, every ingenious illusion, every
framework he had attempted to build around his littleness, every
laborious unsuccessful aspiration, every meagre comfort, even
the all-demanding, all-repaying, adored and adoring face of
Helen. For a long time he had been growing poorer, but now at
a blow he was destitute. He had no propelling will any more;
there was no longer anything which could make him go forward,
for his mechanism was broken. He sat there under cover of the
infant willows, and for a long while had not impulse to cease
gripping the pin of the grenade; then panic took him, of this
place, of these nightmare children who did exist, who were not
figments of his imagination. He took the grenade away from
his mouth, and scrambled away left-hand along the fence,
groping anyhow through bushes and stones, until he had clawed
his way into the hollow centre of an uneven mound of masonry,
and lay there exhausted, face downward among the rubble. He
did not know where he was, but that did not matter. He could
no longer see the frame of darkness where the demon children
had been, nor hear their voices; the rest he could not escape if
he crawled to the ends of the earth on his bleeding hands.

For some time which might have been counted in minutes or
days for all he knew, he lay shuddering spasmodically, hugging
the stones and breathing dust into him in great gasps. Then he
sat up, and set his back against a fragment of standing wall,
and stared painfully about him. Perception came to life in him
slowly. He saw the frame of a doorway which no longer held
a door, ramparts of bricks, beams, mortar fragments, slivers of
glass close under his hands, all penned within the square shape
of a room which was shorn off short at about three feet from the
ground. He was in a house, then. Expanses of smoky sky looked
in on him, and a few meagre stars, flickerings of gunfire, rumblings of 'planes, an occasional flare. How long had he been
there? A long time, surely, for he was stiff with cold. He did
not know what time of night it was, but it was night still, unless
this darkness had become perpetual.

Awareness of things not perceptible through the senses began
in him after another and longer delay, and with a desperation of
pain like recovery from cramp, but still with this same night-
marish slowness. What had he done? What was he now? For

he was no longer a soldier! He had the grenade still clutched in his hand, and still inert after all that reckless scramble, though his hands were bleeding from the broken glass, and his sleeves cut to tatters. He sat and looked at it, and began to sob with a horrid, hard sound his own ears did not seem to hear. It was done; there was no help for it. He could not go back, never to the gap in the fence, never, never to the platoon. He could not make good what he had left undone; even if time could be unwound, and opportunity haled back again, he knew he could not do it. It was all over. He was finished; there was nothing for him but to cower and hide from his own people and the enemy alike, and God alone knew where he would go, or how long he could stay hidden. And if the company attacked with dawn and found him sitting there, what would become of him? A sweat of horror broke on him cold and copious as dew. What had he done to Helen? How would she live with her world exposed to the cold wind, with her heart broken? How could she bear it that he was nothing, had never been anything, but a wretched, inept failure, one of the clowns who serve to make life complex and amusing for other people? How could she face the humiliation of a husband sentenced for desertion? After all they had dreamed for each other, to come to this draggled ruin at last! A true ruin, a just ruin, to which he had dragged her by the hand the day he married her!

He thought he would go out and finish the job, find the track of the machine-gun and walk in it until he died; but when he tried to get to his feet there was no power in him, he could neither stand nor go. He could only sit with his head sunk in his hands, trying to take hold of place and time, to make his body, which had recognised the folly of effort, renew its allegiance. He ceased even to rock himself and shiver, though it was very cold. Sounds passed by his desolation and left him untouched. He did not even hear the renewed stutter of the machine-gun, or the sharp crack of the rifles as the snipers went into action again; not until feet crashed among the broken glass and plaster, and a heavy body fell into the doorway, did he look up out of his trance. Then he lifted his head slowly, and his opaque gaze was steady for a long minute before he recognised Sergeant Benison. Even then it was only the first of a series of inevitable things. He would be dragged back, of course, and put under arrest, unless he could find a death before they reached the lines; but it wasn't the Sergeant's fault. He just got the dirty work to do.

But the Sergeant was not saying anything, only leaning there in the doorway to get his breath, and clutching ineffectively at his left wrist with the fingers of his right hand. He had Deveril's Piat mortar gathered into his arm, which was hampering his movements; and there was blood dripping out of his left sleeve and hanging from his fingers.

"Help me!" he said in a fierce undertone. "Help me!"

Clure moved like a sleep-walker, took the projector from him, and laid it on the ground. His dulled eyes, double their size and burned into his head with shock, stared upon Jim as if he had been something unhuman, but at least his body obeyed. Jim sank down against the wall with something between a gasp and a groan, and began to wring blood in a shower from the ends of his fingers. The lower part of his sleeve was soaked, so that he could not unloose the cuff to lay his wound bare. He struggled with it for a minute or two, and then held it out to Clure, his hand palm upward and slack, with blood drying in the lines of it.

"Undo it for me! I'm damned if I can!"

It was not easy, with cold fingers slipping upon cloth rigid and slimy with half-congealed blood; but meanings were reaching his hands, and therefore must have passed through his brain, for he toiled with a sort of timeless patience until he got the buttons undone and the sleeve turned back. He watched his own fingers all the time with deep interest, as if they belonged to someone else, and were performing some function he had never witnessed before. His reason was withdrawn a long way within, was shrunken together infinitesimally small; but it was still alive, or it could not have received and transmitted the appeal, or commanded even so remote a response.

It was not a grave wound which came to light, a double ploughed furrow the length of the forearm, not deep, but bleeding copiously. Jim groped for a field dressing, and held it out to Clure without a word. The hands went on with their deliberate ministrations; he could feel the mind wondering in a slow agony when he would speak of the unspeakable, the thing which had not been done. He knew why he was supposed to be here. He wondered that his own thoughts did not communicate themselves just as surely to Clure, for they seemed to him to have escaped out of his mind, and to be adrift upon the bitter air.

"Thanks!" he said when the bandage was completed and the cuff buttoned again. "That's better! Give me a breather now. I thought they'd packed up for the night, or I wouldn't have tried it so soon."

250

Clure opened his lips stiffly, and a voice unfamiliar and labouring asked: "Is it still—early?"

"Not midnight yet. You and me have got a hell of a wait, and it's going to be perishing cold. Sit closer! We may as well have each otner's heat."

Clure moved a little nearer, but not within touch. His blank eyes went over Jim from head to foot, and wondered and grieved upon him. The effortful voice asked again: "Was it at you they were shooting?"

"Can't be sure. I thought I was well hidden, and they were just fanning away on principle, but I wonder now if they didn't spot me, after all. I hadn't heard the rifles for over an hour till they let fly at me."

"Your leg is bleeding, too," said Clure, pointing.

"That's nothing much—just a tear on some of this blasted broken glass we're sitting on. I came down a purler over a beam outside. I wonder you didn't hear me, but there was considerable row going on just then. What about you? That mortar shell that got the rest of the bunch can't have done you any good. Any damage?"

What was he doing, this incalculable man? Was he offering him an alibi, inviting him to say he had been stunned by the concussion, and dragged himself here half conscious? Why didn't he come to the point? Did he think it would sound any better for keeping?

"No, I'm all right," said Clure half-audibly.

"Good! Because it looks like being your show. I'm not going to be much help. This arm'll be pretty stiff by morning."

"We're to wait here until morning?"

"No good trying anything before. Though I needn't tell you that if I *was* spotted they may come looking for us—supposing there's enough of 'em to risk it—just about any minute. And if we wait too long, and our barrage begins, we'll be blown off the map anyhow. Nice spot we've got ourselves into!" He looked up at the sky, whence the smoke was drifting away, leaving a great space of stars. "Thank God there's no moon! You were wise to go to ground until it had set."

His voice was brisk and businesslike, and seemed to be innocent of all double meanings. Was it possible that his coming here had nothing, after all, to do with the apprehension of a deserter? He wasn't the kind to take a delight in playing with a poor devil. He wouldn't lie about it if he'd been sent to bring him in.

"Did Major Harben send you?" asked Clure abruptly, unable to bear it that he did not know.

"He doesn't even know I'm here. Nor does Baird. I sent myself."

"Then why——?"

"Well, I knew you were somewhere about, I saw you go on after the shell burst; I thought we'd do better to improve the odds a bit."

And suddenly, when it sounded so true, Clure perceived that it was a lie; not all and literally a lie, but yet a lie in intention, and of an amazing kind. He had come to improve the odds a bit, yes, but not the odds against the Germans. He knew, and only God knew how he knew, what had happened, not the means of it, but the end, not the weapons, but the wounds. He was here to mend the breakage; there was no reservation, no clause of "if he could"; he was here to do it or die trying. And by what extraordinary ways he worked, by what straight and yet what devious ways; no command, no exhortation, no criticism, no comfort, only his hand held out dropping blood, and his voice panting: "Help me!" Clure shut his eyes for a moment, and drew breath hard into him.

Things were beginning and ending and giving birth to new things with such bewildering speed. Only a few hours ago the fairy tale of his life had dissolved like a burst soap-bubble into a little muddy water in the palm of his hand, and left him trying to think of a way to die without relying upon himself for the death, because there was no other way of making all clean again. And then the Sergeant had come, and he had seen himself surviving even this horror, and being made to live with his own shame, and take it home with him to put at Helen's feet. Now that also was slipping away from him; he had nothing. He was emptied upon the ground, and not yet refilled. He had been dead, and was alive again, but only mechanically alive, with no heart and no spirit in him; only this spark, only this small heat of wonder, that Sergeant Benison had so inexplicably lied. He tried to express what was most urgent, not so roughly as to strip aside the lie, but so clearly that he himself should understand the bare bones of the change that had come upon him.

"I saw them," he said. "They were not soldiers; they were children."

Jim was silent, but he turned his head and looked at him with a grave and steady regard.

"There was one boy of fourteen or so, and one no more than ten. Not even the elder one wore uniform. How can it be right?" His voice sank to a breathless whisper.

Jim said: "If I could answer that for myself, it still might not answer it for you, so what's the good? But anyhow I can't. Nobody can." But he understood. His voice was considering and regretful, with none of the orthodox uneasiness so many might display in admitting their own helplessness. He didn't excuse it, or attempt to put it into the background or deny that it still needed answering; he only looked at it with a preoccupied sadness, and turned back to the noises of the night. And yet, knowing what he knew of Sergeant Benison, how could Clure suppose there was anything he suffered by it that the Sergeant had not known? A man who could feel panic and pain across fields and through the night's darkness, and find his way to them—had he, though he kept his eyes fixed upon his duty, anything to learn from Arthur Clure about the many aspects of tragedy, and all their confusions and complaints?

He asked like a lost child: "What do you want me to do?"

"Come and help me to bring in everything Deveril and the rest were carrying. There was a lot of it, and we may need it, and I can't heft things as well as normally."

"But afterwards—tomorrow? What are we to do? You said yourself they'll lay down the barrage from here."

"We're going to be in the garage before they begin. With any luck we'll be out of this and back to the lads when the balloon goes up."

"You mean we shall attack them—with this?" He looked at the mortar lying on the ground between them, and a tremor went through him which Jim did not fail to notice.

"Yes, if need be. With anything we've got. I've got no choice. I came away without orders; I've got to show results, or else."

"They're children!" said Clure, drawing back from him. "I told you!"

"I know. I'm not forgetting anything. It's all right," he said quite reasonably, "don't come if you feel bad about it. I can manage."

But when he paused outside the lolling door-frame to listen to the spasmodic sounds of gunfire and take his bearings afresh, Clure was at his elbow, shuddering still, but keeping step for step with him, more unwilling to let him carry it all alone even than to bear a part of it himself. Three journeys in all they made together, back and forth between the crater and the ruined house with grenades and mortar shells and a Sten gun, and always Clure followed him without a word. Jim knew that he came only because his conscience would not let him leave a wounded man to venture alone; but still he came. Once in a great quietness Jim heard his teeth chattering with cold and exhaustion and extreme distress, and he wondered, in a moment of misgiving, if he had done well to tempt the overridden spirit further; but there was no going back now, and no giving up. It was the only twinge of doubt he had; afterwards, when they had gathered together their little arsenal within the broken walls and sat down in the midst of it, his mind was easier in him. He leaned back into the corner, where the wind was cut off from him, and motioned Clure to come nearer.

"I'm perished, and you must be worse. Sit close and keep warm."

Clure did not hold off from him this time, though he had asked himself no question and come to no decision. Nothing had ever been posed to him, only that first: "Help me! Help me!" to which his body had responded unbidden. No spear had ever been levelled at his breast; he was free even now, or so he was being given to understand, to hold his hand or plunge it in as he saw fit. Which made it the more clear to him, and for the first time, that he could never be free. What was the use of releasing him from the standards of his fellow-men, when that very generosity made its own involuntary claim upon him? And yet this was a changed imprisonment; it made him his own keeper, his own hand held the key that would be turned upon him. No one but himself had wronged him, unless it was an injury to say to him: "You're a man, stand on your own feet and do the best you can." No one but himself had tried to destroy him, unless, perhaps, God had made destruction implicit even in his creation. So he had to make up his own mind, after all. It wasn't a case of giving and obeying orders, just: "Yes, Sergeant!" and: "No, Sergeant!" and: "Very good, Sergeant!" as he had dreaded and hoped it would be. The burden lay upon him, and no one else could take it away. That made him independent, responsible, and free to damn or save himself; if only, if only he knew which way the damned must go, and which the saved.

He sat down, shoulder to shoulder and thigh to thigh with Jim, obeying what had not been a command. Now that all things rested upon him strangely he, too, could rest; he sat

254

suspended in the moment, feeling no desire to anticipate what was to come, not even consciously thinking of what he must do. Night and day would follow each other regardless of him, and so could his actions and reactions take shape, without pangs of birth or burial to begin and end their single and sufficient pain. He leaned upon the big, lean body and kept silence. The stammer of the machine-gun had stopped; but for themselves the night here was unpeopled.

"I could do with a cigarette," said Jim. "Think we dare risk it?" Clure was not expected to reply to that, only to accept the smoke when it was offered, and enjoy it as well as he might, while his companion talked desultorily, letting his tongue and his mind run; for the darkness covering them made him only a disembodied voice, speaking to the one benighted soldier as clearly as to the other.

"I don't know!" he said. "It's funny about these things. First Baartjen on one side, and now these gun-kids on the other. None of 'em can much help 'emselves; she was taught to resist the Germans after her own fashion, and I dare bet some Dutch boys not much older than these even ran to rifles. After cursing about what happened to them, it's hell to be brought up against the thing in reverse, and find yourself cast for the invader and murderer, all ready for other people to curse. I know! I've been there before. But it goes on happening. That's the way it is; all we can do is work out a rough-and-ready way of dealing with it—the best won't be up to much. Or—sometimes it doesn't amount to working anything out; you just plough through it, and go right ahead, and it falls into place."

"You get used to it!" said Clure in a bitter whisper.

"Some do, but that's no good to you, or to me, or to most of the others. It isn't so very many who ever get used to it. No, it just falls into place. It isn't a separate thing at all, only a part of the whole rotten business, no uglier than the rest, for that matter. You don't get used to it, but you wonder why it ever surprised you. Why do we expect a sharp line to be drawn across at a certain degree of awfulness, and nobody to go beyond it? Obviously war chucks all the limits overboard; I don't know why we should look for anything else. Some get it bad for children, some for animals, some for their own friends." He looked darkly down at his bandaged arm, and stirred the fingers uneasily, and frowned at a memory from a long way back. His voice as he went on speaking was deliberate and quiet. "Mine was in 1940, on a road—no, two roads—in

Flanders, when the Germans were pouring west across the country from Sedan to the coast, and we were on the run. The first part of it was a woman running along a causeway, out of the wreckage of a little party of refugees who'd just been shot up by a Junkers; the pilot followed her up until he got her. She was far gone with child. I've always remembered that. The other was just a road. Moonlight it was when I saw it, and as quiet as this. The panzers had been along it early that day, when it was full of refugee families streaming west and south; and they'd been in a hurry. You know how fast refugees move. These had been machine-gunned and then driven over. There were a lot of children among them, too. I never stop seeing those children; I doubt if I could see your two very clearly for 'em. It isn't any question of avenging one on another; it's just a sort of double vision that keeps 'em both in sight. And it gets to look," he said grimly, "as if every time you step aside to avoid one you step on the other, and every time you try to miss 'em both you get in bloodier and deeper than ever. There isn't any solution. There's only a choice of courses with not much to choose between 'em. I picked mine a long time ago, as straight ahead as I could steer and the run of things let me go. There *is* only one way out, for them as well as for us, and that's straight through to the finish and out the other side. It's the most economical, as well as the shortest. We've done a lot of walking round in circles in our time, and it did nobody any good; now we are going ahead, and I'm all for carrying on. Nothing's going to stand in the way if I can help it—nothing with a gun in its hand, man, woman or child."

He paused, pricking his ears to listen for nearer sounds between the distant thunders, but there were none.

"If I talk too much, tell me. I want to keep awake. If you weren't here I'd be talking to myself."

"It's all right," said Clure, "I don't mind."

"But you could sleep, if I shut up."

"No! No, I couldn't sleep. Go on talking."

There was no mistaking the eagerness with which he leaned now upon every manifestation of human companionship. Whether he agreed with, understood, or even listened to what was said Jim never knew; it was the sound of the voice he wanted, and the feel of another shoulder against his shoulder and thigh against his thigh, and the goodwill of a mind moving soothingly with his mind. And this was a time and a place where all things could be shared. Jim shut his eyes and went on talking, not discreetly, scarcely even coherently, letting half-forgotten things flow out of him, losing the knowledge of his companion's response, only spending his memories for something he himself wanted now absorbingly, and was willing to buy at any cost. He talked about that first campaign in Flanders, and what it had done to him; about the months of optimism and the fourteen days or so of unbelievable calamity. He talked about Miriam, which was a thing he had never done before to anyone but Imogen. He went from Boissy-en-Fougères to the coast, he was shot up again in the boat and brought home bereaved and half dead. There was Egypt again, there was Libya, the long, sandy trek from Nibeiwa to Benghazi, and the abrupt recoil before the German advance. There was Malaya again, a green, dank, populous, steaming cauldron of rotting vegetation and hurrying death; there was Charlie Smith moving through it with his long-legged, lounging walk and his gaunt, satanic smile to a grave among the mangroves by the borders of Johore. There was Singapore, a bill never yet paid, where sixty thousand men had lain rotting at Changi; and once again there was escape from Singapore, the rocking of the small boat in an idle sea, and the glassy arching of the sky over her, with Jap 'planes busy in it. Even he talked about the second homecoming, and Simone stammering through her brief story of Miriam's death; and about Imogen a little, but not all the truth of her. Only there would he have been giving away what was not altogether his; the rest was his life, and it went into a night easily, all those five years of it lying down now so quietly together, which once had torn him so many several ways. It did him good, though how he did not trouble to think. It shed the intensity of remembrance out of him, and left him refreshed and eased and curiously light of heart, as if something else had come in as these ghosts went out of him. When it was over, and his own voice had lost its way in the silence, he sat there quite still, watching the height of the sky recede and pale in the lofty hours before dawn, while the night remembered the rivalry of day with understanding and no sadness. He saw that Clure was asleep upon his shoulder, and he was glad, not only that Clure had heart to sleep, but that some of the rich coin he had spent was returned to him unchanged even by a touch. He had not known until he received the half of it back that he had made any sacrifice. Certainly there was a kind of goodness, not accidental nor wanton, that gave him back his own.

He waited until the darkness began to change, to grow

crystal-clear and full of outlines, though as yet there was no hint of the familiar depressing between-light to cloud it; then he slipped gingerly out of his corner, easing his sleeping companion back against the masonry. Even the access of cold did not waken Clure; the stress had ebbed out of him and let exhaustion in. Jim thought: "Shall I wake him? Or shall I leave him out of it?" Yesterday—even at midnight, perhaps— he would have been afraid to let him sleep through it and escape the issue, for how can you be sure a terror is laid unless you are made to face it? But now it was all changed. This issue was already won or lost, before ever the battle was fought. To be spared the testing of the decision now was to escape an ordeal, certainly, but not to leave the end in doubt. One way or another, it was finished already. Let him sleep! Everything was arranging itself, even the price of the victory. Let God, or whatever it was, arrange this also. It might be all the surer that no one should carry this load for him again.

Jim took half a dozen grenades and the Sten gun, and went away quietly, leaving Clure where he lay. From this fallen house it was well to move with care, for the path back to the lines passed between garage and fort, and there were fragments of buildings, not all uninhabitable, close about the spot. Snipers by the dozen might be dozing out the night there, but if he didn't disturb them they wouldn't interfere with him. And surely those two boys who had so confused Clure would be sleeping now. Ten-year-olds do not watch the night out easily; and there was at least one man there to take the responsibility from them. Who knew but the whole thing might turn out easy? So often after much foreboding the event itself slips by almost unnoticed. From the other end of the garage grenades and a mortar had seemed none too much to reckon on to clear up the strong-point; but from this end, the town end, where Clure had led him by a mere outburst of panic, the situation was very different. He could approach unseen and certainly unexpected, could walk clean over the flattened fence with no upstairs window to overlook him, and in by the gap of a blown-in window in what appeared to be the office of the garage. There he halted until his eyes grew accustomed to the outlines of the room, which was almost bare, and littered with dust and splinters of glass and wood. There was a door, only one, right across the room from him, leading into the garage itself, no doubt. There was also someone on the far side of it, for he heard the shifting of feet as the sentry changed his position,

258

and the unmistakable thud of a rifle-butt on a concrete floor.

He stood quite still, which was a thing he could do indefinitely, until he had collected whatever evidence his senses could provide; then he moved inch by inch across the floor, feeling with his toes for space innocent of the flung splinters of glass, and felt along the edge of the door delicately with his fingertips. The latch was large, heavy, probably noisy. The key was in the lock on the other side, he thought, for a very faint line of light came in by the hinges and the shut edge of the door, but none by the keyhole. He could not, then, go through to the sentry, but the sentry must and should come through to him. He flattened himself against the wall behind the door, felt for a large piece of glass, and heaved it under the window, where the thickest of the debris was.

It was only a small, sharp sound, but it was enough. There was a pause of almost intense stillness and listening, and then a faint click announced that the key had been turned in the lock. The door was flung back before a dim light and a small dark figure fanning a rifle across and across the room. It was the elder of Clure's two boys; so much the better, for this one, at least, need not die. Seeing nothing but the empty familiar room, he eased his finger upon the trigger, and stepped a little forward from the doorway, which was all the luck Jim needed. His left forearm, padded with the dressings under the sleeve, took the boy across the mouth, stopping his shout before it was uttered, and jerking back his head; a knee in the small of his back hoisted him off his feet, and the rifle, as he released it in sheer surprise, was scooped in by a large right hand and propped back noiselessly against the wall. The door closed upon them gently, swinging to in a languid fashion.

The boy fought wildly, groping above his imprisoned head for Jim's throat, but could get no purchase, and wasted his strength upon a face he could hardly spoil. He wasn't the kind to cave in and co-operate; there was nothing to be done with him but stop his mouth with his own scarf, and tie him up in a sketchy fashion with handkerchief and belt to keep him quiet for the ten minutes or so which were necessary. Which was done, though not without difficulty; and he lay upon the floor, well away from the door and window both, when Jim slipped through into the garage.

The dim light came from a small-power electric bulb burning in the middle of the ceiling, and showed a big floor-space cumbered with a derelict truck and one small car. To the left, a small outer door, and a staircase leading up to the living quarters; at the far end, the main doors above which the machine-gun lay. He judged, though because the light was cut off halfway he could not see, that at the top of the stairs a door on the right would bring him directly into the room the snipers were using. He made what use he could of the concrete pillars which supported the ceiling, and dodged from shadow to shadow towards the foot of the stairs; but in a moment a rifle cracked, and the bullet clanged against steel and whined off again just behind his head. He dropped into cover behind a bench littered with tools, and fired back up the stairs, just as another shot, this time from the direction of the office, shattered the single light-bulb and left them in darkness.

He knew who that was, though the shooting was not characteristic. Without taking his eyes from the direction of the stairhead he asked in a quick half-tone: "Clure?"

"I'm here!" And he slithered along the wall and crouched beside him. "I followed you."

"Good lad! Did you see who's up there?"

"Only one. On the landing."

"Man or boy?"

"Man—in uniform."

The machine-gun, stuttering into action again almost overhead, gave them assurance at that moment that there was at least one more to deal with, besides the child. For a moment after its burst ended there was absolute silence, and then the sound of a door opening and shutting, and a quick thread of light and a movement between, upon which they both fired.

"Another soldier," whispered Clure. "I saw his collar and tabs."

"Right! Keep teasing 'em! I'm going up."

But it was not up the staircase he went. That would have been only a form of suicide, with two well-armed men sitting at the top with every advantage ranged on their side. Instead, he shed his boots, left his gun behind, and slid away into the deepest darkness below the solid wooden bannisters. He went up by these, hand over hand, drawing himself up from stair to stair, while Clure, obedient to his orders, kept up a rapid fire upon the stairhead. Because of the extreme need for silence it took what seemed a long time, and hurt him a good deal, for often he had to hang still upon his hands for as long as twenty seconds before the next burst from the machine-gun made it safe for him to drag himself up another step or two. The main drawback was that the fingers of his left hand were not as pliable and firm as they should have been; but they kept their hold until he reached the top and got his wounded arm safely locked round a couple of stout uprights to maintain him in position for the minute he needed. He was not more than a foot away from the nearest man, for he could hear his breathing, and the rasp of cloth as he moved; but their attention was fastened upon returning Clure's fire, and there was no least glimmer of light to betray the other danger. Jim took out a grenade with his right hand, pulled the pin with his teeth, pushed it gently through the banisters on to the landing, and rolled it a few inches forward. Then, abandoning caution, he loosed his hold, and dropped like a stone, and scuttled under the lee of the stairs on hands and knees just as the grenade went off.

In that narrow place, between the high, confining landing walls, the explosion seemed terrific. There was only one way the full force of the blast could go, and that way it went, flinging two bodies and two rifles before it, and sucking after, in a plucking of air that sang like a stringed instrument, a great shower of plaster and dust and cobwebs. An invisible procession of demons seemed to sweep down the staircase and swirl across the floor, spurning the dead bodies as it passed and sending the dust whirling in spirals in the wind of its going. Before the reverberations of the explosion had quitted the walls, and the plaster ceased to silt downward, Clure was scuttling up the strewn treads and bursting into the room above. He it was who rushed in upon the fair-haired child and the middle-aged civilian who were operating the gun between them; and to him it was that they surrendered, seeing no alternative. For all this while Jim was kneeling under the stairs, shaking to and fro a head that seemed to house that explosion within itself, and was suffering besides from the effects of a sudden drop of fifteen feet or so, for the level of the upper floor was very lofty. He was just getting to his feet when Clure marched his prisoners down, the child stumbling along dazed with sleep, but still defiant, the man strutting and arrogant. Clure was afraid to take his eyes off them except in quick glances, but even in those few furtive looks in his direction there was something new and strange, a terrible intimacy of anxiety.

"Are you all right, Sergeant?"

"I'm fine. You keep your eye on what you're doing, and let's get out of here."

They reclaimed their third prisoner, who was so broken by

chagrin that he would not give any trouble; and they got out as fast as they could, making for the ridge where the company was dug in, using no caution this time, for there was no gun raking the meadows now. The dawn was smoky and strange and cold as yet, hardly paler than the night had been before the moon set; but that was all that Jim was capable of noticing. He walked in a throbbing daze, moving almost mechanically; but he knew he was all right because he had to be all right. Clure couldn't budge him if he dropped, besides the fact that he had to watch out for the prisoners; therefore he must not drop yet. Nor had anything been done to him to justify his foundering at all; the most he had was a scratched arm and a brain addled by slight blast and shock; no self-respecting M.O. would look at him. By will-power he kept himself upright until they were challenged and recognised, and fell into the ranks of the company massing in the scrub. Exclamations breaking over him like rain made him start back into life and look about him. There were a lot of known faces staring interest and wonder. There was Baird suddenly erupted from nowhere, saying blankly:

"Good God, Sergeant, I thought we'd lost you! Where the hell have you been? And what in the name of fortune have you got there?"

Jim was aware that he laughed; and indeed, they must present a pretty comic spectacle, though the affair had as near as damn it been a tragedy.

"Snipers from the garage, sir. It's all clear there now, you can go in and occupy as soon as the gunners let up. And you'll find the mortar—and the rest of the stuff—you'll find them——"

He swayed a little at the knees, crazily faint. Baird saw him going, and said quickly: "Are you hurt, Sergeant?"

"Only a scratch, sir—and knocked a bit silly," he explained with perfect composure, and instantly collapsed together at Baird's feet. He heard the first crash of the barrage break out over the borders of Goch, and had just time to be glad that he was safely out of it; but the last thing he remembered was Clure's wild-eyed face blazing at him snow-white out of the pervading greyness, and Clure's voice calling out to him with a note of desolate urgency in it; and the last reaction he felt was a half-dazed wonder at the vigour of that cry, which he had neither done nor said anything to evoke. He went down into the ungrateful dark as if hiding from that inexplicable utterance;

and when he came back into daylight to find Clure as he had always known him, deprecating of face and hesitant of voice, still it continued to haunt and disquiet him until the day, over three months later, when he made sense of it at last.

PART FOUR

GERMANY

"And I should wake up soon in some place where
The piled-up arms of the fighting angels gleam."
MORRIS: *Rapunzel.*

I

WAITING to cross the Rhine, a mile or so downstream from
Wesel, they fell into a world where nothing was real. A
long straight dyke ran along the skyline before them, cutting off
from view the flat silver flood of the river; and they knew,
because of frequent notices which said so, that to climb to the
top of this rampart of earth was to expose themselves to the
enemy sharp-shooters beyond the water. A long straight road
fringed with long straight poplars paralleled the dyke behind
their positions, and they knew by experience that certain spots
on this road were permanently unhealthy by reason of enemy
shelling and mortaring. But for the daily crop of casualties from
these causes there might have been no Germans left in the
world. The civilians from the area they occupied had either
run upon their own account, or been removed forcibly to the
rear. The cattle and horses and pigs had not, simply because
no one had time to deal with them, nor would it have been
practicable in any case to draw attention to the movements in
the area by adding to them a frantic, bellowing bustle of
exhausted animals being driven off westward. They were left
to wander unfed and untended until they fell down from weakness and starvation, and died where they lay. In a day or
two now, when the crossing was accomplished and the bridgehead safe, the survivors would be herded back to Holland, and
those past moving at least put out of their misery; but now they
shambled in and out of the artificial fog, ghosts of animals in
a spectre of a world, crying at man with weak, weird cries and
haunting his helplessness with their pain; and the Midshires,
who had been forbidden to shoot them for fear of revealing the
positions they had so carefully hidden under fold upon fold of
smoke, fled from them in a superstitious horror they had never
yet felt for the enemy, dead or alive.

It was necessary, in these few days of late March, to cling

fiercely to the knowledge they had that the last great grouping was in hand, and the last great leap preparing. To lose touch with that for an instant was to be adrift in a nightmare, an opium-dream of which the hollow-eyed calves pulling at the dugs of dead mothers, and the lean horses blundering about crippled with wounds, and the crazed cows with their flattened sides and swollen udders were only a single facet. Every dawn the grouped generators poured out their bluish-white smoke into the air in spread hands of vapour disintegrating at the finger-tips; and every fifteen minutes throughout the day canisters of zinc chloride were fired here and there to deepen the obscurity. From behind the Infantry positions the cloud flowed over them and dwelt constant upon the air, making not darkness but a perpetual leaden twilight, blue-tinted, without distances. Men appeared out of this veiled quietness without warning, and passing on, dematerialised again as nimbly as they had taken shape. The sun, which knew only this one cloud during those days, rolled across the sky as mildly as the moon, reduced to the cool silverness of a sixpence; and a faint, surprised warmth came down through the murk and touched them fitfully with comfort and reassurance. Only at night were the generators suffered to rest; and then the mysterious cloud was gradually lifted, and the earth emerged darkened but clean again, and in place of the impalpable white pall over them there was a soaring of air, and stars, and the passage of the moon.

In this fantastic world of quiet nightmare they lived a strange, still life. All was already planned that could be planned; there was nothing left for them to do but sleep and wait, holding their breath against the moment when the penned assault would be launched at last, and varying the monotony by the desultory firing of zinc-chloride canisters, the pursuit of occasional poultry, and the composition of long letters home. They dug themselves in under the dykes and in the deserted farm build-ings, and made themselves comfortable, and slept through the long hours of the day; but at night, when the fog dispersed, they moved forward into their slit trenches upon the dyke and in the flat fields beyond, and obscurely from over the wide flood waters of the Rhine the knowledge of the enemy came to them. He was still there, the German, still waiting for them in hate and determination. They were not done with him yet.

Behind the massed generators at their backs there was activity enough. Fleets of Ducks, Weasels, Buffaloes, Crocodiles were grinding up into position by all the passable roads. Thousands of trucks shuffled slowly through from Holland loaded with sections of Bailey bridge, rolls of Sommerfeld track, wire, tools, all manner of queer, necessary things. Mobile cranes and derricks, capable of hefting 36-foot landing vessels, were grouped coyly in the wrecked village away to their right, under the sheltering clouds of the smoke. Foresters were busy in what remained of the woods, felling the longest and straightest trunks to make slipways by which the pontoons could be launched. If you walked back westward for half a mile or so you were just as likely to run into the Navy or the Royal Marines as the Army, for they'd been coming in in considerable numbers for days past, along with enormous transports which had covered over two hundred miles of damaged roads, God and their crews alone knew how, to bring up flotillas of 26-ton Landing Craft Mechanised, capable of shifting Sherman tanks if need be, and 9-ton Landing Craft, Vehicles, Personnel; primly named, deadly-looking steel giants nosing purposefully for the Rhine.

That was the world behind. The world in front, which they lived in more nearly though they saw it only at night from the trenches along the dyke, was a waste of flat meadows dappled here and there with flood water left behind in hollows after the winter level had receded, and patterned here and there with ruled lines of orchard trees, and occasional shells of houses; but these slight variations did nothing to shake, or brighten, or bring to life the motionless emptiness of that stretch of land. The surface of the river itself, wide and still beyond, with only a flat dark line for its opposite bank, was not more dead than those once populated and fertile fields. All night they would look over it, and see it as sterile as the moon itself; and only scattered bursts of mortar fire, or a chattering spurt of tracer from a Spandau, would remind them that the enemy also sat watching as intently beyond the river. To these invitations they never made any response. Only from the heavy artillery far in the rear a methodical rushing passage of shells overhead kept the silence out of their ears; and at dawn, when the shelling ceased and the smoke was just beginning all over again, it grew so quiet that they could hear the larks rising and circling in invisible and unfeeling rapture over the pastures where the cattle starved to death.

In was in these moments of quietness that Sergeant Benison began to hear voices inside him, and they frightened him a good deal. The first time he grew aware of them was after the mortar-

bomb which killed two of his section had set off in his head
trains of echoes which survived after the dizziness and aching
subsided. He supposed they were simply the natural
disturbances of shock, duplicating that temporary collapse he
had suffered at Goch, and that they would diminish with time
and eventually go away altogether; but they persisted. Nothing
was the matter with him; he hadn't even a scratch to show for
it. Only inwardly the echoes ate their way deep into his substance, and reproduced themselves at will whenever the quietness came down in which they could make themselves heard.
They said that he'd been luckier already than any man has a
right to be, and that it wasn't to be supposed that it could go on
much longer. They said that even if this was to be the end
of the war it could as easily be the end of him. They said it
would be just like him to get killed on the last lap. They told
him it was no use refusing to consider it, that he might as well
face the possibility, if only for Imogen's sake. But the crawling,
liquefying fear they started within him was not all on Imogen's
account but very largely on his own. For everything they said
was true, and he could do nothing about it.

He didn't want to die. He was terrified of dying, not because
the thing itself was so awful, but because it meant the end of
living, and he wanted to live. How had it come into being, this
unexpected appetite for life? How had it come about that he,
who had known times when death was a holiday tantalisingly
deferred, now shrank from it in something not far from panic?
What incomprehensible sickness had taken hold of him? Was
it because of Imogen? Could loving her undo the most fundamental principles by which he had learned to move? Not
through any fault of hers, certainly, not because of any word
or look she had ever given him; but it might be that the thought
of a life with her had been too much of happiness to offer
suddenly to a man who had expected so little from living. Or
was it that the lasting part of himself had outlived disillusion-
ment and returned by roundabout ways to the normal state of
man, which is an optimism very tenacious of life? Did he
actually want to survive the war in order to see what happened
next? In order, even, to have a hand in what happened next?

He supposed a psychiatrist might think him a fit case for
study; or the chaplain, maybe, would consider it his job if he
knew what went on inside this taciturn man. But the echoes
were contemptuous of any such attempts at comfort. What
difference would all the flannel in the world make, they said,

if one of these mortar shells had his name on it? Once he got as far as drifting in upon a service in the biggest barn in the farmyard behind the dyke; but the padre was a breezy, high-coloured young man with a big voice and an air of indomitable enjoyment, to whom no one in decency could confide anything more disturbing than the football scores; so Jim took his sickness away with him and went back almost thankfully to his dug-out under the swell of the dyke, and wrote a cheerful letter home, and went on living unobtrusively in terror of his life.

The whole thing had something to do with Arthur Clure. He didn't know how, but Clure was there in it, tangled as deep as he was. It was in the way the little man looked at him sometimes, when he thought no one was noticing; like a proprietor, like a familiar, pondering him in an intent way that worried him very seriously. If all had gone well at Goch and after, Clure need never have been aware of him at all; but something in that relationship had gone wrong, and silently they confronted each other with their separated knowledge of it every day, every time their glances crossed. Sometimes Jim thought it was from these encounters he drew the conviction that they could not both survive. Something had happened at Goch which he had never meant to happen; he had given too much of himself away, so much that he was lame now for lack of a vital part. He had maimed himself, and he would die of it. Clure was all right; Clure had never seemed to look back since that night under the garage, nor to remember that he had looked back then; so why should it be he who died?

It was at this point always that he began most clearly to see how undeservedly fortunate he had really been, in having Imogen's love, which might so easily have gone to a better man. And all the little tormenting jealousies and anxieties he had escaped for so long through preoccupation with other things came back and had their revenge on him. But all this was within; he seemed to the rest of the platoon much as usual, only if anything more dour than ever, which under that ever-lasting twilight was not surprising. They all went about like people in a nightmare; if it took a different form with him they did not notice it. And the days carried them along steadily towards zero hour of what they felt in their bones was to be the last great adventure of the war.

It began on the night of March 23rd, at five o'clock on a fine evening, with a barrage that made the soil tremble right

268

down to the Rhine. All sorts of small, unhurried activities began about the same time, for many miles up and down the river in the Wesel sector. Fresh white tapes ran out through the residue of the blue haze, to mark the paths to the dyke and beyond. Columns of tracked vehicles, with assault boats hitched on behind, began to assemble along the rear roads close to the Infantry positions. Assault troops timed to make their leaps between midnight and morning drew their emergency rations and packed up their belongings, stripping down wives and pin-up girls from the boarded walls of their dug-outs. Derricks moved up closer to the dykes, ready to begin unloading heavy landing craft as soon as the assault boats had moved off. Engineers sat down upon their stacked and smoothed tree-trunks for a final rest and smoke before the business of bridging began. All along the river a pause and a tremor ran before the reverberations of the guns, and men drew breath and looked towards Wesel. The orchestra had struck up with the overture, and the rise of the curtain would not be long delayed.

The interlude was unlike anything they had known. The preparations completed themselves deliberately; there seemed no haste, and no urgency. To doubt the success of the crossing was impossible; and this strange new security took away their normal preoccupation with personal nervousness, and left them only a deep and dispassionate interest in all that was to come. From high places and look-out posts they could watch history being made, be spectators even while they were actors in this last great drama of the times, and contemplate without surprise the possibility that some of them would be dead before morning.

The enemy barrage which opened in response to their own was not great, and the Spandau experts on the shore were holding their fire until they could see something definite to fire at. When the darkness came, and the Midshires slithered forward to climb the dyke and look across the river, they could see no sign of the enemy, no boat patrols venturing the water, none of the customary perforations of small-arms fire along the flat line of the shore. The British barrage appeared to be blazing away steadily into a depopulated country, wasting its enormous power upon a body already dead. Overhead the air was convulsed with the rushing of steel as guns and rocket projectors together poured an unceasing stream of fire into Germany. The whole sky was torn away in shreds and borne eastward over the Rhine, tracer like an orange-red net writhing in great weals across the face of it. They lay under this canopy of fire, and could not talk to one another because of the din; but by nudgings and signs and pointing fingers they compared notes upon the ominous lack of resistance, and marked the beginning of the disintegration of Wesel.

The Commandos at Wesel were the first to make the crossing; at ten o'clock, by moonlight, their assault boats put out across the river to land them within reach of a massing point some fifteen hundred yards outside the town. Of their passage the Midshires from their trenches could see nothing, not even a pencil-line of darkness defacing the silver of the moonlit water upstream; but they knew, because everything was working as if by machinery, that at ten to the moment the move began, and by half past ten the assault troops had taken up their positions and were waiting for the next thing to happen; which next thing was the methodical bombing to pieces of the town. This the Midshires saw very precisely, as did all the troops up and down the river, for the clear night made of it a dazzling firework display. The barrage slackened abruptly, and over the diminishing thunder came the sudden insistent drone of bomber engines sweeping overhead; and in a minute a burst of coloured flares circled the target to the crescendo roar of the first 'plane diving. A small town, Wesel, they were assured, very neat, very compact; difficult to pinpoint, but easy to flatten once the target was accurately marked. It took the R.A.F. the prescribed quarter of an hour to flatten it, though the regular rocking impacts, measured out briskly second after second, seemed hardly to continue for so long. A dozen quaking purplish glows of fire burst out below, and a hundred drifting plumes of flak suddenly sprang to life in the upper air, before smoke gathered in an angry cloud and dirtied all. When the shivering of earth and air ceased, Wesel was a furnace of sullen slow fires glowing through a pall of smoke, and a single flare was burning its way deliberately earthward on the side of the town where the Commandos were massed, as a sign that the field was theirs. As the thrum of the returning bombers receded westward, the distant chattering of small arms began in what was left of Wesel, under that angry black and crimson cloud.

Well, that was that. The thing had begun according to plan, and their own zero hour would not be long. Time for a last mug of tea under the dyke, and a last smoke, and a last island of stillness within this appalling persistent ocean of noise. There was always, at the beginning of such an onset, a moment when you looked round the familiar faces of the platoon, Baird, Peterson, Morgan, Mason, Courthope, Clure, all the lot of them you knew better than your own flesh, and took a solemn farewell of them in your mind, in case you should miss the only one you would not see alive again. But this time, drinking scalding tea in the circle of them before the assault boats moved off, Jim saw everywhere through their faces his own face, and silently took leave of it. He knew he was being a fool, but he knew there was no cure. Whatever had hold of him he might outlive but he could not suppress. He had never before found himself brought up short at every turn against his own reluctance to die; but so it was now, and if he could not alter it he must accept it, and add it to the weight he carried. Why not? Many a man among them must live with it night and day and give no sign; and why should he escape it, or find it beyond his scope, if they could shoulder it? After all, there was nothing new about it; most men alive knew it well enough.

They moved off at one o'clock in the morning, the first to cross in their sector. There was half an hour of standing by, close beside the column of assault boats along the road; then a casual passing and repassing of officers up and down the line, a few remarks half overheard, half lost in the barrage; then Baird beside him, and a voice which he knew to be Colonel Friedland's saying mellowly: "Come on, you fellows!" and the great rolling bulk of him swinging away towards the tape-marked gap in the dyke. The tractors lurched forward at a walking pace, the boats slithered along lizard-like behind, and the men walked beside them with a hand out to cling by the low gunwale. Beyond the dyke the moonlit fields opened pallidly, and beyond these the river, wide and white as milk, still well out of its normal limits, but dropped from its high flood. The assault boats were manhandled into the water without difficulty from these flat reaches of land, and rode steady against the shore; and the men climbed in and filled them. Their faces in the moonlight were all alike, pale and very still, with fixed eyes. They went in awe of the night and the occasion; the enemy had ceased to matter.

It was one o'clock to the dot when they moved off, and until they left the land they had not been fired upon, though they must have been observed, and indeed expected; but as the green-white rim of the fields fell away behind them a scattered Spandau fire broke out in a stuttering line along the distant shore, and scarlet threads of tracer hissed across the water and left a broken red reflection behind. They stared ahead eagerly, by these tenuous lines fixing their attention along the rise of the land, upon the hither side of the inland fires which smouldered low under the smoke. There were no casualties during that crossing; the level surface carried them lightly along its moon-glazed flats, the deceptive currents tugged at them ineffectively from below, and the barrage lifted gradually, proceeding inland ahead of them as they came into mid passage. The width of the river here was not much less than four hundred yards, and riding low in the boats they saw this distance multiplied and magnified until they travelled along the bosom of an ocean of lambent light, upon either side very far from land; which was fitting enough, for though the maps disagreed with them they knew this for a frontier; and beyond it they would step into Germany indeed, and be able at last to believe in victory as they had not believed in it at Erdenlich.

They slacked along the far shore at last, nosing in to the rise of grass; and the nearest steadied themselves a second and leaped for dry ground and the rest followed, splashing up the last shallows with cold fountains at their heels. Now as before, now as later, all was done without haste. Their job was to mop up the village which lay a hundred yards or so back from the river, and the woodland upstream, and so move in to meet the Commandos at Wesel; but there was time and to spare for the task. No miracles of speed or proficiency were required of them now. Miracles had been rendered unnecessary. They could mass at leisure on the shore, and move in upon the village without interference. When they looked back from the rise of the fields at the Rhine now dotted with more boats in mid passage, they looked at a dwindling legend, the wall of Jericho laid in ruins.

For two hours after this they still did not see the enemy. He was gone from the flat fields across which they deployed their forces with so much care; he had left even the village, when they reached it and combed it by lantern-light and tracer, and had abandoned with it a house full of his wounded, who announced themselves by a flutter of white from a ground-floor window and a chorus of screams and cries within. The first doctor who made the crossing took over this house as it stood, and set up his Aid Post there; and within an hour British mortar casualties lay beside the German stretchers, marking with their stoical and satisfied silence the lamentations of the master-race. All night until the light grew dove-grey in mist along the river, the tale of the wounded mounted as Germans and British were brought in side by side; and all night the conquerors shut their mouths upon their sufferings, for it was enough for them that they had crossed the Rhine; and all night the conquered, who at their worst had possessed more of courage than of most other virtues, tossed and screamed under their hurts because the crossing of the Rhine was to them a violation and a death. So final, so symbolic was this leashed river which lay now behind the fighting, silver and serene in the fading moonlight.

It was in the wood that the Germans chose to fight, where shadows of trunk and branch and bush complicated the darkness and offered cover and to spare for mortars and guns and men. It was a little Reichswald again, but more sorry and battered, scarred piteously by artillery fire and full of dead men. The survivors were dug well in, and hung on to their positions grimly until they were searched out man by man; but still there was neither haste nor urgency, for the Midshires had been allowed until full daylight to work through the belt of woodland and emerge within sight of Wesel. They went about it methodically, filtering through the cratered shades by ones and twos, combing every bush, and rooting out from camouflaged trenches and dug-outs a stream of wretched prisoners half crazed with shock. Some of them came from cover and gave themselves up unhurt; some were wounded already, and had no option but to surrender; but most fought until they were driven from hiding at the bayonet's point, and went down stiff-necked to the temporary cage in the village, to be shipped back at first light to the western bank of the river and a long captivity. And foot by foot the Midshires worked their way through the wood towards Wesel, and waited for the light.

The weight at their backs was growing all the time, steadily gathering its impetus without any appearance of concern, for all that was visible was a continual trickle of assault boats across the stream, and under the far bank an insignificant activity of cranes lifting the first L.C.V.P.s into the shallows. A single ferry was nosing tanks over the river, clumsily, fussily, like a duck urging an unwilling foster-child to swim. But this was all, and it made no show. The bridge-builders would not emerge until daylight; not a single truck, not a tree of their felling, nor a solitary pontoon, showed along the flat shore. They had become adept, like all the Army of the Rhine, at

273

disappearing into the background. Nevertheless, though there was so little to be seen, the sense of the thrust thus launched mounted disproportionately in the minds of the spearhead troops who went before it, until they felt the whole power and purpose of England firm at their backs. Jim had not felt it so since 1940, and then it had been an illusion. Not even at the landings in Normandy had he been held upright like this, though the propulsion had begun then; first the touch of that ancient hand, long-suffering, slow to anger, tenacious as the hills; now the sweep of it moving him forward at will. And now, when he should have been able to rest in it, now he must remember at every impulsion: "It can use, but not save. In spite of it, one little slug could be the end of me, as well now as ever."

He had time to think this while he was saying other things, because it was fastened into his mind beyond eviction. It ran like a burden in him while he was climbing out of a crater in the wood, and chivying prisoners into line for Courthope to take back to the village. Two men had just been carried back to the Aid Post on stretchers, one of them with his face covered; a third was lying in dappled shade under trees, being patched up in haste by a medical orderly, and groaning on a steady, deep note broken only for breath. Any one of them could as easily have been him. There, but for the grace of God——— And but for the indifference of God the bloke on the stretcher could have been saying the same. Everyone thought for himself first; he wouldn't be human else. But that was a blind alley, if ever there was one. Once you began considering death as something to dodge, and to hell with the rest, you saw it wherever you turned your eyes, and the face was always your own. Once you began to fear it, you suffered it continually; every relief, every self-congratulation as some other poor devil was carried away, only renewed the agony all over again. No, Imogen could never have done this to him, nor caused him to do it to himself; there must be something else operating within, some sickness, some failure of the mind. He was afraid it might become visible to others in time, and he dared not think of that. Once something happened which made him suspect that it had already been noticed. They were working through the margin of the wood under a heavy mortar fire, and a near-miss had made them drop into the churned mud; and before Jim could rise there was young Teddy flat at his elbow, asking breathlessly: "Sergeant, you all right?"

"Sure I'm all right!" he said, jerking his head up. "Why not?"

"Oh, nothing, only it was pretty near."

But why select him for the enquiry, when it had been just as near to half a dozen others? Why should young Teddy, whose sole business was to acquire a little sense and worry about nothing beside, suddenly start wondering if Sergeant Benison was all right? Why should Arthur Clure look at him, after every impact, with that intent and terrifying look? He felt it now in his back; and when he turned his head, there were the eyes fixed upon him as always, large and steadfast and bright. It was there he had given up the mainspring of his peace of mind, like a bloody fool, meddling too complacently with another man's problems. What could he expect in return? Wouldn't he have been hard put to it not to hate any man who had taken such liberties with him? But it was done now; they'd all have to abide by it. Maybe Clure wanted him to break, so that that night in Goch might be wiped out. Maybe Clure was waiting to be the one to reach a hand to him when the collapse came. And who could blame him if he was? No Jim, at least; he might be in a bad way, but his sense of justice was still functioning; and by God, he'd take the hand when it was offered, and give him his revenge.

"You keep your mind on what you're doing," he said sharply, "and never mind me."

"O.K., Sergeant! I only——"

But Teddy was learning sense too fast to finish the sentence; he let it slip away unlamented into the patterned moony aisles of nut-trees as they picked themselves up and went on. And as for Arthur Clure, he never spoke what was in his mind, only stayed close, and kept his eyes fixed, and waited for his time.

When the early light came they were through the wood, and working along the fields towards the margin of the town. This time, with no artificial fog to mar it, the morning came fair and clear, only the sluggish smoke of fires smearing its pale and radiant air, while the upper heaven was as bright as glass. From the meadows the Midshires could see at last a fair section of the river winding away upstream to where Wesel bridge lolled broken-backed in the water, with sunlight gleaming through its girders; under that bridge more flotillas of assault craft were busy transporting more men, and as for the town itself, it was already in the hands of the Commandos. All they could see of it was the outline of the house-roofs low by the water, splintered now into matchwood and piled up at all angles like spillikins. Some of the fires were out; only an angry russet smoke hung thinning overhead, and an occasional pulsing glow, diminished now by daylight, made a quivering along the still air below. On the western shore of the river they could see the lifted noses of cranes and derricks swinging, and about them a great movement of men; but it needed glasses to enable them to pick out any details, the corrugated appearance of the mud-banks where the peeled tree-trunks were being laid down, the slithering descent of pontoons, the blunt nose of the first bridge elongating itself along the water, the engineers coming down in pairs with anchors slung between them, the amphibians making arrowhead tracks back and forth into the currents, all the paraphernalia of a new temporary town founded with one end in view, to transport the greatest possible amount of heavy armour over the river at the earliest possible hour. For the thing now was not to break out of the bridgehead in any haste, but to bring across forces so formidable that the success of that move might be beyond question before it was even attempted. Within a week they might leap through Münster as they had leaped through Northern France and Belgium; but now they went deliberately, cementing everything they did. Patton, far down south, could afford to sledge-hammer his way deep into Germany without even pausing to think, for he had smashed all immediate resistance west of the Rhine. Hodges at Remagen might have pushed as hard if he could have kept his unexpected bridge a little longer; luck had had a hand in the game there. But here at Wesel it was a cold matter of calculations; the enemy had withdrawn his forces intact across the river, and was waiting to fight hard for what was left of his illusion. It was simple arithmetic to assess what he had, and to have more, to judge what he would expect, and to launch upon him worse than was expected.

They had almost forgotten the barrage, but when it ceased abruptly at a quarter to ten the silence fell upon them like thunder, and for the first five minutes of the quietness they did not notice how their heads sang after the long bombardment. They could see larks in their ascending round, and strained to hear them, but the song was too frail by far to make any impact upon their dulled ear-drums; and in ten minutes more, as a degree of the deafness was wearing off, stranger birds than larks came sweeping flight by flight over the Rhine, flying low, with their jumping-doors already open. The paratroops were off inland, to enlarge the bridgehead to the positions of the enemy artillery. Everyone on the ground stood still to watch them pass. The mist rising from the river made it difficult to follow them home, for they came out of a white gleam, and passed into a white gleam, and so wave on wave continued to pass for an hour or more; but towards the end of this time the sun was dispersing the haze, and it was possible to watch them heel over the dropping area, and rock in the feathery puffs of flak, and even to catch here and there the pinpoints of light upon the filling parachutes. Towing 'planes unshipped their gliders and turned back westward, while the abandoned Horsas circled and plunged to earth. There were some losses among them, for a few lurched and disintegrated in mid air, and more, probably, overturned in their skid-tracks on landing; but by eleven o'clock the shower of flak had almost ceased, as early paratroops cleared the ground for those who were to follow, so that the last waves of gliders came in unopposed, and made their descent at leisure. The Midshires, watching, remembered Valkenswaard, and the airborne landings in Holland, which had been everything these were not, and yet had looked so like them. Yet out of that magnificent gamble had come this calculated and assured strategy, as wild parents breed methodical children and yet stamp the opposed substance with their own image.

Throughout the middle of the day the sky was thronging with Allied 'planes, for by now the flak batteries had all either been put out of action or fallen to the Red Devils up in front. Even on the ground resistance had fallen in this immediate area to a spasmodic activity of isolated units, supported by some mortars, but having little or no artillery backing left. The Midshires touched hands with the Commandos in the heap of bricks, splinters and ash which was Wesel, and moved off inland about noon to try and find their way to the paratroops, five miles or more away. This time, thank God, there was no river in between. They passed through a village where a few middle-aged men and their womenfolk were creeping out of the wreckage of their houses, and children looked round their mothers' skirts numbly, staring as they had seen other children stare after bombing, all dilated eyes and sharp bones. No one in these territories seemed to have any fear of the invader, but only a sort of uneasiness in his presence, from lack of practice in being occupied. They watched, looking sidelong that they might be less clearly seen to watch every slightest move made by the newcomers; and wherever they caught English eyes they smiled quickly, and looked more than ever ingratiating and eager to please. The men raised their hats if an officer's eye dwelt upon them; the older women nudged their children to a sort of half-attention, the younger ones tidied their hair and smoothed their skirts and began to make nervous play with their eyes. Only one middle-aged housewife stood bolt upright in the broken doorway of her house and glared hatred at the Midshires as they passed through, and catching Jim's eye as he came abreast of her, very deliberately spat upon him. He had more respect for her than for the rest, and thought it likely she would need less watching, too; a person who spits in your face is less likely to shoot you in the back than the other kind.

There were going to be more difficulties of adjustment here than belonged to one side, though. The lads were used to being the friends of children, for instance, wherever they came, and had hardly yet met the problem of this other kind of child, for the fighting zones had been cleared, as a rule, of civilians, and nowhere except on the west bank of the Rhine had there been a lengthy halt since they entered Germany. The women, too—some formula had to be found for dealing with them. They could not be treated as fighting enemies, though they were enemies sure enough; nor must they be helped and comforted as if any injury had been done them. The hands which had done services willingly for French women and Dutch must not fall unawares into the habit of doing as much for these; and not everyone had a Miriam to stand in between. He knew it was too early as yet to bother about the halt which had not materialised; the time to keep an eye on the platoon would be when they were still. They went through this village now with hardly a glance aside, their noses to the trail; even young Teddy could pass by a blonde of seventeen or eighteen and never see her. Or did he see her and make up his mind not to see her? You couldn't be so sure about Teddy as once; he shied off first impulses pretty suspiciously these days. At least he went right ahead, his eyes narrowed to look for red berets rather than blond hair.

It was almost five o'clock in the evening when they sighted the first. They were five miles inland by then, and had reached the landing area, as they knew by infallible and lavish signs, for the whole landscape was littered with gliders, ammunition boxes, shells, stores, matchwood wreckage, and draped with tatters of parachute silk. Coming out of a copse aflutter with white and orange ribbons, they saw their first paratrooper walking leisurely towards them, and even at a distant view his gait first, and then his grin, broadcast that all was well here. He was a very big man, well over six feet, with the red beret pulled well over his right eye; and he strolled erect and monumental over open fields still raked with occasional fire, content with himself and his works, though half his shirt was torn off him, and a sliver of flesh with it. He greeted them with a jerked thumb, and the grin widened.

Baird, nosing ahead like a terrier, asked how far forward Division was, and was told that it was not more than half a mile on.

"How're you doing?" he asked. "Have much trouble?"

"Oh, not so dusty! It was warm at first, but it didn't last long."

"Is it safe to go right ahead?"

"Safe as houses, sir, if you watch your step across the ditches and run like hell through that bit of hanging wood."

He accepted a cigarette, and asked Jim to tighten up the bloody bandage knotted on his shoulder; and having accepted these services, conveyed himself away at the same untiring pace towards the Rhine, leaving them to make the best of their way forward until they struck Divisional H.Q., which they did somewhat after six o'clock. It was dusk by then, and the inland fires were making smudges of dark purple low upon the iris-tinted evening. A mist, fine and pale, was hanging over the river's course when they halted for the night in that very ridge of woodland through which they had been warned to run like hell. The last half-hour had made all the difference; there were no longer any Germans in the wood, but only the red berets everywhere. Even the dead had been moved out, to leave a clear field in this most advanced position. The Midshires dug in for the night in a daze of tiredness and satisfaction, and settled down to get what sleep they could before the dawn moved them on again.

Jim walked the length of the hanger before it was dark, from the crater tucked under the lee of it at the eastern end, with seventy-odd prisoners and one bored paratrooper squatting in it, to the splintered plume of trees at the western end, draped with silk and nylon rope and bristling with fragments of a glider which had come to grief there. Looking forward, he could see a rolling expanse of meadow and coppice, scattered village roofs, farm buildings, and the ornate bulk of at least one mansion with its neat skirts of orchard about it, all growing filmy and remote in the twilight. Puffs of flak were blown upward out of this portrait of peace, and splayed along the sky upon the tails of British aircraft; but apart from these reminders the countryside seemed empty of resistance in one day. Looking back, he had lost the river but for the upper river of haze which flowed along over its course; but he could see the smoky smoulder of Wesel glowing again in the dusk, and between that point and himself the same homely scenery turned fantastic with the shells and carcasses of gliders, lying in the fields at every angle, with splintered wing-tips, burst bodies and black voids within their noses, as if a plague of locusts had passed over, and great numbers of them had been beaten down here by a killing wind.

He was irresistibly reminded of Arnhem. So little, and yet so much, separated the two adventures. The one had been a failure, the other an unqualified success, so history would say; and yet it was Arnhem, the failure, the tragedy, the triumph, that people would remember and celebrate, as for thousands of years they had remembered Troy. He walked a little way towards where splashes of white and red silk marked the forward foxholes of Divisional H.Q., strange coloured dots in the fields. All manner of people were coming in now, by jeep and tank and Bren-carrier, with stores and reinforcements in plenty; and for these sky-fallen men there was no terrible shadow of day after day of waiting for help, until their food was gone and their water supplies reduced to the meagre harvestings of rain and dew. They had already been relieved; they sat in the brushwood hollows over fresh brews of tea, eating new rations, and resting from their labours with cigarettes, their last wounded already taken care of, and their well-handled affairs now passed into other hands. Vividly Jim remembered the silent, dirty, exhausted men tramping back from the Lek beside him on the night of September 25th. Here was another progression, another continuity in this specialised sort of living, where every day was the germ of a coming day, and every year of a following year; where reverses were the heralds of triumphs, and bore upon them a prophetic radiance; and where one man's dying set in train currents of energy and valour and power to keep many men alive.

When he came back to the platoon it was almost dark, and only a subdued murmur and movement marked where men went among the trees. The barrage had opened up on a steady, unexcited note, and tracer was burning through the mist, but by comparison with the previous night it was calm, almost silent.

Someone moved and drew nearer to him through the shadows, but did not speak to him or call his attention except by being so deeply aware of him. He did not turn his head to see who it was who took care to be near him before the darkness fell; there was no need. He knew the feel of Arthur Clure's eyes on him; it was becoming his constant companion, so that when he was away from it his equilibrium seemed upset, as if he had gained again the lost part of his integrity, and was at a loss how best to carry it.

2

Next day the four separate landing-points between Rees and Wesel were merged in one great bridgehead, thirty miles wide; and in two days more the bridgehead, steadily expanding, had become a salient. Already the mysterious fulcrum upon which all their motion swung in such calculated balance had stolen forward imperceptibly, and left the river behind; and with the dwindling of the Rhine fell away behind them all manner of doubts, wonderings, insecurities; yet with so much left to do, all was now over. There remained only the long, descending tension, the unwinding of a thread whose end was already in sight. All their long five years of fighting back and forth over the span of the world came down at last into this thirty-mile salient and the power pent up within it, as a lifetime dwindles into a moment at the approach of death.

On the 29th of March Montgomery's armour broke out at last like a spring released, and bore forward in a great surge across the face of Germany; and on their heels went the Infantry, packed into trucks, Bren-carriers, Ducks, lorries, riding passenger upon tanks, anyhow to keep the speed. No more foot-slogging this trip; this was as breathless as the impetus loosed at Falaise, and even more final.

It was an incredible journey from the moment that they gathered speed. There were long stretches of farming country where scarcely anyone seemed to realise what their approach meant, where well-fed, smiling girls came out and fixed white flags to their gateposts, and seemed to think life should go on, apart from this small technical concession, exactly the same as before; and to behold their serene unconcern was to be reasonably sure that it would. Food was handed out on demand to the invaders, without sullenness or reserve, in these parts; it was plain that these people, so long as they themselves were comfortably off, held the war, lost or won, to be no affair of theirs. Yet their indifference made them superficially attractive, and to live among them could have been deeply confounding; so Jim was glad that the speed did not slacken as yet, and every comely ingratiating face was lost as soon as discovered. There were villages and small towns just stirring from the torpor of shock after bombing, or after the flight of their own armies; where a handful of overworked non-coms. ordered and pushed and chivied the whole population back into living, and were obeyed at first numbly, then slavishly, then with an opaque, insolent servility which flattered some and nauseated others. The women it was who remained disquietingly in the memory afterwards, for there were more of them, and the greater part of them were young, and in spite of their servility quite unreconciled to defeat. Wherever there were scenes of disorder, and particularly of looting, nine out of ten people involved were young women. After bombing their main anxiety seemed to be to get what plunder they could from the damaged shops and warehouses of their less fortunate compatriots, and they would fight for a pair of silk stockings or a jar of molasses as viciously as wild-cats for their young. Soiled and dishevelled and predatory, they were almost reassuring to Jim then, for they had no time to be anything but repulsive. It was in the country places they were most unnerving, where the war had not touched them, and they came out from their kitchens bare-armed and fair and inquisitive to welcome the strangers, so unaware of wrong or shame that it was almost as if this was a second advance into the Netherlands, where only the innocent waited. Yet they came and went in a glimpse only, wasting their smiles upon a flash of passing steel; and before the column reached the Dortmund-Ems Canal and the town of Rheine, where again they were compelled to slacken and fight, they had seen other faces which armed them against these.

This new manifestation began at a small factory, where they arrived on March 31st, a no-account place no one had cared to stop and smash; yet it was burning merrily as they drew in there and halted for a while to let the armoured traffic clear from the road. There was music coming from within the loading-shed inside the gate, and music was so unexpected there that they dropped out of their trucks to investigate, and found a crowd of hands from the factory dancing to the sound of two violins, a 'cello and a broken-down piano. There were at least two hundred people there, in the poorest of clothes, with shabby shoes and thin bodies, but with so much of joy in their faces that it was at once clear these were no Germans. The Midshires were no sooner seen than hands seized them and drew them into the throng, and they embraced Frenchwomen, Czechs, Poles, Dutch girls, Austrians, and whirled away with them in a waltz. No explanations were ever given, no greetings ever exchanged in words; but they knew that these were freed slaves of the last tyranny of history, celebrating by the only available means their release from servitude. This was a joy more awful than their tragedy, almost, and could never be expressed in any known language; but the Polish girl in Jim's arms, young, handsome and haggard, talked to him in her own tongue as they danced, talked for ten minutes without ceasing in a rush of passion, with a pulse beating wildly in her throat, and tears running down from her open eyes over her wan cheeks and smiling mouth; and he could read into the outlandish syllables the whole story of her deportation to this place, the fate of her family, left behind or dead somewhere in Poland, her life here without love or light or hope, her long labour and humiliation, and her ecstasy now, so much more wonderful in its birth than the grown reality could ever be. When the traffic jam cleared and the Midshires were called away he suddenly bent and kissed her mouth with the words still alive between the lips, and she drew breath hard under his touch, and kissed him again with all her might, because he was not German, and she loved all the rest of the world. Then he put her into the arms of one of her own countrymen, and went away with the warmth of her still in him, and a queer foreboding pain in his heart; and he wondered how long this joy would last, and by what miserable stages it would crumble about her ears.

From that day the roads were full of them, the forgotten people, the new Ishmaelites, the new children of Babel. They came from the east, moving slowly, at first in groups of ten or a dozen together, then by hundreds, by thousands, in continuous processions; very patiently they came, for many were weak, and some were crippled, but steadily they moved towards the west, towards where there was help and shelter, food and clothing and medical aid to tide them over until the field was cleared and they could go home. Some had bundles tucked under their arms, some had made or looted small handcarts and piled into them the belongings of four or five of their number, which they took turns to push; but most had nothing but what they wore, the nondescript rags of once proud uniforms, scraps of bright colour glowing pathetically through the dirt still, drab Todt Organisation overalls, shapeless civilian coats picked up from the pitiful along the road, for even here there must be pity. They spoke all manner of languages, and some even carried their nationality blazoned upon their clothes, "Ost" for all those from the eastern territories of the Reich, an initial "P" for the Poles. They limped towards the west, a humbled but not a broken people, smiling at the armour that drove them from the road, waving their hands, imploring news, comradeship, a little pardonable exuberance of love after so long of being outcasts; and the Midshires threw down over the tailboards of their lorries every cigarette they could muster, every month-old newspaper and year-old magazine, every scrap of chocolate, and half their rations into the bargain, and were with difficulty restrained from throwing down the other half.

The Russians it was who asked most vehemently for news. Where was the Red Army, they wanted to know, before they even accepted food or cigarettes; and the information that Rokossovsky was in Danzig and Gdynia, and Tolbukhin had crossed the Austrian frontier, would send them on again with a more elastic step and a broader smile. In rags and misery they retained unshaken that dazzling childlike pride of race which had moved them to such prodigies of heroism at Stalingrad and Sebastopol, the faith that could move mountains and turn back floods.

And indeed, there was something both moving and inspiring about this weary, shuffling pilgrimage westward out of the battle-zone. It was planned, it was orderly, it was unanimous; they moved not only to get to the rear areas where help was, but to clear the fighting areas for the British coming in; and as they went they helped one another, sharing loads, supporting cripples, carrying children, waiting with the sick and exhausted, burying the dead. There was hardly a good office man can do for man that they had not performed for one another on that march. History had done her worst here with hunger, disease, cruelty and degradation to reduce man below the animals, and still he manifested within him the likeness of God.

Jim, watching them from the back of the lorry, wondered how things would work out for them. Hope was so new that they could get drunk on it; but when the fumes wore off they would find their homes in Hungary, in Yugoslavia, in Russia, in Greece still a world away, and those whose job it was to help them preoccupied with a thousand and one other cares.

Moreover, the comradeship which had thrived in hell might fray to pieces in limbo, and separate them miserably into nationalities, creeds, factions and languages. Freedom, which in her first ecstasy had put colour back into the world and youth and hope back into the heart, might turn out in a month or two to be just another ageing drab limping along beside them. Certainly she would never again be to them so beautiful and kind as she was now; and perhaps the luckiest were those who died by the way of a joy too great to be borne.

On April 2nd the British fought their way into Rheine against a ragtag-and-bobtail army of Volkssturmers, embryo N.C.O.s from a training college near by, Wermacht men on leave, students, and a handful of regulars, who had occupied a high wood which commanded the approach roads, and fought well to hold their position. It needed only half an hour's shelling by tanks and mortars to pound their hill to pieces, and the Infantry walked through and collected what was left of them, and took them on into Rheine.

This was just another bombed town like all the rest they had seen, half its population gone, the other half sitting about the street in that state of perverse apathy they all seemed to lapse into when victory slipped out of sight, waiting for Allied Military Government to come and assume responsibility for them. Personal tragedy lost itself in that impervious expectancy. What was it that had been left out of the German make-up that all the rest had in some degree? Not courage, but the spark that directs courage into its true channels, that gives it intelligence, purpose and responsibility. These, like those terrible defective children who grow immense in physical size and have no minds, would hang like a dead weight upon the victors, doing nothing for themselves, demanding to be fed, housed, cleaned, amused, and returning nothing for the energy they absorbed. It was frightening to look at them and think how they could make victory itself a negative thing. Win or lose, the responsible peoples, the adult peoples, always carry the burden.

It was a relief to get clear of the town again, though hold-ups were more frequent now, and even the farming country presented its problems of behaviour. Once they were halted close to a market-garden, while armour tore past them, and a girl of about eighteen came out with hyacinths and jonquils in her arms, and began to offer them along the line of transports, smiling up at the men confidingly, sure of her welcome.

She could have been English; she was fresh and neat, with fair hair shaken back upon her neck and shoulders, and blue-grey, unembarrassed eyes; and they looked at her sheepishly and didn't know what to do. Time and again they'd been warned about fraternising with the German women, long before they'd stood still long enough to get a look at one in repose; but here was a pretty, harmless eighteen-year-old holding up flowers to them, and to draw back would be churlish. One here and there began to accept, and stood turning the wretched blossoms helplessly in his hand, or thrust them hurriedly into his pocket-top or button-hole; and the girl, encouraged, continued her walk down the length of the convoy, until Baird, rolling along the verge in a jeep, saw her at it. He got out of the jeep very deliberately, and walked to meet her as a determined man might walk to his execution; his face was white, and you could almost hear him feeling for the right German words, but she seemed to see nothing wrong, for she smiled at him engagingly, and advanced her hand with a jonquil in it towards his chest. Baird stepped back, and brushed her touch off him with fastidious fingertips, and said something short and to the point in German. She understood him all right, for her face went blank with shock and resentment, and in a moment she turned and ran back through the garden and out of sight. Those in the nearest truck almost fell overboard in their eagerness to overhear, and having picked the syllables off the air like orchids from the vine, hawked various versions of them round for days in the hope of getting a translation, but without result. What Jim noticed most was the surprising fact that it had half killed Baird to have to hurt the girl, even with words; he went back to his jeep as rigid as a poker, and wiping off sweat. He had recognised that it had to be done, and he'd made no bones about it; but it shouldn't have worried him so much.

As for the others, they were half relieved at having the scene ended, and half regretful that Baird should have interfered at all. After all, she was only a kid, no harm in her, surely, and it was childish to try and deal with a problem by forbidding it to arise. With which Jim agreed, though there wasn't much else Baird could have done in the circumstances. But in another day events took care of any tolerance or kindness the most innocent German living could have inspired in Jim's section.

They were perhaps seven miles out of Osnabruck at the

time, and driving upon a stretch of very badly mauled road which they had taken to relieve the congestion of faster armour upon the main roads; and towards midday a skid upon spilt oil tipped Peterson and the lorry he was driving into a dry ditch, and broke the lorry's back axle and Courthope's left forearm. A breakdown truck lugged them out of the ditch and into a farm-track, and a too-friendly German civilian hurried to volunteer the information that there was an automobile factory not half a mile away, where they could loot spare parts as copiously as they liked. Harben agreed that it seemed a pity to jettison a perfectly good lorry when in all probability a few hours' work could see it on the road again; and accordingly the rest of the company moved on, leaving Jim, Peterson, Mason, Morgan, Clure and half a dozen more to effect the repair of their transport and follow into Osnabruck when they could.

It was a fine, cold day, and an undamaged stretch of country, partly meadow and wood, partly built-up with working-class houses and small factories of various kinds. Jim took Peterson, Clure and Teddy Mason along with him in search of the car factory, leaving Morgan in charge on the road; but when they came to the shell of the works they found it deserted and stripped of what was immediately portable. There was a good deal of stuff left, though, all they would need, and at least one old car which would still run. They went from shop to shop and office to office, and found only superficial signs of bomb damage, some boarded windows, and a crater or two in the fields near by. They were crossing the concreted yard when from nowhere, from an empty corner of shadow almost under their feet, a girl erupted as if from a star-trap, and presented the business end of a rifle at them from her hip, in a way which proved the use of it was by no means strange to her. She cried out at them also, sudden and fierce in a language which was not German.

Teddy had lifted the muzzle of his own rifle instinctively, but let it drop again next moment, reacting to the report of his own eyes even before Jim's hand on his arm had urged the same argument. She was no German. That fierce, broad face, as wide across the cheekbones as its length from brow to chin, had all the passionate individual life in it which those bland, blond fräulein faces lacked. She was young, but God alone knew how young—nineteen or twenty, perhaps; her dark hair was parted in the middle and tied back with a strip of red rag, and the short ends curled up and knotted into glossy black rings upon her neck. She had direct eyes, square-set and deep, and a mouth ruled straight in her face above a straight white jaw. Her look was itself a levelled rifle. She wore an old, patched military tunic, so colourless with washing and smeared over with grease and dirt that only the faintest gloss of red and green showed the presence of two medal ribbons over her breast; and her skirt was short, full and dingy black above cracked leather boots. She was below the middle height, and sturdy, but so ill fed that in face, shoulders and body they were aware of her bones rather than of her flesh. There was one more noticeable thing about her. Teddy saw it first, and his fixed eyes and quick-caught breath drew Jim's attention. The hands that held the rifle levelled were scratched and torn, and all the finger-ends in particular smeared with blood.

She looked them over quickly, and made up her mind about them with equal promptness.

"Angleeski?" she said hopefully.

"Da!" said Teddy unexpectedly, and coloured vividly at his own temerity, for it was positively his one word of Russian, and if she or anyone else expected more of him they were due for a disappointment. He repeated defiantly: "Da, Angleeski!" Everybody knew that much, anyhow.

The rifle-barrel dropped instantly. She made an explosive noise apparently indicative of approval, whirled upon her heel, and plunged back into the narrow concrete stairway from which she had emerged, beckoning them with a gesture of her hand to follow her. There was no hand-rail, just the steep cleft in the yard leading down to a flagged level and a door; and here, coming to her side at a run, Jim saw how she had torn her hands to pieces, for smears of her blood marked the concrete setting of the door, and the lock was scratched and scarred with her efforts to spring it. A long chisel lay upon the floor, a clasp knife with both blades broken, and a short steel rod, bent out of shape. None of them had made much impression upon the lock. She indicated it with a sweep of her arm, wasting no more words, since they were plainly of no help; and it was clear that here was the first if not the only source of her immediate anxiety.

"What's in there?" asked Teddy, crowding after.

"How should I know? Whatever it is she wants it out."

"Pretty badly, by the look of it," agreed Teddy, eyeing her fingertips.

"Get off my elbow a minute," said Jim. "There's only one quick way in here. Lend me that Sten, Pete."

He looked at the girl as he steadied the gun sidelong against the lock, and she met his eyes and shrugged. They understood each other very well.

"Why didn't she blow it in with the rifle?" asked Teddy, who had not yet outgrown the obvious, for all his progress.

"Because it wasn't loaded, of course! Stand back and shut up!" He looked at her again, and indicated with a gesture of his hand that whoever was within must be told to stand away from the door. She nodded quick understanding, and dropping to her knees, shouted incomprehensibly into the keyhole; nothing but an obscure murmur came from within, but it seemed to satisfy and comfort her, and she sprang up and flattened herself against the opposite wall, out of his way, as he obeyed her look and let fly. The lock curled up and smoked, and echoes went chattering and leaping upward between the narrow concrete walls. Jim put his shoulder against the solid wood of the door, and let his weight go against it, and it gave and let him in against the cleared space of the wall. He was aware of eyes in darkness, of a great many people drawing frantic breath and leaning towards the light; then out they came, flooding past him and up the steps from the air-raid shelter, very quiet, very orderly even in their extremity. What they left behind was a lingering, drowsy and very unpleasant death by carbon monoxide poisoning, or an even longer and more awful one from hunger and stagnation; the smell of it was there already, rushing out of the cavern after them, nauseating to the senses. He tried to assess the number of them as they emerged, and made it something like a hundred people, men and women, probably all the slave labour of the factory. Most of them were Russian, or Slav, anyhow, which was as well, for the girl with the rifle was quite capable of making herself responsible for them. And where did she come into the picture? Why wasn't she locked in with the rest, if she belonged here? They were stuck with a dozen questions to ask, and not a word in common between them, and in any case no time. But what a girl!

They climbed the steps after the others had passed. The girl was up in the yard, in the middle of them, swopping short, sharp question and answer with men and women as ill clad and ill fed as herself; and certainly they all knew her, for a dozen were round her at once clamouring with questions, and she was putting them off, riding over their queries with strident, shouted orders. Plainly she had something more on her mind before there was to be any rest or relief for her. She made some urgent demand, not once but repeatedly, and finally seized the arm of a young boy who answered her, and hustled him through the crowd to confront Jim.

"This is a rum do!" said Peterson, looking her over between admiration and awe. "What happens now?"

The boy, about sixteen, and all shaven head and hollow eyes, uttered haltingly: "I speak English. You talk now. Yéva Porfirievna say you give her bullets for gun."

"Maybe," said Jim cautiously. "What's her name again?"

"Yéva Porfirievna Grishkina. She say she must have bullets."

"Well, ask her why she wants 'em."

The girl, appealed to, spoke vehemently, her eyes never leaving Jim's face. The boy, groping after words, repeated slowly: "She say will send us away—that way—we be safe. She need gun—must go back there, quick. There camp—people be killed if no one come."

"Camp? What sort of camp? Prison camp?"

"She say yes—only women and children there—not men. She say they all be killed if no one stop."

"Ask her if a car can go there," said Jim, thinking of the crock in the shed.

"Yéva Porfirievna say yes—can go."

"Then tell her we'll go there. She can show us the way, and then leave with the rest of you."

The girl made indignant reply to that, and was translated in haste.

"Yéva Porfirievna say quicker she drive. Must save time. But she say you come. Need much help."

At the risk of antagonising her still further Jim demurred again. "Her hands must be doctored, she should go with the rest."

"Yéva Porfirievna say she is a soldier."

She looked at Jim eye to eye, determined, domineering, inflexible. Yéva Porfirievna Grishkina looked every inch a soldier. He made up his mind.

"Pete, give her some ammunition, quick. I'll bring round that car—if it'll budge."

"What about the lorry?" asked Peterson. "We could bring the rest of the boys up if we got that moving."

"Can't wait for it. She knows what she's talking about, all right. Help her to get rid of this crowd—not that she'll need any help!"

Indeed she needed none. Running back towards the sheds, tinkering with the car, still he heard her voice uplifted, hectoring, threatening, bullying, overriding the dazed minds of people half drugged already with suffocation; and he knew by the comparative silence, before ever he coaxed a spark of life from the neglected engine, that she had got them moving down towards the offices and outbuildings of the factory, which they would certainly loot on their way to the road. Small blame to them if they did, for they had precious little of their own to take with them, and they would have to live somehow until they reached the Military Government zone. However, Yéva was quite capable of giving them good advice in the matter. The hour had produced the man there, all right.

The car, which was large, and might have belonged at some time to a staff official of the company, consented to start at last. He took it round to the entrance gates of the yard, and found the procession of the rescued already on the move, and Yéva Porfirievna very busily and contentedly loading a clip of cartridges into her rifle and thumbing over the safety catch. The blood had dried on her hands, and was blackening; she did not seem to see it, so firmly was her attention fixed upon the job in hand. When she heard the car she came to meet it at a run, and almost pushed him aside from the driving seat; and the comparative slowness of the rest of them in climbing aboard behind caused her to turn on them a fiery look which lifted them in in a hurry. Before the door closed she had the car away with a jerk that made its ancient chassis groan, and was tearing her way along a narrow lane between young lime-trees, heading as nearly as possible due north.

Jim kept silence on that drive, unwilling to disturb by a word her desperate concentration; but behind their backs there was talk enough, as Teddy and Peterson and Clure plied the Russian boy with questions. His name, it appeared, was Dmitri Nicolaievitch Pestinov, and he was from some unpronounceable place in the Ukraine. He hadn't even been old enough for the Red Army, but the Germans had taken him for forced labour, and he'd been here at this factory two years, and nearly a year at some other place before that. He must, thought Jim, listening, have been tough to survive.

"But who on earth shut you in that shelter?" asked Teddy,

as they swung round a sharp left bend into a broad concrete
road, unfenced and by the look of it newly laid.

"The Germans," said the boy simply.

"What, the Germans from the factory, or soldiers?"

"From the factory—when you come too near. They have
guns, make us go down and lock door. Then they go
away."

"But—but nobody might ever have found you," protested
Teddy. "What good would it do them if you all starved to
death down there? They're still beat. Why should they want
to kill you?"

"Always want to kill," said Dmitri, patiently underlining
what in his estimation should have needed no saying.

"What, just for sheer spite?"

"Use your loaf!" said Peterson. "They weren't put down
there for fun."

"Well, hell, I knew they were bad enough, but—with
absolutely nothing to gain—that's what gets me!" And he
subsided to try and assimilate it; there was still a lot he didn't
know. There were things none of them knew yet, except
perhaps Yéva Porfirievna Grishkina, Red Army man, who sat
there gaunt and small beside Jim's shoulder, with fixed,
ferocious eyes upon the road ahead, that long, ominous, grey-
white road. She drove very boldly and very badly, obviously
ready to smash the car and kill half its crew if that would carry
her any more rapidly to the end of the journey.

"What about her?" asked Peterson. "Did she work at the
factory, too?"

"Yes, she worked on repairs."

"Then how did she come to be out o' the shelter? I bet they
didn't love her any better than the rest."

"Yéva Porfirievna she is in staff garage when they round us
up. Only one guard there. She kill him, run off in woods.
When they go she come back for us."

"Bloody lucky for you she did, too! What a lass!" he
remarked to her oblivious back. "Killed him, did she? What,
with the rifle?"

"No, she find that in office—after. But no bullets."

"She knew which end of it was which, though," said Teddy.
"Wonder what she'd have done if we'd been Germans, after
all?"

"Held us up just the same, and bluffed through it; and got
away with it, likely. Who can tell at a glance if a gun's loaded?

They'd be taking no chances, not they! But Ah wonder,"
he said fondly, "how she did kill yon guard?"

"I ask her," announced Dmitri obligingly.

"Nay, let her alone, we don't want to take her mind off
job, Ah'd like to live through this ride."

He had his wish, for the ride was ending, and so was the
road, in a great enclosure of barbed-wire fencing pierced with
very high iron gates. They saw it first as a long, squat grey
mesh strung across the scene and swallowing up at right angles
the concrete road; there was a slight, crescent-shaped rise of
country framing it, with some woods atop, but this furtive
and shadowy thing lay flattened along the hollow, evading
notice. It carried two chimneys at one corner, not very high,
but high enough to give their smoke to a considerable wind
instead of letting it drift down to earth again within the shelter
of the ridge. At first, when their eyes were drawn to it, they
could make out nothing of the detail within, but only the fuzz
of wire, maybe ten feet high and bent over inward for the
last foot; as they drew nearer a ridging of roofs appeared
above the wire, all alike, slate-grey above buildings of drab
brick, a great number of them, arranged along three aisles.
Outside the wire barrier, at a dainty distance within the edge
of the trees, there were half a dozen prosperous-looking villas,
all with their windows discreetly turned away from the camp.
A quarter of a mile beyond these there was a farm, sitting
complacently among its green fields. Here it was spring, but
in the broad iron gateway the season seemed to pause and
draw back. Under the wire the grass died into a yellow,
withered growth humble along the ground, and within was
a wintry expanse of earth, trodden hard and dust-grey by feet
which were forbidden to go any farther. From fence to fence
there was no colour but the drab of that perished soil and
the faded, smoky black of old rags lying upon the ground; these
and a dead clay-whiteness cast up by nightmare glimpses
among the black, for which at this distance there was no
explanation. And over everything a dimness of unreality, the
distance-colour of miserable memories or obscene dreams, a
gloss of dirt, of rottenness, or putrefaction, which made the
place horrifying without the need of showing a reason. They
all felt it; even Teddy fell silent, staring ahead with dilated
eyes and dropped mouth. Labour camps they had seen, even
a P.O.W. camp, but this was a different thing. Then, as they
drew nearer, they were visited by a curious, sickening odour,

not yet strong but intolerably persistent; and from the cattle-strewn pastures of Normandy and the Rhine they knew it for the smell of death and decay.

Yéva Porfirievna did not slacken pace. Right up to the gates she drove them, and Jim rose and braced himself against the back of the seat, levelling the Sten gun and shouting for entry. Two men in brown uniforms peered through the bars and hesitated over their rifles; but they knew what was required of them, for the barrel of a submachine-gun pointed at a gate-keeper's belly is "Open!" in any language. Certainly four British soldiers and two Russian labourers in a single decrepit car did not constitute a very serious threat to the camp in themselves; but who knew if the entire British Army might not be just over the horizon? Moreover, the two gatekeepers would be the first to suffer, and they saw no reason why the ultimate fate of the camp should be of more importance to them than their own lives. No amount of self-immolation could alter the end. One of the men made a gesture towards the gate, the other towards his gun. Jim could have dropped him easily, but chose rather to put a burst of shot into the ground under his feet. The wires of the fence cried out like a smitten harp, the guard screamed, leaped back and fell headlong, sprawling on his back along the ground; and Yéva Porfirievna Grishkina laughed.

It was the loveliest sound imaginable, and one of the most reassuring, full and round and sweet, but it so startled her that she broke off in the middle of it, catching her breath upon a sharp gasp. Perhaps she had not laughed for a matter of years, and to do so now, and of all places here, terrified her; she became furious, and cried out to the remaining guard at her most strident and shrill, but it was the laughter and the gasp Jim remembered. Then, as the gate swung open, another unexpected echo took up the threnody from within the wire barrier, a dry, chirping, cackling sound like a half-grown chicken. It came from a bundle of striped and greasy rags lying under the wall of the nearest hut; and as Yéva stopped the car within the gateway the bundle of rags, still chirruping and shaking, sat up and stared at them with great hunger-sick eyes from which the lids were rolled back far into the skull, and they saw that this also was a woman, or had been one, and that she also laughed, and that to her also laughter was beyond imagination a stranger.

Beyond her, here and there along the ground, lay those

other soiled drifts of rags which had shown from a distance
such bewildering eruptions of bony whiteness. They saw now
what these were, and stood at gaze in a stupor of horror. The
white was not of bone, certainly, but of skin so closely drawn
to the bone that it seemed the same thing, and was not even
visited by decay, being devoid of flesh. These also were women,
like the first, but in a happier state, for they were dead.

3

The most awful thing about this awful place was that it was
not related to anything, that it did not tie on anywhere to any
picture of life as they had known it; and they had known it
pretty queer and pretty grim. Certainly they had got here by
a flat concrete road, in a palpable car, and travelling at a speed
not beyond credence even in waking men; but at some period
during that drive the moorings had slipped, and they were
adrift in a vacuum, an island outside humanity. Yet this was
real enough, real as a nightmare is real, through body and mind
and senses all at once, with a dreadful exaggerated authenticity,
only nowhere having any relationship to anything east or west
of it, or before or since. From the moment when they came
into it in mid afternoon to the moment when they left it by
dawnlight they lost touch with normality, and the air they
breathed was contagion, the exchanges of their eyes strangeness,
and the ground they walked on panic. But their bodies, from
force of habit, went on functioning; to how much purpose they
did not know, did not even wonder.

They never knew a name for it, nor how it had been filled,
nor for what purpose; none of the women in it had an age, or
a name, or a past or a future. How they had come there none
of their deliverers ever knew, nor what was to become of them
when they left it. There was the place, there were the people,
unexplained, not reasoned about nor understood, only in
unimaginable need; and there was no time, after the first
sickened stare, for anything but action.

Jim fell out of the car and jerked his gun into the gate-
keeper's ribs.

"The Herr Kommandant!—quick!"

The man stuttered compliance, in which only one word meant
anything to anyone but the boy Dmitri, who clung closely to
Jim's side, his thin body shaking with excitement.

"I speak German too—a little. I work here two years."

295

"Good, stick by me!" He called back over his shoulder, without shifting his eyes: "Clure, you stay here and keep the gate. Let nobody out unless you get word from me. Here, catch hold o' this bloke's rifle! Now, you—the Herr Kommandant's office—quick!"

Nightmare or no nightmare, they knew what to do. Clure, with one of their two Sten guns, stood over the car, as they went away from him, with face bleached like parchment, looking as dead as the dead. There was no time to remember any suspectibility of his. He would do what he had to do, or he could go to hell; but he would do it without fail, as the most unexpected people do when events overtop their own preoccupations without warning. As for the second guard, even his one half-hearted gesture of resistance was over; bidden to set his rifle against the wall and stand away from it, he hastened to obey, and stood rigid at a docile distance, watching the barrel of Clure's gun, and making no further move.

The rest went inward, following the gatekeeper, who walked stiffly and with haste because of Peterson's rifle-barrel nuzzling his back; and in the five minutes of following him they saw more than they wanted of hell. As soon as the first brick aisle received them there began to be shuffling shadows moving alongside, between the long, low huts, keeping out of reach, evading notice as best they could, muttering uneasily among themselves, for in their experience all visitations were evil. They were dressed in dirty, striped blue and white overalls or miscellaneous fragments of their own clothes, all worn to the same greasy drab condition; some of them were mere hobbling erections of rags, from which the enormous eyes watched ravenously, and glimpses of clay-white skulls from which the hair had fallen away, and hands and arms like birdclaws, flashed among the discoloured tatters and hid again as soon as seen. Some without concealment walked across the gatekeeper's path, looking nowhere, going nowhere, moving as if the wind blew them, apparently unconscious of hunger, distress or danger, for their minds had long since been put out like candles; and of these there were many, and they were the most terrible of all, because of the air they had of having elsewhere some mysterious business, which concerned no one but themselves on earth. Some were disfigured, their faces scarred and bruised; some groped and listened, being blind; some had babies in their arms, wound in the least filthy of their rags, and these seemed the youngest and nearest to humanity, and for that reason were almost reassuring to the sight. The gate-keeper thought nothing of any of them. When one of the mindless creatures roamed too closely across his path he swung his arm to brush her away as if she had been a poisonous fly; and Peterson dug the gun into his back with such ferocity, and roared at him so suddenly, that he snatched the blow back off the air in terror, and shrank aside out of her way. She seemed to see nothing, to hear nothing; she drifted on, shouldered her way stumblingly past the corner of a building, and went out of their sight.

"But, good God!" said Teddy in a breathless whisper, pressing closer to Jim's shoulder, "what have they done to them? How do they get like this? For God's sake, what sort of a show have we butted into?"

No one attempted to answer him, unless it was an answer that the Russian boy lifted his shoulders. Peterson had cursed a little under his breath at first, having too little force left in him to curse aloud, besides the circumstance that this place drained away all colour from the sight and expression from the voice, and made passion curiously futile. Silence was the most economical reply to any remark here; whatever energy survived would be needed for other things than talking. It was effort enough to speak when it was needed, as when they came at length to a small square paved with flags of concrete and flanked with decent brick buildings, and walked into the office of the Commandant.

The first thing that met them was an overpowering scent of Parma violets, and after the ominous odour of death and decay and burning which hung upon the outer air this came as a fantastic shock, a sensual outrage. The second was the nervous stare of two pairs of eyes converging upon them as they entered the doorway. Before he had even had time to separate the two people in his mind, Jim knew that he and his party were expected; if not they, then others upon the same errand, and if not today, tomorrow. Their welcome was ready, rehearsed, agreed upon; there would be no fighting to do here. For days these people must have known their camp would fall soon within the tide of British armour; how many feverish consultations upon conduct, considerations of flight or surrender, disagreements, despairs, lay behind these two uneasy, calculating stares he could only guess, but the room stank of fright beyond the power of Parma violets to disguise.

A man and a woman, the man sitting behind a large desk

looking official and sullen, the woman well back in an armchair beside an electric fire, withdrawn as far as possible into her fur coat, and flickering her lashes like fans in an agony of fear. She was youngish, perhaps in the thirties, and good-looking, no doubt, when she was less afraid, but now her face was blanched under its make-up so that the rouge, used even so delicately, burned in two abrupt patches of deep rose upon a chalk-white face, and the brightness of her eyes, feverishly blue, gave her a look of waxen stupidity such as an expensive doll might wear. Her fair hair hung in a long bob on her shoulders, smooth and pale as primrose-petals; she looked from head to foot well fed, well dressed, clean and fastidious. Yet she must have walked across the camp to get here, no doubt under escort for fear one of the crazed creatures should pass too near her. The man was scarcely older, big, heavily built, solid-featured, with narrow eyes set deep under overhanging black brows, and a mouth like a rat-trap; he turned and turned a paper-knife on the desk before him until it shot from under his fingers and whirled away to fall at Dmitri's feet, and when it was gone he looked indefinably feebler and less sure of himself, as if his one bit of camouflage had been stripped away.

Jim levelled the Sten gun at him across the desk and motioned him on to his feet. The hands, big, square-ended, with blunt fingers, went up instinctively to shoulder-height. He began to speak, vehemently pouring out words.

"What does he say?"

"He say he has orders to surrender the camp to you."

"His orders weren't necessary. Tell him to be quiet and stand away from the desk." The order was translated and apparently understood, for he shut his mouth with the aplomb of a broken sound-track, and stepped smartly back into the open. "Peterson, see what he carries on him. Have a look in the drawers of the desk, too."

The Commandant's person yielded a small revolver, and the desk a Lüger, both fully loaded. Surrender or no surrender, they felt better when these were in their hands.

"Good, now we can talk! Ask him, Dmitri, how many people he has in the camp."

Dmitri reported, after a brief exchange: "He say maybe four hundred women, maybe not so many."

"God's truth, doesn't he know? Tell him I want figures, not theories."

The Commandant began to sweat visibly. When he stirred,

wafts of Parma violet drifted out from his every movement and blew sickeningly over them. He, the woman, and the room must have been sprayed with it. He talked earnestly, humbly, ingratiatingly. Dmitri translated in short contemptuous sentences; the boy was only just coming alive, and beginning to realise how the situation was reversed.

"He say he has no staff left, only six men, twelve women. He say they take away all others four days ago. Many prisoners also they take away. I think these here all meant to die—no good for labour. He say no, but I think so. He say no proper records left. No guards now, no stores, no water. He say not his fault, he do his best."

"Ask him why no arrangements were made to feed those who were left behind. Ask him how the place could get into this state in four days."

"He say," replied Dmitri like a machine, "he got only fifty people ever. He say he has done what he could, they never give him proper supplies."

"Tell him a court can hear his excuses later. He's going to take us round the camp and show us everything. We want all his keys. As we go he'll tell his guards to deliver their arms here, in this office, and line up outside in the square. If any of 'em disobey, they'll be shot out of hand. If several disobey, we shall know he's trying to string us, and he'll be shot himself. Tell him so!"

He was told; he licked his dry lips and signified that he understood. It was not necessary to say that he would do his best to avoid this last eventuality; there were last-ditch Germans, perhaps, but he was not one of them. He did, as an afterthought, glance uncertainly at his wife, and gave Jim another idea.

"Your home is one of the houses outside the camp? Who lives in the others?" He drew towards him a sheet of paper from among the litter on the desk, and reached over for a pencil.

"The doctor in one, the women guards in two others. The rest are now empty."

"And the men?" he asked, writing.

"Their barrack-house is on the other side of the square here."

"It holds how many?"

"Fifty."

"Good, that really means fifty if they were to be Germans, I suppose. And it ought to be reasonably clean. Tell him,

Dmitri—no, tell his wife—she's to go down to her house, get all the Germans she can find, men, women and children, I don't care, and strip down all the bedding from those houses, and have it ready to be shifted up here before night. All the bedding, and all the food. When that's done she can bring her party up here and stand 'em in the square with the men to wait further orders. We need labour. Tell her to make a good, quick job of it, or else! Here, this will pass her through the gates."

The woman, more terrified than ever, burst into a flurry of speech, wringing her elegant hands together as if she would pluck the fingers out.

"What's the matter with her?"

"She is afraid to go through the camp alone. She say they will kill her."

"Tell her we're reasonable people. If she's torn to pieces on her way to the gate we shan't expect her to have the bedding ready."

Dmitri, smiling ferociously, translated this not only into German, but also into Russian for the benefit of Yéva Porfirievna, but she stood erect and silent at Jim's right arm, as she had stood throughout, and only the slightest contortion of her mouth showed that she had understood. The German woman, afraid still to go, was more afraid to refuse to go, and hung agonised in her furs, shifting from foot to foot, looking from her husband to the invaders, and back again. He was no longer God in this place; he could not help her.

"Tell her to go. It's an order!"

She looked round wildly, and seeing no escape, obeyed, though she hesitated in the doorway until they followed.

"Now, you! The staff barracks first, and the stores; I want to see what we've got."

The square was as empty and still as when they had entered it, but from every shadow between the huts the women gazed and wondered, and dared not hope. The German woman had overestimated her importance; not one of them turned to look or stirred to follow her as she drew her coat about her and began to walk rapidly towards the gate. It was only her own fears that followed so hard upon her heels, and caused her suddenly to break into a blind, stumbling run. One mindless wanderer crossed the track in front of her, and passed her without a glance, though the wild swerve she gave should alone have drawn one look towards her. No one, not even her husband, could doubt she would reach the gate safely, for all the prisoners who could reason were reasoning upon the newcomers. As they prodded the Commandant across the square towards the barracks a soft, shuffling noise passed over the air behind them, and the unutterable, stale, sickening smell of putrefaction moved in a wave as the women drew nearer. Possibly some of them knew the British uniforms; but they had learned that there was no counterfeit too small or mean for the German mind, and this might be only another lure to the gas-chamber or the furnace. They kept their distance, watching with their famished eyes for the first trustworthy sign. If an army had come they would have known themselves delivered; but only four men, a woman and a boy had come, and for what dark purpose who could guess? They followed and watched, creeping from shadow to shadow as the day drew to its early close; and with this murmurous half-visible army in escort Jim and his party made the tour of the nameless camp.

The Commandant was servile, anxious to placate them, full of excuses, but in no way ashamed of what he showed, nor disposed to attribute any guilt for it to anyone, least of all himself. The barracks was roomy, bare, and none too clean, but at any rate there was space, and there was heating, and two or three able-bodied women and a lot of hot water and carbolic could make it hospital-clean in an hour or two. Yes, he admitted, that was so, but he had no able-bodied women except the guards, who were fully occupied attending to the prisoners; and the water supply had broken down.

"There is water at your house?" asked Jim.

"Yes, it is another system."

"Then you can carry it—and you and your wife can use it."

The man laughed, in sheer incredulity, and as hastily tried to cover the indiscretion with a burst of coughing. Jim made then a resolve that these two should indeed scrub out the barracks on their knees; but after he had seen the living huts he changed his mind.

The stores and kitchen were well equipped, disproving at once every word the Commandant had said about his supplies. With four hundred starving women outside, here they found food enough, fresh, tinned and dried, to feed them well for at least a week; yet only two women were there, desultorily cooking for the staff, in a distrait atmosphere of untidiness and dirt. There was ample room and more than ample apparatus, including two huge water-boilers, but no attempt to use any of it, just as in the so-called hospital they found any amount of medical stores and no one fit even to tie a bandage. The doctor was an old man with dirty hands, who smelled of spirits; he might have had qualifications once, but he deserved none now. His patients, thirty-seven in number, lay on filthy biscuit mattresses laid side by side along two low shelves built out from the wall, with single grey blankets, stiff and slippery with grease, covering them; and the floor was paraded by two well-fed S.S. women who swaggered between these shelves in top-boots and half-uniform, looking more like executioners than nurses, which they claimed to be. All the patients were skeletons, some hairless, some toothless, four clasping dead babies, two themselves dead. The S.S. women said that they knew it; the men had already been informed, and there was nothing more they could do.

But this was only the beginning; it was the array of living huts that really opened their eyes. They were all alike, brick-built, lit from high up in the walls, and very badly, presumably to lessen the chance of escape; they must have housed probably two thousand women before the crossing of the Rhine made it expedient to remove the evidence farther east as rapidly as possible. Now half of them were empty except for rats, lice and the overwhelming stench of death, which was horrible enough in the open air, but beyond description between walls. It met them as they entered the first hut, sickening and dulling their senses; and the Commandant flourished his violet-scented handkerchief in vain against the waves of it, and tried to back away. For him there was nothing here to see; those bare shelves of boards built up against the wall like pigeon-holes, those half-naked bodies too weak to move in life and too fleshless to decay in death, those skull-like heads and enormous hollow eyes were all nothing except that the smell of them made him feel ill; he had done nothing to them, and proposed to do nothing for them. In any case most of them would inevitably die, so why waste effort? No doubt he was wondering in his impervious mind how these people could bear to be near such creatures; and indeed it was more than their stomachs could stand for long, and first Teddy and then Peterson had to withdraw hastily and vomit their hearts out upon the waste land along the wire, though they both came back greenly to the charge as soon as the paroxysms were over. Jim went near to following them several times, nearest of all when a youngish woman came tottering forward out of a darkness full of eyes, and thrust a bundle of rags into his arms, imploring him in a cracked whisper for her "kindlein". He saw by her eyes that she was mad with the negative madness which possessed people here; only one thing had retained its nature in her broken mind, and that was her child. And when he turned back the ragged cover he saw what she was no longer capable of seeing, that the child was dead, had been dead for several days. A momentary nausea as much mental as physical came over him, but he put it by. Pity was no good; nothing was any good to her, and even for those who could be helped more was needed than pity. He let her take the terrible bundle from him again, jealously, as if she had forgotten the very hope which had caused her to hold it out to him. They went on and left her murmuring over it.

They saw, as they had demanded to see, everything; the unfilled trench grave at one end of the enclosure, to which the new dead from the hospital were just being carried and consigned like so much rubbish to a dump; the rows of half-clothed corpses, so emaciated that all looked alike, articulations of bones tightly covered with parchment skin; the deserted huts where rats gnawed at the sleeping-shelves in spots where blood or food had been spilt, or ordure dropped from dysentery victims lying above too weak to move; the furnaces still reeking from the last bodies they would ever burn, where human ash lay about in barrels and pails and powdered the floor underfoot, and half-consumed bones glowed in the narrow trough stretcher through the open hatch; the unspeakable wash-rooms and latrines; everything. They saw them at speed, partly to keep themselves sane, but chiefly because the object of the tour was not to collect evidences of anything except the nature and scope of the effort now required from them. Once Jim had tried to send the Russian girl back to the office, so that she could avoid the worst of it, but she only shook her head and looked past him with her fierce, intent dark eyes, and he let her alone. As for the boy, he was needed; he had to see it through.

Well, they knew now. It remained only to dispose what force they had, and make all haste to get more. As for the rest of the battalion, now entering Osnabruck, they might have been in another world; there was no possibility of following them until this place had been handed over to a competent authority, and the only way to get one was to pull one off the road. Someone must take the car at once, and go and fetch

Morgan's half-dozen men up here to help, while Morgan stayed behind to collar the first medical unit he could find, and any other passing force that might be useful. Clure, thought Jim, might as well be the messenger: there was no need for him to hang around here, and he could drive well enough to get him down to the road safely.

What had he got then? The blonde woman was so frightened she would certainly obey orders, and might even be induced to do some work. There might be one or two maids from her house and the doctor's; there were twelve S.S. women and six men; call it twenty-four people in all. They ought to be able to make some difference. Food first, certainly; and there was no milk, of course, or only what the staff houses could supply. Someone would have to go to the farm. And a party to bury the dead. Not Germans! Let them scrub out the unspeakable huts where the dead had lain, but never again touch the victims. He felt strongly about this, and couldn't understand why. The dead women wouldn't care who carried them to the trench, yet he cared very bitterly. But was it fair to ask, say, a kid like Teddy to do a job like that? No, he'd take Peterson, maybe, and they'd do it between them, later, when the rest of the section was here.

Peterson, plucking at his sleeve, asked as they went back towards the gate: "Jim, why don't we take 'em down to the houses and just burn this hell-hole, instead of bringing all the stuff up here?"

"We daren't. I daren't risk it. There may be all manner of infection; we can't turn it loose and risk starting God knows what epidemics. And besides, if once we began moving in and out of the gates we'd lose half the women. You can see for yourself. Their lives wouldn't be worth much if they wandered away now."

"They're not worth a lot as it is," said Peterson sombrely.

"All the more reason to hang on to what chance they have got."

"They'd be better dead!" burst out Teddy passionately. "Look at them! Why, they're not even human! I know it isn't any fault of theirs, but they've been pushed down below animals, and—well, good God, if it was me I'd beg you to put a bullet through me and finish the job. So help me, I would, sooner than go on living like that!"

"You'd be a fool, then," said Jim gently. "They've not gone so far as you think—not so far that they can't come back."

Teddy didn't argue; he was too far gone with sickness and shock to try it, and besides, his one desire was to be convinced. Living would be a less precarious business once again if only he could believe these ruined creatures could ever be reclaimed. What good was it to be man, the master of creation, if you knew you could be reduced to this?

They went back to the gate, retrieved the guard who was still standing rigid under Clure's levelled gun, and looked down the long grey road, but it was empty of traffic.

"I want someone to drive back to Morgan," said Jim. "Clure, you'd better go."

The little man hesitated, and curiously the effect was of deliberation rather than indecision. He looked at Jim, and his eyes were steady and no way perturbed either by what they had seen or what it was too plainly designed that they should not see. He looked at Teddy, shivering in the early chill of the evening after sickness and sweat, greenish-white to the lips.

"Just as you like, Sergeant. Only I've never driven a car like this before. I think it would be a lot quicker if Mason went."

The words were prompt and casual enough, but the eyes were imperative; and why shouldn't he do the nursing and the sparing and the considering if he chose, as well as any other? It was no man's monopoly. Yet who would have thought he would be ready to turn down a chance of escape? Jim doubted if he could have done as much, had the positions been reversed.

"All right, it's all the same to me. Get going, Teddy, fetch the rest of the lads up, tell Morgan how to get here, and explain how things are. Tell him to stop the next convoy and get somebody to come and take over. What we need most is medical staff and plenty of it. Understand?"

Teddy nodded. Speech had become a dragging effort. He looked at the road, and drew breath gratefully as he scrambled into the driving seat.

"You remember the way?"

"I can find it."

"O.K.! Put a jerk in it getting back—and better warn 'em what to expect."

Teddy nodded again, turned the car with a burst of smoke and noise, and drove away down the long, straight mark of the road. They closed the gates after his going, but did not fasten them; someone would have to stay on guard there until all the fetching and carrying had been done, and by then there would most probably be fresh troops here to relieve them. In the meantime, they must separate their forces and begin work on the biggest mess any of them had ever had to clear up.

It was beginning to hint at dusk when they mustered again in the square and were given their orders: Yéva Porfirievna with the two cooks, the Commandant's wife's maid, and two of the S.S. women to the kitchens, to extract some sort of meal from the stores in the shortest possible time; Clure to oversee the carrying up of water and bedding from the houses; Peterson to slave-drive more intransigent S.S. women into making a thorough job of cleaning and disinfecting the barracks first, and then the hospital; Dmitri, after he had translated all the orders, to keep the gate, with the Commandant's revolver to back his authority; Jim, with what people were left, to attempt to make some of the empty huts habitable. He took the Commandant and his wife with him, the woman somewhat recovered from her first terror, and outraged that she should be expected to put her well-kept hands into soapy water and set about scrubbing of filthy benches and filthier floors. She talked a great deal of indignant and agitated German to her husband, clutching his sleeve tightly in her white fingers, until Jim levelled his gun at her leisurely over his arm, and the Commandant snapped at her to be silent before she got them both killed, or words to the same effect. However, she worked, having no alternative. She had a strong stomach; it was only with rage and self-pity that she even wept, knowing herself in half an hour draggled, soiled and weary, perhaps for the first time in her life. Her well-cut nails broke, the strong soda and carbolic frayed the skin of her hands, and her long hair brushed up from corners all manner of curious foulness, and smelled evil. She was not happy that night, but it was only for herself she grieved.

Afterwards, when Teddy came back with the rest of the section, the situation was greatly eased; there were enough of them then to send down to the farm for milk and eggs and vegetables; there was plenty of hot water, for both boilers were working; there was decent house-room for about a hundred women in the barracks, by turning all the available space into sleeping-quarters; and there was soup being ladled out into any cup or bowl or cracked basin that would hold it, and handed out with hunks of bread to those who were strong enough to take it; and for those who were not there was warm milk and water sweetened and thickened with a little bread, which Yéva Porfirievna carried from hut to hut with her own hands, a great enamelled jug steaming on one arm and her rifle over the other. Even then they had only touched the fringe of it, but for the moment they had to pause there and take stock, for every one of them was needed at the kitchens as soon as the smell of food began to reach the women. They came out of hiding ravenously, like starving cats sidling towards the scent, resolute at last that this was good, and not a trap. It was even possible, with the help of Dmitri summoned from the gate, to single out from among the prisoners some who were stronger, younger, more reliable than the others, and could help to marshall their companions, to fetch and carry for those too weak to walk, to take responsibility for a hundred and one small but vital jobs. Before darkness came it had been made clear in many infinitesimal ways that they were not, indeed, gone so far that they could not come back; they were on their way back now, every time a thin hand was put out to steer one of the crazy creatures away from the wire, every time they steadied shaking cups for one another, or helped the crippled ones to limp towards food. The spark survived and was quick to grow. They began to talk, in unpractised voices, in many languages, not always intelligibly, but sanely. They recovered humanity, sex, nationality in an hour.

It was at this distribution of food that Yéva Porfirievna, who had been silent ever since they entered the camp, burst into full voice again, half in German, half in her own tongue, and after three valorous hours of struggle with dirt and resentment and time in the kitchens, during which she had established something like a Red terror on her own, opened like a flower turned to the sun, and began to show another side of her nature. On the job she had been as single and fierce as a hunting tigress, passing by her own degraded kind without a look or a word; now she had something to offer, and with the same trenchant thoroughness she poured out news, encouragement, brusque comfort with her soup and bread. Teddy noticed her as he came in hefting a drum of milk from the farm, and stood for a minute after he had delivered it, to watch her from cover with a wary but fascinated wonder, so intently that he started when Jim came to his shoulder.

"She's terrific, isn't she?" He held a cup of coffee she had pushed into his grubby paw with hardly a look. "Terrifying, though! She'd never have to do more than look at me, and I'd jump through the hoop all right. Did you see her pushing those S.S. cows around?"

"Yes, I saw. She's made a difference here!"

"But she's too self-sufficient—I mean, she's like a little machine——" He seemed curiously damped by this reflection.

"Is she? She looks damned tired to me."

Teddy said doubtfully: "I suppose she must be."

"And she's dished out grub to everybody else, but have you seen her eat anything herself? I haven't. I think she's forgotten."

"Good lord, you mean she's had nothing at all?"

In a few minutes, from across the kitchen, Jim saw him making his way to her with a mug of soup and a slice of bread. The encounter was curious and poignant. She looked up at him in astonishment as the handle of the mug was presented to her hand, and seemed suddenly to consider and admit that the need of food might even have reference to herself. A wave of colour, unexpected and becoming, blazed through her face like a brief flame and passed, leaving her paler than before. She met his embarrassed smile with a long, contemplative stare, as if she hoped to see clean through him, and then abruptly buried her nose in the mug like a ravenous child. Jim went back to his job in a weariness at once lightened and accentuated by the memory, for with Yéva Porfirievna all manner of other remembered things came to life, and suddenly this microcosm of hell was tied fast to the waking world by at least one slight unseverable cord. She would not be forgotten with it, nor shut into the darkened part of the memory with it. To see eyes like hers, or just such an uncompromising, tormented mouth, would always be to revisit this place, to see beyond her shoulder other eyes like the empty holes of a skull, and mouths dropped open all alike in a hideous caricature of song; just as to see her now when she flushed and stood at gaze was to remember Helen and Imogen, and all the pleasantness of women outside this rim of wire.

They went on working; they had no alternative. They had rigged lanterns against the darkness, and went on with their carrying and cleaning well into the night. Once the Commandant had asked, through Dmitri, where the S.S. men were to sleep that night, since the hospital was being evacuated into their quarters, and been as crisply told that the problem did not arise; there would be no sleep for them. He had made no further protest, not even on his wife's behalf. The work went on.

Yet how it came about that Arthur Clure was his partner in

the burial of the dead Jim never quite knew. He had wandered down the long trodden walk above the open trench, and suddenly there had been someone walking beside him; and together, with no words, they had lifted the first limp, light corpse out of the scattering of soiled rags upon the ground, and carried and laid it beside the rest. Throughout the hours they worked together, until the relieving convoy was sighted along the road, they never spoke of the piteous things they carried. The darkness was kind; having light enough for their need they carried no lanterns, and what they saw was less horrible than they might have feared, though the cold touch of scarcely covered bone chilled them through, and the heavy stench stirring upon the night wind made their heads swim with loathing and nausea. Together they finished the clearing of the open ground, and turned to the gates, where the first trucks were just coming in. It was near midnight; their responsibilities were almost over.

And what did they carry between them now, as they walked across the broad space towards the gate-house? What was Clure thinking? Had he voluntarily stayed and subjected himself to this burden merely to establish his own status with himself, to spare Teddy, or in Teddy's place another, to continue his jealous watch upon Sergeant Benison, or because he had reached the point of wanting this and any other experience, whatever was to be had of humanity between birth and death? Had his vision changed, then? Had he exchanged the pervading fear of his own limitations for the intimate, honourable and commanding fear of death? Tired after long strain, having survived profound personal stresses, he might well turn again almost with gratitude to the first fear which transforms the later and lesser ones almost into friends, and in the end is itself the closest and most constant of companions. But if this was what they shared, they carried it silently still.

Jim handed over his charge. There were a lot of chaps coming in, fresh as paint in beautiful new Red Cross trucks, and ready for anything, or so they thought. A couple of captains went round the camp with him; said he had done pretty well in the time, but——; frowned disapproval at the sight of the Commandant's wife still on her knees, in laddered stockings and floods of tears, with soiled hair and grimy face; all but apologised to the lady and permitted her to go back to the office forthwith; raised their eyebrows at the apparition of Yéva Porfirievna sitting by one of the kitchen stoves with an orphan baby wrapped in a towel dying in her arms; were efficient, complimentary and not unkind, but with the reservations proper from the professional to the amateur. He was glad to have the weight off his hands. The thing would be properly done now, with ample equipment and supplies; already any amount of stuff was coming in and being unloaded, and the camp hummed with activity. As for him, he found himself, now that he was out of a job, half-drunk with tiredness, and too sick to ask any questions yet, or make any plans. He supposed Yéva and Dmitri would not stay here, but move west after their friends; and in the morning he and his party would go back to their abandoned repair job, and this hideous accidental interlude would be over. But there must be scores of these camps, maybe hundreds, many worse than this, scattered along the way ahead of them; and in some of them deliverance would come even later and less effectively than here, perhaps with the Commandant's wife holding the gun and Yéva Porfirievna scrubbing the huts out. God help us, we love anything that's well established!

He walked out of the office aimlessly, leaning his face to the cool wind that blew freshness even here by sad little gusts; and the wind drew him to the rim of the camp under the flank of the wooded hill, where the web of wire stretched pale across the moving darkness of bushes. He was cold, stiff, aching from head to foot, and a fool not to look for some passable corner of store or kitchen and drop to sleep; but now that no exertion of his could help or influence he wanted no part of this place, no traffic with it but service, no memory of it but frenzy. This was halfway back to the other world, and this he could bear; the sky over it had stars, like any other sky, and there was even a thin, discouraged grass rooting in its soil. The extreme corner of hell, looking towards purgatory; which, by comparison, is heaven itself.

He did not hear her come; she walked quietly in her down-trodden boots; only suddenly she was there, some yards away upon his right, standing by the wire, looking out. She had not seen him, because she was not looking for him or anyone. She stood there looking small, tired to death, passionately discouraged, her shoulders sagging a little; and the starlight made her face shine as only still things shine by night, tranquil water, or faces of hewn rock smoothed off by weather, or the glossy surfaces of leaves. She was crying from sheer weariness, motionlessly, soundlessly; and first he thought he would go to her, and then he remembered that this was no job of his, for he was learning sense at last. And Red Army man Yéva Porfirievna looked from the sky to the trees, and from the trees to the earth, wonderingly, with a very little but very live hope. There was a flower in the grass under the mesh of wire, a little pale orchis of no account, fast shut now, only just visible against the ground. She went down on her knees, and carefully began to strain her hand through the strands, trying to reach it. He saw with a peculiar, painful clarity the effortful motion of her blackened fingertips struggling along the grass, patient, impotent and intent; and to his distorted senses the hand and the orchis grew for an instant so vast that they shut out from him the world and the sky with all its stars. He had never meant to turn Yéva Porfirievna into an allegory, and the visionary moment troubled him with enormous unlimited distresses, so that he could not cross to help her because there were generations, universes, light-years in between. Then the moment nearest to sleep passed by him. She was there, a human creature like himself, expending a great deal of energy upon a foolish, pathetic object, and falling short of it.

Teddy came out of the shadows of the camp quietly, dropped on his knees beside her, slid his long arm easily through the wire, and nipped off the stem of the orchis between his fingers. He offered it slowly, sitting back upon his heels, as grave as she, while she drew back her empty hand and stared at him mutely, with the tears standing on her cheeks; and then she took the meagre little ghost of a flower and held it to her face, and bowed herself over it brokenly. He put his arm round her, and she cried for a long time; and Jim went away very carefully, for fear either of them should know.

4

In the morning she came to the gate to see them go, her tunic brushed, her face glossy and calm, her black curls gleaming. She shook hands with them all as they fitted themselves into the car, and stood at attention as they drew away through the gate; but she did not wait to wave to them or look after them once they were gone, and young Teddy, turning his head to crane back for the last of her, saw her march away into the camp, her shoulders squared, her chin out, ready to tackle anything. Maybe he let one sentimental thought go after her, but if he did it was the only one, and the next thing that came out of him was a gusty sigh of relief at the thought of getting away from the whole show, including even Yéva Porfirievna; and he certainly never got more of her thoughts than the last glance carried to him as she turned on her heel and walked away. She had other things to do besides dwell upon minute kindnesses received from temporary friends and allies. It wasn't for either of them to reflect upon the significance of these ridiculous things, a mug of soup, a hunk of bread and a meadow orchis, whose influence would probably outlast and out-fruit any amount of treaties and high-flown declarations of international friendship; that was something which had happened inside two minds not addicted to self-examination, and it could be left to work out its own inscrutable courses. The world would not be the loser.

And now they had the one job they had left over from yesterday, though it was like coming upon it full circle round the world after years of travelling. It took them just over two hours, during which time they did not talk more than was necessary, partly from a grim thickheadedness that had settled on them like the worst sort of hangover, but chiefly because they were thinking more than they liked to admit. They never compared notes in this matter, unless perhaps privately in their most privileged circles of two or three friends, but it never needed saying that it was no good any attractive well-groomed blonde flashing an eye at any of this section any more. They'd all had it! Yellow hair, cool blue eyes, delicate skin would always recall to mind the Commandant's wife passing by the emaciated dead with only a fastidious shiver, and shedding heart-broken tears over her chipped fingernails. It was no use giving them the old flannel about atrocity propaganda from now on; they'd been there!

They came alive gradually on the way into Osnabruck, re-discovering the everyday world by the roadside in house and hamlet and factory and farm, astonished that things were not more changed. There was the wide sweep of the plain, gently rolling away north-east towards Bremen, smudged with sultry fires where railway sidings, iron-works or supply depots made bombing worth while, dotted with dishevelled villages and towns, a few roofs here and there reduced to a lace-work of rafters, but most of the house-property undamaged; and everywhere in this countryside a sleek, servile, selfish, two-faced people keeping both eyes fixed firmly on their own advantage, and therefore unable to see any such open nightmare as the camp under the hill. If the fact of its existence was ever shoved pointblank under their noses they would swear they had no knowledge of it. No one could go near the farm, no one could walk over the hill without seeing the living skeletons ranging along the wire; but they would swear with tears their ignorance and consternation, and in some quarters, beyond doubt, they would be believed. That was the way the world was run, even by the well intentioned; but God help them if ever they tried the same tale on any of this section.

Osnabruck, when they reached it, was a town of M.P.s, Eisenhower proclamations, and a few persistent snipers; the now familiar announcement that the Allies came as conquerors but not as oppressors stared at them from every hoarding, and was still going up here and there as they drove in. The first M.P. they struck disclaimed all knowledge of the 7th Midshires, but supposed they were still in the town if you could find 'em for Commandos; the second handed them on to a brisk little major in a chaotic office in the centre of the town, who instantly gave them chapter and verse and hustled them out of town northward, where armour was streaming ahead for the Weser and Bremen; and towards nightfall they contacted their lost company in a fantastic German mansion on a knoll by a small river, some ten miles out of Osnabruck.

The German family—there must have been some money there!—had bolted without waiting to be either bombed out or turned out. The place was intact, all park and pillars outside, all fake marble and gilt and red plush and classical murals inside, Gothic with knobs on. One wing of it was a Casualty Clearing Station, but the rest was free for all comers, and A Company had established squatters' rights on a suite of rooms overlooking a sweep of garden, a railway cutting and a blazing oil-train derailed some hours before. The purple-black smoke made a truly Gothic backcloth of dropsical demoniac clouds, from which Mephistopheles might have materialised at any moment without doing violence to tradition. The largest room had a ceiling painted with a pastoral scene crowded with pneumatic nymphs and Glaxo-fed cherubs, at which they gazed in dumb wonderment until their necks grew stiff and threatened to fix themselves for ever at the same exaggerated angle; and in the centre of this apartment, which was littered with the platoon's kit and blankets, lay Sergeant Alcombe, flat on his back upon a plush and gilt couch, with his arms folded behind his head, and his half-closed eyes exploring with dreamy pleasure the abundant curves of the goddesses above.

"Hush!" he said. "Don't disturb me! I'm picking my pin-up girl."

Teddy followed the sleepy gaze upward, and shied like a

313

nervy horse at the display of flesh. *"They* didn't live on civvy rations! Who d'you think you are, anyhow? Paris?"

Alcombe sat up slowly. "What happened to you, Jim, anyhow? Harben's down the corridor—first on the right and straight through to the inside room. What price this for a billet, eh? Everything laid on, even girls—if you can call 'em girls!"

"Not so dusty! I think I'd better push off and talk to him right away. Is Baird with him?"

"Wouldn't be sure now. He was half an hour ago."

He was still. They listened together to Jim's story of the interlude, which might have taken place in a crater of the moon for all the relationship it seemed to bear to this place with its ornate and transcendental silliness. He had always found them both good listeners, but this time they were exemplary, saving comment and question alike until the end, and sitting grave and attentive through the somewhat lame recital as if it had been a reading from the Bible. Alcombe, no doubt, was getting the same tale in other words from the rest of the returned wanderers, in strophe, antistrophe and chorus. Not that the words they used to describe it would be any nearer to their thoughts than his were, as he made pale attempts to reduce that remembered horror to so much cool, lucid fact, in items which could be proved or disproved but not argued about. What sort of a picture they got he could not guess, any more than he could stand on both sides of a door at the same time.

"I see!" said Harben, when it was over, and he looked thoughtfully up at Baird and back to his own linked hands, deliberately considering the story. "The men are all right? What about the chances of infection?"

"Well, we took what precautions we could, sir, but I'm bound to say there is that risk."

"There'd been dysentery, you say?"

"Yes, but no present cases that we could find. There'd been something like two thousand women there at one time, but life must have got a bit easier for the ones who were left when they took the able-bodied away. I suppose for labour somewhere else—these weren't worth salving."

"Well, if the medicals turned you loose we'll have to accept that. But make the most of tonight, we move on again tomorrow. This place runs to baths; I should grab the chance if I were you, God knows when we'll get it again."

"Thanks, we shall, sir—if we can get near 'em."

314

"Make you out a priority docket if you like, Sergeant," offered Baird with a fleeting grin.

"Won't be needed, sir, tnanks. I'm ready to scrap for it. That's all, sir?"

"Yes, that's all, Sergeant. Except—you seem to have done pretty well with a bad deal. How did the men tackle it? Any comments?"

"They were all fine. No exceptions. I couldn't have wished for better. I wouldn't pick anyone out as having done more than the rest, or better—but Clure surprised me most."

"He came out on top, did he?"

"Bang on top."

"I see! Clure, too! Thank you, Sergeant! I'll have a word with Clure, if you'll send him along."

"Very good, sir," said Jim, and went away in some astonishment to find him. This was an unwonted concession. Harben's words with other ranks were usually of a very uncomplimentary character, and even where he saw no need for censure he was seldom known to find any for commendation. Maybe he was mellowing now that it was nearly over; or maybe Baird had gone so tar as to advance Clure's case to him as one for more than ordinary care and encouragement. Well, the man who had chosen to help to bury the dead because of a necessity in him to measure himself against the hardest things he could find might not care very greatly about a compliment or two, but at least they would do no harm, especially from so unexpected a quarter.

Clure was sitting on a cushion on the crimson-carpeted stairs, with a cigarette smoked down to its last half-inch between his fingertips. Informed of the Major's summons, he raised his eyebrows, drew carefully upon the fag-end for a last time, and stubbed it out under his heel.

"Oh! What have I done now? Or what haven't I done?"

But you could tell he didn't really care. Something had happened to his over-anxious mind, something which emancipated him from considerations of what Harben or anyone else might think of him; or at least, if there were still people whose approval he desired with all his heart—and while Helen lived there must be at least one—yet Harben was not among them. He went along to collect his snub with curiosity but no trepidation, and came back with his unexpected bouquet rather as a schoolboy accustomed to bottom place in his form comes home at last with a prize for application, divided between bewilderment and derision. So, at least, Jim interpreted the look that flashed in his direction as he sat drinking tea under the inflated ladies; and he felt almost personally guilty of some profound indiscretion, as if it was his fault that this signal of approbation came too late to be valued. He avoided having to answer that look all the evening.

The bathrooms, they found on investigation, were in keeping with the impressiveness of the house, but by no means cheerful or comfortable; however, there was hot water, which for economy's sake, and because the queue was long and eager, they shared two at a time. This was easy, for the bath was of a size suited to the ceiling nymphs rather than to hard-trained men on army rations. Young Teddy, splashing and steaming at the other end of it, harked back suddenly to what was over.

"What a bit of luck, getting this today of all days! I feel clean again—cleanish, anyhow. I say, Sergeant——"

"Hullo?"

"Why do they try and make out Russians are any different from the rest of us? I mean—all this bunk about the Russian enigma—— And all the time they're just the same as other people, only——"

"Only rather more so," suggested Jim.

"I was going to say only a hundred per cent. Comes to the same thing."

"So you didn't find Yéva Porfirievna hard to understand—even without a word of the language?"

"Cripes, no! She was great stuff, though, that kid! Say her name again—I like it."

"Yéva Porfirievna Grishkina. So do I, for that matter."

"Yéva! Is that the Russian for Eve? I knew a girl in Farnham called Eve."

"Well, don't get 'em mixed up when you write."

Teddy surprised him then. Sitting suddenly forward behind a bow wave that washed up the bath and smacked against Jim's chest, he said abruptly: "How did you know? I mean—well—I've got her name written down, you know; and an address in Kiev—if it's still there, she hasn't had a word for two years; and her regiment, and all the dope. I got Dmitri to ask her and write it all down this morning, before we moved. I gave her mine, too, but I don't suppose she'll keep it, I know she isn't bothered—why should she be?" This, from one into whose arms all things feminine were wont to fall, was revolutionary; but then, this had been no ordinary meeting.

"She'll have more important things to do than write to me, and anyhow, I'd need an interpreter; but still——"

"Are you going to write to her?" asked Jim, judging that he was permitted to be interested.

"I don't know. It seems daft. I'd like to, all right, but what are the chances of ever reaching her if I do? And anyhow, she may be married; I never asked her that. Besides— well, good God, we couldn't even talk to each other! And yet— I don't know——"

He continued to ponder it distractedly until the queue recalled his attention to more urgent affairs, and hauled him bodily out of the bath. Probably he would still be pondering it as he dressed and wandered away to his blankets. In a week or so it might be completely forgotten under the tide of events, unless some chance wave cast it up upon the congested beach of his memory again; and in all probability he would never, after all, write to Yéva Porfirievna. And yet an encounter like that might not be so easily soothed away out of the memory. Nobody knew. It was all in the future, and could safely be left there, without a regret or a heart-burning whichever way it went in the end; for the really important part of it had already happened.

There was a moon that night, clean and distant in the smoke-fringed heaven, shining upon the oil-train, burned out like a burst sausage beside its switchbacked rails, and smoking now only very sullenly; and as coolly, not a quarter of a mile away, upon the elaborate garden of the house, lavish with cypresses and marble and flagged walks and overweight Teutonic goddesses, in every particular redolent of wealth and security. Jim walked along a black and white alley of trees and statues, and gazed at the thinning plume of smoke at the end of the vista. A few 'planes passed over, almost negligently, as if they had been moths of some lost midnight in a fantastic dream. For the moment nothing was quite real, yesterday being ended and tomorrow not yet begun; but at the end of the alley there was another stray like himself, sitting on a marble seat under the cypresses, an incongruous Tommy with a Woodbine in his mouth. He sat very still in his dark corner, and was not immediately identifiable; but when Jim came nearer he knew the shape for Clure's, and was aware that the eyes in shadow had watched him all along the avenue, and were dwelling steadily upon him now. The white bar of the moonlight passed between them; a muttering of guns eastward frayed the edges of the stillness ineffectively, and troubled their attentive minds only lightly, as if from a great distance.

"Hullo, Sergeant!" said Clure.

"Hullo, Clure! Give me a light, will you?" He leaned to receive it, and drew his cigarette into a strenuous glow. "Thanks, that's better."

"Something fresh, isn't it? You to be needing a light? What happened to the lighter?"

"I wish I knew!" Jim sat down beside him upon the chaste uncomfortable stone, and stared hard at an abundant marble nymph dazzlingly white among the black trees. "I lost it somewhere between Rheine and here, that's all I know. Must have bounced out of my pocket or something; I never noticed it go."

"The only one in the company that worked, too," said Clure. "Now we'll need matches." An immense yawn convulsed him. "Lord, I'm tired!"

"Well you might be, you didn't do any sleeping last night—did you?"

"Not much!" But that meant none; with the feel of the dead on his hands still, and the stench in his nostrils, how could he sleep?

"Why not turn in now? We may not see anything like this again in weeks; better take advantage of it while we are here."

"That goes for you, too, you know," said Clure. "Or are you different?"

"I'm going in just as soon as I finish this smoke."

"What's the use? You won't sleep. It's too near the finish—or too far off, I'm damned if I know which." He leaned forward and trod out his cigarette-end upon the flags with gentle, deliberate pressures of his boot-heel. Everything about him had changed in some degree; his voice was no longer either eager or deprecating, though its tone had not altered; and his movements were not so restless as once, nor so jealously sensitive to watching eyes. And his words were all of them in some sort new, words he would never have used six months ago, and used without reflection now; as if he was the man he had always been, but enlarged by some tremendous legacy from someone else's mind. "After the firing stops," he said, "I'll do my sleeping."

Jim was silent, chewing over that accidentally ominous statement.

"How much longer do you reckon it will be?" asked Clure.

"A few weeks—maybe less. Your guess is as good as mine.

Neither of 'em's up to much, anyhow." He leaned back, and the stone struck cold into his shoulders; he had not noticed the live cold of the wind, but he shrank from this because it was dead. It reminded him of other dead things, better forgotten, and turned his mind inward upon thoughts he no longer wished to postpone, since time was so short. Now that he came to consider his own situation, he found himself a curiously friend-less man. There were plenty of chaps from whom he could ask casual services, but hardly one who could be let into the personal places and given the real baby to hold. Sloan was gone. Peterson had never quite taken his place. There was no Charlie in this outfit. Anyhow, if he felt he must expose his weakness to someone, why not Arthur Clure? He owed it to him, after all the liberties he'd taken of him uninvited. Besides, a weakness confided can be a strength to the sharer of it. We live on each other, he thought, we're dependent all our lives; the mistake is to try and be independent. Then we starve, and other people starve for want of their share in us. He felt his hold even upon privacy, even upon loneliness, relax, and his weariness grew upon him and hung like a loose, easy garment. After all, we are members one of another.

He said, quite slowly, letting the words sort themselves out as they came, with long pauses between: "I'm glad I happened to drop on you like this. There's something I've been meaning to ask you, but it comes pretty queerly at this stage, after all the holes we've been in." Here there was a long wait, but it did not seem troublesome to either of them. "Fact is, I'm not easy. I've got a hunch. It may be second sight, or it may be only bellyache, God knows, but I've got it into my head that I'm not going home." He waited; there was neither movement nor exclamation beside him, only he felt how unsparingly he was watched, with an intentness beyond astonishment. "If I'm just making a bloody fool of myself, well, all right. But suppose I'm not. If anything happens to me, I should be glad if you'd go and see Imogen. Will you?"

"Yes," said Clure, "I will. But it won't happen."

"Maybe not. Only I've got this feeling that it will. And I'd like to be sure that she'll get more back in the way of relics than a War Office telegram. Not that it'll do her any good," he said, "but she'd like it all the same. There'll be some things to take, too, that I'd rather you took. Not much, just a little packet, it won't bother you a lot. What d'you say?"

Clure said: "I promise I'll do whatever you want. But it

won't happen, you know, Sergeant." And he sat with his elbows on his knees and his hands loosely clasped, looking at Jim across a mere yard of moonlit air with the bewitched gaze of someone a world and a thousand years away. "I know how you feel," he said slowly. "It's because we've come to the tail-end of everything. You don't have to rouse yourself against the odds any more, and the things you really want get so near you begin to get superstitious about 'em. The nearer they look, the farther off you're sure they are. Too good to be true! That's how it is. A heathen idea, but then, most of us are heathens."

"Have you been bitten by it, too?" asked Jim.

"Maybe, maybe not. What does it matter one way or the other? If it comes, it comes; recognising it won't shove it off."

"No, I've found that out." But he thought that Clure, for all his silence on the subject, had found it out first. "It's partly that what I really want I never had the sense to want properly while I was within touch of it. You know how it is. You could tell Imogen—I mean if the need did arise—how I felt about her at the finish."

"I could try. But the need won't arise."

"You're as sure as I am," said Jim, marvelling. "Well, we shall see who's right, I suppose, if we wait long enough. Anyhow, if you'll take it on I shall be easier in my mind. I know it's a hell of a job to unload on to anybody, but it's one job I can't do myself."

"I'll take care of it," said Clure, "as well as I can." His voice was low, but not hesitant nor awed; there was something in it that could almost have been triumph.

"Thanks! I appreciate that. It's a hell of a feeling keeping this sort of thing bottled up inside just because it sounds idiotic. So it does sound idiotic, but why shouldn't it? I'm human, I can make a fool of myself if I like. Anyhow, I feel easier now I've got it off my chest."

He thought within himself: "Well, if he wanted an advantage of me he's got it. Surely we can call quits now." And he turned his head and looked at his companion suddenly, surprising the expected gleam in the intent eyes, the deep, hungry, bright satisfaction of a fed man looking back on starvation. Yes, he had done it; he had delivered himself bound into Clure's hands, had shown him his nakedness voluntarily, given him fast rights in his weaknesses; and Clure knew it, and was glad. They were even now, and he would be satisfied. As for Jim, the look went into him like a bayonet for one instant of jealous, indignant pain, and then what he had said became true. No errand would ever be more scrupulously carried out than this, undertaken so readily, so eagerly for a hated man; because to do him such intimate service, even after his death, was a sufficient revenge for past impious benefits endured at his hands. Who would have thought there was so much bitter pride in that small, dutiful body? The assuaged eyes exulted upon him without concealment, just as he had foreseen they would, just as he had hoped they would. It was no lie that he was easier, by one more vanity unwound from him; and Imogen would be dealt with faithfully.

"I don't know what made you pick on me," said Clure deliberately, "but thanks, anyhow. It's a compliment I didn't expect." He moved a little, and the advancing shadows hid his face, but still it was clear that the focus of his gaze had not shifted. "By the way—that nosegay the Major handed me —I can't get over it. Was it you who gave him a good account of me? I suppose it was?"

"Why, does it make any difference?"

"It might."

"I answered what he asked me, that's all. There wasn't a dozen words in it, all told."

"Still, you gave him to understand that you—thought well of me?"

It sounded like a phrase of bitter mockery, and he believed it to be that, and no other, but he could not be sure; and there was, in any case, only one possible answer.

"Yes. Why not?"

"Oh, why not? As long as I know where we all stand!" And he smiled, and the smile was perceptible, but not its quality, so that Jim went away from him at last still in doubt of what that last remark had meant. Not that it mattered greatly; what was done was done, and he could afford to let it alone now. He thought rather, as he walked back to the house with Clure's good-night in his ears, of what was to come tomorrow, and all the days to come until the blank wall at the end of his foreseeing either let him through or crashed down upon him. It would all resolve itself; he had nothing to do in that event but to abide by it. In the meantime he still had work to do.

Before he slept—and he did sleep that night, deeply and without dreams—he put together all the things he had about him that belonged by rights to Imogen, and made them into a small parcel with her name upon it. They didn't amount to much, in bulk at least; a few of her letters, a photograph of them both together, and one of her in uniform, a little leather wallet she had given him two years ago, and his last letter to her. If she ever received it it would be his last. He had written it precariously upon his knee, sitting under the light at the foot of the ornate staircase, and a pretty lame thing it was, but so it would have been if he'd had all the time and privacy in the world, and it would do, for Imogen would know how to read it. He sealed it into the parcel, and went to sleep with it buttoned into an inside pocket; and the next morning they pushed on towards Bremen. Whether it was the finality of having set his affairs in order, or merely the mounting hallucination that had hold of him, he was more sure than ever in his heart that he would never reach it.

5

They entered Bremen on the 24th of April, the same day that Zhukov and Koniev made contact in the heart of Berlin, and they left it again on the road to Hamburg on the 28th, the day Mussolini was shot in a waste place outside a village of Northern Italy; and in the entering they lost a fair number of men, and in the clearing of the town some few more, but Jim Benison was still alive when they drew out by ploughed fields and crumpled railway lines on the last lap of the road to victory.

The U.S. 3rd Army were in Czechoslovakia by then, and the 8th Army in Italy were about to enter Venice; and in Berlin, where the whole hideous conspiracy against man had been hatched, suburb after suburb was being lopped off from the trunk, Potsdam, Spandau, Rathenau, Tempelhof, Neukölln, bleeding to death by methodical slow degrees the Chancellery where the world's enemy still sat underground making and discarding plans, evolving martyrdoms and resurrections, seeing visions of the fiery chariot that should snatch him up to heaven, and raving that there was no such deliverance. It would come as an insurmountable shock to him that he could die like other men, like the few snipers picked off in the streets of Bremen, casually as so many rooks at harvest. He should have ascended in a cloud, or disappeared in a clap of thunder, instead of being ignominiously blown to pieces by a Russian bomb. Or maybe, at that, he wasn't in Berlin at all, for all his last-ditch

322

utterances, but well away by air days ago, heading out for the Argentine, or Spain, or any other of the places where worn-out dictators find homes. Eitner way, his day was over; his bubble had become a wisp of slimy sediment in the hand, his empire a chaos of disorganised self-seeking where men and women who were not even hungry tore one another for the loot of food-shops, and fawning girls with inimical eyes vied with one another for the notice of men they feared and hated. To this, though there must have been a strong predisposition in them or the thing could not have been done so readily, one man's vision had brought them.

Howbeit, no reliable news came out of the fabulous shelter under the Chancellery, nor was it possible to guess that within twenty-four hours the German armies in North Italy and Austria would have surrendered at Naples, the first confession of absolute defeat. Here on the roads north-eastward out of Bremen the war was still in being. All the Midshires had to do was keep moving, keep firing and forget how near or how distant victory might be; all of which they did, turning their backs upon the alternately sullen and obsequious people of Bremen, and the Deschimag yards where sixteen U-boats lay ranged in rows like so many chrysalids waiting for birth. These were past almost as soon as sighted, with the wide streets and the immense concrete shelters and the desperation and the spleen; and they were streaming away for the Elbe. But for all the speed they could make, time and events were rushing by them headlong upon the inevitable end, and though they chafed and agonised that the last impact was still deferred, yet they were dizzy and a little sick with the rush of its approach.

South of Hamburg they entered Uelzen and Stederdorf; and on the third day of May, the day Hamburg surrendered, they came to a large half-industrialised village, towards evening, when the light was growing long and lean. It looked much like any other large village, perhaps more than the usual allowance of it factory and artisan dwellings, and unless the light maligned it it was uglier than most of its kind. There was a long, flat road into it, well surfaced and newly planted along the margins with young poplars before the first houses began; and on these slim trees the sun had been warm all day, so that the heady fragrance of their foliage hung drunkenly sweet, drowningly sweet upon the evening air, and became for most of them, after that night, an indelible memory of the last flare of their burned-out warfare. For as their lorries drew towards the end

323

of this immature avenue, almost within touch of the first white
flags dangling from upper windows, the driver of the foremost
braked sharply, someone yelled that the road was barricaded
across ahead, and then an anti-tank gun opened upon them a
direct fire at killing range, laying the lorry split and sagging in
the dust, with half its cargo dead or injured. The survivors
and those behind went to earth in haste, flat in the grass under
the drowsy sweetness of the trees, where the perfume stirred
under them and fell down over them, saturating their senses.
There they drew the wounded into cover and laid the dead
decently, and peered ahead between rounds to try and discover
what was going on. Baird's platoon had been in the lead,
Alcombe's lot first; Alcombe was dead, and eight more with
him, and there would be a good many more casualties if they
had to lie here under the muzzle of that gun for very long.
There were, besides, rifles operating from the upper windows
where the improvised white flags hung gently waving in the still-
ing air. The village had been arranged as a trap for the next
convoy, and they had sprung it full tilt, as any following unit
would certainly have done, for had not armour opened up this
road not many hours ago? Who could have expected it to
spring shut again at all, let alone so soon?

Baird came up the ditch at a crouching run, and flopped
down upon his stomach beside Jim, who was slithering forward
along the edge of the grass.

"What the devil goes on?" he panted, half winded by his
flat drop. "Can you locate that damn' gun?"

"Haven't yet, sir, but it's somewhere behind that barricade.
They've blocked the street completely—looks as if there's
timber, stone, scrap-iron—any amount of stuff there. Watch
out for your head, too, they've got riflemen parked up and
down the road."

"So I see!" agreed Baird, grovelling under a thorny crackle
of fire. "But who the hell are they? You haven't got a look at
any of 'em?"

"Not yet. I thought this road had been cleared for use,
anyhow?"

"So it had. Armour went through this afternoon, and late
at that. The place is supposed to be deserted. I wish to God
it was!"

"Would the local folks let the armour through and then go
to the trouble to work this on us—at this stage?"

"Not likely. Besides, where would they lay hands on an

324

anti-tank gun and so many rifles at short notice? Maybe there's some military training school or something near by. They're always the hottest—remember those embryo N.C.O.s at Rheine. And they might have the stuff."

"Yes, but would they be this good?"

"God knows! A couple of stray regulars might make the difference. All I know is we've got to get through, there's no way round."

"Not for traffic, not a chance; but we might work round through the fields and get to the rear of 'em."

"We might hell! There's no cover, not so much as an eyelash. Think they'll only be watching the road?"

"Might not be enough of 'em to do more, sir."

Baird groaned and bit his nails, looking from the bare bright road to the bare bright fields in an agony of indecision, for the move was certainly his, and it looked fatal either way. And all the time that they lay there hugging the ground and watching the gun smash up their transport, the delirious sweetness of the budding poplars showered down over them like a gracious drug persuading them from violence to peace, and where bullet or splinter cut the young green shoots the wounds gave out waves of new fragrance. England would smell like that this month, while the magic was fresh; but some of them would never enjoy it again.

"I wish I knew what to do!" said Baird.

"Let me make a run for it. It might come off." They had a Piat plugging already, but without effect, and a couple of Bren teams were angling for a line along the upper windows.

"What, straight up the road?"

"Why not? It comes to the same thing." And he felt his inside shrink and grow cold with dread at the thought, and said to himself: "This is it. This is the place and the time." He was ashamed and afraid both, and yet it was true, by the road or the fields it came to the same thing. There was only one way past this fear, like all other fears, and that was into it and through it; then a man might get some peace, one way or the other.

Baird looked round for Harben, and Harben was nowhere near, hadn't come up with the jam yet; he had it all to himself. He made up his mind.

"Give me some grenades, quick, I'm going myself."

"Why not let me, sir? I used to be pretty speedy."

"What d'you reckon it is? Eighty yards—a hundred? I

325

bet I could give you five seconds and still lick you."

"Time me if you like," offered Jim.

"No, you stick around here and be ready to pick up the pieces. Here, hand over the eggs!" He hugged them to him in the sweet, ripening grass, and edged himself gingerly forward towards the road. "It's all right, I know the Major'll slaughter me—if the Jerries don't get there first." A machine-gun had joined the forces at the barricade; he listened to the malignant chatter of it, and winced, then hitched his feet under him, sprang up and ran.

Just forward of them, where the houses began, there was a deep doorway that seemed to offer some shelter, and for this he made, running like a hare; but there were riflemen on both sides of the street, and no doorway ever built could cover him from them all. Whoever had laid out the defence had done it thoroughly. They saw and heard bullets begin to whine off the wall above where Baird threw himself to earth, and thud home or splinter sharply into the door. To stay there was impossible. He picked himself up again, and tore head-down along the street, straight for the barrier; and before he had covered half of the distance the machine-gun dropped him, casually, in one short, sharp burst of fire. He sprang into the air and seemed to drift backwards upon a sudden wind before he fell, and rolled, and lay still in the gutter.

"They've got him!" cried Peterson at Jim's elbow. "My gawd, the best o' the whole damn' bunch, too."

"He's not dead," said Clure, straining ahead after him. "I just saw him move."

"Are you sure? My oath, I thought they'd all but cut him in two!"

"Yes, I'm sure. He's alive, all right."

"Will I go and bring him in?" asked Peterson.

But damn all, the war was as good as over, wasn't it? A man with four children couldn't go and get himself killed now, at this late hour, when everything was done bar the shouting.

"No," said Jim, "you hang on here. I'll go."

He thought, as he crawled forward to the margin of the first small front garden, how ridiculous it was that there should have to be heroism even now, and saw in a curious double vision how great this incident was in the happening, and how small in the sum of things. The machine-gun chattered, splaying bullets across and across the road. He calculated the speed of its arc of fire, and ran as it swung away from him, doubled

326

upon himself and shrinking every way from the spatter of rifle-fire that broke out upon him. He heard then something for which he had not bargained, the scurry of feet following him, and half turned to shout back over his shoulder: "Get to hell out of this!" but did not see in that breathless glimpse who the other fool was; and when he dropped prone over Baird's body his obstinate shadow was still with him. Even then he did not look at him immediately, being preoccupied with Baird. The machine-gunner had got him in the body, just above the waist, and broken the bone of one arm into the bargain, but he was still alive, and good for a lifetime yet if he could be got out of here safely. There was nowhere on either side the street here where he could lie out of range of the snipers on the opposite side, not one arched entry or front-garden shrubbery big enough to hide a cat. He would have to go back to the platoon. All the same, to the barricade was only about the same distance; it seemed a pity to Jim that he should get so far in fear and trembling and still have to go back empty-handed. He turned his head upon his arm under the declining swathe of the machine-gun, and looked across Baird at his companion; it was no surprise to find himself eye-to-eye with Arthur Clure. Even here, it seemed, he couldn't lose Clure; he meant to be in at the death.

The little man was out of breath, and his eyes had a strained transparent stare about them that was brighter than the lengthening light. They blazed at Jim across the unconscious Baird, and blinked sweat from their lids, and stared again. They had no time to pause and recognise their mutual, peaceful, defeated fear; only they lay panting under the spasmodic spleen of bullets, and between them contrived to buckle Baird's broken arm at his side with his belt, that it might not be worse displaced in moving him. Prone in the dust, this was infinite labour, but they managed it without more damage; and their eyes, encountering once across the dimming air, were like eyes in a mirror, wary and fascinated yet familiar, as if each of them watched himself with a stranger's impersonal interest, and no foreknowledge of what he was about to do. Overhead the drooping white flags flapped languidly and mournfully in the small wind of the evening, and the poplar fumes came eddying over them and in at the upper windows, where the enemy lay over their rifles, with a lulling, impartial gentleness, unaware of wars. It was strange to remember now so poignantly, so bitterly, that the world was at its spring, and life

327

about to draw breath and leap to a new adventure, and no place for you anywhere in this dynamic splendour. Strange to come to an end when everything was about to begin, and all for one more limited objective which would be theirs without a shot fired in a week, in a day, perhaps; but he was here, and the wall of his hallucination seemed quite to cut off the breeze from his face and leave him struggling for breath, so near was the moment. There was only one way, and that was through the moment, through the wall, through the barricade if he could get so far. He eased his sweating, dusty face on his arm, and measured the distance forward and back; and all the time Clure watched him, and he felt the other obsession matching his own step for step, inscrutable and immured from his knowledge, looking at him jealously through Clure's eyes.

"Got to get him back out of this," said Jim hoarsely through the dust. "Listen, can you hoist him?"

Clure looked at him and shook his head, but made no other move.

"What's the matter? You all right?"

"I'm all right. Just got a slug in my left arm—I can't lift him. You go back. I'll cover you as well as I can."

There was no help for it, then, for Baird must be got away; and yet he was loath to go back.

"He's not heavy. Try and take him! Try it! Your arm's not broken?"

"No, but—losing blood—I can't get much power. We'd never make it."

"All right, cover us close! Don't stay far behind!"

He felt for the best hold on Baird, and eased up the dead weight of him, crouching from the stinging of rifle-bullets and biding his time until the sweep of the machine-gun slid from over him. Then he hoisted the lean young body upon his shoulder with a long, balanced heave, and began to run with him. He heard Clure open fire behind him, but for his own part he did not once pause nor look back, nor try to put a finger into the job he had given to another man, only ran staggering and crouching with his own burden until he fell into the arms of Peterson and Teddy Mason and Morgan all reaching forward to receive him. Baird was drawn away into the grass under the rise of the ditch, where he could lie safely. Jim grovelled winded for a moment, and then raised himself a little on his hands and looked round for Clure; who was not with him.

It was as if he leaned back upon something he had believed fixed and firm, and fell heavily to the ground. His balance was gone, the eyes had been withdrawn from him. He felt gropingly aside left and right, and halted for a moment at a complete loss, on the edge of a question; and then he never asked it after all, for suddenly he knew where to look. He clawed round in the grass, and craned to look back along his track, and there was Clure just raising himself out of the gutter upon one hand, leaving his rifle lying. He had something hugged to him in that supposedly injured left arm of his, and his hold on it was firm enough for a sound man. The injury had been a fiction adopted to send the Sergeant back out of harm's way with Baird, and leave the coast clear—for what? For this crazy gesture, this ceremonial suicide under the barricade. Jim lifted himself fiercely and shouted after him:

"Clure! Come back! Come out of that, you damned fool!"

But would he? Not he! He was deaf and blind to everything but the thing he had set out to do. He had his eyes fixed upon the confused irregular line of the barrier, almost lost against the background of the approaching dusk; and he was running towards it, crouched low, a small mark but a distinct one, too sharp to miss. No shout could reach him now; he had set in motion, by what feat of self-compulsion only God knew, something none of them could stop.

Harben was there suddenly, lying quiet under the poplar trees, watching under frowning, drawn brows, asking no questions.

"Let him alone! What happens happens, there's nothing we can do about it. He'll have a better chance if we leave it to him now."

But he had no chance, no chance at all. They seemed to have been watching him for an age, while he ran middling fast, and yet he covered no more than twenty yards before he lurched in his run, and clutched himself about the chest with his free arm, and was seen to be jerked backward by a palpable hit. Then his knees gave, and he was down. He made so small a heap in the middle of the road that in the increscent dark they could hardly see him.

"He's done!" cried Peterson. "The poor little beggar's down!"

Jim was on his feet, leaning forward to the road. "Let me——"

"No, wait!" said Harben sharply. "That's enough!"

329

"He may be alive, sir. They're playing clean over him."

"There'd be two to fetch in then. No, wait a bit, Sergeant."

"He is alive, sir," reported Teddy excitedly. "Look, he's trying to get up!"

He was certainly hunching himself together in an immense effort to rise, for the small dark heap grew and heaved about its armful of grenades.

"All right, fetch him in if you can, God help the pair of you! Go with him, Morgan!"

They were away before the words were well out of him. It was not he who waved them imperiously back this time, but the only other man with any right. Clure lifted himself suddenly and turned his face towards them, and though his expression was lost now utterly, every following movement cried out at them eloquently enough for voice, face and all. Something seemed to enter into him at the sight of them, and to drag him to his feet and hold him rigid. He stood there erect, his back turned upon the searching fire that laboured upon him, and with a wide gesture of his free arm threatened them off from following. It seemed as if he cried out to them, too, for there was certainly sound, peremptory indistinguishable words, the vigour of which reached them though the sense was lost in some wound which had robbed him of his full voice. All the noise he could make as he screamed at them to go back and stay alive was a hoarse, bitter croaking like a sick crow; nor did he wait longer than to be sure that they would not obey him. If they could not be stopped that way, he knew of other ways. How he stood, how he moved without falling again, they could not guess; but he turned clean upon his heel like a spinning top, and set his face again towards the barricade. They felt how he fixed his eyes and set his course, once for all, while he could still see; and because he could not run any longer he walked forward upon his objective, bolt upright, going stiffly, hugging his grenades. They shouted after him and were not heeded; only that hard automaton's walk of his grew faster, stiffer and wilder, like a jointed doll come to life, he was in such haste to get himself killed in time to leave them men alive. He knew what he was doing. All the fire shortened upon him; they ran in his shadow and were immune. Around him bullets were thick as bees in a blossoming lime, and the machine-gun was chattering frenziedly, but having taken his course he did not swerve from it again, nor halt, nor seem to be in any way vulnerable any more. How many wounds he already had, how

330

many he received in that advance, there was no means of
guessing; but a man could no more walk through that fire
unharmed than fly to heaven alive. Yet he went straight
forward through it, lurching in his walk, biting on the pin of his
first grenade, a dead man before his death. He did not relax
his terrible concentration to attempt a throw he could not
control. Running like rabbits, too blown to call to him any
longer, they saw him, in the last few yards, pull out pin after
pin, and reaching the first talus of timber and scrap, suddenly
open his arms and pitch forward behind the shower of his flung
weapons. Beyond the barricade there was a shout and a running, both brief. Then the first explosion shook the air with
convulsions of dust and wind between the house walls, and after
it four distinct detonations following close, and long rumblings
after, that ran on and on, back and forth in anguished echoes
from wall to wall, and from wall to wall again. On their faces
in the dust, choking and gasping, they hugged the road and
waited, and after a long time of groaning and sighing the
almost-silence came back, and the cloud began to settle in the
familiar gritty, silting murmur, monotonously sibilant, like
interminable whispering of ghosts. And then it was all over,
finished, as final as the grave.

They picked themselves up, and stumbled through the hanging dust to find him, clambering and slipping upon shattered
ramparts of stones and rolling rubble, trampling German bodies
in their haste and blindness. A howling cripple in a torn grey-
green uniform ran towards them out of the smoke and screamed
surrender, but they pushed him out of their way frantically and
groped on; and in the confusion of the mid street, crumpled on
his side against a baulk of timber, they found Clure.

Jim dropped into the dust beside him, and lifted him against
his thigh, and it was like lifting an old coat with no body in it,
so light and limp and insubstantial he was. His right hand,
which had held the last grenade, was off at the wrist, and
blood streamed steadily out of the flattened sleeve; his face
was partially crushed; how many of his bones remained whole
they dared not try to discover, but they knew he was smashed
beyond repair. The thread of breath that moved through his
lips could not endure more than a matter of minutes, nor did
they expect to see him open his eyes, or hear him speak, again;
but in a moment the smoke-blackened eyelids drooped back
from unfocused pupils that stared at Jim and seemed not to see
him for a while. The eyes were clear and clean still in the

stained ruin of his face, and long-sighted as ever fixed first
upon the pale zenith, and came only by degrees upon nearer
things. Harben came up while he was still fumbling with
drawn, bloody brows for the face of the man who held him
in his arms. Half of the platoon was there, and a rabble of
broken prisoners, but no one interfered and no one was noticed;
even the Major kept out of it, standing in the background
unseen, watching the dying man.

His fixed glance in its laborious journey back to earth withdrew itself reluctantly from the breadth of the evening and grew
anxious upon the eaves of the houses, the empty, shattered
windows, the pattern of the brickwork emerging mottled from
the smoke. His lips moved a little, vaguely, but made no sound.
Then a spark lit within the shadowy stare, very far down,
and came slowly to the surface in recognition. Without moving,
for movement was beyond his power, he seemed suddenly to
lie more easily, more closely, in Jim's arm. He tried again
to speak; Jim bent his head to take the breath from his lips
and draw it into words if man could do it.

"Sergeant——" It was like him to stick to every bit of a
rank even at this pass. "——it's you?—you're there?"

"I'm here," said Jim.

"You're—all right?"

"Yes, I'm all right."

"Did I——"

"You did it fine. You did all we needed."

A sigh, so long and slow that his breathing seemed to stop;
then he began again, and for a moment more clearly.

"Sergeant——"

"Yes?"

"——my wife—will you—— You asked me to go—will
you——?"

"I'll go and see her," promised Jim into his ear.

"——tell her—she'll believe you——"

"I'll tell her; I'll tell her everything. She'll be proud."
More words, if you could have poured thousands of them into
his consciousness, were no use to him now, for time was too
short to hold them. All he could accept was the bare skeleton
phrase, and it was enough, he expected not even that. The
word "proud", the sound of it, the feel of it, went into him
deep; he said it over once or twice to himself without utterance,
only the shape of the syllable shaking his mouth. His face,
soiled and darkened with blood and dirt, seemed to dwindle

strangely in the dusk, leaving the fixed eyes vague and wide upon Jim's eyes; and the spark of recognition disseminated slowly into a glimmering luminous content, absent from pain. He lay so for a few minutes, and this bewildering light sank inward gradually from their sight, so still, so tranquil to the last that they could hardly follow its withdrawal or catch the moment of its loss; so that Jim knelt holding him for a long time after he was dead, and did not know. Only when at last a breeze came clear through the twilight, scented with the poplar leaves, and blew dust into the open eyes and dulled their fading light, and still they lay open and content, only then did he sit back slowly, and lay down the light, discarded body very slowly out of his arm. He was gone, like all the rest; Arthur Clure was gone after Miriam Lozelle, and Brian Ridley, and Charlie Smith, and Priest, and all the others, gone into the everlasting procession of them once for all; and whatever was left was in other men, and they were responsible for it henceforward; and from them the account would be required.

But the look in the eyes, the fixed, luminous look, who was to repay God for that?

6

They spent the first half of the night there, clearing the road and rounding up the few obstinate snipers who continued to fire on them; and then they moved on, and came to their destination in the early, colourless dawn of May 4th, a clean, decorous, almost undamaged provincial town with ample houses and shy people. There they found an enclosure for their prisoners, and decent lying for their dead; and for themselves a few hours of rest, even some sleep, before they moved on again or reckoned their gains and losses.

Less than five miles away from where they lay two anxious German staff officers were waking in Montgomery's camp on Luneberg Heath, and eyeing the track through the silver birches by which their superiors would return that evening with authority to effect the surrender of a million men in arms; after which they would be prisoners of war, but alive. Ten men of the Midshires had had less luck. No amount of signatures upon instruments of surrender could bring them back to life. The chaplain with his ineffectual little white wooden crosses was the only one who would do them any service now.

The Midshires were quiet and subdued. They talked a little

of Arthur Clure, saying the tenth part of what was in their minds, and even that excessively badly. Poor little beggar, they said, who'd have believed it? Who'd have thought he had it in him? And you could see them thinking back upon all the leg-pulls they'd worked on him, and all the tolerant contempt he'd had to put up with from the wise boys who knew it all backwards and could do everything with both hands tied behind them. And after all, he never had learned to squeeze a trigger instead of jerking it. But—my God, there was more to it than that, it seemed, a lot more! This part of it they chewed over in their blankets and kept to themselves, especially the very young and very knowing among them. Where they lay awake in their quietness there was a feeling of shock upon the air, like the smell of a thunderstorm passing by without breaking. They would tread very circumspectly from this on, feeling after the things they didn't know backwards and weren't sure they could do. In its way their silence was as good an epitaph as any.

Major Harben struck almost the same note, though in a different way. He sent for Jim in the first light of the dawn, as soon as they were settled in their barren abandoned factory, and they had some conversation together upon the subject which filled both their minds. Harben was tired, and for him, dishevelled; he sat upon a packing-case in the small, stripped office where he had set up his quarters, and smoked cigarette after cigarette to keep himself awake. He looked up when Jim entered, and seemed to draw his mind back from a long way off.

"Oh, hullo—yes! Sit down, Sergeant, if you can find anywhere to sit. Try the window-sill. It's about Clure, of course. I saw the end of that buiness. I want you to tell me the part I didn't see."

Jim told him all he could remember; he did not think there was much detail missed out. The Major listened without a word or movement, and at the end of it he said: "Well, it defeats me! I don't mind telling you, Sergeant, I never saw anything like that, and never expect to again. If it had even come from anyone else I wouldn't be so confounded. I suppose it's good for me to have all my judgments turned over on their backs, but—— Well, I'm beaten! You seem to have known him as well as anybody. *Were* we all mistaken about him? *Was* he the sort of chap who does that sort of thing?"

"Is there a special sort?" asked Jim in a low voice.

"Very probably you're right, and there isn't. But did *you* expect Clure to do anything so superhuman?"

"I don't know. I didn't—expect—anything. There were so many opposite influences. Nothing he did would have surprised me."

"He wasn't normally what one would call a good soldier?" suggested Harben with a faint and rueful smile.

"No, sir. But he tried to be. Some of those who are don't even have to try."

"Being totally devoid of imagination is a help there."

"Yes, sir; and he wasn't."

"And—I may be putting too much into your mouth, but I gather you're implying, Benison, that some of those who become what we call heroes don't even have to try, either?" Jim was silent. "And he—did have to try?—heavens hard?"

"I think so."

"Poor devil!" said Harben, and abruptly got up from his packing-case and began to walk the floor uneasily, as if it was hot. "And it came off, too. But at this late hour, and on such a comparatively slight occasion, why, in the lord's name——? What could make a man screw himself to that pitch, damn it, when it's all over bar the shouting?"

Jim sat watching the straight, square shadow pass and repass restlessly over the floor, and debated within himself jealously how much or how little of Clure he should show to this man or any other. He wasn't sure if he wanted Harben to understand even so much as he himself knew; but neither did he want men who did not understand to go on misinterpreting to ever-widening circles of other men. To represent Clure as naturally brave was to lose half his heroism.

"If he was afraid," said Harben, "and it's my belief he was, small blame to him, either,—but *if* he was, then why go on with it? He didn't have to. Nobody'd laid it on him. It was the most deliberate thing I ever saw. Why did he do it? Did he just want to be a hero for his own satisfaction, or what?"

Jim hesitated. "Well, in a way, yes, he did. But not just for his own satisfaction. He has—had—a wife who thinks a lot of him. I think he's had an obsession about letting her down. He hadn't any opinion of himself, you see, sir. There wasn't much he wouldn't have done to justify her in being proud of him."

Harben stopped walking the floor for a minute, looked at

him slantwise through the smoke of his cigarette, and moved on again abruptly.

"I see! Yes! That was what you meant——"

"Yes, sir." Jim wondered if he had said too much, but it was too late to take anything back. The Major thought it over to himself, frowning perplexedly, obviously unsatisfied; then he said quite slowly: "But if she was already convinced why should he want so much to convince her all over again? Nothing had ever happened to change her mind. I know he was regarded as—not brilliant, perhaps; but he'd always done what was asked of him. Hadn't he?"

Jim said: "Yes, sir!" with appropriate woodenness, himself hardly remembering the chill of the night air in that ruined house on the outskirts of Goch, where for all he knew the whole splendid desperation had started. But for some reason it suddenly seemed to him more intimately tragic, less obscured by trailing clouds of unexpected glory. Clure was a dead man who should have been alive; the rest was irrelevant, and this was piteous.

"Even if she had been there to see," said Harben, hammering out his point fretful-fine, "I could have believed in it. A thing like that done under her eyes—yes, I can see the force of that. But to throw his life away on the off chance of a report reaching her which would convey at least something of it—— There was no one watching whose approval he can possibly have been prepared to die for. I tell you, Sergeant, I'm still at a loss."

Well, let him remain so. Why not? Others had groped in their time. Jim said only: "There were immediate reasons as well. We'd lost nine men, and several injured, and there looked like being a lot more damage if we didn't stop that gun. What he did needed doing—only maybe not necessarily that way."

"Oh, yes, I'm remembering all that. Yes—he shall have all the backing I can give him. She'll get his medal to wear, if that's any good to her. God knows what it will be, it depends on the mood they're in; but if I can get him a V.C. I'll do it. He earned one, and I suppose his widow will value it." He shook his head, suddenly, as if a fly had been worrying him. "All right, Sergeant, thanks, that's all. Go and get some rest."

So he would have done, gladly, if there'd been any to be had. But if Harben was at a loss, where was he? He'd lost something and found something in one lightning-flash, and didn't know what to do without the one or with the other. He was still alive, and the conviction that he would not survive had been shocked into the background of his mind, and withered away there, and was gone; and with its going he had recovered so great, so sudden a calm that he felt marooned in it as in an illimitable sea. He could not yet rest; there were adjustments to be made before this abrupt peace could be anything but oppressive, or this unwatched loneliness anything better than strange and bleak. He remembered, lying sleepless in the sullen dawn, how the Airborne Division had come back from Arnhem in September, moving stiffly, speaking slowly, looking through things and out the other side. They had been farther than he, but he knew the way it took them; he was on the same road now.

That May evening momentous things were happening among the birch copses of Luneberg Heath. At about six o'clock a group of German officers, very correct, very nervous, came down through the silvery woodlands in sober procession: General-Admiral von Friedeburg first, between two British staff officers, a lean, austere man with cadaverous eyes and a rigid bearing; then General Kinzel and Rear-Admiral Wagner together; then Colonel Polleck and the young staff officer Major Friede, good-looking, deferential, laden with two bulky briefcases and a sheaf of papers. They came down past the flagstaff where the Union Jack fluttered a little wearily in the chilling wind, to where the Field-Marshal's caravan stood, and von Friedeburg mounted the steps and went in alone. He was within for perhaps a quarter of an hour, during which time his companions waited in silence; then he emerged, and the procession re-formed and moved across to a tent which had been prepared to receive them. It contained a square table covered with a grey army blanket, and six hard chairs ranged about it. The staff officers shepherded them to their places, and they stood there waiting beside their chairs. In the borders of the tent, and without, journalists and photographers began to gather. Then a sudden spare man in battledress and a black beret shot out of the caravan and crossed the rough grass after them, and at the first sight of his sharp features and long questing nose everyone in the tent seemed to suffer a mild electric shock, to become more alive than before, the British more eager, the Germans more nervously aware of defeat. He sat down alone at one side of the table, brushing off their rigid salutes with hardly a glance, and they all sat, and fixed their eyes on him, and waited. The Field-Marshal laid a single sheet of typescript before him, cleared his throat, adjusted his tortoiseshell spectacles, and began to read aloud, as drily as if it had been a laundry list, the terms for the surrender of all German armed forces in Holland, in North-West Germany including the Frisian Islands and Heligoland and all other islands, in Schleswig-Holstein and in Denmark, with all naval ships in those areas. Then he sat back and called them up one by one to sign it. From under the rain-flaps of the tent cameras twisted and flashed in General-Admiral von Friedeburg's face, making him draw together the thick black brows over his deep-set eyes, as he added his signature to the Instrument of Surrender. Then the others: General Kinzel, Admiral Wagner, Colonel Polleck, Major Friede; finally the Field-Marshal, who all this time had stood by with his hands in his trouser pockets, took them out again to finish off the document with his sturdy, uncompromising handwriting opposite their five varied flourishes. "B. L. Montgomery, Field-Marshal. 4 May 1945, 1830 hours." He paused to strike through a blurred figure 4 and write it again, initialling the amendment BLM with deliberate neatness; then he leaned back and removed his spectacles, and remarked briskly: "That concludes the formal surrender. We proceed to details." But the details were not yet for publication; the tent-flaps were let down, and the Press dispersed to collect pictures of the men who had escorted the German envoys through the lines, and the H.Q., and the groves of birch, and the 3.7-inch A.A. guns up-ended like clumsy telescopes ready for their grand salute in honour of the occasion. The show was over. The General-Admiral was to survive one more such scene three days later at Rheims, before he died a suicide at Flensburg. For the others, they disappear, like many more, into the twilight of the demi-gods.

It must have been at about the same time that the Midshires were burying their dead. Arthur Clure was newly in his grave when the tent-flaps came down like a curtain upon the surrender of Luneberg, not five miles away. His war was more surely over. As they came away from the newly turned earth and the ranged pale crosses they heard in the distance, shaking the air, the guns of Luneberg begin their salute.

Jim turned towards the sound, and stood at a street-corner, listening. It was a fine, cold evening, the sky lofty and colourless, marbled with light cloud; and in the pervading stillness the reverberations of Montgomery's guns seemed to send tremor upon tremor out from Luneburg like ripples upon a pool, to startle and shatter against the zenith. Here there were no silver birch-trees, no pomp and punctilio of salutes and escorts and respect between enemies, only the bleak street and the few sad, hurrying, furtive people, and the familiar Eisenhower posters; and suddenly those quivering reports linking out across the evening in a rhythmic chain, announcing so clear, so still an ending. He looked along the street, past the uniform houses and the shuttered and blinded shops, memorising half in wonder and half in an analytical carefulness, seeing and storing up within him every detail; the corrugated light along the wood fences of the factory, the two damaged warehouses leaning inward gauntly over the single bomb-gap, the silent railway sidings overlooking the street on the left, the abandoned rolling stock, the mauve candle-flames of daphne mezereon in a small front garden, tired smoke trailing low, all but motionless in the failing wind. All the winds of experience were failing, all the fires of intent burning out in just such a weary, bewildered smoke. Traffic had ceased for the moment; only a weedy boy on a bicycle passed, head-down in a hurry, and a middle-aged woman and a girl walked along the pavement, looked curiously and coldly in Jim's face as they passed, and went away silently as shadows. Somewhere an unmistakable British canteen improviser was vamping up chords along the tune of "I'll be Seeing You", upon a good piano which would not be good for long under that sort of hammering. A Volkssturm recruiting poster flapped a loose corner dismally from the wall across the street. An ambulance convoy went through slowly, flashing its red crosses dimly in the fading evening. Across the railway bridge painted white letters two feet high cried to the blank reverberant sky: "Unser der Sieg!"

"Ours is the Victory!" Hitler was dead, miserably, like a rabbit trapped in its hole, dead in the Chancellery under burning Berlin, unless Dönitz and rumour lied; and the Grand Admiral striking attitudes in Flensburg was only the mute at a funeral. Berlin was eaten alive, a city swooped upon from the air, gnawed from east to west, Charlottenburg gone, Scheoneberg gone, the last wretched shell-drunk defenders creeping out to surrender themselves to the Russians. Italy was lost. The 8th Army were with Tito in Monfalcone, and Trieste had offered capitulation. Burma was as good as lost, Pegu, Prome, Rangoon all crumbling away into Allied hands as all the tides went out together. In Prague, as the U.S. 3rd Army drew nearer in their sweep, the Czech patriots rose again, and the blood of Miriam Lozelle quickened other veins, as in France the great dead had raised up already armies of deliverance. It was all over, the grand conspiracy, the thousand years of domination suddenly lost through the fingers like sand, the German world dwindled away to enough narrow dust to make a German grave, and bitter dust at that. Nothing remained but this: an empty street, a timid old civilian shuffling along and taking off his hat humbly to the silent English sergeant, a single bomb-scar, a disused railway littered with plant, a chill evening, and guns firing over something dead. "Ours is the Victory!"

Whose, then, he thought, since it isn't theirs? Ours? He knew he held none of it. He was empty, drained, and cold; and more than this, he was overtaken now by a strange vertigo, so that the outlines of the German town, so hard and strong against the bright, cold sky, seemed to heave and quiver like distances under a heat-haze, like Jebel Kebir in the mirage, four years ago at Petrol Parva. He was sick with trying to see at once fore and back, back over a long recessional of apparent loss and secret gain, forward into a time as blank and bright as this very sky. He had lived with war, war had been his life, for so long. What else was there of sufficient urgency to take its place now and maintain him upright? Ours is the victory! And is that all, a technical conquest inscribed upon a small sheet of parchment in half a dozen florid signatures? And those smug, sly German women coming ingratiatingly in to ask favours and lodge complaints, to live fatly, snivel fittingly, and stab a Russian or a Pole or an Englishman in the back when no one's looking. Sponging, living off us, riding on us, and whining that we crush them; and all the time waiting until they feel strong enough to attempt it all over again. "Unser der Sieg!" Was it theirs, after all?

He walked along the street slowly. It was growing dark, and in the dark his lightheadedness grew until it drew near to panic. Everything was running down, was declining, was ceasing with a diminishing sigh around him, leaving a blankness, a void in which he could not breathe. And this was victory, this lying down with the dead. There must be more than this. Imogen, whom he had feared to rob and to lose, was farther from him now than when he had written her that last letter she would never read. He had nothing now, until this numbness passed, but what was within him; neither lover nor friend nor companion can enter into the last, loneliest place, nor would you let them in if it were possible, for it is full of darkness and pain. Only the dead, perhaps, whose life has passed into you, set foot there

by right; and they are a part of your being because you are
what they made you. Miriam—Charlie—Arthur Clure—strange
company within, in that stony, astonished coldness where the
victory hung so heavy and dismaying upon his heart; and yet
they would not leave him nor take away their hands from holding him. Because you are what they made you? That ought to
let God in, by any reckoning. If there is a God, after all? And if
he cares to come in where God knows—and who should know
better?—there's no comfort to be had.

Well, he thought, what do you do when this comes on you?
What do you do when you have it, and it isn't what you had
hoped for? What do you do when the world stops trying to roll
over you, and suddenly rolls away, and you fall and hurt yourself? Women cry, and get it out of their systems that way. Or
do they? Not all. Some sneak away and hide like this, until
they've worked out some other way of living, until they can
face even the people they love best, and never show a scar. And
it all works out; the readjustment you think out of all reach
takes place naturally before you realise it, and in time things
slip into gear, and you forget how this felt while it lasted; but
while it does last no amount of reasoning will reason it away.
He could assure himself he was suffering from nothing more than
the reaction after six years of sustained and cumulative strain;
but it felt like the end of the world after as before. Until it
passed, or at least until he discovered some means to dull it, he
dared not go back to the factory to face innumerable disquieting
eyes the doubles of his own, or endure silences that cried out and
produced no answer but their own echoes empty at the heart.
He'd walk the town all night, if need be, to escape that; it
wasn't sleep he wanted.

He had wandered into a quarter he had not entered before,
and people were looking out at him fearfully from behind their
drawn curtains. There was the flutter of trees, and a small
tower looming through them; a church, he supposed, at least it
had the shape of a church. Well, you can sit in churches, there's
that about them; even if they're not your particular brand of
church, even if you don't take much stock in any of the brands,
you can sit quiet in them and nobody bothers you. This one was
damaged, for he saw perforations of sky clean through both
slopes of the roof, and glimmerings like stars puncturing the
tower. Small, squat, fortress-like, but an abandoned fortress;
older than the town, he thought, for its thick walls and massive
door, the stocky buttresses and the erratic batter of the stone-

work did not suggest the twentieth century, whereas the town was a mere mushroom.

He tried the door; it was latchless, and gave to his weight. Within, there was enough light left from the splinter-holes in the roof to let him pick his way along an aisle littered with mortar-rubble, between carved bench-ends eaten with worm and marked with rain. It was desolately damp and cold; but there was one small lamp burning before an image, away towards the altar. He went forward and looked at a shattered wreckage of glass and stone and wood, climbing up chipped steps to a sanctuary washed colourless and bleached with rain, green-stained at the weather-limit and glistening in faint layers of slime. There was a big wooden crucifix, still upright but hanging slightly forward out of line, the only thing left almost intact among the ruin. The light from the lamp climbed up it in long, twining planes ridged with intense shadow, embracing it, imploring it. Not a beautiful thing; a hard, human agony, emaciated body, starting muscles, contorted face, the last horrible extremity of pain; no uplifted eyes, no halo, no angels. Well, maybe it was more like that; at least it brought it nearer home. Very new, he supposed it to be, by the extreme rhythmic simplification of the figure; then he looked more closely, and saw the erosion of the wood, and the minute perforations which showed that here also the worms had been at work, and he knew that it was old, centuries old, older than the church itself. There is, after all, nothing new; only old things renewed. What's wrong with that? It's comfortable to contemplate old things, things that neither shift nor change, hills, trees, weather in the sky, things antique and permanent and profound. Not because of their age in itself, but because of what survives in them for ever fresh and living and growing. Even man is old, and yet endlessly renewed. War is only temporary, recurrent but spasmodic; peace is static and broken. What continues and draws man along with it is something else, an everlasting progression, passionate, constant, the instrument of life; and even if you find it sometimes in the shut places of the heart you know no name by which to call it, and no mark by which to recognise it again. Only it may have for you faces of men you have known, and women you love. Or it may, for the very lucky, have God's face. Who knows?

He put up his hand and touched the wooden forehead under the thorns worn smooth and innocent with age. The cold damp there made him snatch his fingers away again with a superstitious start, for it felt to him like sweat, though he knew it was only weathering. He found himself a dry corner of a bench, and sat down, and contemplated the fearful thing silently for a long time; and the anguished face, drawn and knotted and near to physical death, grew out of the darkness toward him with an imperative power, the only lit thing in his sight. The climbing light, unsteady in complicated draughts, agitated it into movement, contortions of pain, tremblings of the haggard features; and the wormholes showed up as speckles flat upon the surface, like flecks of blood. Yes, this was much how it must have been, if there was any truth in it. This was how other men had looked on the threshold of death. This was how Charlie Smith had looked, grey and old and exhausted under the dripping trees of the Johore jungle, the drawn, attenuated mouth running blood thinly at the corners as here the shadow ran, the eyes fallen far back in the head under too-large lids, and the lean cheeks become caverns of bluish shade. And how if the dead do not rise? How if this immortally dying, endlessly tormented man had never risen, after all? Though after my skin worms destroy this body, yet in my flesh——But suppose worms had indeed destroyed more than this wooden shadow? Then there was nothing. Then Miriam was only a sweet influence in his mind, all her courage, all her goodness drawn down into a little mouldering dust under the flowering soil of Artois; and Charlie Smith had made men for his own fate, to dwindle away from the stature he had raised them to, and dwine, and crumble, and be mere earth under-foot. Then there was nothing worth the lifting of a hand, not liberty nor wisdom nor love itself, nothing but the indifference of a clod to be desired, and a self-absorption to which a fed belly would be enough of pleasure. He looked at the crucifix, and thought within himself, how if this is all?

The guns had stopped a long time ago. It was very quiet, as befitted the hour of the ending of warfare. He knew only that after every despair, after every despondency, the convic-tion of good revived in him, steadying like a flame recovering after a wind has passed. It steadied so now, suddenly, rearing itself whitely in his mind. In an hour it would be blown low again, and all would be dark.

He ceased, while it burned, to reason or wonder, or even think at all. He sat there before the Calvary with his chin on his fist, narrowly regarding God.

PART FIVE

ENGLAND, 1945

'Said Aglovale: "Yet God made me so."
"Nay," said Nacien, "you are not made, but making. One
only came made from the womb. Not before the day of
your death will God have made you."'
                    HOUSMAN: *Life of Sir Aglovale de Galis.*

I

IMOGEN was in Midshire with his parents when Jim came
home on leave late in July. She wrote that she was out of
a job, the ambulance service having recently dispensed with
her, and would come down and meet him when he landed; but
he told her in return not to be a fool, but to wait comfortably at
home for him, instead of half killing herself in crowded summer-
holiday trains and paying for the privilege of being crushed flat.
From which she rightly deduced, or he was afraid she did, that
apart from a quite genuine care for her comfort he had things
on his mind which made it inexpedient that she should be in
London to meet him. In any case she knew about Clure, and
would guess at one of the jobs Jim had taken on; and she
raised no argument, but remained pliantly at home, and let
him do things his own way. She didn't, of course, know
about Private Bostock's boy who was in trouble, and one or
two minor commissions beside, but Clure was enough to go
on with.

Jim was mortally afraid of Mrs. Clure. All the way over,
among an uproarious company of homing warriors laden with
liberated watches, cameras and binoculars, and bent on making
the most of every moment, he rehearsed and amended and
despaired of what he should say to her, and tried in vain to
guess what she might say to him; and all the while he knew that
it was abject waste of effort, for no interview ever panned out,
in his experience, the way it was intended to, and only his
dread of this one kept him struggling to prepare for it. In the
end it would work itself out. But he couldn't somehow bring
himself to the leave-party's level of careless enjoyment, all the
same.

He was glad when they reached London, and he was able
to stow his kit and get on with the job. There was a train
out for the Midlands around four o'clock, so he had just over
five hours to get the weight off his mind; and after a packed

leave-ship and a worse-packed train he was doubly glad to stretch the cramp out of his legs. All the same, when he stood at last outside the door of Helen Clure's Hampstead flat he would have given a great deal to get out of this job he'd taken on. Bostock's private troubles were nothing to this. There was nothing the matter with his kid, only more enterprise and a lot more cheek than any one fifteen-year-old should have, and a soft-natured mother who should have had half a dozen instead of stopping at one, and evened up her affection between them. She threatened him too often, and carried out her threats too seldom; Bostock's first leave would straighten things up a lot, and his demob.—and he was well placed, being an older man—would soon put the whole thing right. But nobody was coming home to put things right behind this polished wood door of Number 17, Vaizey Court. Jim felt his inadequacy more bitterly now than ever, confounded as he was by his own difficulties of adjustment. He'd even come back shy of Imogen. But he was here, and after all, it was not for him to consider how he felt in the matter.

He pressed the bell, and after a pause the door was opened by Helen Clure herself. He knew her at once from her photograph, a pretty, fair woman in black, looking at him questioningly for a moment, while her large eyes studied his face, his uniform, his stripes, and added them up to the person he was. It was not a smile that visited her wan face, but something as welcome, a clear light of recognition. At least she was glad to see him; anybody wearing these flashes would get the same reception, he supposed, for her husband's sake. She held out her hand.

"Sergeant Benison? I'm so pleased! Do come in."

Everything here, he thought as he followed her into the living-room of the flat. was curiously more sophisticated than he had expected it to be. The flat was not large, nor lavish, but the arrangement of it had involved time, money and taste; and as for the woman, the small head-and-shoulders portrait of her had contrived to suggest that she had grown soft and matronly, whereas he found her slender and elegant, her black suit beautifully cut, her white blouse swathed delicately over small breasts and pinned at the neck with a pearl pin. But the face was the same, pointed and smooth and pale, as subtle of texture as a white wild rose, but a little faded, a little relaxed from its first freshness; and her eyes were bewildered still, and always would be, for everything outside this little kingdom was

345

confusion and conflict to her. He noticed, as soon as he entered the room, Clure's photograph in a thin black frame upon the mantelpiece. He saw her eyes fasten on it, and hold there, shining. She was more restful than he had expected her to be, perhaps because she had exhausted every emotion already, for the death was over two months old. She could sit quiet, and keep her hands still and her voice liquid and low; that helped them both.

"I wrote you from Hamburg, Mrs. Clure, before I started, but the mails are very slow. Did you get the letter?"

"It came yesterday. Do sit down, won't you? There are cigarettes on the table there."

"Will you smoke?" He offered the box, but she shook her head.

"I don't, thanks. But do light your own. I—it's just habit; I filled up the box again. I hope they're all right? They're what he always smoked, you see, it didn't occur to me to get any others."

"They're fine, thanks. You're sure you don't mind?"

"I like it. No one has, for a long time now." She said these things quite simply, not dragging in the dead man, for he was already there. Jim judged from this that he was a privileged person here, considered to have a foot in the door already; and how, unless Clure had talked to her about him, could he have achieved that intimacy before she had even seen him? There was Imogen, of course, but he did not believe that Imogen was his sponsor.

The widow sat opposite him, the light oblique upon her face, and looked at him directly. "It was good of you to come. I know it isn't an enviable job, even so long afterwards. You were—there—weren't you?"

"Yes," said Jim, watching the smoke rise between them. "I was one of the fellows who'd have been dead but for him. Major Harben wrote to you, didn't he?"

Her eyes seemed to shine, not brightly, rather as if with a reflected light. "Yes—a wonderful letter. I shall always keep it."

"He told you, then, I expect, that your husband would be recommended for a decoration?"

"Yes. He said—it was certain. He said he deserved the highest."

"So he did. I saw it at close quarters. The people who'll have to assess it here didn't, though, you see; they may not realise what it was worth. But if the Major has his way it'll be a V.C., no less." He was afraid to look at her for a moment, because she became so still; but when he raised his eyes at last he saw her blanched, pathetic face dazzled with gazing at glory. If he had had words at command he could have given her great happiness, praising and praising without measure at the dead man's name; for every word would have been meat and drink to her. And here was he barely articulate, the worst man on God's earth to have undertaken the job. He fumbled for elegiac phrases, and there were none in his nature. Surely, though, surely she knew what was going on in him; or why did she seem so satisfied with so desolately little?

"I'm no good at this," he said lamely. "But you know yourself how few V.C.s there are—how much it's valued. Whether they award it or not doesn't really matter so much. You can take it from me that's the class he's in."

She drew breath hard and was still. "Please—tell me about it. The Major didn't go into details; and besides, you knew him. He often mentioned you in his letters. I—I should like to hear it from you."

He tried, in short, broken sentences, labouring badly; and to him it sounded as bare and brusque as he would have had it noble and lucid. All the time she leaned forward, watching him with that dazzled look, and hanging on the words as they formed on his lips, as if he fed her both honey and gall. She didn't interrupt, even by a movement; now and then he wished she would, for there was a tension winding up inside him that he would have been glad to arrest by any means. She lived on hers. It was easy to see how every remembered detail of that evening under the poplars was transport and torment to her, and how she welcomed both. When he reached the last scene she sat back with a long sigh, and closed her eyes for a moment.

"I'm sorry, I'm no hand at describing things. You'll have to ask me whatever you want to know."

She asked, her face in shadow: "Was he very much hurt? What had—been done to him?"

He told her that, too. He felt the tears spill over from her shut lids, but she made no complaint.

"Did he have—great pain?"

"It's hard to say, but I don't think he felt very much of it. I think he was numbed."

"You were with him until he died, weren't you?"

347

"Yes. I held him until he died. It wasn't long—ten minutes, maybe a little more. It happened very quietly; I don't think he'd know much of it."

"Did they talk of him much?—the others?"

Jim heard them. Poor little beggar, who'd have thought he had it in him? The last man in the world! He said: "Yes. Yes, they did." But he didn't try to enlarge upon it. "None of us had ever seen anything like that before. I doubt we never shall again. Naturally we spoke of it. We thought of it a lot more; we still do. You can't always find the right words, but there's nothing to stop you thinking."

"I always knew," said Helen Clure simply. "He was very quiet, very unassuming; there were people who thought him ineffective, just because he hadn't a great opinion of himself. But I knew what he was capable of. I always knew what was in him."

"Yes, I know. There were some among our chaps who thought of him that way, too. The very young ones, the very clever ones—what can you expect? They're wiser now." He looked down into the glowing end of his cigarette, frowning upon it, feeling his way. "It isn't only what he actually did, you see. Anything like that—well, it goes on getting results, to my mind. Maybe sixty to a hundred of us saw that done, some closer than others; lots of youngsters among us. It's bound to have an effect on them. A thing like that, done for other people, it goes on reproducing itself through other people. Nobody knows where it may end, but it isn't ended yet." He slanted a look at her, and went on talking. She had one hand up to hide her eyes; he saw the thin gold bangle on her wrist take the light. "I know this is a long way off the track, but it's a thing I've got a hunch about. Seems to me that among the gang of us who benefited by your husband's throwing his own life away there must be some who'll hand on the benefit, sooner or later, to other people. It's like a brush-fire where there's plenty of roots and leaf-mould. It travels out of sight, only breaking out here and there, but it takes a lot of putting out. Those kids won't forget it. They'll pay it back some day, to somebody else. It happens. It's happened to me. He started something bigger even than he knew."

He looked at her then, and she had not moved. She said from within the shadow of her spread hand, in a breathless voice: "I think you're very good at this, Sergeant. You make me very proud."

348

Well, it was what he had promised Clure, wasn't it? "She'll be proud," he had said, and she was. He could imagine her at the Palace, walking up the red-carpeted ramp to the King's dais, in her well-cut black, rigid with the responsibility she bore, insatiable for her husband's glory. She'd make a good job of it, too, for his sake; and probably be petrified with terror every minute of the time, poor wretch. He wondered, rather wearily, if Arthur Clure was satisfied; maybe he would be when he saw his Victoria Cross pinned on her breast, and her eyes, enormous, dazed, reflecting back the world's sympathy and admiration. He had given her that, and it was a thing he had dreamed of only in his most visionary moments; maybe he would still think it worth a mere anxious life.

And had she always remained faithful to that unquestioning belief she professed in him? Or had there, for all her love, been times when she had had her doubts? If so, all was resolved now. Everything final has a certain aspect of peace.

"You should be," said Jim soberly. "I'm proud of having even known him. A good many people will boast of having known your husband, Mrs. Clure. I've wanted to tell you that. You know it already, but still I'm glad to be able to say it. There's not much any of us can do more than that."

She took her hand away then, and showed him a pale but composed face, something glittering through it which was almost a smile. "You have. You've done me more good than you think. He valued your good opinion as high as anyone's. Did you know that?" He hadn't known it; he didn't know it now. She was being nice to him, because she wanted to be nice for ever and ever to anyone who spoke of Arthur as he had done; that was all. "You look doubtful about it. Never mind! He would have liked to hear—what you've said—especially from you. And so do I. No, don't worry, I shan't say any more. Except, thank you for everything."

"There's nothing to thank me for, I wish there was. If there should be anything Imogen or I can do, here or over there, you'll call on us, won't you?"

"I shall come to you first of anyone," she promised.

He felt it was time for him to go. She had got what she wanted from him. When he made the first move to take his leave she pressed him to stay, but he knew she didn't want him. She wanted to be left alone between the photographs of her dead husband and her dead son, with whatever new picture she had before her eyes disembarrassed of the alien who had

349

opened it to her. He believed she had got something from him, but any other man would have done as well, and silence would talk better now in her ears. He excused himself, and she let him go gracefully enough.

"You haven't seen Imogen yet? Then of course you'll want to get away. She wrote to me a week ago. I haven't had time to answer her letter yet. Will you thank her, and give her my love?"

He said that he would. She went out into the hall with him, and again gave him her hand; but her heart was away from him in a solitude, hugging the legend.

"Good-bye, and thank you!" And her eyes looked through him, smiled abstractedly in passing, and forgot him again; except that some reflection from Clure's radiance clung to him, and would not let him go clean out of mind.

"Good-bye! Don't forget, if there's anything I can do——"

"There is something, but it may not be possible. There'll be—the investiture. I know it's looking ahead; after all, they may not make an award. But if they do, and if you should be in England when—when I have to go—will you be my guest? And Imogen, too. I should like it, if you will."

Taken aback, Jim began to stammer. "But—are you sure—? There must be people with much more right. It's only a question of one or two, you know——"

"Yes, I know. No, there's no one with more right. He would want you to be there. You will, won't you?"

"Why, if I can, and if you're sure you mean it—I shall be proud, of course. It was only that——"

"I know," she said, "but I do mean it. Then it's settled." And she drew her hand away, and sighed, as if she had accomplished some heavy duty, and let him go.

He went utterly confounded. All across London he tried to work it out, and got no nearer to discovering any reason he should be offered such a privilege. Was it Imogen who carried him into favour under her wing? He couldn't understand. There was no one with more right, Mrs. Clure had said. "He would want you to be there," she had said. Would he? To prove it home to the one person who'd damned himself by witnessing his failure? Jim could almost have believed that; but if that was the reason she was the last person to know anything about it. She, of all people, would never have been told one word of it. And why else should Clure want him there. It was too hard for him, but it wouldn't let him alone. It annoyed him that so simple and awful a tragedy should have to be complicated by obscure little cross-threads of human motives, and yet he couldn't help getting hold of them and trying to follow them up. The devil of it was that he got nowhere.

All through the four-hour journey north, cramped in the corridor most of the way, he worried at it unreasonably, until he had frayed himself into a temper none too well suited to a man coming home. But at the end of it, when the train slacked into Caldington and decanted him upon an empty platform in the honey-coloured middle evening, he lost the weight of it from his heart in a breath, in a gush of sweet air; for there was Imogen coming down the steps towards him, and all his morbid troublings went out for the moment in the welcome of her eyes.

2

They sat in the rough heathery grass on the brow of the waste ground until the light faded, and the sliver of silver which was all that remained of the river had sunk into the thirsty twilight. Then the cool came down on them suddenly, and they stopped talking freely together, and were quiet, looking away from the town, down the long gentle slope into the valley. The Sheel was no more than a cast veil in the green drapery of willows and olive cushioned fields below, and all the rich colours were becoming one colour, a shadowy iris-grey, and all angles were lost, and all distance became a nearness, and all nearness a distance. The hills against the west floated, every modest rounded height rather adrift from the sky than uplifted from the earth. All detail sank from sight in that dim purple sea; there were only the broad, bland, tranquil, lasting outlines, the realities, the victorious brave bones of the land.

There it was, then, England the queer place, the unshakable place, the impervious place; all that seemed evanescence was stone, all that shifted like mist was rock, and the dimpled softness sat resiliently upon foundations that went down to the centre of the earth, and had rooted more firmly for every passing year. There she was, the immovable country, serene, dreaming of earthen things, harvest and stubble and plough and harrow and seed, the sequence in which war and peace were only incidents, to be ridden, endured and exhausted like storm and wind, and even in their tumultuous passing not greatly to be regarded. Out of this the iron had come that held fast at Dunkirk, and Falaise, and Arnhem; and would emerge to strike such sparks again as often as need was. And yet more was there, a deep under the deep, not so easily to be assessed. And even that was not enough for Jim's trouble. He rolled over on his face in the turf warmed through by the sun, and pressed his palms and his chest and his thighs against the stable earth, comforting himself with the feel of it; and the only complication and littleness which persisted was within him, but it was obstinate, and neither twilight nor dark could coax it out of him.

"They won't move you out east again, will they?" asked Imogen. "I couldn't bear that, just when we've almost got everything fixed, and you pinned down."

"No, they won't do that. We've got job enough where we are. No, Germany'll be my address for the rest of the time I'm in."

"I'm glad," she said. "They couldn't have the heart to spoil things for us now."

"You don't seem to be worrying about the fraternisation business," said Jim. "Everybody else seems to think we spend our time running round with a blonde in either arm. Trust me?—or what?"

"Trust you. But I know you hate it. It can't be for long, Jim, surely. They've started on the groups, and yours is only twenty-two—"

"Twenty-three."

"Twenty-two. I looked it up. Oh, Jim, do you know, it's not like I expected it to be—this business. You should have seen London on V.E.-night!"

"Went mad, did they?" he asked a shade bitterly.

"They didn't, that's just it. Oh, they played the fool, of course. There was a lot of noise, and everybody was happy. They climbed a lot of lamp-posts, and wore silly hats, and paraded the town all day, and all that. But they didn't stampede. There was hardly a casualty in the whole of the two days. They knew what they were about, all right. There wasn't any going mad this time. And—Jim—I don't think they mean to be stampeded about anything. All that artificial hysteria about the election—or didn't you suffer from that?"

"Oh, lord, yes, we had all that—— Red letters, Laski

bogy, Gestapo and all that. We got so sick of it, it even stopped being funny."

"I know! It fell flat here, too. It was like an inoculation that didn't take. Jim, I really believe they know what they want this time."

"Do they know how to get it? I don't!"

He was aware that he grew monosyllabic and morose, but for the life of him he couldn't snap out of it. She would sense it as fast as he, probably be one jump ahead; and he was sorry. But she would know how it was, and if anyone could unknot him, she could. She sat quite still, not bothering him, not rushing him, letting him fret and grieve and prowl about his circumscribed solitude until she had made up her mind how best to get at him; and then she would do what had to be done, whether it was soothing him or scarifying him, and whatever she did would be right in the end.

"It seems almost as if the Japanese business will finish soon, too," said Imogen, talking to let him emerge if he could. "We've got all Burma now, and most of Borneo; and the bombing over Japan's been terrific. How long would you give it? Another month?"

"Don't know. Daren't try and guess. Not long, anyhow."

"It's queer, isn't it," she said, "to look back now? It used to seem so straightforward, and it turned out more spiral than any corkscrew. I can hardly even remember how it felt then."

"Yes," he admitted bitterly, "the ground did shift."

"Well, we're here! It wasn't where we expected to be, exactly, but there's no help for it. Anyhow, we got something out of it. Maybe it was better worth getting than what we were after."

"Maybe!"

Yes, he'd got something out of it, all right, a crop of memories as vehement as toothaches, and a few inches of growth, perhaps, difficult things to assess now; but what had Miriam got, and Charlie Smith, and all the dead men out of mind? As far as he could see, all that was left of their vigour and valour and grandeur was the few who remembered them, the very few who would never, could never, forget them. How many had laid this weight upon him? For how many, since the first and dearest began it in dying for him, did he now carry the unimaginable load? My God, he thought, were they fairly paid? Did they get value for what they spent? He was newly come from the widow of the last of them, and the debt smarted in him hot as fire. He felt he was bankrupt; no man, no ordinary man, could hope to pay off debts like these, even if he spent his life on it.

Imogen said: "Jim, what's the matter?"

"Oh, nothing much! Germany blues, I daresay. It should work off in a day or two; I haven't got the stink out of my system yet."

She leaned over, not abruptly, and took firm hold of him by the near shoulder. There was this wonderful thing about Imogen, that she didn't feel any urge to soothe him with those irritating, sensitive, butterfly brushings of her fingers to which most women seemed to run by way of showing their sympathy. She never touched him until she had made up her mind, and then she did it as one having a right. Her gestures towards him had a dignity and vigour which made her as tall as him. He liked that; he liked it now, the feel of her hand holding him.

"Don't talk to me like that, Jim. It isn't good enough."

"I know!" he said into the grass. "Don't make me, kid! Better forget it and let me alone for a bit; it'll all work out."

"Meaning you don't want to talk about it?"

"I don't know what I want, and that's the truth. Everything coming adrift like this—and the way it did it—well, it's just knocked me off my pins, I suppose. I haven't got my bearings yet. And then this particular business——"

"Which particular business?"

"Clure, of course!" he said fractiously, as if she ought to have known.

"Oh!" said Imogen very quietly; and sat looking down at him for a while without more words, her hand still on his shoulder. Then she asked in the same low voice: "You went to see Helen, didn't you?"

"I promised I would. He asked me——"

"Yes, I know. Did she make you tell her—how it happened?"

"All I could remember. I hadn't forgotten much."

"No, I—don't suppose you had. She wouldn't give you a bad time, though—not like you might have had."

"Not as bad as I expected," he admitted. "But I'd rather have had a kick in the teeth, any day. You can't imagine what it's like—that sort of job—even when they're as quiet as she was."

Imogen said: "Can't I? I was with her the day she got the wire."

"But you're a woman. You could do it all differently. And anyhow there was nothing she could ask you for but sympathy; you weren't on the spot when it happened. Still, I never thought of you having to——"

"Why should you? It's all right, Jim; it wasn't the first time."

Yes, Imogen had deaths in her memory, too, many a one before this. It was only too easy to forget that. He raised himself on his elbows, and looked at her earnestly through the dusk. What must it have been like to live through the London blitzes as she had done, not on a gun fighting back, but running round with an ambulance picking up the pieces? She hadn't complained, but then she never did complain. She looked back at him gravely now, half lost in the dimness against the shadowy green of the broom-bushes; so small, so slight, that in such a light she could still be taken for a child. Seeing her so, he could almost feel the last six years slipping by him, back into the void of strange imaginings from which they had come; but that sort of dizziness wouldn't last long, and he didn't know that he wanted it to. Nothing had ever yet made him wish a day out of his life. No going back, whatever happened; they would go on from here, even if it wasn't the ground they would have chosen. He could supply the detail the twilight hid; the fine etched lines of strain and wakefulness at the corners of her eyes, the short, deep cleft at either end of her mouth, the weathered maturity of her skin. Women and men alike, they come to their full stature by strange ways.

"Imogen," he said, "I don't know how this started. I'm no good to you."

"You're all I want," she said.

"So you tell me, and I believe you; but I wish you'd been luckier, girl!"

"Luckier!" she said, and smiled. "Does that mean you want to call it off, Jim?"

"My God, no! Never in the world!" He drew himself close against her, leaning his forehead against her shoulder; through the thin cotton fabric of her dress her body felt cool and smooth. "You're cold! We ought to go home."

"No, not until you tell me what's on your mind. What did Helen say and do to you? I know there's something. It's about him, isn't it?"

"Yes, it's about him." He turned his cheek into the hollow of her shoulder, and began to tell her; not only the confused

355

story of this last interview, but the whole history of the relationship, leaving out only the incident at Goch, which was Arthur Clure's secret, not to be disclosed even to Imogen. Once he had pushed the first sentences off his tongue the whole thing came out in a flood, running faster and more confidently every moment: how Clure had taken to haunting him, watching him closely, following him about, after the trifling help Jim had lent him by Imogen's favour at Arnhem and after; how he had acted towards him at the concentration camp, and in the garden of the German house outside Osnabruck; how he had taken upon himself to destroy the barricade single-handed and save the company a costly attack; how he had died; and how his widow had looked at Sergeant Benison and said: "No, there's no one with more right; he would want you to be there." He was sick and tired of mysteries. He poured it all gratefully into her receptive sensibility, and his mind ached with relief even while she pondered it in silence. Last year's broom-pods rattled drily on the green bushes in a rising breeze. The air grew cold and restless, stirring about them uneasily.

"You're hard to satisfy," said Imogen at last, more to herself than to him.

"How's that? I only wanted to swop a lift or two with him. Why couldn't it just rub along like that, and nobody any the worse? I never meant to start a long-term feud——"

"But haven't you left something out?" He said nothing to that, being unable to trot out the lie with sufficient conviction at such short notice; besides, how could she possibly know more than he had told her? "There was one thing you never mentioned; something that happened at a place just beyond the forest, after you went into Germany——" She felt him jerk upright beside her, and instinctively steadied him within her arm. Straining to see her clearly, he thought her eyes shone with a blind, brilliant light, but they looked beyond him and he could not be sure.

"What do you know about that?" he demanded in dismay.

"Almost everything, I suppose," said Imogen.

"But how? How? Who told you? Nobody knew but the two of us."

"And you didn't tell me? No—you didn't tell me."

"But—*she* couldn't. He'd have cut his tongue out before he let *her* find out about it."

"No, don't worry. She still doesn't know; she never will."

"Then how——"

"He wrote to me," said Imogen in a level tone. "Soon after it happened. He told me all about it. Your version would be easier on him, I expect, but I was able to make allowances for that."

"But why should he do that? It wasn't that it didn't matter to him; it did, like hell! Why, for God's sake, should he write and tell you?"

She said, turning the glimmer of her eyes upon him suddenly: "Don't you understand? He wrote to me because he wanted to praise you, because he wanted me to know what it was I was in love with—because he wanted to be sure I appreciated you——"

Trembling, he said breathlessly: "It's crazy! He wouldn't do it. The very thing he dreaded most in the world had happened to him, or as near as damn it happened. Nothing could be half so important as keeping that dark——"

"Yes," said Imogen, "one thing could. You could."

The breath went out of him so hard that he couldn't speak, but only sat staring at her piteously, his world in chaos round him.

"I know," she said, "because I want to do much the same. I know because I feel about you the way he felt. Why shouldn't he watch you closely? Why shouldn't he follow you about, and go tearing after you when you went into danger? He wanted you to live, didn't he? He wanted you to come home to me, and marry, and be happy. He wanted me to love you properly. That was why he wrote to me—to tell me how wonderful you were—in case I didn't realise——"

"No," said Jim fiercely, "it's impossible! What he wanted was to get even—to be quits with me. I always thought that; I still think it." He took her by the shoulders, and held her hard, and she felt how he was shaking. "Imogen, don't! It can't be true! I know you wouldn't fool me, but this can't be true. It's a mistake you're making."

"I had his letter," said Imogen gently.

"Where is it? You've made too much of it. Can I see it?"

"No—even if I'd kept it. But I burned it after I'd read it. It was his secret; I made it safe." She leaned forward, and shut her hands steadily over his wrists as he held her. "Listen, Jim! I'm not fooling you, and I'm not making any mistake, either. She doesn't know. All she knows is that he spoke well of you to her, and that you were his friend. No, I won't be quiet! I know what I'm saying. I want to say it. It's the

357

first time, and it'll be the last, but this once you must listen to me. You weren't so clumsy as you thought you'd been with him. You didn't make the mess of it you thought you had. It was much simpler. You were good to him, and took risks for him, and he knew it; and he didn't hate you. There wasn't anything second-rate in that little man. He was grateful. He—— Oh, God, why should we fumble about after another word when there isn't any?—he loved you! Why shouldn't he? Other people have! I have! That's why he was always near you. That's why he watched you. He was afraid something would happen to you, and he didn't mean that it should if he could help it. I think he forgot how to be afraid for himself; you do when you care enough about someone else. When you went out after the lieutenant, he went with you; and when he saw you meant to try and go the rest of the way, he took good care you shouldn't take any such risk. Oh, I don't know how he meant it to end; maybe he believed he could do it, maybe he didn't trouble to wonder whether he could or no. But when you ran after him, and he knew it was you or him— well, you've told me what he did. He destroyed himself to make sure you shouldn't be destroyed. Oh, and for how many other things you can guess as well as I can—better. Maybe he saw glory. I don't know. Maybe he thought what he was robbing his wife of, and what he was giving her in exchange. Maybe it was a relief to be sure at last of something definite, something everybody could see. I don't know, I don't want to know. But I do know he got almost everything he wanted out of it; a life for you, and a hero for her; and for himself— there wasn't anything he wanted more than for you to approve him, and he had it—hadn't he?—right up to the moment when he died in your arms. I think he was satisfied," she said fiercely, "I would have been!"

Half a dozen times he had tried to break in, shaking and sweating with abject anxiety to deny, to disclaim, and every time some flash of memory had shut his mouth again upon a voice he could not trust struggling for words he could not command. He remembered that look of Clure's, the look and the cry he had never understood, as the daylight collapsed before him and let him down at Baird's feet in the furze. He remembered the intent eyes following him, and it came upon him now that affection hunts as tirelessly as hate. He remembered Harben saying curiously: "If she had been there to see I could have believed in it. There was no one watching whose approval he can possibly have been prepared to die for."

"Do you think he was the only one?" said Imogen. "Other people would have done as much for you if they could, and been glad. Do you think you can shut yourself in and escape affection for ever?"

He had shut his fingers upon her until they hurt, but she was too intent upon him to know or care. He sat still, staring at her in a sick fascination, and for all he had learned, and suffered, and done, his eyes were a lost child's eyes, frightened and lonely.

"Of course he would want you to be there!" said Imogen. "What's strange in that? Why shouldn't he? If I had any honours I'd put them under your feet, too."

Jim said: "Oh, Imogen!" in a long, groaning sigh of help-lessness and wonder and shame, and slowly slid his hands down her arms to the wrist, bowing himself forward over them. She let her hold upon him be broken, her arms opened to him at his will; his arms about her body now, hers closing again about his shoulders, and against her throat the soft, repeated flutter of his lashes and the restless movements of his eyelids. She held him fast; his weight was comfortable to her though she ached with it. She felt his breath warming the little cup of her neck, and the seamed scars at his temple branding her cheek; and these things she remembered afterwards as deliberate gifts between them, more lasting than caresses. She knew she had made him wretched and ashamed, had humbled him as low as she had exalted him high. What of it? She had had her say, and she was satisfied; and he would take no hurt. He wasn't the first to know this passion of unworthiness. Lancelot after his miracle, they say, crept away from the applause and wept by himself in the church. So they do still, the best of them; But God gets something out of it in the end. She held him on her heart, and the taste of praising him was sweet and lingering in her mouth, and she was very happy. He could spare her this for this one time; she would never even reach for it again.

"There, forget about it now! Just understand it, and then forget it, quickly! After all, what is there new in it? He only did what generous people do. He only adored in you what you adored in Miriam."

The name drew a long sigh out of the lips that warmed her breast. Was it possible, was it at all possible, that another human creature had found in him what he had found in Miriam Lozelle? Imogen felt him stand at gaze upon the threshold of a world into which she could not follow. How small a part of his memories were her memories, and how limited a part of his mind was set open for her; yet she was content to sit and wait for him to bring all the unknown part of his experience here to her breast, and look for house-room within. As he would, when the cold bit him and the winds grew keen; for she could keep all warm and living which might otherwise die. The air is chill and rare in which you remember things alone.

He said wearily: "But I did nothing. Even when I tried I mostly made a poor show of it. You mustn't say that I—— Oh, my God!" he said on a broken sigh, "didn't I owe it? I've taken so much from so many people——"

"And given so much to so many——"

"Don't, Imogen!" he besought her, his voice shattering.

"No, never again, I promise. When we go from here we won't speak of it again. Oh, Jim, my dear, it's all right, you know. He wasn't swindled. Let him alone now—let him rest."

She believed, he knew it then, he felt it in his heart, that Clure did rest, as secure from extinction as from life; all her dead went to a serene, eager heaven, not to a grave of timeless dust and evanescent flowers, not to a green, stinking swamp-slime under mangrove-roots. They were still up to something, somewhere, more alive than the living. He had been about and about the world looking for what she had always had, what she had offered him in her hands many a time, and he could not take. Couldn't he take it now, and be content? It was right for her to live with it all her life, and for him to come to it with labour after long wanderings. Why not? It was still one and indivisible, like the ordinary kind of peace. And surely he had it now; he felt it as if with his fingertips as they reached and strained her body to him, and the first cool and sweetness of it was on the lips quiet now against her heart. What was the use of trying to reason about it? There are things which come without being called, and hold aloof when they are sought. The trouble was lifting from him like the mist off the valley in the morning sun. So after all, things do go on. The spring wears out, but is endlessly renewed. A war which has eaten six years of your life suddenly runs down like a worn-out machine, but out of it new interests emerge and struggle, and only a little quick pain fills the pause. Death is only another pause. Things go on. He felt under his palms, within one small human creature, all the permanence of the world. Nothing was lost; nothing ended. He was satisfied.

He sighed at last, and raised himself. She had felt the tension go out of him, draining away with it the panic of humility and distrust over which she had exclaimed as over a child. That was finished. What now? Did he know himself any the better for her mirror held up to his eyes? She searched his face, and saw only the mysterious mask the twilight made of it, calmer than life. She thought, nothing worthwhile is ever completed; nothing beloved is ever exhausted. He'll last me a lifetime, she thought, and after he'll still be fresh and new.

"Imogen, help me!" he said.

She said: "Yes, of course, if I can."

"You can, Imogen." But he didn't say what he wanted of her, nor how she could bestow it. There was no hurry. It was all just ahead of him, just leaning within his reach. "You're cold," he said remorsefully. "Shall we go home?" It was all so quiet, the storm quite gone by him; she felt stillness settle upon them after the passing of the twilight wind, and without and within the cool impersonal night came on. Little things came back into mind, banns and house furnishings and Jim's release group, which she knew better than he; and after them other things, greater than these, treading on their heels and over-shadowing them, his return to Germany, the tedium between leaves, the uncertain future of the world. Even peace would be only another name for conflict and distrust, in which their small fate became insignificant; and yet they had everything they wanted or needed, here between them, here within the hands with which they held each other. Their own love at the core, and about it and about the sustaining peace which drew not from their experience, not from their courage, but from far apart where the skies and the stars find their calm, and far within where the imperishable, unreasonable inspirations are, from something which to him was shadowy and grateful and nameless, and to her was close and clear and God.

"It is getting cold. Yes, we'd better get back. They'll think we've got lost, or something." She thought within herself, as he lifted her to her feet, how half of what she had meant to say was still not said; and she was glad. The lapis sky, the wan stars pricked fine in it, the aromatic sticky sweetness of rest-harrow in the grass where they had lain, the distant fluting of a blackbird down the fields, these had near, clear voices. There was a speech between her mind and his now as they walked which used the same free, fluent language, and could do wonders with silence. And in the last privacy of the heart where she neither would nor could pursue him, where humiliation and joy, human frailty and human goodness, terrible memories and dear, all draw together and become one loneliness, if ever he doubted and cried out for comfort he would not be without an answer.

FINIS